Whence the Healing Stream Doth Flow

Other books by Robert Jones

Limited to Everyone: An Invitation to Christian Faith,
The Seabury Press 1982

Prayers for Puppies, Aging Autos & Sleepless Nights, with drawings
by Gay Guidotti, Westminster/John Knox Press 1990

God, Galileo, and Geering: A Faith for the 21st Century, Study
Guide to the writings of New Zealand scholar
Lloyd Geering, Polebridge Press 2005

*Proud to be a River Rat: Characters and Calamities along the
Lower Russian River, Vol I,* Kindle Direct Publishing 2019

*Proud to be a River Rat: Characters and Calamities along the
Lower Russian River, Vol. II,* Kindle Direct Publishing 2021

Whence the Healing Stream Doth Flow

A Story of the Welsh in America

A Novel

Robert Jones

McCaa Books • Santa Rosa, CA

McCaa Books
684 Benicia Drive #50
Santa Rosa, CA 95409

First published in 2021 by McCaa Books,
an imprint of McCaa Publications.

Library of Congress Control Number: 2021916369
ISBN 978-1-7363451-8-4

Printed in the United States of America
Set in Minion Pro
Book design by Waights Taylor Jr.
Author photo by Stephen Gross

www.mccaabooks.com

For Arline

1

So Here We Are In Scroggtown

"THEY SING LIKE ANGELS AND FIGHT LIKE SNAKES." That's what Davy Davis said to Russell Llewellen when Russ got back to Princeton Seminary from candidating at a Welsh Presbyterian Church in the hard coal country of northeastern Pennsylvania. Russ asked Davy why he would say such a thing, and Davy said he was born and raised in hard coal country and grew up in a Welsh church. "I wouldn't go back there for anything," Davy said. Davy, too, was graduating in the class of 1959.

"Well, you've got the singing part right," Russ said, "I know that much."

Candidating is going to a church and preaching a sermon, and the whole congregation chews it over and votes on whether they want you to be their minister or not. And so, after the service at the Welsh Presbyterian Church of Scroggtown, they put Russ all alone in the church basement, which was also the Sunday School room, banquet hall and kitchen, while almost two hours of sermon chewing went on above him. Finally an elder came down the stairs to report the congregation had voted him in. Right off, Russ could tell, it could make him kind of beholden to them.

Next day, Russ packed a suitcase, took the bus to Trenton, and bought a little blue Saab by signing a contract to pay $67 a month for three years. In his new car that was hardly big enough for two people and a small dog, he headed west toward Los Angeles to marry Ellen. Russ and Ellen had met little over a year earlier at a church camp on the central California coast near where Russ grew up. His father was in business there, having bought the small men's clothing store where he had worked as a young man. He prided himself on giving people what he called "full value for their dollar," and, as far as Russ could tell, that's what he did. On Sundays, his only day off, he took Russ and his brother to Sunday School and the church service for what he called "moral training," and, often as not, went out to the course and played nine holes of golf while his boys were at church. Sunday afternoons he took his boys fishing or swimming at the beach or something. Their mother, happy to be going for a little ride, sang along with the car radio in her strong soprano voice. Tunes like "Roll out the barrel, / We'll have a barrel of fun" and the one about Sister Kate who can "shake it like a bowl of jelly on a plate" were among her favorites.

Father Llewellen allowed the boys to "grow out" of Sunday School early on and took the family to church only on Easter, in part, Russ thought, to show off their new clothes from his store. Russ was aware his father would have preferred him to take business courses rather than literature and theology, but he paid Russ's tuition at college and seminary and never once complained

Russ' mother was a different story. During his last semester at Cal, when Russ drove home to announce he was going to become a minister, she all but shouted, "What? We never raised you like that." She had been raised Mormon, and though she had much to say against the church of her childhood, like a good Mormon she didn't think churches needed professional clergy and she told Russ so. "Even our bishops work at jobs to support themselves," she said. "Remember when your grandfather died, the bishop came and did the funeral for us. He was an insurance man. He wouldn't take a nickel. We don't believe in paying someone to pray for us."

"Thank God Presbyterians aren't like that," Russ said.

"Who's to say Presbyterians are right?" she came back. Russ let it go.

ELLEN WAS TWENTY YEARS OLD and had spent most of her life in southern California, having just finished her second year of college. Lithe, blond, athletic, she was perfect for places where people wear skimpy clothes and lie on warm beaches a good bit of the time. Russ, on the other hand, was a little pudgy from the heavy dining hall food at the seminary, and, though he was almost six feet tall, he had the stooped bearing that comes from spending too much time in libraries. In this, he was like Ellen's scholarly father, who taught Bible courses at a Christian college near Los Angeles.

At the summer camp where he met Ellen, Russ was in charge of the recreation program, a job they gave to seminarians. This got him out in the sun and removed some of the accumulated pallor of academic life. One sunny day, as he stood on the rustic porch of the camp administration building, Russ got a glimpse of Ellen as she moved along a narrow path beneath some redwood trees. Having never been given to long seasons of prayer in seeking the will of God, Russ said under his breath, "Lord, let her be the one."

Russ found out Ellen was the counselor for a group of kids from some church or other and tracked down where her cabin was. Thinking to get her attention, he pretended to be the inspector who judges which cabin gets the prize for neatness, and, when no one was looking, he reached under Ellen's pillow and confiscated her pajamas. These he attached to the rope on the flagpole so that, when the campers gathered for the opening ceremonies that morning, they were directed to pledge allegiance to Ellen's pajamas instead of the stars and stripes.

That got her attention all right. She thought it was childish and totally uncalled for, which, of course, it was. Still, she went to the movies with Russ before the week was over. They saw each other as much as they could until fall and wrote thick, serious letters during the school year, Russ in Princeton, Ellen at college in

Santa Barbara. Just before Christmas vacation, Russ sold his old Volkswagen bug to buy a plane ticket to the west coast. For a couple of weeks they had something like a courtship and started talking about marriage. Before the vacation was over, they set a date in early August.

Ellen's family was against it. Ellen's mother expressed her opposition by canceling the wedding dress Ellen ordered. When Ellen found out, she was furious. "I'll be married to James Russell Llewellen no later than September 12," she announced, "dress or no dress, people can come or not."

"That's ridiculous," her sister said. "Your name will be Ellen Llewellen. It's all ls." Still, Ellen's little tirade got things going. Within days, the invitations were printed, the cake ordered, the church lined up, and Ellen went for fittings at the dress shop, everything running a month late.

Ellen's kindly and studious father said little about it except, "Well, a young pastor needs to be married when he takes his first charge." But Ellen's mother was concerned for her daughter in many ways, not the least of which being that Russ would graduate from a seminary whose professors, she had heard, cast doubt on the literal underpinnings of such doctrines as the Virgin Birth of Christ. On the night before the wedding, in fact, Ellen's mother asked Russ what he believed about the Virgin Birth, as if this was the crucial test for determining the suitability of a son-in-law. Mimicking one of his professors, Russ answered without hesitation, "I stand firmly with the Apostle Paul on the matter." That seemed to satisfy the inquisition for the moment. Russ didn't go on to say, as his professor had, that the Apostle Paul never mentioned the birth of Jesus except in one verse where he wrote, simply, that Jesus "was born of a woman." However, Ellen's mother consulted Ellen's father, who knew the Bible through and through, and so she was soon on to Russ's attempt to hide behind the good Apostle.

Nonetheless, on September 12, Ellen and Russ were married in her parents' church with eight bridesmaids and groomsmen, maid of honor, best man, flower girl, ring bearer, two ministers, one of which was Ellen's father, and hundreds of guests attending. Russ wore a rented tuxedo, and Ellen wore the white, full flowing, formerly canceled dress. Her blond hair swirled upon her shoulders, and her face seemed to glow behind her veil. People said she looked like Grace Kelly, but Russ thought she was much prettier than that.

The dress was so full it took up the whole aisle as Ellen walked into the church on her father's arm. All during the service, Russ felt he was being kept at a distance by billowing swirls of nylon, taffeta, and lace. When they knelt for the closing prayer, Russ' left knee came down on the folds of Ellen's dress, and with the final "Amen," Ellen rose first, ready to be on her way. A loud "riiiiiip" was heard throughout the church, and, while they stood kissing, great heaps of underskirts fell to the floor around Ellen's feet. She daintily stepped out of them and marched up the aisle on Russ' arm. Russ thought she looked even better with the dress draped closely around her.

They spent their first night together in a Holiday Inn just east of Arcadia, a southern California town much like others except the Santa Anita Race Track is there. Ellen wore the cream colored linen suit she had changed into at the church, and Russ wore an inexpensive brown suit he had bought for the occasion. They got to the door of their room carrying their small suitcases, and Russ thought he would do what he had seen in the movies. He reached down and picked up his bride, but with fumbling with the door and tripping over the suitcases, he lunged into the room and dropped her unromantically on the thin brown rug under which was a concrete floor. Bonk. Ellen looked a bit startled but said nothing, and Russ could only manage a subdued giggle. He said he wanted to take a shower. It was beginning to hit him that, in over a year, the two of them had hardly been in the same town for three weeks all told, let along the same room. But soon they were in the same shower, and then in the same bed, and that was that.

Next day they stopped early in the afternoon in Kingman, Arizona, for another shower and a little "nap" before dinner. By Tuesday they were still in New Mexico. The next night, in order to get back on schedule, they slept for a few hours without taking off their clothes in a less than first rate motel on the edge of Amarillo, Texas. It was just as well. The sore places needed a chance to heal.

Russ had been to Scroggtown that one time when they voted him in, but Ellen had never seen the place. As they headed northeast, Russ kept telling her not to be disappointed by where they were going. "It's nothing like you're used to," he said. "We're headed for a beat-up coal town where the main thing is to hold on to your job so when the humidity builds up at the end of a summer day you can afford a couple of beers while you sit on the front porch in your undershirt and wait for a breeze."

But Ellen was not going to be talked out of her adventure. "I don't even own an undershirt," she said, "and I don't like beer." She began humming a song from a movie she and Russ had seen together, something about there being a place for them. She seemed to know a million songs. Every time they crossed a state line she sang a song for the occasion. "Deep in the Heart of Texas," "Oklahoma," "Meet Me in St. Louie, Louie," it didn't matter, she knew a song. In Missouri, Russ sang parts of the "Saint Louis Blues," but Ellen knew the whole thing and looked askance at Russ' wobbling ways with the notes. She sounded happy and hopeful, and Russ took it for a good sign.

Somewhere in green, muggy, rural Illinois, the rich smell of mowed alfalfa in the air, Russ saw a red barn and grabbed Ellen's thigh. This started a game whereby every time they passed a red barn they grabbed each other someplace, and the little blue Saab wove its way down the two-lane road missing farmers on tractors, school buses, and milk trucks by margins that were closer than safe.

Not long after they joined the turnpike east of Chicago, Ellen broke into a song about Gary, Indiana, which was the town they were passing through. It's a lively song, and she sang it for miles in her irrepressible way. But as they drove by the steel mills on that smooth, sweeping road, Russ noticed the smokestacks were not smoking, long lines of flatbed cars stood idle in the railyards, many locomotives were parked off to one side, and nothing moved. It had an ominous feel in spite of Ellen's blithe song.

They spent the night near Pittsburgh. The steel mills there were quiet too, the recession of '59 having taken hold. Still, in the morning when they started out, Ellen sang a rousing "Pennsylvania Polka" as they drove through the rolling hills. She enjoyed the forest greenness and the occasional red barns. She enjoyed the Howard Johnsons with their orange trim and "cute little towers on top." Her light-heartedness kept Russ from thinking the heavy thoughts to which years of grinding study had made him susceptible.

And so at four o'clock on a Saturday afternoon in mid-September, Russ and Ellen left the Pennsylvania turnpike at Clark's Summit, paid the toll, and headed east on the two-lane road that leads to Scroggtown. Russ knew what time it was from the clock on the tollbooth. They had been married one week, almost to the minute.

Russ was just as happy Ellen hadn't noticed the clock. She would want to stop and mark the spot where they passed this one-week anniversary by setting a rock on top of another, shoving a stick into the ground, or something. Then she would want to hug and kiss in honor of the cute little tollbooth or the narrow little road, or the haze rising off the green hills. Throughout the whole long trip she had been bubbling with enthusiasm for everything she saw. It all had meaning for them as a couple, she seemed to think, and she wanted those meanings pinned down. But Russ had to preach his first sermon in his first parish the next day, and he was getting anxious about it.

They drove through a tunnel of limbs and leaves, through dark shade and specks of sunlight, through a kind of passage between what was and what was to be. Huge maples and poplars lined the road. Their little blue Saab, barely a month old but already with seven thousand miles on it, thumped and putted and seemed to find every pot hole in its path. Through the trees, they saw white farmhouses, huge red barns, and deep lush meadows with black and white cows in them motionless as porcelain figurines. By the river they saw another red barn. Grab, grab, giggle, giggle, then up over a rusting metal bridge across a gorge full of gray water, hit the big chuckhole on the other side, and bump into town. The car went putt-ta-putt-putt, its three-cylinder, two cycle engine sounding like a big lawn mower and smoking like one too, which it was supposed to do when slowing down.

"So here we are in Scroggtown," Russ said. "What do you think?"

"I think it's beautiful," Ellen said, "in its own kind of way."

SCROGGTOWN IS SET IN A VALLEY with wooded hills on four sides. Gaps in the hills let the river, the main roads, and the train tracks through. On a patch of flat ground near the river, the rickety, tottering tin roofed towers of the Scroggtown Coal Company rose above the scene. Rusty mine cars rested on narrow gauge tracks that eventually disappeared into the hillside. Near the mine were ashy dark gray mountains of smoldering slag, and smoke the odor of eggs gone bad wafted up from them. Sometimes bluish, sometimes yellowish lines ran through the slag heaps at various levels like the lines on a topographical map. When a breeze hit just right, it seemed as if a charge of electricity flashed along these lines, giving a sense of messages sent from another world.

Clustered along the river were shops, houses, churches, schools, and funeral parlors jumbled together so that it seemed the town had slid downhill into itself and buildings got caught on each other to stop their slide. Main Street was brick storefronts, huge elm trees, crisscrossing power lines, and above it all the yellow-brown haze from the smoldering slag heaps. The road map showed Scroggtown with thirty-six thousand people, but it didn't show Scroggtown's streets, so Russ stopped at a service station, bought Cokes, and had the red headed high school kid who worked there fill the car with gas. Then Russ put a quart of oil in the gas tank, and the kid almost flipped.

"Hey, watcha dooin' like that for?" he said.

"With this car you put oil in with the gas," Russ said, "one quart to a tankful. You get thirty miles to the gallon and never have to change the oil." The car was small and shaped like a bull-head fish, so the back seat was nothing but a narrow bench, and the trunk was tiny too. A large portion of the new couple's belongings were jammed into that car, their wedding book wedged under the passenger seat, their Melmac dishes stuffed in loose wherever they would fit, and their silverware packed around the spare tire. There was no way to see out the rear window because of clothes, blankets and pillows piled on the back seat.

"YOO MOOvin' 'ere?" the kid asked, gawking at Ellen but talking to Russ. Russ told him they were. "Why you want to moove 'ere for? The mines are shuttin' down. Everybody's leavin'," the kid said. He talked like no one they'd heard before, lots of emphasis on the "oo" sounds. Ellen glanced around like someone who had just landed in a foreign country, but she kept smiling. That day, in ponytail, white pedal pushers, and striped turquoise top, she was pixie-like and looked maybe all of sixteen. The kid gawked at her the whole time they were there. Russ ran his hand through his short brown hair, stretched his five-foot-eleven-inch frame as far as he could, adjusted his glasses, buttoned his half open shirt, and pulled together every semblance of dignity he could manage. Then he informed the young man he was the new minister of the Welsh Presbyterian Church and asked if he could direct them there. The kid had never heard of it, so Russ and Ellen putted off to find their way on their own.

It was hot and sticky now, humidity building toward the end of the day, clouds forming to the west. Clumps of cars moved in little spurts from corner to corner down the narrow, pothole pitted street. The traffic signals dangled from wires, so they bobbed up and down and were hard to see. Half of them didn't work anyway. Trucks were double parked in every block. Main Street was, in effect, a one-lane thoroughfare. Russ could see it might take an hour to get through town like this, so he stopped and made a phone call from a booth next to a drug store.

He found out their apartment wasn't ready and was given directions to the widow Elsie Edward's place where he was told they would be staying for a few days. On the way to Elsie's they passed the Welsh Presbyterian Church, and Russ pointed it out to Ellen. It stood close to the street on a busy corner, square, thick, steep roofed, and solid, with towers on either side of the front entrance, one shorter than the other. Kind of gray, kind of brown, the church took on the colors of everything around it, like the street, like the water in the river they had crossed, like the smoldering slag heap.

Uphill from the church Ellen and Russ came to Elsie's two-story, light green shingle-sided house, and Elsie actually seemed to whir as she trotted out to meet them with a warm greeting and open arms. A woman in her sixties, short, round-faced and plump, she moved in quick spurts as if powered by an electric motor. She showed Ellen and Russ to an upstairs room barely big enough for a double bed and two suitcases. It had pink and beige wallpaper and tiny pictures of mountains and snow scenes here and there on the pale green walls.

"Oh look," Ellen said, "a chenille bedspread, just like I had at home." God bless her, Russ thought, how could anybody be so chipper? Elsie just beamed. Her house, though large from the outside, seemed crowded inside. Everything was stairways and halls. Much of the furniture was oak or mahogany, thick, dark, and sturdy. In the parlor a number of large old lamps, small tables, and stuffed chairs with knitted quilts over them left hardly any room to walk.

While Ellen took a bath, Russ rummaged through the Saab looking for the sermon he hoped to preach the next day, but it wasn't turning up. "Four years of college and three years of seminary, and I don't know what I'm going to say tomorrow," he muttered. From years alone in library cubbyholes, he had acquired the habit of talking to himself more or less out loud.

RUSS HAD WRITTEN FOUR SERMONS up to that time, but only one was for a real church. The others were for preaching class, and the professors had criticized them so thoroughly he had no confidence in them at all. The sermon for the real church was called "When God Says 'Yes,'" quotes within quotes and everything, but he missed the service where he was supposed to preach it. It was still fresh and unsullied, if that's any advantage.

The reason for this is that, during the last week at Princeton, when the seniors in the Class of 1959 were trying to find enough money to pay off the seminary so they could graduate, a call came from a church in Mays Landing, New Jersey, for a substitute preacher, twenty-five dollars and dinner with a parish family after the service. Russ jumped at the chance and quickly sat down and wrote his sermon. On the appointed day, he put on his dark gray Dacron suit, snitched a black choir robe from the seminary chapel, and got the keys to his roommate's maroon 1950 Plymouth sedan. Good old Hoppsy, Russ thought, he's nothing if not generous. Hoppsy Hopple was a year behind Russ in school. Nobody called him by his first name because Hoppsy fit his last name so well.

Russ drove Hoppsy's bulky, slightly rusting, but surprisingly smooth running Plymouth to Route 1, turned south, and was on his way. In his rush, he circled Cape May on the map, a resort town on the Jersey shore maybe forty miles south of Mays Landing. When he drove into Cape May and pulled up in front of a big, white frame Presbyterian Church, it was almost eleven and the bell was ringing for the final call to the faithful. He grabbed the choir robe and ran up the steps into the narthex, sermon in hand. The choir was already forming for the processional.

"Sorry I'm late," he said. "I'm supposed to preach the sermon."

"Not here you aren't," came a deep, ministerial voice from behind the choir. Sure enough, there was the minister all robed and ready to go.

"So now what do I do?" Russ asked.

"There's another Presbyterian church over the bridge. That's probably the one you want. You get going, and I'll call and tell them you're on your way," said the robed one.

"Thanks," Russ said, and he was off and running amid snickers from the choir. Too bad he hadn't asked which way over the bridge. Too bad he hadn't checked his destination in the first place. Too bad a lot of things. It took fifteen minutes to find the other church, and when he got there and peered in the big front door, somebody in a black robe was up in the pulpit preaching away. Russ rolled the choir robe into a ball and backed off, out twenty-five bucks, not to mention the gas. He threw the choir robe in an unholy heap on the back seat of the Plymouth, slammed the door shut, and headed north on Route 1. When he saw the sign for Atlantic City, he turned off the highway and drove into town. "Long as I'm here, may as well see the sights," he mumbled to himself.

IN ATLANTIC CITY, RUSS NOTICED THE STREETS were named for the states, so he went down California Street in honor of where he was from, found a place to park, got out, and started walking. People of all sizes and shapes, many in swimsuits, were hauling stuff toward the shore. Books, balls, bottles of suntan oil, wicker baskets full of cut up chickens, whole hams, or uncooked hot dogs, also chairs, umbrellas, changes of clothes, ice chests, watermelons, six-pack after six-pack of beer, everybody was carrying something. Russ was glad to be empty handed.

He passed a bar called Windy's that had a neon sign representing clouds blown by the wind, if you used a lot of imagination. Music boomed through the open doorway, and inside, a band played "Kansas City, Here I Come." A big guy in a skimpy swimsuit was singing about getting one of those "crazy lookin' women there," and people were dancing like crazy on a big floor in the back. Russ went in and ordered a gin and tonic just like he could afford it. The bar was full of women, and they all wore shorts or swimsuits. He took off his preaching tie and stuffed it in his pocket, rolled up his shirtsleeves, and tried to look casual. Usually Russ had no trouble looking casual, but he was having trouble with it right then, he could tell. Then he noticed women were dancing together. He hadn't seen anything like that since high school sock hops when the girls wanted to dance and there weren't enough boys around. But these were grown women his age and older.

"What's going on here?" he asked the woman sitting next to him at the bar.

"What d'ya mean, 'What's going on here?'" she said. "We're from central Philly. We come here weekends. That's what's going on here."

"Oh," he said. He had been going to school too long. He knew it even as this young woman spoke. Twenty-five years old, and he'd spent twenty-one years in school. Summers he had worked in apple orchards, lettuce fields, and packing sheds near where he grew up. Those were the only jobs he ever had except for mowing the neighbor's lawn and stocking shelves in his father's store at Christmas time. And he had washed dishes for his meals in college and seminary and worked at the summer camp where he met Ellen. The rest of the time he spent learning languages, reading the great literature of the world, grinding through huge theology books, and trying to get better at golf. It would be hard to imagine why he thought he knew a lot about life, but till that moment, that's what he thought.

So there he was sitting in a bar in Atlantic City, the band now playing "Your Cheatin' Heart," grown women dancing real close with each other, when he was supposed to be giving the benediction to a congregation of Presbyterians in Mays Landing, wherever that is. He bought the young woman a drink and another for himself. Not bad for a guy out twenty-five bucks and no prospects.

Russ gulped his drink and headed out to the boardwalk. People were everywhere—distinguished gentlemen in white linen suits and tasteful ties, fashionable ladies in complete ensembles and fetching straw hats, others in dungarees and cut-offs, halter tops, wild shirts of swirling colors, and Bermuda shorts that didn't match anything else they had on. Many wore cardboard sunshades advertising beer or cigars. Straw hatted grandmothers smiled and nodded from big rolling wicker chairs pushed along by younger members of the family. Kids ran in and out through the crowd. Everyone munched popcorn or hot dogs or cotton candy, and they all seemed to have plenty of money to spend on nothing more serious than having a good time.

The beach was a mass of bodies of every description and some of no description at all lounging on the sand or running among the towels and blankets and bright colored umbrellas. It was like looking into one of those dime store kaleidoscopes and turning it slowly so colors slide over each other and form a pattern for an instant before tumbling into an entirely new splash of colors.

Russ had never seen so many people together in one place. Miles and miles of people. And all their games. Baseballs, footballs, volleyballs, beach balls, and red, yellow, and blue Frisbees sailed and bounced and rolled over and among the crowd. And dogs everywhere, hundreds of dogs jumping and barking and splashing in the surf, even though there were signs forbidding them. All this fun, all this abandon, all at the same time as churches would be letting out all over town. For Russ, the scene rolled itself into one big question: How in God's name am I supposed to compete with that? He stood staring at it for a while then quick walked back to the car and headed for Princeton. With the sun far in the west, he parked Hoppsy's car and left the choir robe lying crumpled on the back seat, glad to get back to good old ivy covered Hodge Hall where he felt he knew what was going on.

"How'd the preaching go?" Hoppsy wanted to know. Hoppsy was sitting at his desk reading and taking notes on little lined cards, the kind of thing Russ and Hoppsy and their fellow students had gotten very good at. Read, jot, and pile the cards in little stacks, that was the drill.

Hoppsy Hopple was tall, muscular, blond enough to be immortal and generous to a fault. They had roomed together happily almost two years, which may have been a seminary record. Russ told Hoppsy he didn't find the church, didn't preach, and ended up in Atlantic City drinking gin in a bar full of crazy women from Philadelphia. He told Hoppsy he didn't know if the preaching business would ever amount to much, given all those people on the Jersey shore right during church time. And he told him he would put gas in his car later because he was broke.

"You don't sound like yourself," Hoppsy said. "We'd better go out for pizza. I'll buy." Pizza was Hoppsy's solution to everything from a mild depression to a weak Christology. Hoppsy drove to Kingston, the next town up the road, and as they sat at the counter of The King's Inn sipping beer and waiting for the pizza to be done, Hoppsy informed Russ about gay bars and how the tavern circuit is where gay people find their sense of community, one reason being that churches shut them out.

"Hopps, I like the scholarly part," Russ said. "I like books. Hell, I'm more interested in ideas than people." Hoppsy just grinned and listened.

"I find it all so damn interesting," Russ went on. "Greek verbs, Athanasius, Freud, the Persians, Paul Tillich, Cotton Mather, I don't care who. I never seem to muster a burning desire for any one thing, never attain purity of heart, like Kierkegaard said. I like it all, and I especially like this little town with its old stone arches and its clanging bells and musty libraries and horrible weather."

"You ought to stick around then, Russ old toot, and not go out jousting with churches," Hoppsy said. "Go see your favorite professor and do a doctorate with him."

"My favorite's Yippie," Russ said, "and he's retiring."

"Yippie" was what they called Professor Emile Cailliet, pronounced Ki-yay, "Yippie" being short for "Yippie-i-o-ki-yay." He had long white hair that stuck out all directions, and he walked with his hands behind his back gazing up at the sky. He was said to walk into parked cars. He taught philosophy, anthropology, great books, and other courses that many in the seminary thought weren't needed by ministerial students. Russ found these courses the most interesting ones there and wrote long, intellectually impassioned papers for Yippie, all of them well received.

Russ knew Hoppsy was right. Princeton was his kind of place. He began to go Ivy League at Berkeley where he started wearing button down shirts, striped ties, tweed jackets, and Scotch grain shoes. And that's where he stumbled into a summer course that got him interested in poems. He was introduced to theology by reading Chaucer and Milton and Eliot and Auden and the like, and went to seminary, in part, to learn more about the God the poets kept mentioning. During his senior year, Russ did a huge independent study project for Yippie comparing and contrasting the Hebrew prophets and the Greek tragic poets and was sure he was on to something, but when Yippie announced his retirement, there was no place for him to go. Almost by default, he let it be known he was interested in taking a church, one of the last in his class to do so. Shortly after that, the Welsh Presbyterian Church of Scroggtown phoned, and Russ went to candidate. "Maybe this is what they mean by divine guidance," Russ said to himself at the time.

And so now he was in Scroggtown, called, signed up, married, and looking through the Saab for a sermon to preach in a real church. Lord be praised, he found the manuscript of "When God Says 'Yes'" under the tire jack, and it was only slightly crumpled.

2

Gettin' Up the Hwyl

"AND LET US REMEMBER, GOD SAYS YES TO LOVE, God says yes to laughter, God says yes to life. Amen." So did James Russell Llewellen come to the end of his first sermon in a real church. A typical seminary inspired sermon it was—three points, some alliteration, a story or two, an introduction and conclusion, which means everything got said three times. In spite of all that, heads nodded as if a phrase or two had gotten through.

Russ felt a thousand eyes were fixed on him, and though it was a bit less than half that many, it was a heady feeling. Because he didn't have a clerical robe, he wore the dark brown suit he had changed into after the wedding, a bit rumpled though it was. Ellen sat by a window near the front of the church in the tailored cream colored jacket and skirt he had helped her wriggle out of that night in the Holiday Inn, which now seemed long ago and maybe in a different land.

"The final hymn is number 104, 'Guide Me, O Thou Great Jehovah,'" Russ announced, not realizing he had called for the unofficial Welsh national anthem.

"Guide me, O thou great Jehovah, / Pilgrim through this barren land," they sang. A good sentiment, Russ thought, for beginning a pastorate far from familiar surroundings. "I am weak but Thou art mighty, / Hold me with Thy powerful hand." Proper sense of humility there, he thought. Russ was smiling down at the people from the pulpit, and they were singing up to him. Clear tenor voices rose from the left front pew where the six elders sat, all of them men in dark suits or sport coats, white shirts, and somber ties. It seemed like the main qualification for being an elder was to sing the tenor part vigorously with a well-tuned voice.

Then came the first chorus, and the singing rose and fell in ever more powerful waves: "Bread of Heaven, Bread of Heaven, / Feed me till I want no more, / Feed me till I want no more." With a deep breath, the congregation readied itself for the second stanza. "Open now the crystal fountain / Whence the healing stream doth flow...." There was no denying them. People stood on their tiptoes, threw their heads back, and strained their necks into the song. The elders closed their eyes and sang with their mouths in perfect circles, each note drawn out as far as it would go, each word given its full ringing tone. They slowed it way down so every syllable stretched and reached and filled the room with reverberating sound. Russ had never heard such singing, certainly not among Presbyterians.

They came to the last stanza and sang quietly in a haunting whisper, "When I tread the verge of Jordan, / Bid my anxious fears subside." Yes, let them subside, Russ thought. But beyond all conscious thought was the stirring witness of those voices. "Death of death and hell's destruction, / Land me safe on Canaan's side." For these people it seemed the Promised Land of Canaan was right there in their little church, in the lives they were living and the faith they expressed in song. They had landed in that Canaan from the troubles of the old world, or their forebears had, and now Russ and Ellen had landed there too. That was the sense of the Promised Land he was receiving as these people sang their hymn. It was nothing like what he got from his Old Testament History class, which located such a place centuries ago in a Middle Eastern desert.

Then it was all boom and glory. "Songs of praises, songs of praises, / I will ever give to Thee, / I will ever give to Thee." They

got to the end of the refrain, and the short, thin, white haired chorister in his maroon robe waved his right arm in one big circle,
and they began to sing it again, letting the sound build and grow,
letting it fall and become quiet, then letting it rise once more in
all fullness. The walls seemed to be expanding and the windows
seemed to be shaking. The chorister led the singing as if all the
people were the choir, and the people responded to every rhythmic sweep of his right hand. They sang it again and again. All the
significance of those simple Psalm-like words was pulled out and
made available to the gathered souls of that congregation of Welsh
Presbyterians. Russ wondered why they needed him to preach
to them.

When the final tones of the hymn faded away and people stood
in silence, heads slightly bowed waiting for the final blessing, Russ
opened his mouth but could hardly raise any voice at all, nor could
he lift his arms to bless them the way he had been taught to do
in seminary. That was just as well. A custom forbids raising one's
arms for the benediction until after ordination, and Russ hadn't
gone through that formality yet.

"The Lord bless us and keep us from this time forth and forever
more. Amen." He said it so softly only a few could hear. It was all
he could manage.

IT TOOK A LONG TIME SHAKING HANDS at the door after the service.
Everyone wanted to get in a word of welcome for the new minister. Many said they could have listened to him longer. "Don't hold
back," they said. "We want to hear your good words, you know."

Last out was Buck Davies, one of the elders who sat prom-
inently in the front left pew. He shook Russ's hand with special
enthusiasm. Buck was a short, thickset man in his early forties,
nicely dressed in tan slacks, brown sport coat, and dark green tie.
He had a good shock of dark hair, and a clear, rhythmic speaking
voice not all that different from the lilting tenor Russ head from
him during the last hymn.

"It was fine the way you helped us get up the hwyl today, Reverennnd, that's very Welsh you know," Buck said. The Welsh word came out something like who-ll spoken quickly, all in one syllable. Interesting language, Russ thought to himself. And Buck pronounced Russ' title with lots of emphasis on the ns, the word rising in pitch as if part of a song. It was the first time anyone had called Russ that, and it seemed like a long, drawn out thing to be called.

"You mean the last hymn?" Russ said.

"We call it gettin' up the hwyl when the spirit starts to move like that."

"All I did was call out a hymn number."

"Ah, Reverennnd, but what a number. And what a hymn." Buck was smiling broadly, his eyes dancing in his long thin face. "And you called the number so well." They both laughed at that.

"The chorister led the whole congregation in the singing. I've never seen that before."

"In a Welsh church, Reverennnd, the chorister is but a little lower than God. He'll do as he sees fit."

"I notice you use the old green hymnal," Russ said. "There's a new red one out, as you probably know."

Buck looked off a bit of a scowl and said, "First of all, Reverennnd, the green hymnal has more Welsh hymns by far. But also, we Welsh, you'll find, are pretty close with a dollar. We don't go out of our way to spend money on what's not needed."

"That's not a bad thing," Russ said. "But it looks like you've spent some money fixing up the church. I suppose that was needed." Russ sensed it would be easy to get at cross-purposes with Buck Davies, and he sensed he was not doing a very good job of avoiding it.

"Used to be terribly gloomy in here, Reverennnd," Buck said, "everything dark brown. Just this year we completed our renova-tionnns." He fairly sang the word, like he did with "Reverennnd."

26

Russ asked Buck if he or one of the elders would like to do part of the service next week, but he wouldn't hear of it. "You do it your way, Reverennnd," Buck said. "We're all just simple folks here. We're here to follow you." Something about the way Buck said this made Russ think there might have been a smirk behind his words. In an informal chat after class, one of Russ' professors said that every church has a "buck elder," one who has been at the eldering business so long there is nothing he doesn't know about it, and who, in ways no new minister can understand, runs the church without seeming to. To Russ, Buck Davies looked like he might fill the bill. But the main thing Buck was interested in right then was showing off the renovations.

"We refinished the pews, making them blond. And we lightened the walls. Brightens things up nice and cheerful." Buck was fiercely proud of his church, Russ could see. And he was right. Things were bright and cheerful. The church must have been full of shadows and gloomy corners, just the way Calvin would have wanted it, Russ thought. It gave him heart to think the brightening of the sanctuary might signify a move toward brighter attitudes among the people.

The pulpit was in the middle of a raised platform, an old, heavy affair of solid oak with leaf-like carvings along the sides. It had been meticulously scraped and refinished with a light ash stain. On top of it was the huge black leather-bound Bible. There was no room for anything else. Russ's sermon notes had rested on the pages of scripture, a fitting symbol no doubt, but the notes curved down into the center of that big book which made them hard to see. The old Welsh preachers, apparently, didn't take anything into the pulpit except their voices. Russ was only the second minister of that congregation who didn't speak Welsh, Buck told him, shrugging a little as he said it. Russ shrugged back.

Directly beneath the pulpit was the blond oak communion table, heavy looking and almost square. It had a single brass candlestick on it along with the now empty offering plates. Someone

27

had quickly whisked the money into an official looking brown leather sack right after the final blessing.

Behind the pulpit were three high backed arm chairs with green cushioned seats. They too had been refinished in a nice light color. The chair in the middle was larger and more comfortable than the others. Behind the chairs was a railing that set off the choir loft, which curved back in an alcove a couple of steps higher. If you looked at the room from top to bottom, you found choir, preacher, and people in descending order, the unspoken hierarchy of a Welsh congregation, Russ suspected. Behind the choir loft was a large window of rippled amber glass surrounded by beige wallpaper with purple florets in it. A peaceful glow, as if divine light streamed in through the choir loft, which, Russ supposed, was the whole idea.

In the back of the church, above the rear pews was a small balcony. "It's where the young people like to sit," Buck said, "but you have to watch them or they fold the worship bulletins into airplanes and send them flying over the congregation during the sermon." Russ said he could hardly wait for that. Above the balcony, a large round rose window let in multi-colored patterns of light that danced here and there throughout the sanctuary.

A big round clock facing the pulpit was mounted in the middle of the balcony railing. "The clock is there so the minister will know when the roasts are starting to burn in the ovens of the parish," Buck said with a chuckle. "You wouldn't want to ruin our Sunday dinners by preaching too long, now would you, Reverennnd." Russ wondered how he would ever fill the time allotted to him. It seemed they expected a sermon to go a good half hour or more, and he had trouble getting enough material for ten minutes. So far as he could tell, the sermon and the hymns were the main attraction; everything else was sort of filler, a far cry from the carefully unified services he prepared for worship class at the seminary.

They came to where the elders sat together in the first pew to the left of the pulpit, the only place separated by little swinging gates.

"So the elders have this special pew," Russ observed.

"It's the Holiness of Holinesses," Buck said, "only elders allowed there." Buck smiled as he said it, but his tone was dead serious.

Then there was the pride and joy of a Welsh congregation— the organ. They had just gotten a new one, spent over two thousand dollars on it, Buck said. "Remember, Reverennnd, if you want to get a Welsh church pullin' together now, you start an organ fund."

The new organ was a small blond oak console with pedals and chimes. The way Buck touched it, Russ guessed they bought the organ first and renovated the church to match. Richie Evans, a young music student they were proud of, was the organist. Russ noticed Richie playing without looking at the music much of the time, closed his eyes even, and moved his head back and forth to the tune, unlike the staid church organists he had seen before.

Russ noticed a little brass plaque on the pulpit that said, "In Memory of Reverend C. Robert Jenkins, Pastor of Welsh Presbyterian Church, Scroggtown, Pennsylvania, 1897-1909, Given by his Son, Lloyd R. Jenkins." On the organ, on the side of every bank of pews, on the gate to the Holiness of Holinesses, on the great high backed chair behind the pulpit, even underneath the clock on the balcony railing, there was a little brass plaque. Everything in the room was a memorial to somebody. The presence of the dead pressed in upon the holiness and was as clearly felt as the light streaming in from the windows. Russ sensed himself in the midst of a Protestant shrine.

"Buck, it's wonderful in here," Russ said. "The people have done themselves proud."

"We did it for the Lord, Reverennnd," Buck said, as if mere human accomplishment is not to be lifted up for praise.

"And the Lord must be very pleased," Russ said, hoping it was what was called for under the circumstances. It seemed to Russ the circumstances could be more involved than they seemed, as if any minute it was possible to say something that would be taken the wrong way. He was glad when Buck led him downstairs to join the others for what he called "a little lunch" in honor of the new minister and his wife.

RIGHT AFTER THAT FIRST SERMON Russ discovered one of the constants of preaching: It can make one readily passionate. Maybe it's the relief it's over or the sense of liveliness that comes from being in front of people. Maybe it's some old connection between religion and procreation now forgotten. Whatever it might be, Russ felt it. He imagined that Sunday afternoon was the scrunchiest time of the week in a vast number of parsonages throughout the land. But Ellen and Russ were not free to go. What Buck called a little lunch was in fact a long table laden with the specialties of the parish—three kinds of meatballs, two chicken dishes, a baked ham, several pots of beans, jello salads of many colors, macaroni salad, and two potato salads, one hot, one cold. Top it all off with dark tea and Welsh cookies, which are round, quarter inch thick little cakes with currants in them that are not baked but fried in a skillet.

As they ate, Ellen and Russ rubbed knees under the table and felt themselves terribly wicked, but soon the parishioners knew very well what was going on.

"My you have rosy cheeks, Mrs. Llewellen. Is it too warm in here for you? We could turn on the fan," someone said. Then wink, wink, wink all around the room.

"No, I'm just fine," Ellen said.

The new preacher and his wife ate way too much. They were expected to try everything and approve of it all. Their approval was confirmed by having seconds and thirds. Someone was always filling their plates with ham or chicken or potato salad.

"You need to keep up your strength, Reverennnd," one of the ladies said as she dished out more meatballs. "You and your little wife. We can't have you wasting away on us now."

"Yeah, a little wife like that could use up a lot of his strength," came a gruff whisper from the back table just loud enough to be heard. Some of the men laughed, and Buck made a point to stand up, clear his throat and look around the room in a mock glare of reprimand.

Finally, the gathering started to break up. No speeches, no introductions, no fuss. They all knew each other and they had brought in young ministers before. That Russ and Ellen didn't know them didn't seem to matter.

"You go on and get your rest now, Reverennnd."

"You're off to a fine start, Reverennnd."

"We've been praying God would send us someone like you."

"Lovely wife you have there, Reverennnd, she'll be a great help to you in your work."

"Ellen Llewellen, what a wonderful Welsh name." Some of them pronounced the double "ls" with a kind of "t" sound worked in, "tl" or something like that. Russ tried but couldn't get his tongue to do it. "Can't even pronounce my own name, apparently," he mumbled.

Ellen and Russ smiled and shook hands in a kind of daze. They didn't know what any of this Welsh ethnic consciousness was about. In California, the Welsh names—Morgan, Davis, Jones, Williams and the like—were considered regular American names, but in Scroggtown, obviously, they meant something. Russ began to think that being voted in by the congregation had a lot to do with his last name, as Welsh a name as there is. And he wondered what Ellen felt about being a "big help" in her husband's work. He sensed the farthest thing from her mind was becoming part of what is known as a "clergy couple." Still, it looked like that's what they were being taken for already.

Again, the last one to shake hands was Buck. He was extremely solicitous now, walking along to see Russ and Ellen to their car.

"You've got a challenge here, Reverennnd, but with God's help, you can do it," he said. "I'm a mere elder, but if you need me for anything, don't hesitate to call."

"Thank you," Russ said and gave him what must have been a quizzical smile. Buck already seemed much more than a "mere" elder.

"Oh Buck, there you are!" A booming voice rolled over the neighborhood from across the street, and a tall hefty man in a three-piece black suit waved their direction.

"There's Brother Henry," Buck said. "You'll have to meet him."

Brother Henry, with arms flapping and coattails flying, seemed to cross the street in one big step. And still his voice boomed, though now he was right in front of the three of them.

"I had to come by and greet the new minister and his wife," Brother Henry said, the sound of his voice rattling the windows of the drugstore on the corner across from the church. "So, Llewellen, how did it go on your first day? You preached the Word, I trust."

"I hope so," Russ said in a voice that sounded far away compared to Brother Henry's.

"He did just fine," Buck said. "Reverennnd and Mrs. Llewellen, let me introduce you to The Reverennnd Doctor Henry Reese, who for over thirty years has been pastor of the First Presbyterian Church of Scroggtown. Brother Henry has been a great help to us while we've been without a minister."

To go with his black suit, Brother Henry wore a black hat, black tie, black shoes and the whitest white shirt Russ had ever seen. When he tipped his hat to Ellen, he showed a fine crop of slicked down gray hair. If there were bishops in the Presbyterian Church, they would look like reprobates in the presence of Brother Henry, Russ thought.

Brother Henry asked Russ to join him for breakfast the next morning at The Coal Bin, a nice new restaurant on the north end of Main Street, he said. Russ accepted and Brother Henry bounded away.

"Heavens, Buck, does he always talk that loud?" Russ asked.

"Well, Reverennnd, it's good for a preacher to have a voice like Gabriel's trumpet," Buck said. "The people need to hear that clear call from the Lord."

"But shouldn't there be some volume control?" Russ asked.

"You're right. Brother Henry's got very little volume control, and everybody hears every word he says from the pulpit or anywhere else."

"Hard to keep any secrets that way," Russ said.

"Why Reverennnd, ministers don't need secrets. At least Brother Henry doesn't. He's a paragon."

"Am I supposed to be like Brother Henry, Buck?"

"Nobody's like Brother Henry. Don't even try to be like him. Before he preaches a sermon, he drops to his knees like a sack full of bones and prays for maybe five minutes up there while everyone looks at him. Then he bounces up all of a sudden and preaches a darn fine sermon. But we're so taken with watching him pray, we forget to listen to what he has to say. Brother Henry takes his work very serious. Some people call him crazy Brother Henry, but he's not crazy at all. You'll see."

RUSS AND ELLEN SAID GOODBYE to Buck and drove to Elsie's house. Elsie wasn't home yet, so they went to their room for a little something more than a nap. About six o'clock, Elsie woke them from a sound sleep to say a little lunch was ready. The ladies at the potluck had sent leftovers so the new reverennnd wouldn't go hungry, she said. Once again they ate jello salad, ham, potato salad, and Welsh cookies. They drank dark tea and listened to Elsie talk about people who had lived and died years ago, including, her dear dead husband Wally. The clock on the balcony railing was dedicated in his memory, Elsie said.

Early the next morning, Russ put Ellen on the bus to Wilkes Barre where she was to register for her junior year of college. Off she went in orange plaid skirt, rust colored sweater, and white shoes, her blond ponytail bobbing up and down behind her just like a college kid. It felt strange to Russ not to be going to school himself. He couldn't remember not going to school in the fall. And he wondered how they would pay Ellen's tuition, make the car payments, and have any fun on the $3600 per year plus housing he had agreed to.

From the bus station, Russ drove down Main Street to meet with Brother Henry at The Coal Bin. The décor inside was in shades of dark slate and deep blue, the colors of coal. The waitresses' uniforms were combinations of the same colors except they wore little white aprons. The lighting fixtures were like huge miners' lamps, and instrumental music came through speakers hidden near the ceiling in lumps of plastic meant to resemble outcroppings of coal. The menus, jet-black printed in white, were the shape of the little rail cars that brought coal up from the mines.

Russ joined Brother Henry at a table in the center of the room. He sipped from a cup of hot water as he told Russ he never took anything more stimulating, even at breakfast. He also let it be known that he never drank liquor, never smoked, never chewed, and never went with the girls who did in all his fifty-five years. Russ sipped a cup of coffee while Brother Henry told him this.

They ordered ham and eggs, and when the platters came, Brother Henry stood up and boomed in his one and only voice, "Let us pray." Russ, startled, dropped his knife and fork on the spot. So did everybody there. Brother Henry lifted his eyes to the black and blue ceiling, knitted his forehead in a pained expression, and roared out his prayer: "Oh God most gracious, we thank Thee for this scintillating morning and the myriad opportunities of this new day, for this delectable food set before us and the loving hands that have prepared it, for those who serve us here and those who wash the dishes, for those who come and go among us throughout the day...." It went on till Russ's coffee was cold, till all the coffee in the place was cold, till the eggs started to look a little sad, and the toast began to curl. Still, when Brother Henry said the "Amen," people applauded enthusiastically. Russ wanted to crawl under the table, but Brother Henry thought it was great. The waitresses went around and warmed up the coffee and people came up to Brother Henry and shook his hand.

"Nice prayer, Brother Henry," they said. "You get us started right for the day."

It turned out his breakfast with Brother Henry was to get Russ squared away for the Presbytery meeting next day. A Presbytery is a legislative body made up of ministers and elders from all the Presbyterian churches in a particular region. It has most of the powers of a bishop and is especially careful when it comes to ordaining new clergy. At the meeting of Presbytery, Russ was to undergo what Brother Henry called his "trials" to see if he was fit for the gospel ministry.

"I assume you have sent to Presbytery the items they asked for on your application," Brother Henry said.

"Yes, I did that some weeks ago," Russ answered.

"Good. Prepare a statement of faith for us, but don't make it too long, and try not to get into anything controversial. It would only bog things down. And brush up on Presbyterian polity. That's what they'll be interested in. I'll stop by for you at nine o'clock sharp tomorrow morning." Then Brother Henry up and left without stopping at the cash register or even leaving a tip. Russ found out that The Coal Bin gave Brother Henry a free breakfast any morning he came in. He was the main attraction. People would call and ask if Brother Henry had prayed yet. If not, they left their shops and offices and headed to the Coal Bin for coffee, hot rolls and a rousing prayer.

3

The Trials

NEXT MORNING AT NINE SHARP, Brother Henry was parked in front of Elsie's house ready to roll in his black 1952 Chevrolet sedan with white sidewall tires. The car was in perfect condition just like Brother Henry was, a no nonsense preacher car. The tires even suggested clerical collars.

They headed north out of town into the low hills, away from the slag heaps and rusty metal towers of the mines. The sun shined upon the just and the unjust and warmed the fields and cows and huge red barns. The woods were just beginning to be tinged with amber and gold, and the beauty of the day helped Russ feel ready to face his trials, as Brother Henry called them.

Brother Henry stopped at several little towns along the way and picked up other ministers. Tunkhannock, Mehoopany, Wyalusing, Russ had never been to places with names like these, Native American names reflecting some hard history in these parts, he thought. The towns were half hidden by great arching elms, poplars, and maples, and the highway north was their Main Street. As the morning progressed, six ministers squeezed into the car with Russ in the middle of the front seat. There was precious little space for anything, including air.

All of these ministers were men in their forties or fifties, and they all wore dark brown suits, white shirts, and tightly knotted beige or brown neckties. Furthermore, they all had rich, resonant voices, as if at any moment they would form the bass section of a choir and sing the low parts of holy hymns and chants. Russ, in his brown honeymoon suit, was a younger manifestation of the species. Except for Brother Henry, it looked like Presbyterian ministers came from the same mold. Brother Henry wore his basic black three-piece suit, his starchy white shirt, coal black tie, and his proper black felt hat, which he kept on while he drove.

The towns all had bumpy tree-lined streets, a few stores and gas stations, taverns with Good Gibbons Beer signs in the window, and several churches of various sizes and shapes. The main streets were overhung with wires, and the road signs sometimes stipulated two speed limits for the same stretch of road.

The biggest church was often Presbyterian, the Methodist next, and then a Baptist church and smaller independent chapels. In Scroggtown, the Catholic Church was the biggest by far, but out in the country, the farmers and their friends were mostly Protestants, it appeared, and they kept their churches and the grounds around them as neat and tidy as they kept their barns and fields. Right next to each church was the manse, always built of the same material as the church. White frame church, white frame manse. Brick church, brick manse. Composition siding, both the same. Russ wondered how many of these preachers stumbled into their churches late at night thinking they were home or ran up the steps of their houses thinking they were at the church.

"See that, Russ," one of the ministers in the back said, pointing to a sign indicating the turnoff to Camptown, "that's where the famous racetrack is, where the ladies go doo-dah all day."

"Yeah," another said, "where I come from the ladies hardly ever go doo-dah." He sang a stanza of "The Camptown Ladies" song and made sure the ladies went doo-dah.

Russ glanced at Brother Henry to see how he might be taking this jocularity. He was smiling. He apparently liked to hear his colleagues ramble about frivolous things, though he didn't contribute anything of the kind himself.

"How many miles on this car, Henry?" the minister sitting next to Russ wanted to know.

"One hundred and four thousand," Brother Henry replied, his voice filling the empty spaces in the car many times over. "It gets eighteen miles to the gallon and never uses oil."

"That's the shortest speech I ever heard you make, Brother Henry," came a deep voice from the back, and it set the conversation toward a comparison of automobiles. The ministers told how their cars were running and what they were doing about the car allowance from the church and how they were trying to work the depreciation deduction and maybe even get the ten per cent tax credit for capital investment. Russ didn't know what they were talking about, but it seemed to be extremely important to them. When it came his turn to say something he told about the Saab. They weren't sure about putting oil in with the gas, and they thought thirty miles to the gallon was impossible. They believed in Chevrolets and Fords, because their parishioners would resent it if they showed up at church in anything more luxurious. One of them told how he had made the mistake of buying a Pontiac a few years back, and the offerings fell off noticeably until he got rid of it and bought a used Chevy. "People figured I must not need their money if I could afford a car like that," he said.

Then they got on to how the offerings were coming in and what materials they were using for their fall stewardship campaigns. Somebody wanted to know if anyone was going to get a raise. To Russ it seemed they took this almost as seriously as they took their cars.

Knowing coffee was on his list of the forbidden, the reverends tried to kid Brother Henry into stopping for a cup, but he pulled his hat down and hummed a verse of "O Sacred Head Now Wounded" to ward off his persecutors. So they went on to talk about golf and trout fishing. They knew as much about these subjects as they knew about stewardship and the tax laws, which was considerable. Every little town had a golf course nearby, and some of them let the clergy play free if they start early on Monday morning, Russ learned. He didn't think it wise to mention he had played on his college golf team.

Just before noon they pulled into a village a few miles south of the New York state line. Everything seemed old and everything seemed to fit. All the rooflines were at the same steep angle, every building was painted white, and most of the windows had green shutters. This was true of the few stores on Main Street, the gas stations, the houses, the Presbyterian Church and its manse, and the restaurant across the street from the church where they went for lunch. Half the Presbytery was there eating enormous amounts of coleslaw, chicken and dumplings, apple pie and ice cream, and drinking mugs of pitch black Presbyterian coffee to keep themselves "from sleep and from damnation," as the hymn puts it, after so heavy a meal. Brother Henry, of course, ordered hot water instead of coffee

The room was noisy, crowded, and stuffy, reverberating with deep liturgical voices. Reverends went from table to table greeting old friends and patting each other on the back. Surely there's no friendlier bunch than a roomful of ministers stuffing themselves with chicken and dumplings. Presbytery was like a reunion, Russ could see, and Brother Henry was at the heart of it. "Say a prayer for us, Henry, so we don't choke on our food," someone said. To Russ it seemed Brother Henry knew he was being kidded and also knew this meant he was an insider, even if a bit different.

AT ONE O'CLOCK, TO THE TOLLING OF A PONDEROUS BELL, a long irregular line of ministers and elders, all but three of them men in dark suits, walked across the street and entered the arched green doors of the church. The three women wore dark skirts and sweaters. They assembled with prayer and song, deep ministerial voices eagerly intoning the hymn "Now thank we all our God / With

hearts and hands and voices," as they followed the steady prod-
dings of a fine old pipe organ played with stops wide open.

The church could have been a movie set for a Protestant heaven.
Everything was white and spotless and glowing with the light of
a golden, early autumn sun through the clear windows. Outside,
Russ could see stubble fields and the subdued amber and gold of the
woods stretching toward eternity. Two banks of straight, mahogany trimmed white pews filled the long, narrow sanctuary. The
pulpit, the lectern, and baptismal font were also white with mahogany trim. From the ceiling hung cut glass chandeliers in perfect
proportion to the room, and on the walls were brass sconces fitted
with tall white candles. A rank of silver organ pipes was set in the
wall at the back of the chancel. The lines were clean and unclut-
tered, everything at right angles to everything else, a starkly simple room where faith had a chance to get at the basics, one would
think.

After some preliminaries, Russ was ushered to a parlor that
had cracks in the ceiling and a slightly faded picture of Jesus on the
wall. The committee for checking on prospective ministers gathered around a white wooden table, Brother Henry in charge. He
had a great collection of Russ' term papers from seminary, some
of his written exams in their little blue booklets, the transcript of
his grades, and letters from his professors stating their opinion of
him. Everything was there, including Russ's stumbling effort to
compose a contemporary hymn rather than memorize a prayer
for worship class. Looking at those papers on the table was like
waiting naked in the doctor's office before the pushing and poking
begins, Russ felt.

"Your papers are in order, Mr. Llewellen," Brother Henry said,
"but members of the committee would like to ask you some questions about certain matters they feel are important. For instance,
what about your Hebrew? I see you received one of your lowest
marks in Hebrew."

Brother Henry, naturally, kept up with his Hebrew. He could probably pray in Hebrew, but about all Russ could remember was that in Hebrew "who" is "he" and "he" is "she." Even with his woeful lack of churchly experience, Russ could tell there was no use mentioning the reason he got the low mark in Hebrew was because, on the night before the final exam, W. H. Auden was reading his poems over at Princeton University, and after a truly Calvinistic inner struggle, he decided to go listen to Auden, because chances were he'd never have another opportunity to hear him. After all, it was the Age of Eliot and Auden, as one of his college professors had emphatically proclaimed, and surely one must hear a poet of the age if the occasion presents itself. Still, Russ could see, Presbytery was not the place to rely on the glories of English verse as an excuse for slighting Hebrew.

Brother Henry produced a Hebrew Bible and said, "Please read something for us? Mr. Llewellen." Russ turned to the back and started to read. At least he remembered to start from the back, because in Hebrew that's the front. And he remembered to read from right to left. "Beresheet bara Elohim...," he began. He could feel it coming back to him. The words spit and sputtered from his mouth the way Hebrew does, and he went on for several verses.

"That will be entirely adequate, Mr. Llewellen," Brother Henry said, "now give us your considered version of the English, if you please." It seemed to Russ that Presbytery had a language of its own. Even Brother Henry didn't speak this formally most of the time, but at least he was able to speak more quietly in this mode, and Russ was glad of that.

"There are those who render it 'By wisdom God created heaven and earth,'" Russ said, "but certainly 'In the beginning God' is a valid translation of the first words of the Bible." He took off from there, stating that, at the place where newer translations say, "the Spirit of God moved upon the face of the deep," it was better translated, "And the Spirit of God brooded over the primeval waters."

"Why do you render it that way?" Brother Henry wanted to know, just as Russ had hoped he would, because, if nothing else, he knew that one cold.

"The verb we have here is used for the action of a hen hovering over her chicks," Russ said. "It's striking that right at the beginning, the Bible gives us a feminine image for God's creative activity. In my translation, I'm trying to express the protective caring that the word implies and also the cosmic newness of the situation. We have a watery scene upon which light is about to shine for the first time, bringing forth all creatures and things, and the language is that of a hen protecting her tiny chicks just as they have hatched. I thought…"

"Fine, fine, Mr. Llewellen, that's extremely fine," Brother Henry said. "We can see you know something of the character of Hebrew words, even if you have not mastered the language. Next to Welsh, you know, Hebrew is the most noble of human tongues." Brother Henry was in his booming voice again, his words ringing through the room. The other committee members leaned back in their chairs and chuckled. They went around the room asking Russ things he should have learned in Sunday School as a kid but didn't, because he didn't much go to Sunday School as a kid. He didn't go at all, in fact, after he started playing golf at a ridiculously young age.

"What are the three Offices of Christ?" somebody asked.

"Prophet, Priest, and King," Russ pulled out from somewhere, though he couldn't remember any course where it was put exactly that way.

"What were the main issues in the Reformation?" was the next question.

Russ trotted out the list: the authority of Rome, the abuse of indulgences for getting out of Purgatory, the singing of hymns by the people, the translation of the Bible into German, and the priesthood of all believers, which means people can go directly to God without reliance on the clergy. Russ wondered what would happen to the reverend clergy if that principle was taken to its furthest conclusion. He could see this was not the place for that conversation.

The longest discussion was about Presbyterian polity and the notion of the "corporate bishop." They wanted to be sure Russ knew were the power lies. "In duly elected groups," he said, "always in groups, forever in groups, for better or worse in groups."

"And what do we properly call these groups?" Brother Henry wanted to know.

"Judicatories," Russ said. "Sounds like a diagnosis, doesn't it. We Presbyterians, we've got the judicatories." Some members of the committee chuckled a little, but others pointedly did not, including Brother Henry.

The final question was to name the four boards of the national Presbyterian Church. Russ got Foreign Missions, National Missions, and Christian Education, but forgot the Board of Pensions and had to be reminded of it. "I hope the Board of Pensions doesn't forget me," he said, and this time everybody laughed.

"Unless I hear objection, our committee will recommend that your trials proceed on the floor of Presbytery," Brother Henry said. "The very best to you." He led the committee in a booming prayer while Russ wondered what it meant to be tried on the "floor" of Presbytery.

When the prayer was over, they took a break. The whole Presbytery had gone outside to sip coffee and gobble up home baked cookies provided by the Women's Fellowship of the congregation. A number of jovial conversations were taking place, few if any about church matters, far as Russ could tell.

WHEN PRESBYTERY RECONVENED, Russ was escorted to the front of the sanctuary and invited to read his statement of faith. He was not offered the pulpit or lectern, so he stood on the first step of the chancel and spoke with as much force as he could muster. It seemed to him his whole body was shaking, but when he looked down, his legs remained solid and still. He took care to hit as many high points as he could—God, Christ, Spirit, Church, human purpose and destiny—without coming down too forcefully on one side or another of the controversies of which the seminary had made him aware. After a while his nervousness left him, and his voice dropped down to where it could express a measure of conviction. He finished with what he thought was a ringing declaration about the God of the Bible being all wrapped up in humanity.

Absolute silence. It was as if he had read the grocery list. Nobody moved or spoke or even coughed. It was a long, hard, brain-numbing silence that seemed to stretch to another age. The dark-haired and gray-haired heads out there in the pews were slightly bowed. No one looked Russ' way.

Finally, someone in the back rose and asked Russ to give a little of his own "pilgrimage," as he called it. Russ told about being captivated by English literature at the University of California and, along with some fraternity brothers, finding his way to the Presbyterian Church in his desire to know more about this God the poets sometimes praised and sometimes treated with disdain. That brought a definite sprinkling of frowns in the assembly but also some obvious signs of interest.

"Can you tell us of any specific religious experience?" another presbyter asked.

Russ gulped. He looked at Brother Henry, hoping there was some kind of protection from the question, like in a court of law. Brother Henry raised his eyebrows and nodded, as if to say, "Answer it, you fool."

"When I was a junior in college," Russ said, "some fraternity brothers invited me to their home in Sacramento for a weekend. One of them played the banjo, and we had a wonderful time singing folk songs far into a Saturday night. Next day, somebody said, 'Let's go over to the fairgrounds to the Billy Graham rally. That should be good for a few laughs.'" Russ knew he had to be careful about Billy Graham among Presbyterians. Some thought he was

Christ's next of kin, but others felt it beneath their dignity to mention his name with anything but a smirk.

"Once we got there," Russ went on, "it didn't seem like the time or place to be making fun. And the singing was magnificent. When the offering basket came by, I found myself putting in my last dollar." The Presbytery snickered at that and Russ smiled back. "The sermon was about Moses coming down from the mountain, finding the people gone astray, and telling them to choose where they would stand, either here with faith and purpose or there with confusion and despair." Russ gestured with both hands to the right and to the left. "Somehow I felt it applied to me," he said.

"We were quiet going back to Berkeley that night," Russ continued, "and it seemed to me a strange and peaceful glow filled the car. I felt it was time to decide some things about my life. That a sermon could affect me like that was a big surprise, and all the people singing, it gave me a sense of something grand and purposeful. I felt I wanted to be part of that somehow. And so I got involved in the church and my life unfolded in that direction. That's why I'm here." Russ' voice had gotten steadier and quieter, until, at the end, he was speaking in a firm whisper that carried to the back of the room. People were leaning forward, some nodding and smiling.

An older minister rose to ask Russ how he would go about comforting a family in the loss of a loved one. Russ had no idea, but his mind went quickly to the day in seminary when they practiced funerals. They stretched out a classmate on three folding chairs, thrust a fake flower into his hands, and took turns praying over him. The flower held by the "corpse" jiggled as he giggled. Russ told his questioner he would quote from the Psalms, and that seemed to satisfy the gentleman.

It went on like this for another half hour. Would he be faithful in attending Presbytery meetings? Oh yes. Would he get his reports in on time? Russ didn't know what reports he had to get in on time but said he would do so most certainly. Finally, a distinguished looking minister near the front rose slowly to his feet.

Dr. C. Calvin Clarke, pastor of a large and important church in Wilkes Barre, was a portly and imposing man with a great wave of pure white hair above his round, almost jolly face. He wore rimless glasses and a suit much like Brother Henry's, except it was dark blue with thin, tasteful stripes. All other questions dried up right then. The fact that Dr. Clarke was from Scotland and his voice was tinged with the heather added to his clearly evident stature.

"Now Mr. Llewellen," he began, "you have given us a most comprehensive statement of your Christian faith, for which we are indeed grateful, and you have well-accounted yourself in answering the several questions my colleagues have put before you. Nevertheless, it seems to me, Mr. Llewellen, that you are oft times a wee bit cautious in your remarks, so that it occasionally becomes difficult for one to know for certain what you truly might be thinking on this subject or that. For instance, if I correctly recall your comments on the Incarnation of our Lord in your otherwise adequate statement, I don't believe I heard any mention of his miraculous birth. Over the centuries, Mr. Llewellen, as I am sure you are aware, the Christian Church has linked its understanding of God's Incarnation in Christ to the record of his birth from the womb of the Virgin Mary. What is your understanding of the Virgin Birth, Mr. Llewellen? Will you kindly enlighten us please?"

So there's the question that will decide my future, Russ thought. Whether or not I become a minister depends on what I think about this old doctrine. It's the same question Ellen's mother asked just before our wedding, for God sakes. Who would have thought?

Still, on the floor of Presbytery, Russ sensed the question was not just an orthodoxy test. He knew that most of the ministers there had read the same things he had read about the gospel passages that tell of the birth of Jesus, but the lay elders likely had not. And he suspected his smart face answer to Ellen's mother would not get him very far in this setting.

"As I understand it," Russ ventured, clearing his throat and speaking carefully, "in the famous passage from Isaiah that says 'A virgin shall conceive and bear a son' the Hebrew word translated 'virgin' has the basic meaning of 'young woman'." Clearly, the ancient Hebrews were not expecting the Messiah to be born of a virgin, so to use the verse from Isaiah as a precursor to the Christmas story is to wrench it out of its original meaning, something our fine Presbyterian scholars tell us not to do.

"Now, when we go on to the Christian writings, we find that, on the whole, they do not relate God being incarnate in Jesus to the story of the Virgin Birth. 'In Christ all the fullness of God was seen to dwell,' is typical of how Saint Paul speaks of the Incarnation. That being said, we must recognize how in Luke, and perhaps in Matthew, we may have references to Mary being a virgin when she gave birth to Jesus. But, in those days, leaders of all kinds often had stories of remarkable happenings woven into accounts of their births. Great philosophers, including Plato, Olympic athletes, and some of the Caesars were held to be born of virgins who had been visited by gods. And so the function of such stories in the gospels may well have been to make sure Jesus compared favorably with other important figures of those times. At the very least, it is clear that stories of prominent figures being born of a virgin were not all that unusual in the ancient world.

"However, this does not mean the gospel accounts are unimportant." Russ was rounding into form now, feeling himself in the familiar mode of reciting in a seminar at school. "The Christmas stories link Jesus to the greatest of the great, to common shepherds, and to the wisest of the wise, thus showing the deep devotion with which Jesus was held by second or third generation Christians. We do well to exhibit similar devotion."

"Mr. Llewellen," Dr. Clarke said, slightly shaking his head, "you have made it quite clear what you believe the Bible says about this doctrine, but you still have not told us what you yourself believe. What do you believe about the Virgin Birth of our Lord, Mr. Llewellen, if you would be so kind as to tell us?"

"It seems to me, sir, that the evidence shows that early on the Doctrine of the Virgin Birth is not an absolutely necessary prerequisite to a belief that Jesus was sent from God, but the beautiful and ennobling birth stories amplify our faith and call forth our praise."

"Perhaps you did not understand me, though I thought I was speaking plainly," Dr. Clarke insisted. "My question is not what you feel the evidence shows, but what you believe in your heart. That's what we're after."

The presbyters again bent forward in their pews, this time as if waiting to pounce. Some of them, Russ knew, had no use for the historical-critical method of Bible study taught in the seminary, and others were great champions of anything new. He was afraid it would come to this. Almost anything he said could bring trouble from some quarter. He didn't know what else to do, so he cleared his throat, took a full breath, looked the good Dr. Clarke squarely in the eye, and said, "I stand firmly with the Apostle Paul on the matter."

"And where, Mr. Llewellen, does the Apostle Paul stand?"

"He never mentions it," Russ said half under his breath. A quick twitter of laughter came from here and there in the room, but it quickly dried up.

"Am I to understand that you accept the witness of Saint Paul over Saint Luke, the author of the third gospel, in the testimony to the Virgin Birth?"

"Yes. On the basis that Paul is the earlier witness."

"You are aware, I assume, that Saint Luke was a physician."

"But there is no evidence he was a gynecologist."

This brought guffaws from several places in the room, and a number of audible gasps. A smirk of pleasure crossed Dr. Clarke's face. Russ wasn't sure if this meant he had blown it or if this was exactly what Clarke was after, a little sparring, a rubbing together

48

of wits allowing the sparks to fly. Dr. Clarke slowly turned to face the Presbytery, paused for a good ten seconds, and said, "Fathers and brothers, what do we make of this?"

One after the other, ministers and elders rose to have their say. Some expressed shock that a candidate for the ministry would not forthrightly confess the doctrine of the Virgin Birth as a cornerstone of his faith. Others were equally incensed that anyone would cast aspersions on the competence of the good Dr. Luke. Still others said they were impressed that Russ knew as much Bible as he did, given what they had heard about the seminary these days. A few thought it was high time Presbyterians stopped worrying so much about this old doctrine and got on with the business of serving people, which, after all, is what the church is for. And a good many used the occasion to give their own answers to Dr. Clarke's question or to answer questions not even hinted at in the discussion up to that point. There was mention of demythologizing the New Testament and remythologizing the entire faith, a discussion on the nature of symbolic language, and a number of fervent calls to get back to the one, true, literal interpretation of scripture which is the only way people will ever make sense out of anything.

Russ didn't know what to think. Obviously, the Presbytery included every theological position under the sun. It was a swirl of spiritual diversity. He looked over at Dr. Clarke for a clue to what was happening, and, by God, Dr. Clarke winked back at him, as if to say "Isn't this great fun."

The Presbytery wrangled for a good long while, and finally Russ declared, "Mr. Moderator, I would like the Presbytery to know that my views fit well within the range of opinion being expressed here today." The Moderator nodded, and Dr. Clarke rose to his feet at once. When he got the hush he expected, he said, "Mr. Moderator, it appears that, as he has just assured us, the statements offered by Mr. Llewellen in response to my question lie firmly upon the theological spectrum in this Presbytery. I therefore move that these trials be arrested and the candidate be approved for ordination to the gospel ministry in the Presbyterian Church." The motion was seconded, and Russ was asked to leave the room.

It took a while. Russ stood alone in the narthex and read the entire church bulletin board including a couple of letters from missionaries in Korea before Brother Henry came to get him. He ushered Russ down the aisle, and all around him his new colleagues broke into quiet applause, at least most of them did. When they got to the front of the church, Brother Henry offered a long resonant prayer that called to mind so many solemn duties and sacred privileges that Russ began to feel weary on the spot. Almost everybody joined in the "Amen," and the Moderator asked Russ to share with the Presbytery his plans for ordination service.

Russ looked shocked. He glanced at Brother Henry, who shrugged and looked the other way, shaking his head.

"I thought it would be presumptuous to make such plans before I had completed my trials," Russ said. Truth be known, he hadn't even thought about it.

"The Presbytery must approve your plans today," the Moderator said from the pulpit, gavel in hand. "We must know when, where, and who will participate."

"Let's make it a week from tomorrow night," Russ said, "eight o'clock at the Welsh Presbyterian Church of Scroggtown. I would like very much for Brother Henry, Dr. Clarke, and, of course, you, Mr. Moderator, to take charge of the service."

The Presbytery voted all of this with resounding "ayes." After a brief closing prayer, the meeting was over, and the smell of turkey and dressing wafted through the sanctuary. They ate another huge meal, this one even better than the first because it was prepared by church women who, Russ could see, were dedicated to excellence in all they do. After cake and coffee and rounds of good-byes, six ministers scrunched into Brother Henry's car for the ride home.

IT WAS ALMOST DARK, THE SUN A GLEAM through tangled branches and autumn leaves, the colors blending into a deep rich brown.

Feeling relieved and tired, Russ looked out at the falling night. In the back of the car, the ministers continued the discussion Dr. Clarke had started, commenting more on what this or that colleague had said and how he had said it than on any doctrine at hand.

"Notice how Clarke's brogue is less pronounced at Presbytery than in the pulpit," somebody said.

"Yeah, and if you meet him on the street, he's got no accent at all," said another.

"He told me once," said a third, "'if a' lose ma' brogue it could cost me five tousand a year.'" And so with chatter and gossip, the reverends made their way home, Brother Henry taking it all in, hat pulled down, eyes glued to the road.

It was after ten when Russ got back. Ellen and Elsie were in the parlor drinking tea and eating Welsh cookies. Ellen was being talked to. She had a book open on her lap trying to study, but it wasn't going well. Clearly, Elsie had worn her down with one story after another about dead people who years ago had said things and done things that were entirely unremarkable.

"Guess what," Russ said, "you're going to have to call me Reverend from now on."

"All right, Reverend, it's time for bed. Early class tomorrow," Ellen said. They climbed the stairs hand in hand.

4

The Lord Giveth and Taketh Away

AT SEVEN THE NEXT MORNING, Elsie was pounding on the door. "Reverennnd, Reverennnd, the funeral home is on the phone. You've got to come right away."

"Apparently the dead get up early around here," Russ grumbled. He didn't know where his robe was, in the Saab someplace, he guessed, and he wasn't going to pad around Elsie's house barefoot in his honeymoon pajamas, the bottoms of which had gotten tangled around his left leg during the night, so he threw on yesterday's shirt and trousers and went downstairs.

"Ah, it's like my dear dead husband Wally would come down the stairs when a young man and in a hurry," Elsie said. "I always liked to see him like that. Made me think he was very important." She handed Russ the phone.

"Good morning, Reverennnd, sorry to disturb your rest," came an important sounding voice. "I have a funeral for you today at ten o'clock. I'll have a car for you at nine if you like. The service is at the Hungarian Church."

"That will be fine," Russ said. "Yes, please send a car." He hung up the phone and turned to Elsie, "What's the Hungarian Church? That's where the funeral is."

She said the Hungarian church was a tiny Presbyterian congregation that had been without a pastor for a long time, so Brother

Henry and the minister from Welsh Presbyterian helped them out. "You'll like them," she said, "but they're different, you know, Hungarian."

Russ called Brother Henry who, in his one and only voice, said he knew the family and would be glad to come along. With his ear ringing, Russ headed upstairs to get ready. Ellen was coming downstairs in a brown skirt and a yellow sweater, ready for school.

"Happy honeymoon," Russ said. Ellen didn't smile.

At nine o'clock, the shiniest, blackest Cadillac Russ had ever seen pulled up in front of Elsie's house. It had a sign in the side window that said "Davis and Giacopetti Funeral Home."

"Welcome to Scroggtown, Reverennnd. I'm Davis. I take care of the Protestant cases, my partner does the Catholic cases." Davis held the back door open for Russ to get in. Till then, Russ hadn't realized he was on a case.

Davis was short, sturdy, thin-faced and red headed, everything except the red hair typical of the Welshmen Russ had seen in the neighborhood. His suit was shiny black like the car, and on the little finger of his left hand he wore a black onyx ring with a diamond in it. Russ told him to stop by for Brother Henry, at which Davis gave an audible sigh of relief. Clearly he had not been looking forward to a novice preacher handling one of his cases.

In his perennial black three-piece suit, Brother Henry was ready, as always, for a funeral or anything a minister might be called upon to do. Russ wore his brown honeymoon suit, more rumpled than ever from yesterday's trip to Presbytery, but it was all he had until he could get to Princeton and pick up the things he left at the seminary. He felt frivolously attired next to Brother Henry and the funeral director. Brother Henry opened a black, leather-bound copy of the *Book of Common Worship* and placed a red satin ribbon at "The Funeral Service."

"There," Brother Henry said, "all set." Russ was impressed.

"You mean with a book like that you just turn to the place, and you're ready for a funeral?" Russ asked him.

"Oh, you get on to it, Llewellen. If you don't have one of these little books, you better get one. Everything you need is here, weddings, baptisms, funerals, special prayers, even your ordination service. I'm surprised they didn't require you to have one in seminary. But since you're not prepared, why don't you just say a prayer today. I'll nod when it's time."

"Fine," Russ said, both relieved and a little piqued. Brother Henry had just taken over his first funeral. But there again, Russ realized, he probably would be familiar with such a book had he not been attending lectures on contemporary poetry at the university on some of the days he was supposed to be in worship class at the seminary.

They lumbered through town in the huge, heavy car that seemed always to be in low gear. It turned left and right and left again down the pothole streets. Russ wasn't sure at first, but, as they bumped along, it seemed to him all the houses, power poles, and everything else in town tipped a little one way or the other. Nothing lined up exactly, and it made Russ slightly dizzy to see it. He asked Brother Henry if he was imagining things or was everything a little off perpendicular.

"Ah, Llewellen, you've noticed. Yes, things are a bit off around here," Brother Henry said, his voice filling the car many times over. "They are not supposed to mine within a hundred feet of the surface, but who's to say they don't get closer than that. In the old days, miners were paid by the ton, so if they got on a good seam they might follow it too far. Then the ground settled and made things crooked." Brother Henry chuckled at this. "Sometimes cracks form and gasses seep up into buildings. It's even happened to churches. Once in a while, someone dies while sound asleep from what are called mysterious causes, which likely means gas from an old mine came up through a crack in the basement. May the Lord protect us all!" Brother Henry intoned this little prayer as if he presided at Holy Services in a huge cathedral.

Russ asked if anything was being done about this, and Brother Henry said there wasn't much to be done. He told Russ how the anthracite mines like the ones around Scroggtown were closing down because oil was taking over. He told how some of the mining companies had declared bankruptcy and weren't paying pensions, let alone taking care of cracks in the ground. "That's why they call this a depressed area, Russ old boy," Brother Henry said. "Here and there we're slowly sinking. We have problems that reach back into the difficult history of this valley."

"How about those smoking mountains of slag. They smell awful. It can't be good to breathe that stuff," Russ said.

"Ah yes, Llewellen, the culm dumps. The word 'culm' is from an Anglo Saxon word meaning 'soot.' And you're right, it smells awful and can raise a terrible cough if you inhale it very long, which I suppose we all do in this valley when the wind blows toward us." Brother Henry went on to tell Russ that Mrs. Endo, the lady who died, had eighteen children, seventeen of them still living. A son was killed in the mines years ago. She was Protestant but her husband was Catholic, Bother Henry explained, and they were married in his church. She promised the priest she would abide by Catholic teaching when it came to family. "She certainly kept her promise," Brother Henry said.

The Magyar Presbyterian Church of East Scroggtown, a small, low roofed building with a squat round bell tower, sat back from the sidewalk a good way. Like the surrounding houses, it was covered with dark brown sesame seed siding. That's what they called it, sesame seed, which was asphalt tile with grains of light-colored material stuck to it. A graveyard that looked as if it had been quickly straightened up for the occasion surrounded the church on three sides. Toward the front, beneath a magnificent oak tree, was an open grave, and next to it was a mound of newly dug dirt. A dozen folding chairs had been placed in front of the grave. Enclosing the church and cemetery was a black wrought iron fence with sharp pointed spikes sticking up about eye high.

The hearse and a station wagon full of flowers were already there, and black-suited men ran in and out of the church carrying floral sprays. Sixty or seventy people gathered around the iron gate, all in dark clothes. The gate opened on an uneven slate walkway that led to the slate steps of the church. Brother Henry waded into the crowd of mourners and shook hands and hugged people. In his booming voice, he introduced Russ as the new minister of the Welsh Presbyterian Church, letting everyone know for three blocks around that a wet-behind-the-ears clergyman was on the scene. Brother Henry made sure Russ met the bereaved husband, Mr. Endo, a ruddy, thickset man looking to be in his seventies, who seemed thoroughly stunned.

Davis opened the back of the hearse and slid out the bronze metallic casket on little built-in rollers, causing tiny squeaks. The people fell silent. A large spray of white chrysanthemums rested on top of the casket. Pallbearers, all in dark suits with white carnations in their lapels, lined up three to a side and took hold. At exactly ten o'clock, the church bell rang from its tower. BONG— and the pallbearers took one step forward together, each one looking somber and important. The chrysanthemums bounced as the casket moved. Again, BONG, and the pallbearers took another step, and the chrysanthemums bounced again.

"Come on, Llewellen," Brother Henry said, "we lead." Brother Henry and Russ stepped ahead of the casket and began taking one step to each peal of the bell. The mourners gathered behind the pall bearers in twos and threes, forming a line down the sidewalk. The entire procession moved forward in a jerk every time the bell rang, BONG—step, BONG—step, on and on. In this solemn manner the retinue marched through the gate, up the slate walkway, up the front steps and into the church. It took a long time to get everyone inside.

The interior of the church was dark and musty. Deep amber windows let in an oppressive light, and the pews were simple straight benches that came only half way up people's backs. The pulpit had been redone in dark plywood in a way that only approximately matched the rest of the woodwork. With serious care, the pallbearers set the casket on a small stand below the pulpit. Around the casket were more cut flowers than Russ had ever seen in one place. "Loving Son" or "Adoring Daughter" was written in gold on white ribbons hung across many of the sprays. The biggest spray of all, entirely of large red roses, had a ribbon saying "Faithful Husband."

Then Davis removed the chrysanthemums from the casket and carefully lifted the lid. The little dead lady inside looked dry and ready to turn into powder. Her dress was lacy black, her hair a dusted silvery white, and too much rouge had been rubbed into her cheeks. A tiny white Bible was folded into her hands. People craned their necks to see her better, and a definite murmur spread through the pews.

"There's Mamma."

"She looks so peaceful."

"Just like she was sleeping."

It seemed to Russ she was anything but peaceful. It seemed to him she wasn't even real, and that if anybody sneezed, she'd blow away.

Without warning, Brother Henry stood up by the pulpit and BAM, dropped to his knees on the platform. That got everyone's attention. Five minutes of silence went by while Brother Henry, his face in a pious grimace, prepared himself with prayer. People coughed, settled down, and the murmuring came to an end. Brother Henry rose and opened his little book, drew in a breath, and, without further glance at the book, gave forth the words that were there: "Our help is in the name of the Lord who made heaven and earth. Like as a father pitieth his children, so the Lord pitieth them that fear him. As one whom his mother comforteth, so will I comfort you and ye shall be comforted, says the Lord."

Some of the younger grandchildren put their hands over their ears, but Brother Henry's mighty voice had a steadying effect on everyone else. Russ was most aware of the vowel sounds and how they fit in Brother Henry's mouth, each phrase exactly equal to the breath it took to speak it. Brother Henry boomed out Bible verses as if death was being swallowed up in victory right then and there. Russ quivered to think how his prayer might sound over against Brother Henry's great outpouring.

After reading from the Psalms and several passages from the Epistles and Gospels, Brother Henry nodded and Russ got to his feet. This time it wasn't some wise guy stretched out on folding chairs in front of a seminary class. There was a real live dead person in the casket, and the grief of her children filled the room. Russ clutched hard at the edges of the pulpit, looked down on the mourners, then looked up over their heads.

"The Lord giveth and the Lord taketh away," he blurted. He had heard it many times in cowboy movies when the preacher intones over the grave of the loser in a gunfight. It was all he could think of.

A huge sob rose up from the congregation. Russ closed his eyes and pushed on, thanking God for this woman he had never seen alive, thanking God for her loving family, thanking God for this place of rest and peace. He finished with "Bless our tears this day, O God, and bless us all in the days to come. Amen." It felt like nothing to him, like he had filled the air with fluff. He was surprised to hear everyone say the "Amen" with him at the end.

Then Brother Henry preached a sermon that Russ never would have expected. It was wonderful. It spoke of long acquaintance with the family and concern for their wellbeing over many years. He spoke about Mrs. Endo's sons and daughters when they were children and how they always had big reunions at holidays with music and dancing and games. People smiled, and the grandchildren snickered to hear about their parents being ordinary little kids. He likened the dead woman to several women in the Bible who had many sons and daughters. He went on to talk about eternal life, all kinds of eternal life, in memory, in progeny, and in the promises of God. Brother Henry could really preach. He made it seem like what he said was so true that the resurrection unto eternal life was the surest bet in town. Nobody cared that his sermon was overly loud and woefully long, except maybe undertaker Davis, who stood at the door checking his watch. When Brother Henry finished, he raised his long arms to the heavens and gave a short blessing. That ended the service.

Undertaker Davis came forward and, with solemn and precise movements, closed the casket and locked down the lid with a small crank he carried in his pocket. The chrysanthemums were placed on top of it as before, the bell began to toll, and people followed the casket out of the church by the one-bong, one-step process with which they had entered. They walked in this halting fashion toward the grave beneath the huge oak tree, its leaves dry and turning brown. In the warmth of early autumn, sons and daughters wept openly. Young children comforted their parents, even though the children were crying too. People of all ages clung to each other, stepped forward to the tolling bell, and sobbed. Every few steps, a high-pitched wail arose from somewhere in the back of the procession. This called forth more sobbing and coughing. It was all-out grief, and Russ was becoming uncomfortable with so much feeling concentrated in one place. The words of Scripture, his prayer, and Brother Henry's fervent sermon seemed not to have had any affect at all.

The pallbearers set the casket on three thick straps strung across the open grave. Mr. Endo sat in a folding chair with daughters on each side of him and their husbands behind them. Other daughters and sons crowded around, and children gathered under their mothers' arms, just like in Genesis where God is likened to a mother bird, Russ thought. He and Brother Henry stood together at the head of the casket.

"Here, Russ, read this part to them," Brother Henry said, and handed Russ the little book open at a section called "At the Grave." Russ took it and read the committal service in the biggest voice he could muster.

"Earth to earth," he intoned.

"No, no, no," came the wail from the mourners.

"Ashes to ashes."

"Not mother, no"

"And dust to dust."

"No, no, not mother."

The wails of grief hit the holy words head on, and together they made an antiphonal chant that rose into the branches of the great oak tree and into the sky beyond. "Yet in the sure and certain hope of the resurrection unto eternal life through Jesus Christ our Lord," Russ read with all the force he had, but even these phrases were greeted with sobs of "No, No, No." It was a Pennsylvania version of a classic Greek play, Russ thought, the grieving family having become the chorus responding in anguish to Russ' attempt to deliver heroic words.

When Russ finished, the funeral director stepped forward and motioned to the pallbearers. They unpinned their carnations and placed them on top of the casket next to the spray of mums. Then Davis knelt on the ground and turned the large steel crank that lowered the casket into the grave. Click by click, the bronze metal box, then the white chrysanthemums dropped from sight. Still, Davis turned the crank, until finally the straps became slack, and the clicks stopped. The straps were retrieved and set aside. Davis stood up, and so did Mr. Endo. The old man stooped over, picked up a handful of dirt, and let it fall from his hand into the grave. His daughters and sons did the same. Thud, thud, thud, the dirt hit the coffin and echoed deep in the earth.

"Mother, Mother, Mother," came a scream, from the back of the gathering. The youngest son bolted forward, screamed, "Mother, Mother, Mother" again, and dove toward the grave. Davis quick said, "Stop him," and Russ tackled the young man around the knees, locked his hands and pulled up, much as he was taught to do by his high school football coach. The two of them hit the ground, the young man's head and shoulders hanging into the grave. He was still wailing "Mother, Mother, Mother" and reaching toward her casket, trying for all he was worth to get down there with her. Russ held tight to his legs, and then, all at once, the young man became quiet and his body relaxed. He pulled himself up from the ground, took a handful of dirt, and, like his brothers and sisters before him, let it fall onto his mother's casket. Thud.

Russ got up and brushed off his now smudged brown suit, having no idea what might happen next. But the undertaker stood in front of the gathering as if all things were as they should be and calmly announced, "The family invites everyone back to the house for refreshments." It seemed to Russ that most of these people were too upset to eat for a week, but he and Brother Henry got in the funeral car and went over to the house anyway.

"You have to show up at the wake," Brother Henry said. "It's expected."

RUSS COULD HEAR THE MUSIC A BLOCK AWAY. Davis let Russ and Brother Henry off in front of a large, three-story house and went to park the car. From the porch, an accordion pumped out a light-hearted Hungarian dance to which a line of barefoot young women, their hands on each other's shoulders, hopped and glided about on the grass that surrounded the house. Children with hunks of bread and sausage in their mouths chased each other around the yard. The grieving husband sat on the front porch in his undershirt with a bottle of beer in one hand and a big cigar in the other. There must have been twice as many people there than were in church.

"Sorry for your trouble," people said to Mr. Endo as they climbed the front steps toward him. He nodded and puffed his cigar. Russ and Brother Henry shook Mr. Endo's hand and wished him well.

"Have a little lunch before you go," he said in a gruff voice with a heavy accent.

The "little lunch" was spread over three tables in the dining room and living room. Ham, turkey, salami, cheeses, all kinds of salads, red and green jellos, and many ample desserts. "Try some of this, Revrend," one of the sons told Russ. "It's Hungarian Easter bread. We have it for funerals too." It was a slice of something like a large Danish roll with dark poppy seed filling and dusted with poppy seeds on top. Russ tried some. It was delicious.

Russ made the rounds with Brother Henry, the two of them shaking hands and greeting people in tandem. After shaking hands with one of the sons, Russ felt a wad of paper press into his palm. He looked down at a folded five dollar bill.

"What do I do with this?" Russ whispered to Brother Henry.

"Put it in your pocket, Llewellen," Henry whispered back, but Henry's whisper had the force of a mild tornado, so everyone knew what was going on. He watched Brother Henry shake hands with a quick clutch and a swipe toward his pocket all in one easy motion. Russ got pretty good at it before the day was over. All told he collected thirty-six dollars. He could see it might be hard to feel sad at funerals if he knew this was going to happen afterward.

The young man who had attempted to jump into his mother's grave stood with his arms around two of his sisters singing a Hungarian folk song they seemed to have known all their lives. Others who earlier had wept inconsolably now talked and laughed, drank and smoked, and lived it up with family and friends. The old man, as they called him, went through one beer after another, not so much in the manner of someone drowning his sorrows but in a way that indicated this was how he spent most of his afternoons.

"Old Pops," one of the sons said, "nothing changes him. He'll be OK."

A full-fledged bar had sprung up in the kitchen, and booze was flowing freely. A jolly son of the deceased approached Brother Henry. "Something to drink, Revrend? Beer, wine, perhaps a highball? Something to wet your whistle after the fine sermon you gave for mother?"

"I will have a cup of hot water, if you please," Henry said. Everybody nodded. Brother Henry had done exactly what was expected, and they seemed to feel reassured. A beer would have gone down nicely right then, Russ thought, but given Brother Henry's example, he knew what he had to do when his turn came. "And how about you, Revrend, after that beautiful prayer, what will you have?"

"I could use a cup of coffee," Russ said. "I take it black." Russ noticed it went well with the Easter bread.

At Elsie's that night, Russ didn't feel much like eating, but the dear woman had cooked a huge meal of stuffed cabbage. "It's the last supper," she said, "Your apartment's ready. You can move in tomorrow."

"I've been eating all day," Russ said

"You mean you ate at the funeral?" Ellen asked.

"From what I can tell, funerals are mostly for eating. And drinking and dancing. And people kept putting money in my hand. Look, I got thirty-six dollars."

"We Welsh would never carry on like that. That's Hungarian. I told you they were different," Elsie said.

"What do the Welsh do at funerals, Elsie?" Russ asked.

"With a name like Llewellen, and you don't know that?" Elsie said. "We sing sad songs and maybe eat a little ham after, and Welsh cookies, and drink tea. And don't think you'll get thirty-six dollars at a Welsh funeral either. We Welsh can be a bit close with a dollar, you know."

"That's what Buck Davies told me," Russ said.

"Listen to him," Elsie said.

Ellen and Russ went upstairs to get their things together to take to their apartment. "It's a lot different than I thought," Russ said. "I'm not sure I'm cut out for this line of work."

"What's that supposed to mean?" Ellen wanted to know. Her question was quick and snappish. She hadn't come all this way to be with a doubting Thomas minister who might change his mind about his calling after just one funeral.

"Things happen you have no way to prepare for. There I was reading verses about comfort and strength, and by God people were trying to jump into the grave alongside their dead mother."

"You sure about that?" Ellen said as she folded a sweater.

"It happened. This guy almost jumped in he was so upset. I had to tackle him. And they were all wailing and moaning. You would have thought the end of the world had come. And then back at the house, here's this same guy singing and dancing and having a beer. And the newly widowed old man was grinning and smoking a big cigar. It was like somebody said 'shazam' and poof, no more grief, no more tears. It was weird."

"Sounds like you said it."

"Said what?"

"You said the 'shazam'. It must have worked. They got through their sadness."

"All I did was stumble through a corny prayer."

"You probably underestimate yourself, Reverend." Ellen gave Russ a sharp glance. Russ grabbed a wadded-up ten dollar bill from his pocket and stuck it down the front of her shirt.

"You better be careful," Ellen said. "Time may come you'll be so broke you'll pray for someone to die."

"I thought about that," Russ said.

Russ looked at her for a long time. She was so much alive. Her skin was soft and flushed, her eyes a delicate blue. He reached toward her and she leaned into him and they tumbled onto the bed. Her gold hair came loose and flowed upon the pillow. What a sight she was. No death anywhere near. Russ felt her lips and eyelids, and everything was warm and moist. He wanted to immerse himself in Ellen. He wanted to get as far away as he could from that powdery form in the casket. He wanted to avoid the teeming, mystifying emotional reality of what he had seen that day, love and grief and death and life all mixed up together. He preferred death to be death and life to be life and love to be love. Keep things separate and distinct like his theology books listed them in their orderly chapter headings. That was what he was used to, not this tumbled together way people live and die.

He and Ellen banged Elsie's bed against the wall as if it was their own coffin and they were determined to break out of it. Then they got dressed, packed their things and went downstairs to drink tea and eat Welsh cookies and let Elsie talk to them until it got late. It was her reward for taking them in.

NEXT DAY THEY MOVED. All they had were their suitcases, a bag of dirty clothes, and some wedding presents that amounted to a couple of sheets, two pillows and pillow cases, fourteen sets of placemats, eight salt and pepper shakers, the Melmac dishes, the silverware from the tire well, and the wedding book from under the front seat.

Their apartment was four upstairs rooms in a two-story house with white aluminum siding located up the hill from the church on Locust Street. All four rooms of the apartment were painted light green, the floors were dark brown linoleum, and the bathroom fixtures were pink. The kitchen had a stove and refrigerator and space for a small table. Across the hall from the kitchen was a room with a tiny upper window that Russ claimed for his study. A small bedroom faced the street, and next to it was an even smaller parlor with a bay window that offered a pleasant view of the neighborhood. In back was a closed-in porch and a flight of stairs that led to a large, unfinished attic. A radiator stood beneath every window, and storm windows were already in place. This cost the church sixty-five dollars a month, including utilities, and use of half of the garage on the alley that ran behind the sloping back yard.

Along the edge of the property was a border of rosebushes that didn't seem to be doing well. On both sides were low wire fences, and up the hill for as far as one could see, clotheslines stretched from back porches to garages on the alley making an artful pattern of shorts and sheets and shirts and trousers flapping in the breeze. There were no trees in the yard, just some stumps flush with the ground. Landlord Edgar Howells, retired from the merchant marine, let Russ know he didn't much care for trees. "I like to look out all directions," he said, "owing to my years at sea."

Edgar and his wife Margaret lived downstairs. Margaret, a tall thin woman in a flowered housedress, her dark hair in huge curlers, smiled at her new tenants. As Russ and Ellen were moving in, Margaret was sweeping the front walk.

"We had Irish before," Margaret said to Ellen. "They don't clean like us Welsh."

"Yes, we Welsh really like to clean," Ellen said, rolling her eyes at Russ.

They went downtown, ordered a bed and had it delivered that afternoon. They bought a kitchen table and four chairs. These came unassembled, and Russ used tools from the Saab to put them together. Elders' wives came by with pots and pans for the new couple, and Ellie Williams brought a box full of canned goods with the labels torn off. "We like our minister to have a few surprises," she said. Then she told Ellen about the Young Women's Bible Class.

"We never study the Bible," Ellie said. "We call it a Bible class to throw the minister off. You will have to come, Mrs. Llewellen. Or can I call you Ellen? We go by first names here."

"Sounds like my kind of group. Yes, call me Ellen," Ellen said, and broke into a big smile. Dark haired, bright eyed, short, and healthily plump, Ellie Williams had a jolly effect on people. Clearly, religion for her was something to enjoy.

"And you, Reverennnd, we'll call you Russell and a lot of other things after a while, but for now we'll call you Reverennnd. Enjoy it while it lasts," Ellie said on her way out. She bounced around the sweeping Margaret and greeted her as if it makes perfect sense to spend an hour sweeping the same small patch of sidewalk.

"Your walk looks lovely today, Margaret, but I think you missed a spot here by the grass." Ellie said. Margaret quick got on it.

For dinner that night, Ellen and Russ played grab bag with the unlabeled cans. They enjoyed sardines and chili con carne accompanied by yams in sweet brown sauce.

5

How Beautiful the Feet

"OHOW BEAUTIFUL UPON THE MOUNTAINS are the feet of one who bringeth good tidings." The ordination phrase. It was printed in big scroll letters across the front of the worship bulletin. As the service began, the choir sang it in English and Chorister L. David Jenkins sang it in Welsh. The people sitting in the blond pews of the renovated Welsh Presbyterian Church nodded as if to say, "Now this is how ministers are made."

Russ sat in the front pew across from the Holiness of Holinesses and looked at his black shoes which he had not got around to giving a shine. Dusty, scuffed, and worn at the heels, they didn't seem all that beautiful. A broken shoestring held the left one on with a bulky knot.

Russ was wearing his new black preacher robe ordered from Bentley and Simon of New York, a gift from his parents in California who still didn't understand what had happened to him. "At least you didn't become a monk and not get married," his mother had written in her last letter. She also said Russ' dad couldn't get away from the store, so they would not be at his ordination.

The wonderful thing about the robe, Russ noticed, was that it was so comfortable. It draped in long straight lines from his shoulders to just six inches above the floor, so there was no feeling of being squeezed in like suit jackets can feel. And it had black velvet panels down the front, very spiffy in a subdued way. Russ thought it made him look taller. For sure it covered all the spots on his trousers, shirt, and necktie. However, it left his scuffed shoes completely visible. He thought it strange that the only parts of him mentioned so far were his feet.

Ellen sat next to him in a black wool jersey dress, her golden hair pulled back in a neat roll. Elders in dark suits filled the Holiness of Holinesses and behind them were the deacons, mainly the elders' wives, all wearing dark dresses. It was their job to send cards to the sick, prepare the communion, and make sure there were flowers in the church for services each Sunday. They usually get flowers out of neighborhood gardens, but for this occasion they ordered a spray of white gladiolas from Prichard's Flower Shop for either side of the pulpit. The church was packed once again.

When the choir stopped singing about Russ' feet, Brother Henry, Dr. Clarke, the Moderator of the Presbytery, and ministers from other churches in town and from the far-flung churches of the Presbytery, all in black robes, marched in twos down the aisle to the stirring strains of the opening hymn, "God of the Prophets, Bless the Prophets' Sons." The bulletin cover featured a picture of an old and bearded prophet dressed in something resembling a purple bathrobe with his hand upon the shoulder of a young, bright-eyed protégé dressed in something resembling a red bathrobe.

Ellen joined in the singing, but Russ just listened. It occurred to him that a procession of marching ministers looks a lot like a line of waddling penguins. Some of them, in fact, had white stoles draped down the front of their black gowns. It seemed like such folderol to him. His messed up shoes, this line of penguins moving in step to the hymn, these serious elders on the other side of their little gate, their more or less ample wives behind them, Brother Henry now up front on the platform working a pious expression into his face, Dr. Clarke silently practicing his brogue, all of this ordinary human stuff going on, and yet it's supposed to be so holy, so exalted, a once in a lifetime rite as blessed as anything there is. Russ couldn't get in the proper mood.

Buck Davies the elder rose to greet the people, welcome the representatives of the Presbytery, and invite everyone to the reception afterwards. Within the next quarter hour, the ordination phrase about beautiful feet was sung as a lengthy anthem and read in unison by the entire congregation. Russ rubbed his shoes against the back of his trousers, but he could tell it didn't do much good.

Finally, Dr. Clark rose to preach the sermon. He seemed immense and immaculate, much taller than Russ had remembered him. His robe was obviously fashioned of more expensive material than Russ' was, and in addition to the black velvet panels down the front, three black velvet stripes on each sleeve indicated he was to be called Dr. Clarke. An academic hood of flaming red, theology's color, slashed across Dr. Clarke's throat and disappeared in great heaps over his shoulders. He assumed his preaching stance by pointing his left shoulder toward the congregation much like a boxer does when sparring with an opponent. Nothing of the nodding, winking side of him was present now. He preached like a Gatling gun with a Scotch accent, never changing pitch, pace, or tone, and his gestures seemed to come right on schedule like maybe he had practiced before a mirror.

"Don't you just love to hear him," someone behind Russ and Ellen said. "So much the preacher."

"If that's what a preacher is, I'm in more trouble than I thought," Russ mumbled.

"Ssshhh," Ellen said and poked him in the ribs with her elbow.

"I am about a great work, and I cannot come down," Dr. Clarke intoned. Actually, "Cannae cum doon" is how he said it. "Let this verse from Nehemiah be our text for the evening." he continued in the same somewhat exaggerated brogue. "It arises during the time of the rebuilding of the wall around Jerusalem." He spit out his phrases like bullets. His eyes scanned back and forth above the congregation, resting on no one, like he was shooting just over their heads. His voice, Russ had to admit, was beautifully rich and placed well forward in his mouth so you heard every syllable without even trying.

"Look at him," someone whispered, "he's doing all this without notes." Russ shook his head and Ellen poked him again.

"It was a new beginning for the people," Dr. Clarke went on. "They had a job to do for the Lord. It was to rebuild the wall around the holy city, to make safe the sacred temple, to reinstate the ancient ways of worship, and to renew their commitment to moral living. But as soon as they began to build, they met opposition. Difficulties arose. Enemies infiltrated. Reaction set in. And they were sorely tempted to give up.

"Furthermore, Nehemiah, their God-given leader, was beset with distractions. People came to him for help with their petty problems. But Nehemiah stayed at his post. He kept his calling clear before him. He would not be distracted by the many worthy and unworthy interruptions that came his way. 'I am about a great work,' he told them, 'and I cannae cum doon.'" His brogue, his aloofness, his red doctoral hood and billowing black robe, his command of the language, all this made Dr. Clarke a spellbinder, and he knew it. Russ was the only one who had to stifle a yawn as Dr. Clarke went on to make the obvious applications. "We are not to be deterred from our high calling. We are to continue hewing the stones of righteousness for building up the temple of the Lord. We are to rise above all opposition which can threaten from within and without. We are the people of God, and we are about a great work, and we cannae cum doon." Then he broke into a story that fairly dripped with the heather about a struggling congregation in eighteenth century Scotland. Russ thought it didn't apply to the point of the sermon, but the people were eating it up. When he finished his story, Dr. Clarke reiterated his text, and sat down to a reverent hush.

"Mr. Llewellen, will you kindly join me at the front of the sanctuary," the Moderator said in a most human way. He seemed much less formidable now than he did when wielding the gavel at the Presbytery meeting. He stood in a hunched and apologetic posture, a man in his late forties, temples starting to turn gray, his tone in complete contrast to Dr. Clarke's. He smiled an inviting smile as if to show his pleasure in what he was about to do. Ellen nudged Russ, and he rose and went forward.

"You will now give answer, Mr. Llewellen, to the questions which the Presbytery, in the name of Christ, head of the Church, requires of you." The Moderator held open a copy of the *Book of Common Worship*. Whatever the questions, Russ knew that the answers had to be the answers printed in black and white right below the questions in the little book.

"Do you believe the Scriptures of the Old and New Testaments to be the Word of God, the only infallible rule of faith and practice?"

"I do," Russ said, having learned in seminary that the question had been discussed and fought over through all of Protestant history. That word "infallible," Russ' professors had said, was there to separate the Protestant way from the infallibility of the Pope in Rome.

"Do you receive the Confessions of the Presbyterian Church as containing the system of doctrine taught in the Holy Scriptures?"

"I do." Russ answered even though his years of study had shown him it's possible to construe many forms of doctrine from the Holy Scripture, and Presbyterians governed themselves by one among others. But these were the constitutional questions, compressing everything he had tried to understand up to that time into affirmations based on a Presbyterian God who, Russ sensed at the moment, may very well wear a black robe and speak with a Scottish brogue.

As the litany of standards and beliefs came forth in compact and uncomplicated form, Russ accepted them as grand summaries of centuries-long debates that he knew were far from settled. It went on for page after page, for age after age, it seemed, this public, ritualized rendering of his inner search, which he knew was by no means over. But at this point, Russ could tell, debate and fine distinctions are set aside. He answered in a theological daze.

Russ went on to promise he would be diligent in the exercise of all private and personal duties, to adorn his office by exemplary conversation, and to walk with piety before the flock over which God had appointed him. He responded as the long line of Presbyterian ministers always had, whatever reservations they may have harbored at the time. That there is wide diversity among those who make these responses had been amply demonstrated in the lovely white church with the green shutters where he stood for his trials, and Russ took comfort in that.

When the questions were complete, the Moderator bid Russ kneel on a small square cushion he had brought just for that purpose, and the other ministers present were invited to gather around. The Moderator laid his hand on Russ' head, and the others laid their hands on the Moderator's hand or, extending back, on each other's shoulders so that all these black robed reverends were connected to the Moderator's hand lying ever more heavily on Russ' bowed head. Russ knelt there under the holy weight of those hands with his scuffed-up shoes sticking out behind him. He could feel the pressure of those hands, some of which had been raised to speak against him at his trials, some raised to speak in his favor, those varied preacher hands that had gestured this way and that from pulpits Sunday upon Sunday for decades. Everything comes down to a time and place, Russ could see, a crossroads of divergent pathways.

"Almighty God, send down thy Holy Spirit upon this thy servant, whom we, in thy name and in obedience to thy holy will, do now by the laying on of our hands ordain and appoint to the Office of the Holy Ministry in thy Church," the Moderator prayed, still reading out of the little black book. The prayer turned out to be a long one, and Russ caught only bits and pieces of it. It seemed to him his head had lifted off his body, and he was looking down on this scene from well above the balcony and listening to the

Moderator's voice echo in the room as if it was spoken in some ancient cave.

The prayer took up a recitation of virtues and graces which only Jesus could possibly possess, but which Russ was supposed to exhibit from that moment on. Perseverance was mentioned and cheerfulness and patience and wisdom and industry and "all courage and skill." Russ felt the impossible, guilt-bearing expectations ooze into him through those cascading words and pressing hands. He felt his life being compressed into this moment. Whoever he was and whatever a minister is supposed to be were being fused together, however imperfectly, under the pressure of those hands. He tried to get a glimpse of Ellen through the tangle of arms around his head, but he couldn't see her. He wondered what she thought about all this. He didn't know what to think.

When the prayer was over, the Moderator led Russ up to the platform and, with Russ standing by the pulpit, delivered a "Charge to the Pastor," a little homily on how the new minister was to carry out the vows just taken. Russ was amazed to hear the Moderator say what seemed to be the opposite of what he had just prayed. He told Russ to be sure to take time off, not to worry about getting everything done, to play golf and go fishing and leave the phone off the hook and spend time with his wife. It was a marvelous talk, and Russ determined then and there to take it to heart. How he might reconcile that with what had been prayed and promised earlier he had no idea. The charge over, he simply returned to his seat next to Ellen.

Now it was Brother Henry's turn to give the "Charge to the Congregation." CLUNK! Brother Henry's knees hit the floor next to the pulpit. Some of the people jumped half out of their pews. Ellen was especially startled. She hadn't seen Brother Henry in action before. Russ patted her thigh and said it was all right. She took his hand and put it back in his lap. Then everyone sat still for several minutes of silence as Brother Henry knelt and prepared himself to bring a stirring word. At last, with his finger waving, his robe billowing, and his face fierce as Jeremiah's of old, Brother Henry leapt to his feet and, in effect, told the elders in the Holiness of Holinesses and the deacons behind them and everybody in the church that they must watch out for Russ and take care of him, for, after all, he didn't know very much.

"This young pastor and his lovely new wife are just getting started," he said. "They will need your earnest Christian charity in gaining that most necessary ingredient for effective ministry—experience." He shouted the word "experience" three times. "Too many of our young pastors become woefully discouraged in their first assignments, and they are lost to the service of the Church. Let not such a blot stain the record of this congregation."

"Lord God," Russ muttered, "What does he know that I don't?" and Ellen gave him another elbow in the ribs.

"Your new pastor," Brother Henry went on, "will need time to study, time to brood, time to ponder the great mysteries of faith." Russ had begun to feel he was about all pondered out, but Brother Henry had other plans for him. "Therefore," Brother Henry said, rising to his tiptoes, grabbing the pulpit with both hands, and jutting out his ample jaw, "you are not to disturb your minister before eleven o'clock in the morning except in the case of dire emergency. And you, Mrs. Llewellen, must get yourself a pot of cobbler's wax and paint the chair in your husband's study with it so that when he sits down there he sticks at his desk and prepares himself for the holy responsibility of preaching the Word of the Lord." The ministers on the platform covered their smirks with their hands.

"What am I going to do until eleven o'clock every day?" Russ whispered to Ellen.

"Oh, we'll think of something," Ellen whispered back.

When Brother Henry finally sat down, Buck the Elder announced the final hymn. "All Hail the Power of Jesus Name,'" Welsh version," he said. They sang it to a lilting tune they call "Diadem" which Russ had never heard before, and the sound of their singing rose up and filled his ears. There it was, the old

Welsh feeling for music now pouring itself out for this newly created Minister of the Gospel. The chorister waved his arms, and the sopranos sang a descant over the refrain while the basses dove deep into a chant-like "Crown him, crown him, crown him, crown him, crown him Lord of all." It was like waves in an ocean of praise. The black robed ministers smiled and nodded their approval. Russ began to sing along, giving more and more of himself to the lilt and lift of the hymn. He even dove in with the basses and hit some of those marvelous low notes that rumble through the refrain.

When the hymn was over, the Moderator nodded, and Russ went to the front of the church, raised his arms, and pronounced the benediction. "May the Lord bless us and keep us; may the Lord's face shine upon us and be gracious unto us; may the Lord lift the divine countenance upon us and grant us peace, from this time forth and forever more. Amen." For some reason, Russ felt remarkably at ease doing this.

The people were ready for that blessing. They had been in church almost two hours. The aisles filled with folks before the ministers could waddle out. Richie Evans at the organ launched into his postlude, which was the tune the Welsh call Calon Lan. People sang it quietly as they moved out of the church. Some sang in Welsh, "Calon lan yn llawn daioni..." and others in English, "A clean heart o'erflowed with goodness, / Fairer than the lily bright; / A clean heart forever singing, / Singing through the day and night." It sounded just right, Russ felt.

Russ and Ellen were led downstairs to the basement where they, the Moderator, Elder Buck Davies, Dr. Clarke, and Brother Henry formed a reception line. The people introduced themselves as they came by.

"I'm Robert Roberts and this is Mrs. William Williams, Reverennnd. We hope you enjoy it here." Then came a Thomas, a Francis, a Jones, another Jones, and another, a Hughes, a Jenkins, then a Lewis, a Reese, a Lewis Reese and a Reese Lewis, then a bunch named Davies and Davis and several Davy Davies, more

Joneses, and yes, a few Llewellens, "but we spell it with a 'y', that's Welsh you know."

"Reverend Morgan made the church double when he was here," Buck said to Russ after the people had all gone by. "You know how he did it? He never forgot a name. Got to know us all right off." Here's the real charge to the pastor, Russ thought. Bully for Reverend Morgan.

"So many names are the same. How am I going to keep everyone straight?" Russ wanted to know.

"You'll catch on," Buck said. "See that one over there with the white hair, Davy Davies, well there are three Davy Davies, so we call him Cotton because he always had white hair, even as a kid. Cottontop Davis. If anybody refers to Cotton, that's who they're talking about. Or else it's his son, young Cotton. Now young Cotton has dark brown hair, but still we call him Cotton Junior. And over there's Tommy Thomas. We call him Goosie Junior because his father used to make a sound like a goose and pinch the ladies' ankles as they walked up the steps of the church. Young Tommy never pinched ladies' ankles, but still he's Goosie Junior because of his father. Goosie Senior isn't too well these days. Got the black lung. You'll have to go see him."

Buck kept it up way past the saturation point. There were several called Red—Red Davis, Red Morgan, Red Williams—but none of them had red hair. There were a few freckle faced youngsters Russ found totally indistinguishable, and the babies, round-faced, and plump, all looked pretty much the same. Russ wondered how they kept from taking home the wrong kid.

The people were mostly the same size and shape as well, short and stocky with faces that seemed a bit drawn out and dark eyes that could twinkle and, at the same time, seem a little sad at the corners. As they got older, the men often developed huge bushy eyebrows. Their hands seemed unusually heavy, and their fingers were short and thick. Russ looked at his own hands and noticed they were much the same in size and shape as many of the

Welshmen, though his years as a student had not hardened them like the hands he had shaken earlier.

"Hi. We're the Whitlocks. I'm Carson and this is Judy. We've got the Congregational Church down the street. We'll give you a call when all of this settles down a bit." Unlike the other Reverends in the room, he had on a gray tweed sport coat and darker gray slacks and Judy wore a green shirtwaist dress. Terribly normal, Russ thought, and he hoped they really would call. Then it was on to the homemade cakes and Welsh cookies and tea.

A pounding of spoons on teacups interrupted the proceedings. Hank Henry, Clerk of Session, the one in charge of the records and files so important to a Presbyterian church, came forward slowly with a gift wrapped in black paper and tied with a white ribbon. "On behalf of the Session and the entire Congregation of the Welsh Presbyterian Church of Scroggtown, Pennsylvania," he said in all seriousness, "it is my privilege to present this gift to our new pastor with our prayers and best wishes for a long and fruitful ministry." Clearly, he had been practicing his speech for days. To hear him speak was to know how much his church meant to him and how proud he was to be the one to make this presentation. Russ could tell that even if he couldn't always take all this religious stuff completely to heart, he was a damn fool, or worse, if he did anything to belittle or slight the depth with which these people held their church. With all sincerity he thanked Hank and everyone there. It was obvious that this was the big moment so far as the people of the congregation were concerned.

"Gwan, open it," Hank said. "We don't stand on formality here." With Ellen's help, Russ got the ribbon off, undid the paper, opened the box, and lifted out a dark blue leather bound copy of the *Book of Common Worship*. He was glad it wasn't black like Brother Henry's. There was also a little kit that contained a tiny bottle, a plate not much bigger than a silver dollar, and four small communion glasses. "It's for taking the sacrament to shut-ins," Hank said. Russ held up the book and communion set and looked at Brother

Henry and smiled. Brother Henry nodded back, as if relieved that this new minister was beginning to acquire some of the trappings of the trade.

"Thank you all for these gifts," Russ said. "As you know, they are just what I need." At that, everyone applauded and smiled.

The evening started to wind down. Ministers packed their black robes into long thin carrying cases, and people began pushing tables and chairs around getting them ready for Sunday School. Russ went about thanking people. It seemed to him to be the thing to do. He thanked them for coming, for baking cakes and cookies, for brewing coffee and tea. He tracked down all the elders to thank them for the prayer book and communion set. He went to the kitchen and thanked those who were doing the dishes. He thanked the sleepy youngsters for staying up so late. People patted him on the back and wished him well. He thanked Richie Evans for playing the organ even though that was his job and he got paid for it. He thanked the chorister and the members of the choir. Many of these were the same people he thanked for baking and cleaning up the kitchen. He thanked the ministers for taking part in the service.

"Now he's a minister for sure," the Moderator of the Presbytery said to Ellen as Russ thanked him for leading the service. "Undoubtedly, one of our main tasks is to say thank you, thank you, over and over again, thank you. Any minister who lasts at all learns that he can mess up the Lord's Prayer, forget the Apostles' Creed, preach terrible sermons, and even drop the offering plate, but he better not stop saying thank you. We thank those who deserve it, and most especially those who don't, because they're the ones who need it most. And we learn not to thank someone too much or someone else will be jealous of our thank you. It's a real art, saying thank you. Someday it may be a science. If so, ministers will be the scientists."

"I hadn't thought it was so involved," Ellen said.

"Oh, I would guess more ministers get in trouble over thank yous than over integrating the public schools or praying for peace in time of war," the Moderator said. "Sooner or later you're bound to mess up, forget someone, or just get tired of it. That's when they start saying your sermons aren't Biblical enough or something. My theory is that most of the trouble in churches comes by way of the Thank You Department."

"Do they give a Thank You course in seminary?" Ellen asked. "Seems like they should."

"No, but you're right, they should. Thank You 101. Any of us could teach it.

"Well, a special thank you for being here," Russ said to the Moderator.

"That a boy, Russ, you're getting on to it," the Moderator said, and with that, he left. Soon after, Russ and Ellen left too. It was a cool night with moonlight and a rustle of leaves. On the corner, Carson Whitlock was talking with Brother Henry.

"Let's all get together sometime for breakfast at the Coal Bin," Brother Harry was saying. "We could help Llewellen here get acquainted with the rest of us in the Association."

"Fine," Carson said, looking at his little date book. "I'm free on Wednesday a week from today. By the way, Henry, were you serious about not calling Russ until after eleven?"

"I was never more serious in my life, Carson. The young man needs uninterrupted time for study," Brother Henry proclaimed. And with that he bounded off in the direction of town and his red brick manse next to the red brick church he served.

"We'll be in touch with you guys tomorrow at eleven," Carson said to Russ. "Wouldn't want to interrupt anything."

"That'll be fine," Russ said, "until then I will be stuck to my chair, brooding."

A whiff of culm smoke was in the air as Ellen and Russ walked up the hill toward their apartment, but the neighborhood seemed cozy and peacefully tucked in under its elms and poplars and sycamores. Yellow leaves caught the light from street lamps, and here and there a dry leaf crunched underfoot.

"Let's see what the new reverend is made of," Ellen said when they got to their door. "It's too late to study."

"Yeah," Russ said, and he lifted her across the threshold. This time he didn't drop her.

6

Knock First

NEXT MORNING, THE PHONE RANG at eleven on the dot. Russ answered it in his bookless, deskless study. It was Carson Whitlock. "Judy and I would like you and Ellen to come by for dessert after youth fellowship on Sunday night. How's that for you?"

"Sounds fine," Russ said. "We'll be glad to come. Say, Carson, how do you keep these people straight? They all have pretty much the same names."

"So you've noticed that. Welcome to Wales. We'll talk about it Sunday," Carson chortled.

No sooner did Carson hang up than the phone rang again. "Oh Reverennnd, I hope I'm not disturbing your rest or anything," a woman's voice began.

"No," Russ said, "I just got off the phone." People had taken Brother Henry's words to heart, it seemed.

"Well," the voice said, "I'm Mildred Morgan, Mrs. Thomas Morgan, though before I married my name was Jones. The Jones boys you met last night are my brothers, or at least some of them are. Our father was Jeremiah Jones, who was an elder in the church for many years until he died. That was in 1953, December 16, I remember it like it was yesterday. Our mother was a Davis."

"I met so many Davises and Joneses last night," Russ said, "I don't think I'll ever get them sorted out."

"Don't worry about that, Reverennnd, we're all the same here, all related somehow or other. Just be careful when you're talking about somebody, because you're bound to be talking to a relative of theirs here on Welsh Hill." She laughed as she said it. "But what I called for was to tell you that Sally Roberts, my husband's mother's aunt is in Memorial Hospital, and I wish you could go see her."

"I can go this afternoon. Nothing serious, I hope," Russ said.

"The female trouble, Reverennnd. I know she would appreciate seeing you. She hasn't been to church in years. The bleeding you know."

Russ knew better than to say things like "Nothing serious, I hope." They told him in pastoral ministry class not to pry into people's troubles, but let them talk about them if they wanted to. Furthermore, everything's more or less serious if you're in the hospital. It was a dumb thing to say, and Russ knew it. He wasn't "on" yet, not "professionally alert," as they called it in that class. He was still in his slippers and bathrobe sipping coffee, in fact. "I'm messing up already, but I just learned I'm living on Welsh Hill. That's worth something, I suppose," he mumbled to himself.

Ellen was in bed reading. They had slept long past the time for her to get to school. He was thinking about where he would put all the stuff he had to bring up from Princeton, the books and bookcases, his desk and the old stuffed chair he liked to read in. He felt the need to look into some of his books again and remind himself about what he was supposed to be doing. But here in the parish, people considered him a ready-to-go minister, and he had come up with an earful of the woman with the flow of blood whom the gospel says Jesus cured when she touched the hem of his garment. That story was both a help and a hindrance to Russ as he got ready to see Mildred Morgan's husband's mother's aunt. "Am I expected to perform a miracle?" he mumbled.

A few minutes later, the phone rang again. "Oh good, Reverennnd, I hope I'm not disturbing your rest, but my sister's niece's cousin's son is in the hospital in Scranton. Terrible colitis. I'm sure it would help a lot if you could go see him."

This went on the rest of the morning. It seemed like everyone Russ had met the night before had a relative with something seriously wrong. What he was supposed to do about it, he had but a faint idea.

"Looks like I'll be spending the rest of the day at the hospital," Russ said to Ellen. "You would think everybody in the valley is sick."

"Probably one of the plagues," Ellen said. "What did the Whitlocks want?"

"Oh yeah. They want us to come over to their place Sunday night."

"Good. They seemed like people you could talk to. Where do they live?"

"Next to the Congregational Church I think."

"Right next to the church. Ugh," Ellen said, shaking her head. For the first time she seemed less than enthusiastic about what was going on.

"You OK?" Russ asked.

"I've got to study for this English test," she said. "Go see your sick people."

RUSS ATE BREAKFAST, WHICH WAS REALLY LUNCH, put on his increasingly rumpled brown suit, and went off to the hospitals. It was a cloudy day, and the wind was blowing a few red and yellow leaves off the trees. He had to go right through town where the streets were crowded and backed up. It seemed like fewer stoplights were working than before. As he putted along in the Saab, it occurred to him it was Thursday already, and he hadn't even thought about a sermon for Sunday.

The hospital was nestled against the hills across the river on the south side of town. The trees around it were old and full and showing fall colors. Beneath the glorious leaves was a small white building, and Russ climbed the slate steps and opened the big glass door. He saw cracked plaster walls, worn tile floors, somewhat green, somewhat gray walls, everything faded, everything crowded in, people on folding chairs waiting in front of counters with signs on them saying CLINIC, OUT PATIENTS, or PHARMACY. Russ didn't know what to do. He wandered around in the halls for a while, finally asked some questions at the front desk, and walked in on Sally Roberts while she was taking her sponge bath.

"Oh Doctor, I didn't expect anyone," she said. A gray haired lady in her sixties, Russ guessed, was sitting on the edge of the bed completely naked wiping herself with a wash cloth, breasts drooping and flabby.

"I'm not the doctor," Russ blurted, turning red around the neck and jowls.

"Then what are you doing here?" Sally Roberts wanted to know. She grabbed a towel to cover herself.

"I'm the new minister at the Welsh Presbyterian Church," Russ said, backing out the door.

"You should knock first," Sally said.

"I'll be back a little later," Russ said.

"Yes, I think that would be a good idea," she said. She was shaking her head and half smiling.

"At least it doesn't look like she's going to call the authorities and have me arrested," Russ muttered to himself out in the hallway. After several minutes, he went back to Sally Roberts' room. This time he knocked first.

"Come in," she said. "Oh Reverennnd, it's you." She broke into a big smile. "My niece called and said you might be coming. I'm sorry I wasn't ready when you came before, but I have to take lots of baths, you see, owing to my condition. Here I am an old lady, and the bleeding has started again. It's so much trouble. I don't know what's to become of me. Maybe I'll be like Sarah and start having children in my old age." She chuckled and her eyes flashed, then she sagged against the pillow like she was tired out from the effort to be pleasant. Russ noticed how easy it was for her to weave into her own situation the story of Abraham's wife Sarah who, it was said, gave birth to Isaac when she was ninety years old.

There was a pale yellow curtain halfway around Sally's bed, and her bed table had a sweating pitcher of ice water on it. Russ found a straight wooden chair painted with several coats of white enamel, pulled it beside the bed and sat down. He remembered that much from preacher school. "Find a chair and sit down," he was told. "Don't seem rushed and ready to leave."

Well, it wasn't a matter of prying anymore. Russ learned more about Sally's illness than he cared to know. She told him it had gone on eight months, there wasn't a napkin in the world that could hold all her bleeding, and she was getting tired of these bulky diapers she had to wear. Russ could see how she could be discouraged, but he had no idea what he was supposed to do about it, so he pursued his own questions.

"When Mildred Morgan called, I thought she said you were her husband's mother's, what? her aunt? or was it her sister? I have trouble knowing who's who?"

"Well, that's right, she's my husband's mother's kin, but I call Mildred my niece. We don't worry about all the connections being held strict around here. You'll see. We're all aunts and uncles, nieces and nephews, either by blood or marriage. It's a wonder we're not all feeble minded. In fact, Reverennnd, just between you and me, I think many of us are." She laughed out loud, and Russ laughed too.

They talked for almost an hour. Neither God nor Jesus was mentioned once. Russ heard about people dead for years, people who had grown up in Scroggtown and moved away, people who now lived in Los Angeles and worked for the airlines. He heard about doctors and pills and the best kinds of rubber sheets and how much it all costs. From time to time he echoed the advice of his pastoral psychology professor by saying "Oh, that must be discouraging." or "I guess that upsets you," but she never bit on any of it. She just talked about her family and her friends and her illness for a long time and didn't seem to want anything except that Russ should listen. Finally Sally said, "Please pray for me, Reverennnd."

"Yes, I will," Russ said, and got up and left.

The rest of the calls went pretty much the same. Russ listened to them talk without getting anything very pastoral said at all. It took about an hour for each visit. By the time the afternoon was over, he had gotten to only half the names on his list.

"THE PHONE NEVER STOPPED RINGING," Ellen said when Russ got home. She was upset, pink cheeks, set mouth. "Here's a bunch of people who are sick or in nursing homes or someplace. I tried to get it down. I didn't get much studying done, I know that." She handed Russ a list of names and phone numbers.

"My God, there go the next two days. When do I do a sermon?" Russ said.

"Oh yeah, and call Hank Henry," Ellen said, calmer now. "He said it's urgent." Russ got right on the phone.

"Reverennnd, can I come over tonight on a matter of urgency?" Hank said.

"Sure, Hank, right after dinner if you want."

"Good, Reverennnd. I'll be there."

Russ didn't like the sound of Hank's voice. He wondered if Sally Roberts had reported him as a snooper after all.

"Evening, Reverennnd. Evening Mrs. Llewellen," Hank said as Russ led him up the steps into their apartment. "Hope you're starting to get settled in. We want to do everything we can to make you feel to home." Russ took Hank's old felt hat and put it on a chair, and they sat at the kitchen table because there wasn't any furniture anyplace else except the bedroom. Ellen went in there with a book and closed the door.

The office of Clerk of Session was made for Hank Henry, all orderliness and propriety and going by the book. Short and angular, Hank worked as a carpenter in the only mine nearby that was still working, making things fit together that didn't always want to fit, doors and braces and the like, both above ground and below. He had small dark eyes, black hair with flecks of gray, and his short, stubby Welshman's fingers curled as if holding some invisible tool. On his lips there was the slight suggestion of a smile, an expression Russ noticed on many of the Welsh he met. It was as if they had the goods on you or had something marginally pleasant on their minds. It was hard to tell which.

"Would you like some coffee, Hank?" Russ asked. "It's only instant but I boiled the water myself." The doors of all four rooms of the apartment were within a few feet of each other. They would hit if you opened two of them at the same time. It was impossible to talk in one room and not be heard in the other. Ellen heard Russ offer Hank coffee and came out of the bedroom and put cups and spoons on the table. When the water boiled Russ poured it into the cups and added the instant coffee. Ellen went back in the bedroom. Russ set out cream and sugar, both of which Hank used a lot of. They talked of the weather, of what Russ had heard from his parents in California, of the just completed fishing season in the streams and lakes nearby. In the Church, it seems, one doesn't just get down to business.

"Well," Hank said finally, "I hear you went calling in the hospital this afternoon." Just by the way he said it, Russ knew Hank had heard about his seeing Sally Roberts naked.

"It was a busy day," Russ said. "Seems like a lot of people are sick."

"It really means a lot, Reverennnd, when you're sick, for the minister to come and pay a visit. It's one of the best things that can happen for a sick person."

"The people seemed to appreciate my seeing them," Russ said.

"Sure they do, Reverennnd. It means a lot, and you are to be commended for getting right to your calling. But our people expect the minister to take hold of their hand and say a little prayer for them before he leaves. Do you think that would be too much trouble, Reverennnd?" So it wasn't that Russ had walked in on Sally's bath, but that he walked out without praying for her right there on the spot, which is what she asked him to do.

"I can manage that," Russ said. "I just didn't know."

"Good, Reverennnd. People will appreciate it more than you can imagine. Well, I'd better be going now. Early shift tomorrow. I think I had a hat."

Russ got Hank's hat for him. Amazing, Russ thought, it took almost two hours to find out that when people say, "Pray for me, Reverennnd," I take them by the hand and say a prayer right then and there. "Small price to pay for such a lesson," he mumbled to himself.

As Hank was going down the stairs, he turned and mentioned that a meeting of the Session was coming up in a few days. "As Moderator, you will preside, of course." Russ knew that this was a big deal. He learned in Polity Class that the Session is the duly elected and installed elders who govern the congregation. And the Session includes the Moderator, who is the minister, and neither the elders nor Moderator can act apart from each other. At least that's what the Constitution of the Presbyterian Church says. Russ asked Hank, Clerk of Session and keeper of the records, if he might look at the minutes of past meetings and get an idea of what has been going on in the church.

"I guess there's no reason why you can't," Hank said, "I'll bring the books by tomorrow morning." It seemed to Russ that Hank was not all that enthusiastic about letting him see the books, but Hank knew Russ, as Moderator of Session, was entitled to. Russ had the fleeting thought that maybe he had some power in this situation after all.

Next day, at seven in the morning, Hank knocked on the door downstairs. In his robe and slippers, Russ said good morning to Hank, who quick gave him a large heavy sack containing the Sessional Records of the Welsh Presbyterian Church of Scroggtown going back many years.

"Here ya go, Reverrrennnd," Hank said. "Thought I would drop these off on my way to work." It wasn't lost on Russ that he was still in his pajamas while Hank was all but on the job, and from Hank's tone of voice, it wasn't lost on him either.

Russ quick got showered, shaved and dressed, fixed himself some toast and coffee, and sat down at the kitchen table to go over the records of the parish. Most everything was routine—budgets, communions held, baptisms, new members, deaths, renovations, and the like. But then Russ noticed that six years ago the Session officially rebuked a young man and woman for "sparking on Sunday." A draft of the Statement of Rebuke sent to the couple was attached to the minutes. Also, about three years ago, a motion passed that refused a sizeable contribution from Hughie Saloony, proprietor of the neighborhood tavern. They actually put his name in the minutes that way. And then there was a puzzling reference, dated little over a year ago, to a mysterious ten thousand dollars that never got referred to again. Ten thousand dollars could underwrite the budget of the church for an entire year. "That's something to ask about too," Russ mumbled, and he jotted down several notes to himself.

Russ turned his attention to trying to come up with an idea for Sunday's sermon when promptly at eleven, the phone rang, and he was told about sick people to go see. Ellen had already left for school. "I'm going to study in the library after my test," Ellen said on her way out, "no use coming back here to answer the phone for you."

Russ got into his brown suit, put an apple and banana in a paper sack and went out to make the rounds. He stopped at the hospital first to see Sally Roberts, and after a brief visit, took her by the hand and said a short prayer: "We ask your healing and help for Sally, O God, and we pray for all who suffer here and need your care. Amen."

"Thank you, Reverennnd. It helps so much. In fact I'm going home tomorrow. I couldn't have done it without you." Russ wondered how the doctor might feel if he heard that. And he wondered just how he had helped. Some talk, some laughter, and now this innocuous little prayer, and Sally takes it for the beginning of a miracle.

He went to others in the hospital, to nursing homes, to back rooms in old houses where grandmas or grandpas had been lying for years with the aftermath of stroke or kidney failure or both. He talked to them, listened for a while, then held their hands and said a little prayer. He spent a lot of time trying to find streets that seemed to end and start up again someplace else. He drove the fifteen miles to one of the big hospitals in Scranton to see the more seriously ill. It was a gorgeous fall day, the hills like huge cresting waves tinged with red and gold, so he didn't mind the trip at all. He got in five stops and saw eight people, which was twice what he did the day before, but he could see how even at that rate he was falling further behind. Everywhere he went, though, they said he had helped them. After hearing it so many times, Russ began to think maybe it was so in some strange way, and a satisfied feeling crept around the edges of his soul.

JUST LIKE THAT, IT WAS SATURDAY AFTERNOON, and Russ realized he had to stop calling on sick people and get a sermon ready. "Seems like tomorrow is always Sunday in this business," he muttered to himself. "If I ever write a book, that's what I'll call it, Tomorrow Is Always Sunday. Not much chance of that, though. There's not even time to write sermons."

An hour of study per minute of preaching, the homiletics professor said. Well, Russ had to preach again in about twenty hours, and he wasn't even sure what to talk about unless he could use another sermon from seminary preaching class. This one was the first sermon he had ever tried to write, and it had been more severely criticized than any of them, but he decided he had to go with it. The text was from Psalm 27, "The Lord is my light and salvation, whom shall I fear?" Next week he would be on his own.

"I've used up three years of seminary in three weeks of preaching," he muttered.

The sermon was mostly a story about Russ substituting for a night watchman at a vegetable packing plant one summer when he was home from college and how the building groaned and squeaked so much Russ was sure people were inside carrying stuff away that he was hired to protect. The old shed was huge and pitch dark, so to check on all these noises was impossible. As he walked among the bins of broccoli and cauliflower, he was completely vulnerable to anyone who wanted to pounce on him. Russ admitted in the sermon that he never liked the dark and let on how he was more than a bit afraid the whole night long. But then the first light of day appeared over the eastern mountains, the shadows in the shed were dispelled, and Russ could see there was no danger lurking. He likened that experience to the divine light breaking in upon human anxieties and calming our fears, as it says in the Psalm. That was the entire sermon. The preaching professor said the sermon was crass illustration, and the meaning of the text got lost in the packing shed. He said Russ would have to dig deeper into the theology of God's light and salvation before he tried to preach that sermon again.

Well, Russ hadn't dug deeper into the theology of anything, but he had been calling on the sick for over two days straight, and he had seen fear and darkness in people's eyes, and he had talked to people who had fought their fears with what they called "faith 'n' prayer." "That's what does it, Reverennnd, faith 'n' prayer," they said, and it seemed their faith and prayers were somehow connected to Russ' faith and prayers. And though it made Russ uncomfortable, he sensed that they believed that he believed as they believed, and if they were sure of that, they could be sure of a lot of things, including that God was helping them get well.

Along with everything else, it was communion Sunday. The sermon wasn't particularly suitable for such a day, but Russ had nothing else at hand. At least that little finger-pointing professor who tore apart their sermons had made his students memorize the communion service so they could look at the people when they said the holy words. That night, Russ stayed up late with his brand new *Book of Common Worship* going over what the little book called "Another Order for the Celebration of the Sacrament of the Lord's Supper." He wanted to do at least that much right.

Next day, it was like a different sermon than the one he preached to his class at Princeton. The image of dawn breaking upon the night of fear didn't seem at all crass to the people of the Welsh Presbyterian Church. They nodded as if to say, "Yes, that's just how it is." Maybe his tone of voice had been beneficially tempered by holding those hands and saying those prayers in hospitals and nursing homes. Whatever it was, this time the sermon had a sound and sense it didn't have before.

After the sermon, Russ approached the communion table for the first time as one authorized to administer the sacrament. He faced the people without book or papers. He looked into their faces as they sang the quiet communion hymn, "Here, O My Lord, I See Thee Face to Face." He looked up into the balcony to the teenagers, some folding the bulletin into odd shapes, though it didn't look like they were going to toss paper airplanes out over the congregation that day. He thought of the parishioners he had visited and the ones still on his list to visit, all of them related in some close way to the people in the pews who, with obvious devotion, were singing the hymn.

The hymn over, Russ spoke the Invitation to the Lord's Supper, letting the phrases form in his mouth of their own accord. It was clear to him there was no need to make the words sound important, for they are important in their own right: "All who humbly put their trust in Christ, and desire His help that they may lead a holy life," he began. Very simple words. Not Russ' words. The Church's words. No need for cleverness now or elucidation or analysis. All that was required was a voice. Russ felt himself taking his place among others in black robes who had delivered those very words from that very place behind the communion table of this old church. He sensed that others would stand there and do this after he was gone. And Russ had a fleeting sense that it wasn't up to him to make everything come out right. Sacraments do not belong to the ordained ones who administer them. They belong to the whole Church and its people. He could feel this was so. He had studied the several theories of the sacraments that had grown up in various branches of the Church over the centuries, but he had never felt the impact of the rite until he stood there that day saying those words he had memorized in order to pass a test in school.

A quiet sigh went up from the people. They were accepting the invitation to this Supper with all their hearts. It was clear to Russ they were far ahead of him in such matters.

At the Prayer of Consecration, Russ began to feel again that lifted, stretched feeling he felt on ordination night when hands were laid upon his head. His feet were still squarely on the floor, his beautiful feet, this time in shined shoes, but who he was seemed expanded somehow. He felt so very tall, his head close to the ceiling, and it seemed as if his arms could reach out to both walls and include all the people in a huge embrace. He spoke the traditional phrases as if he was hearing them just before they formed in his mouth. His voice was speaking to him as it spoke to the people. When he opened his eyes after the prayer, he immediately became his proper size and shape again, standing there behind the communion table.

Russ reached for the small loaf of fresh baked bread that one of the deacons had put on a silver platter in the middle of the table. He lifted it up, saying, "On the night before he was betrayed unto his death, Jesus took bread and broke it and said, 'this is my body broken for you. Take, eat, this do in remembrance of me.'" Then Russ broke the loaf in two, and an audible gasp rose up from the people. It was like something in them was being broken, like it hurt them to see this bread torn in two. Eyes were moist. Many bowed and prayed quiet prayers, cheeks glistening with tears. Such devotion, Russ thought. Such devotion as I have never seen.

Four elders stood up in the Holiness of Holinesses as if on cue. They walked forward and held out their thick coal miner hands, their carpenter hands, their accountant hands, their out-of-work hands, and Russ put a tray of cut up bread in each hand. The elders stood waiting, as did Russ. Hank Henry, with the slightest nod, indicated Russ was to sit down in the cushioned chair that had been placed beside the communion table. Then Hank came forward in all solemnity. He held the tray for Russ to take a piece of the bread, and he stood at attention there until Russ put it in his mouth. Only then did the elders move out into the congregation to pass the bread to the people. Russ bowed his head, thinking about the light he had spoken of in his sermon, and feeling the light streaming into the church through the amber tinged windows behind the choir loft.

Two by two, the elders came down the aisle, handed the trays to Russ, and he laid them on the table. Then he took a tray and went over to the Holiness of Holinesses and served the elders. Everyone serves and is served, these gestures seemed to say. Russ leaned over the railing and paused before each elder, and each one, with long practiced dexterity, took a piece of bread that seemed very small in those thick hands. The elders communed as one, and they all bowed in silent prayer together.

Then Russ raised the silver chalice and said, "After the supper, Jesus said, 'This cup is the new covenant in my blood. All of you drink from it.'" He handed the elders four trays of little glass cups full of Welch's grape juice. It didn't seem to matter that it wasn't wine, which had never been served in the Welsh Presbyterian Church of Scroggtown, nor that the holy words suggest a primitive kind of bloody rite that originated, perhaps, in primeval tribes. Clearly, Jesus was present to these people at this moment, whatever the liquid in the little cups happened to be or whatever might be said about the origins of such rituals. It all moved slowly and quietly, like it took place under water. When the elders brought the cup trays back for Russ to lay on the table, his shiny new wedding ring banged against the polished brass edge of one of them. Clang! Heads popped up from deep prayer. Russ determined to watch that from then on. None of the elders, with their thick stubby fingers, had allowed such a thing to happen. Surely the minister could be as careful.

After a brief prayer of thanksgiving, they sang Calon Lan, Richie Evens' postlude at the ordination service. The gentle rhythm of the hymn was a means of rising up from the mysteries of the sacrament, it seemed to Russ. Now the people were relaxed, enjoying their renewed lives. "A clean heart forever singing, / Singing through the day and night." It was just beautiful, and thoroughly Welsh in sound and sentiment. Fine voices meshed and softly pulled the notes, it seemed to Russ, from the far corners of the room or even from the green hills of the homeland. Russ' meager spiritual history began to form itself around the congregation's singing. He could feel it. And he wondered if there was something in him, something he was only now becoming aware of, something in his blood and bone, a Welshness that somehow had passed through generations to his less than settled soul.

Then there was Ellen, young, beautiful Ellen, standing near the front of the church singing away, her face turned slightly upward to give her voice better passage. She seemed a little troubled lately, school pressures beginning to build, and the pressure of all these new things going on, including a growing sense of expectations about being a pastor's wife. But there she was singing the hymn with all her heart. Russ looked at her and trembled. How could he make it all right for her? He didn't know.

As he sang quietly along, Russ noticed that the deep solemnity of the service was starting to lift. The people were becoming a normal-looking group of Presbyterians getting ready for church to be over so they could get home to their dinners. Russ felt emptied out. His hand seemed heavy when he raised it for the benediction.

7

Aunt Sophie

AFTER CHURCH, AFTER SHAKING ALL THOSE THICK Welsh hands at the door, after many comments about the "lovely communion service" and how it came "right from the heart," Aunt Sophie Thomas invited Russ and Ellen to Sunday dinner. On Welsh Hill, Russ was becoming aware, "Aunt" was a designation given to ladies of a certain age who never married.

Tiny, eighty something if a day, alert, and more than spry, Aunt Sophie had the bearing of a chickadee. She hopped and flitted as she walked, her legs thin straight sticks barely poking below her long blue dress and her somewhat shorter black coat. The net veil on her little black hat flew in the air as she walked. It was her church hat. All the women wore hats to church.

Ellen had gone bareheaded that day, tired of wearing the honeymoon straw hat she had worn with her linen suit when they drove off after the wedding. It was the only hat she owned and would have been out of place on this early October day. She may have been the first minister's wife ever to attend the Welsh Presbyterian Church of Scroggtown without a hat on. She hadn't even thought about it, and neither had Russ. There was enough on their minds without that sort of thing. In fact, Ellen had gone to church in school clothes—plaid skirt, white blouse, bulky blue sweater—and on that score alone there were whispers here and there in the pews as she took her seat in the front row across the aisle from the Holiness of Holinesses. All the other women wore dark dresses.

Aunt Sophie seemed not to be concerned about such matters. This may have been because Aunt Sophie could hardly see, though she never let on how bad her eyes were. By memory more than sight, it seemed, she avoided the ragged edge of every slate in the sidewalk. She led the way in sort of a trot.

Most of the sidewalks of Scroggtown were large squares of steel-gray slates set in the ground one after the other. Winter freezes caused them to tip and crack so that, even for those with good eyesight, every step was a chance to catch a heel and go tumbling down. Sophie's heels never got caught. She set her feet down between the cracks every time.

"They ought to fix these cracks," Sophie said as she trotted a step ahead of Russ and Ellen. "Some poor old soul is likely to fall and break a hip, and then you'd have to go visit them, Reverennnd, and I hear you got enough sick to call on."

"You're right about that, Sophie," Russ said.

"I like to hear them, the different sounds of the slates." Sophie said. It was true. Some of them sounded hollow and made a dull ring when they were stepped on. Others sounded solid and made more of a click or clink. Click, clunk, ring, ring, clink, clunk the slates chattered as the three of them scurried along.

"I bet, Reverennnd, even if I couldn't see, I could tell right away where I was by the sound of the slates," Sophie said.

"I bet you could too, Sophie," Russ said, and he looked toward Ellen who was smiling and shaking her head.

Sophie's was a small house all on one floor. A square wooden box is what it was, with porches and pantries tacked on outside the box. The white paint was washed off in places, and the roof's asphalt shingles curled up with thick black moss on them. Aunt Sophie led Ellen and Russ through the back door and sat them at the kitchen table on round backed wooden chairs painted bright green. The table was covered with white oilcloth on which was a bud vase with a small purple flower sticking out of it. Near the bud vase were large clear glass salt and pepper shakers that looked like they had been there for decades. The silverware, of elegant patterns, was old, genuine, and heavy, but none of it matched.

"We're going to have ffrois," Aunt Sophie said. It sounded to Russ like she said froyce. "It's an old Welsh treat." She got a bowl of white batter out of the refrigerator and lit her old, black and white gas stove. Not able to see the flame, she waved her hand over the burners to make sure she knew which two were on. She set the teakettle on one burner and a frying pan on the other and poured a layer of the batter into the frying pan. The batter cooked into a huge thin pancake, which Aunt Sophie served to Russ on a white plate. She got sugar, jam, butter, and cream from the refrigerator and put it all on the table.

"The idea," she said, "is you put butter and jam or sugar and cream or whatever you like on the ffrois and then roll it up and eat it, and you follow that with a gulp of good Welsh tea. We like our tea so that it keeps us awake all day and half the night," she said through a little laugh.

"I've noticed that," Russ said. He had been plied with "good Welsh tea" in every house he had been to while visiting the sick.

Russ did what Sophie recommended with the ffrois while Ellen waited her turn. The minister goes first, he was learning, ahead of women, children, and the elderly. Not the worst custom in the world, Russ chuckled to himself.

While she cooked and served ffrois, Sophie talked about her dear brother Tommy Thomas who was in the sanitarium up on the hill, sick with the black lung, about her dear mother who had been dead for thirty years, about her dear sister Blodwyn who had gone to Wales for a visit, met a man there, and never came back to Scroggtown, about all the dear people dead or alive she knew and loved, which seemed to be everybody on Welsh Hill, past and present, and the Irish, Polish, and Italians of Scroggtown as well.

"I don't see much difference in folks, Revvverrrennnd," she said, emphasizing his title even more than Buck the Elder. "We all seem pretty much the same to me, all of us kind of nuts in our way, but all right too. We all have to get by somehow, and we do church mostly the same. We just call things by different names. Anyways, that's what I think about all these different churches. I know I'm not supposed to think like that, but I can't help it. I can't see why we have to be at odds."

"I like your way of thinking, Sophie," Russ said. He noted that this spindly Welsh Presbyterian was not afraid to tell her minister things she thought he might disagree with. Or maybe she was testing him out in her spunky way. Whatever was going on, Russ could see that Aunt Sophie did some thinking on her own.

As they finished eating, Sophie gathered up the paper napkins and threw them into a round opening on the right side of the stove. The napkins hit the kernels of glowing coal there and blazed up as Sophie set a heavy lid over the flames.

"So you have a combination coal and gas stove," Russ said, "pretty clever."

"Oh yes, Reverennnd. Soon now I'll get my winter coal in. I've just about used up last year's delivery. A little coal in the waste burner, and I'm nice and cozy. The winters aren't so bad so long as we have coal. I can remember when we didn't have it though. Couldn't afford it."

"When was that, Sophie?"

"Mostly when I was a girl, but later too. There would be a cave-in and the mine would shut down and nobody could work. And when the miners went for the union, it was bad. They locked them out and nobody could work even if they wanted to. All that winter we had no money coming in and my father trying to do deliveries at James' Grocery for a little food. It got colder and colder in the house. All us kids would go down to the tracks to pick coal that fell off the trains, but it was all gone before Christmas, and no trains going by to spill any more. A lot of us would live in the same

house then, all cousins and everything, even strangers. We ate nothing but potatoes those days, just like the Irish." She laughed at the thought.

There was no mistaking Aunt Sophie for Irish. Without knowing her name, it was clear she was Welsh. It was in her voice, the lilt of it, the way she said "Revvverrrennnd" when she wanted to make a point, the suggestion of a smile on the lips through which her words came. With Sophie, that smile seemed to come from a kind of inner assurance, a sense of having made peace with human differences and deep knowledge won from long, difficult coping. It was a subtle and at the same time penetrating smile, full of old shivers and chills and the people who suffered them. For a minute or so Sophie just looked out the window, and Russ thought she seemed very wise, very knowing in her uncomplicated way.

Aunt Sophie's kitchen window looked over a sticker bush that was turning red. Also in the yard was a small oak tree with its leaves fading to dirty orange. Then there was Sophie's rotting picket fence and then Main Street where the cars bumped along among the potholes. Across the street was the brown and yellow plaster front of a former grocery store, now a garment factory. From time to time the sun caught a glare from the chrome on a passing car, and it flashed into the kitchen through the branches of the tree. It was obvious Sophie spent a lot of time looking out that window on a jumbled, unpromising scene like so many in Scroggtown. She seemed to get something from it, like maybe her town and her memories were all there within a kind of frame, and the traffic kept going past, and the ministers came and went at the church, and she had them in for ffrois and strong tea and told them things about Scroggtown that could take months to learn any other way.

Aunt Sophie took a plate of Welsh cookies and the teapot and led Russ and Ellen into her tiny living room. Chippendale chairs were mixed in with an old overstuffed sofa with a knitted quilt on it. The lamps had long tassels hanging down from dark shades. The low table where Sophie set the tea and cookies looked rough and homemade.

"Sophie, what was it like when the mines were running full bore?" Russ asked.

"Well, Reverennnd, those were hard days, and yet we wouldn't trade them for other days either. I guess that's how I would say it."

"You mentioned the mines caving in. How did that happen?"

"Explosions mostly," Sophie said, and chuckled even at that. "The gas would build up in pockets, and then a spark or something would set it off. They couldn't tell the gas was there; it didn't have a smell or anything, and it sank down and stayed there. That's why they liked it when there were rats around. That's what my brother Tommy always said. He prayed to have rats playing around his feet when he was in the mine. He gave them little parts of his sandwiches. The rats ran along the floor where the gas would be. If the rats started to wobble, the men knew to get out. And they had canaries in cages up high for the kind of gas that rises. When the canary stopped singing, they got out. Sometimes the gas built up where there were no rats or canaries, or even if there were, they couldn't get out in time, and that was bad."

"So they were working in a kind of trap with gas building up all the time?" Russ asked. He could feel the prophetic impulse to say something about oppression and injustice, but he stifled it in favor of finding out more.

"They still work down where the gas builds up, but they have better ventilation now, better fans and ways of telling where the gas is. We hardly ever hear of explosions now. A lot of the mines are closed, anyway."

"How deep are the mines, Sophie?"

"Oh, I don't know the figures, Reverennnd, but they go way down, or into the hillsides, a mile or two, maybe more, I heard people say. The deepest mines are full of water. They work the closer ones, which is why the top falls in sometimes and we have holes in the ground. That's what happened down to the Knox Mine.

The whole Susquehanna River flowed into that mine, and people drowned. Eddie Polanski, he was down there for two or three days, water up to his chin sometimes. Hasn't been right since and won't go to the mines any more. We gave Eddie a job as janitor of the church even though he's Polish. I voted in favor of that."

"Good for you, Sophie," Russ said.

"A lot of Polish came to dig coal after the Welsh and Irish and Italians, and all of us know what can happen to a miner." Sophie had a sip of her tea and poured more for Russ and Ellen. She sighed, sat back, and went on.

"Reverennnd, when I was a girl, everyone around here was Welsh. There were thousands and thousands of Welsh over to Scranton and more in Carbondale where there was lots of coal. The Welsh came to this valley soon as the mines opened. The company owned our houses and our stores and everything. And all we had was their script, they called it, which we could only spend at the company store, not U. S. dollars we could spend anywhere. We had to pay what they charged or go without. Our rent and our groceries went on the tab, but the pay never covered the tab. So every month we owed more. Remember that song about you get a day older and deeper in debt, that's how it was."

"So people were pretty well stuck," Russ offered.

"It was worse than being stuck, Reverennnd. Little breaker boys, no more than eight or nine years old, had to work all day picking slate for maybe seventy cents, maybe less. Imagine that. It's how families got by."

"What are breaker boys?" Russ asked.

Aunt Sophie looked out the window again and chuckled. "The breaker's that big building you see by the old mine," she said. "Chunks of coal from the mine have to be broken to different sizes. It goes in the breaker and comes out on belts. The breaker boys sat there all day and picked slates and rocks from the coal. What a racket it was in there with the breaker going and the coal rumbling down and all that dust flying. The boys chewed tobacco to keep the

103

dust out of their throats. If a boy's head came up to a man's out-stretched arm, he could work on the breaker. No more schooling for that one. Oh no."

"My father came from the soft coal country in Indiana," Russ said, "He never talked about picking slate, but his brother was killed in a mine explosion when he was just eighteen."

"Then you know something of what it was like," Sophie said.

"How could little kids keep going all day like that?" Russ asked.

"A grown man stood watch and hit them with a broom if they got lazy or started to fall asleep," she said. "Now what kind of man would have a job like that? But actually, they used to do something like that in church if people began to nod off. Not with a broom, but an elder would come along and give a little pinch. They thought if somebody slept in church it was because he was out late the night before. It couldn't be the Reverennnd's sermon was going on and on. No, no, not that," Sophie chuckled. Then she added, "My brother Tommy picked slate before he became a miner. He worked in the mine over forty years. Now he's got the black lung, and the mine's closed down, and they say they can't pay benefits. So there we are."

"Why do you say you wouldn't trade those days for anything?" Russ was proud of himself for asking such a good question.

"Because they brought us together, brought us to church to pray and sing. When there was a cave in down below, a terrible whistle would go off in the middle of a shift, and we knew it was bad. We would all gather 'round the entrance to the mine and wait for the men to come out. If some didn't come out, volunteers went back in to get them. It was an unspoken rule, you don't leave a miner underground, dead or alive. Then we all gathered in the church to sing hymns and pray. We sang and sang all day and into the night, and when we couldn't sing any more, the minister lit a tall candle on the communion table and turned off the lights, and we sang Sandon, 'Lead, kindly Light, amid th'encircling gloom.'" Almost in a whisper, Sophie hummed the first bars of the old hymn.

"We sang it in Welsh too," she went on. "We sang it over and over in the darkness, our eyes on the light of that candle. Down below, our men were following their little miner lights through the darkness. It was like the church and the mine were the same, like we were there in the darkness with those miners looking for light to lead them home. You don't forget times like that, Reverennnd."

"No, and I'll not forget your telling me about them," Russ said.

"We had to help each other or we couldn't make it," Sophie went on. "Had to give to each other and loan things. In those winters when the strikes were on, some didn't make it. Some died, children, grown men, and the women too, they died from hunger and cold though they called it consumption. Breaker boys fell into the machinery and got mangled. Some got their fingers cut off. Men came home hurt. If a hurt miner couldn't walk, they just carried him home and left him on the kitchen table. If he was dead, they left him on the front porch. We had to stick together those days. There's nothing like hardship to make Christians out of us, Revvverrrennnd." Aunt Sophie laughed quietly and patted her thigh.

She left Russ and Ellen for a minute and came back with a box in her hands. "Mrs. Llewellen, you must take this as a little welcome present from me." Sophie took from the box a small white wool blanket with long tassels all around the edges and gave it to Ellen. It was obviously very old. "It was my mother's," Aunt Sophie said. "She used it to keep her legs warm when she sat in the rocking chair to do her sewing. I want you to take it and put it in the car and wrap your pretty legs in it so they won't be cold when you go calling with the Reverennnd."

"Sophie, are you sure you want to let this go?" Ellen said.

"You take it, Mrs. Llewellen. It would make my mother happy to know it was keeping your knees warm in the wintertime. And I want you to have this, too. It makes just two cups, so you won't be wasting water when the Reverennnd wants his tea. That's very Welsh, you know, not to waste." It was a small tin teapot in a hexagon shape that became smaller from bottom to top. There was no spout. You poured right out of the top of the pot by raising the lid with a little wooden lever.

"Thank you, Sophie," Ellen said, "these are wonderful things to have. We don't even own a teapot, so this will be very handy when the Reverend wants his tea." She rolled her eyes at Russ, but she was smiling just the same.

"That teapot has been in the family from Wales," Sophie said. "It came across on the boat in somebody's sack. You won't find one like it around here except in some silly old Welsh lady's kitchen. Now you will have it in your kitchen, Mrs. Llewellen, and you can be a silly old Welsh lady like the rest of us." Sophie laughed and laughed about that. Russ laughed too, and Ellen smiled and shook her head. No use talking about the modern minister's spouse with the likes of Sophie. She had Ellen pegged for going on pastoral calls and making tea for the Reverennnd, and that's all there was to it.

Sophie chirped and bubbled and served the Llewellens tea and Welsh cookies for another hour, and then quite abruptly announced she needed her rest. She showed them to the front door saying, "In the back, out the front, that's how it is at my house," and she laughed and thanked them for giving her so much precious time. Russ figured it was time extremely well spent.

FROM AUNT SOPHIE'S HOUSE RUSS AND ELLEN went down the hill on Maple Street. Gold sunlight slanted upon the rooftops. A few yellow leaves fell with every gust of breeze, and the cracked, uneven slates made their particular sounds underfoot. People were in their yards raking and pruning and wrestling with storm windows. They stopped what they were doing and greeted Ellen and Russ as they walked past. Everybody knew them, or at least knew who they were.

"Afternoon, Reverennnd. Mrs. Llewellen," they said. The men tipped their little caps or garden hats as they nodded toward Ellen.

"It's like they expect us to do this," Russ said, "come by and sort of proffer a distant blessing. Then they tip their hats and go on with their gardening."

"Pretty good," Ellen said, "if all you have to do to give out blessings is walk down the sidewalk."

"Maybe I'm getting credit for pastoral calls," Russ said.

"Do they keep a count?" Ellen asked.

"I don't know, but if so, I'm getting way ahead today," Russ chuckled.

When she saw Russ and Ellen start down her block, a lady on lower Maple Street dropped her shears on the sidewalk and ran up on her porch and sat down in a rocking chair.

"Oh Reverennnd, nice to see you. I was doing a little pruning and my back got to hurting. I guess it serves me right for profaning the Sabbath," she said.

"I expect you can be forgiven for a little pruning," Russ said, "just so long as you're not bringing in the harvest."

"Oh, I wouldn't do anything like that on the Lord's Day, Reverennnd," she said.

When they passed into the next block, Russ looked back and noticed the lady had picked up her shears and was at it again, her back all better. They passed Hughie Saloony's, the neighborhood tavern just up from the old mine. It was a narrow version of the houses around it, its green sesame seed siding much the worse for wear. The main door opened on Maple Street, but the tavern extended back along an alley. There, well down from the front of the building, was door over which a small sign said, "Ladies Entrance." A nice looking house with white aluminum siding and a flagstone porch was attached to the back of the tavern. Because it was Sunday, the tavern was closed in keeping with Pennsylvania's blue laws. Hughie's wife, a mildly plump and chesty woman with an open, inviting face, the tail of her blue work shirt loose around her ample hips, was outside washing the two little windows on either side of the tavern door. One window framed a blue neon sign that said DRINK STEGMAIERS, and the other framed GOOD GIBBONS BEER in red neon.

"Lovely day, wouldn't you say, Reverend?" she said. "I'm Mary Hughes, but they call me Mrs. Saloony. They've got a name for everybody in this neighborhood. Welcome to Welsh Hill." She went right on with her work and made no apology about profaning the Sabbath or anything else. Her hair was wrapped in a blue bandana, but what hair could be seen had obviously been helped to keep its flaming color by the dedicated use of various concoctions available at West Main Rexall. She seemed totally comfortable with herself and pronounced "Reverend" just like it's spelled.

"We're closed today, but I hope you'll come by sometime when we're open and have a ginger ale." She smiled a full smile.

"I'll do that," Russ said.

"That would make you the first minister who ever did," Mary said. "Still and all, I'd like you to come visit my husband Hughie. His sugar's real bad; he's got a leg off from it. The elders can't get on you for visiting the sick, now can they, Reverend?"

"I don't know, can they?" Russ replied.

"Well," Mary said, "Hughie's contributions to the church are never accepted, for one thing."

"Why is that?" Russ asked.

"Because they come from what they call 'the drink.' They think the church and 'the drink' are ever to be separate. They don't have anything to do with us. I won't say anything about the elders who've come calling here on the sly, if you know what I mean."

"Let's pretend I don't know about that," Russ said.

"Good for you, Reverend. See you later." Mary Hughes went back to cleaning her windows. Russ sensed that going to see Hughie Saloony would be crossing a line, but he had already decided that's what he would do.

Russ and Ellen walked back along the lower road by the river, past the old leaning breaker, the defunct white stucco chemical plant downstream from the mine, and lots of rusting machinery.

They walked up to Main on a street with smaller houses on it. Davis Grocery, a tiny store that mostly carried cigarettes, soda pop, potato chips, milk, and ice cream bars occupied one of these dwellings. All of them had clapboard siding with the bare wood showing through in many places. Roofs were in disrepair. Clotheslines stretched in narrow spaces between the houses where it seemed the sun might never shine. There were no front yards at all, or sidewalks for that matter. The houses came right up to the narrow street and stood across from each other, barely twenty feet from one front door to the other. Rooms had been built on the back of the original square boxes so that there were no yards to speak of. Cars were parked nearly against the front doors, staggered so there was just enough room for a single zigzag lane between them. These must be the old company houses, Russ thought. People were obviously living in them, but no one could be seen. Most of the street was in shadows now, and a chill floated up from the river.

"What do you think of all this?" Ellen asked.

"What do you mean?" Russ asked back.

"I mean it all seems so…well, closed in or something. This valley, this neighborhood, the church, the houses pretty much all the same, everything leaning this way or that, and the people pretty much look the same and sound the same. They're all related for God's sake. It's like nothing gets in from the outside. It's spooky."

"Let's just say it's different," Russ said.

8

The Whitlocks

RUSS GOT BACK TO THE CHURCH AT SEVEN for Youth Fellowship. He had no idea what to do with a bunch of high school kids. He didn't have to worry. Only three showed up, two boys and a girl, and one of them wasn't in high school yet. He visited with them for an hour, asked what they would like Youth Fellowship to be, got nothing at all by way of response, and closed the meeting with a prayer for the youth of the parish. Strangely enough, the kids seemed to appreciate being there. They said they would be back the next week and bring their friends, which meant Russ would have to figure out something for them to do. He seriously doubted the young people of Scroggtown were going to be interested in a comparison of the Greek tragic poets with the major Hebrew prophets, which he knew more about than anything else.

Then Russ and Ellen drove up Main Street to the Congregational Church, an imposing new building of bright orange bricks with a spotlight showing off its modernistic glass front. The red tile roof rose in a long sweep upward, culminating at the pinnacle in a stout, understated, black metal cross. It was the highest thing anywhere around, and the whole church seemed to be perfectly perpendicular, while the telephone poles nearby, in the manner of Scroggtown, leaned a little one way or the other. Next to the church was an immense old wooden house newly painted an uncertain color, as if they had tried to match the church and missed. It looked like it was four stories, including attic and basement. There was a light on in the basement as Russ and Ellen walked up the steps. When they rang the bell, the light went out.

"Come in," Judy said. "Carson is downstairs staining a chair. He'll be right up." A trim woman in her forties, Judy wore gray slacks and a red gingham shirt, and her dark hair was in a short bob. She smiled so warmly, Ellen and Russ were immediately at ease. A dry sink with a marble top stood against the wall in the entry hall, and beautiful old hutches, one pine, one maple were in the parlor. Nothing matched, but it all fit, the various woods imparting an inviting warmth and glow. On the floor in front of the fireplace, two girls in pajamas, one dark haired and one with curly red locks, played a board game, rattling the dice, counting off spaces, gloating or groaning depending on the result.

"This is Reverend Llewellen and Mrs. Llewellen," Judy said. "Shirley, Sally, come say hello. Shirley is our seven year old and Sally is four."

The girls got up, faced the Llewellens, and said in turn, "Very pleased to meet you." They stood quietly for the signal they could get back to their game. Carson, dressed in spotted work pants and a gray sweatshirt, came in wiping his hands with a cloth.

"Why don't we go into the dining room where we can talk around the table?" he said. The girls sighed in relief, dropped to the floor, and started to rattle the dice again.

"Five minutes more," Carson said, "then it's bedtime." The dice rattled even faster.

"I love your furniture," Ellen said. "You must be collectors."

"Oh no," Judy said, "we're correctors. We get old pieces cheap and fix them up. Carson's gotten awfully good at it. That's what he was doing when you came. We found a couple of pine chairs up in Vermont last summer. They have to be taken apart, scraped with broken glass, sanded, glued back together, and then refinished. It takes him forever, but at least he's not getting into trouble."

"You don't seem to use varnish," Russ said. "Your things glow instead of gleam." He had taken woodworking in high school, and at times, in the midst of Hebrew and Greek exams, he had thought woodworking would have been a great profession.

"Linseed oil," Carson said, "linseed oil and a little turpentine, and then you rub and rub. It's tedious, but when you're done you've got a finish that goes down into the wood and brings out the grain. You can set a glass of ice on it and it won't leave a ring."

"It's not really coffee," Judy said, as she poured from a ceramic pot. "It's half decaf. You'll see, someday you'll have to cut back on a lot of things. I'll make you pure coffee if you insist, but if you do, I'll never speak to you again. I will make tea though."

Ellen asked for tea, Russ had black coffee as Judy had made it, and Carson took his with three spoons of sugar and what seemed like half a cup of cream. Judy did the same.

"Time for bed now, girls, and no groaning," Carson called into the other room. Click, click, click went the markers on the board, and a quick bursts of "I won," "You cheated!"

"Girls, that's it, bed." Carson said in full preacher voice, and they put the game away in a glowing old hutch. Judy followed them upstairs.

"How do you tell the people around here apart?" Ellen asked Carson. "They all look so much the same."

Like Judy, Carson was about twenty years older than Russ, his flattop haircut getting gray on the sides and thin in front. Dressed for refinishing chairs, he could have passed for a day laborer, nothing preachery about him at all. He smoked Kools, one after the other, though he didn't light the next one until he had put out the last one, and there were gaps when he wasn't smoking at all. Judy came back to tell him his girls wanted their kiss from their daddy. He put out his cigarette by squeezing off the burning head of it in the ashtray so it wouldn't smolder.

"The Llewellens have found their parishioners look alike. Can you imagine anything like that, Judy?" Carson said as he left to go upstairs.

"And they all have the same names, and they're all related," Ellen went on. "I've never been anyplace like this."

"You've said a mouthful there," Judy said with a whoop of a laugh. "Nobody's been anyplace like this. You're just lucky your name is Llewellen and not Paulucci or Murphy or Whitlock."

"C'mon now, Judy," Carson said, just back from kissing the girls goodnight. "Don't prejudice them by what happened to us. Whatever you do, Llewellen, don't try to merge two Welsh congregations together with an English one."

"That's it right there," Russ said. "Everything around here is in terms of nationality. Why, they find out your last name, and they think they know all about you."

"Around here," Judy said, "if they know your last name, they know where you live, where you go to church, how you vote, what tavern you're likely to frequent, and which cemetery you're going to be buried in."

"It sure ain't California," Russ said. "There my best friends were Franceschi and Hiura, and my favorite teacher was Mr. Sanchez."

"Yeah," Ellen said, "where do you go for tacos around here?"

"No such thing as tacos around here," Judy said. "I bet there's not a taco in all of Lackawanna County. Lots of Welsh cookies though. You had Welsh cookies yet."

"That's about all we've been living on. I kind of like them," Russ said.

"Hey, Carson, they like Welsh cookies," Judy said, and shook her head and slapped the table in mock disbelief.

"Take it easy," Carson said. "People have a right to like Welsh cookies."

"You have to understand," Judy said, "when you merge churches, things happen. Stuff gets all messed up because one group doesn't consult with the others. They call meetings among themselves, decide to do something, and then Carson has to go running around heading them off until he can get them together in one place. When that finally happens, there's inevitably a plate of Welsh cookies on the table, as if that makes everything all right."

"I don't know what I would do without Judy," Carson said. "She'll take a phone call and sound as pleasant as whipped butter, 'Yes, Mrs. Morgan, fine Mrs. Morgan, yes just tea and cookies will be plenty, Mrs. Morgan,' and on the basis of a short talk about the Women's Association meeting she'll pick up on something, put her hand over the phone, say to me, 'Hey, Carson, you better get over to the Morgens' right away,' and then she's back on the phone in her whipped butter voice saying, 'I think half and half would be fine, Mrs. Morgan, it's lighter than cream, and so many are watching their figures these days.' I don't know how she does it."

"Well, I sure messed up one time," Judy said. "They got the painting project right past me."

"That was something else," Carson agreed. "We woke up one morning and there they were, peering in our bedroom window with paint brushes in their hands."

"Let me tell it," Judy said. "We were lying in bed about eight on a Saturday morning thinking there wasn't anything in the world to do, and all of a sudden Sally starts screaming 'Mommy, Mommy, there's men here,' and I yelled back, 'Sally, what kind of men?' I was sure she was dreaming. And she said, 'Mommy, it's church men.' And I said, 'Well, what are they doing, Sally?' And she said, 'They're paintin' our house.' I still thought she was seeing things in her sleep, so I called out 'What color are they paintin' it, Sally?' And she said, 'The color of shit.' Those were her exact words. Well, with that we were up looking out the window, and, sure enough, men from one of the churches were swarming all over the house. They had ladders and buckets and brushes, and Sally was right, they were painting it the color of shit. And I don't know where on earth she learned that word." Judy whooped and patted the table again.

"Didn't even ask us about it," Carson said. "Didn't consult with anybody. Just got a deal on paint and decided to spread it on the house."

"It's wild," Judy said. "Sometimes it's just wild."

"Then to top it all off," Carson said, "when we went down to breakfast, we found a huge platter of Welsh cookies on the table, must have been three dozen of them, and a little note saying 'For our Pastor and his Wife.'"

"They think Welsh cookies will protect them from the fires of hell," Judy said.

"Can they come in here without you knowing it?" Ellen asked.

"It's their house," Carson said. "All the trustees have keys. I'll bet your trustees have keys to your place. They're renting it for you, aren't they?"

"Yep, they're renting it for us. Does that mean they all have keys?" Russ said as he looked at Ellen. "That's something I didn't know I'd bargained for."

While they spoke, a little redheaded figure appeared in the doorway.

"You're talking about me and laughing," Sally said.

"We're just telling them about the men painting the house," Judy said. "Have a drink of water and Uncle Russell will put you back in bed." Sally took hold of Russ' hand and they went upstairs.

"I don't like people talking about me when I'm not there," she said.

"Nobody does," Russ said as she got into bed. He patted Sally's back, and she was off to sleep in a couple of minutes. Shortly after that, Ellen and Russ left, having arranged for the Whitlocks to come to their place next Sunday after Youth Fellowship.

"Goodness," Ellen said on the way home. "Carson and Judy are really a team."

"It apparently takes both of them to stay ahead of the maneuvering," Russ said, "a real mom and pop operation."

"Well I don't want any mom and pop operation, Russell Llewellen," Ellen said. "I've got a lot to do besides answering the phone and figuring out what's going on by the tone of someone's voice. And the trustees shouldn't have keys to our house."

"True," Russ said.

Next day Russ got up after Ellen had left for school, ate some bran flakes, listened to the radio, and read the newspaper. At ten, when the mail came through the slot in the door downstairs, he was still in his pajamas. He picked up the mail, which consisted of two flyers and a small, thin magazine called *Monday Morning*. Glancing through it, Russ saw it was all about Presbyterian ministers. Some of his classmates were mentioned, in fact, along with notices of when they were ordained and where they were serving. Russ' ordination was too late to get in this issue, he assumed, but that was fine with him. He wasn't interested in reading about Presbyterian ministers or anything else right then. He was taking the day off, as the Moderator of Presbytery had told him to. He got dressed in rumpled suntans and a sweater, left the house before eleven when the phone would start to ring, got in the Saab, and headed south toward the Poconos.

Quiet, aching October with its gold and amber leaves stretched for miles on either side of the road. Russ saw red barns and farm houses with yellow school busses next to them. The farmers milked twice a day, and, apparently, twice a day the farmers' wives drove the school bus on their narrow and bumpy routes. It occurred to Russ that these folks don't get a day off ever. You can't just up and leave a dairy farm because you're not particularly interested in cows that morning. Nor could there ever be any question about meaning or purpose in such a pursuit. Growing up, he'd helped out around dairy farms, and he knew milking a cow is inherently meaningful whether you do it by hand or hook up a milking machine.

Heading east from the main road and coming over a rise, he saw a golf course nestled in the hills among the farms. He wished

116

he had his clubs, but they were down at Princeton with all his stuff stored in the basement of Hodge Hall. He had played the fine Springdale Golf Club across from the seminary no more than half a dozen times in his three years there, even though they charged but fifty cents a round for students. There just wasn't time.

When he was eight years old. Russ' dad cut down a hickory shafted five iron and made a grip out of friction tape and they went to the golf course. Russ hacked away and tore up huge chunks of grass until by some miracle he made a smooth unhurried swing, caught the turf and the ball at the same instant and it rose into beautiful soaring flight. The feeling in his hands, arms, shoulders, down his body to his feet and into the ground was exhilarating. Ever since, he had lusted after that feeling. For sure, golf had been a part of Russ' life a lot longer than Christianity had.

Russ worked his fingers around the steering wheel as if it was an imaginary golf club as he drove to the course. In the clubhouse, he met Art Koski, the greens keeper, who also ran the lunchroom, the locker room, and the beer cooler. "Call me Artie," he told Russ, "like I was still a little kid, which I guess I am." Artie wasn't very tall, kind of hefty, and had a round smiling face that seemed to make everyone feel better than they otherwise would. In his green golf shirt, blue work pants, and white apron he was ready to tackle all his tasks. He moved quickly about the place as if there was too much for him to do, which it looked like there was.

Russ ordered a hamburger and iced tea. While frying the hamburger, Artie found out that Russ was a minister, and Russ learned Artie was raised Catholic, but since getting this job at the course it was impossible to be at Mass on Sundays. Artie didn't seem broken hearted about it. "Sunday's our big day here," he said.

"I suppose it is," Russ said, fully aware of the implications for his calling.

Russ also learned the green fees were a buck and a half weekdays, two and a half weekends, and it cost three bucks a month to rent a locker, which included a clean towel after your shower. For

Artie, dollars were bucks, and he pronounced it more like "bocks," smiling all the while.

"But, Revernt, we might be able to make you a discount," Artie said. "We'll see now, when yas come out to play." Artie spoke the word designating Russ' title with a short, staccato push—"Revernt." He was extremely jovial, and he obviously loved his job. His face seemed always ready to smile even when he wasn't smiling, which wasn't often. He cleared off Russ' plate, wiped the counter, disappeared into the back, reemerged with two cases of Gibbons beer, went out to yell at somebody for leaving a pull cart too close to the eighteenth green, and came back in to jostle with a newly arrived foursome and sell them a round of beers and sandwiches.

"Would it be all right to walk around a bit?" Russ asked. "I'll stay out of the way. I don't have my clubs with me."

"Sure, Revernt, walk all yas want. You can borrow my clubs if yas like," Artie said, "I don't get to use them much these days." Most golfers don't lend their clubs to next of kin, but here was Artie offering his to a perfect stranger. Russ thanked him but turned him down and went out to see what the course was like.

One hole followed another through red and gold maples and birches. There were places that seemed remote as a clearing for a native village. Russ sat beside the seventh green for fifteen minutes, and no one came past. He found it wonderfully lonely, fall colors at their height all around him and no people, sick or otherwise, to deal with right then.

Russ walked back and told Artie how great he thought the course was. Artie just beamed. "Be sure to bring your clubs next time, Revernt, and we'll have us a little game," he said as Russ was leaving.

In the parking lot, Russ found next to the Saab a black Chevy with "Just Married" written in white all over it. He noticed a woman sound asleep on the back seat.

"One doesn't live by love alone. There's also golf," Russ chuckled to himself as he drove off.

9

Hoppsy Hopple

THAT NIGHT, AGAINST ELLEN'S PROTESTATIONS that they couldn't afford it, they went out to dinner at an Italian place on the south edge of town. They had a salad of lettuce greens with olive oil and wine vinegar dressing for the first time since leaving California. In Scroggtown, the rage was Thousand Island or what they called French dressing, something pink laced with something sweet. Pleased by the familiar flavors, they dug into a huge platter of raviolis with a really good red sauce. They even had a half bottle of house red wine wrapped in a wicker casing.

"Let's go down to Princeton tomorrow and get my stuff," Russ ventured over their dessert of complimentary apple fritters. He was thinking books and golf clubs.

"Fine, my classes are all in the morning tomorrow. We can go in the afternoon." Ellen said, thinking furniture and maybe a few pictures for the bare, light green walls.

When they got home, Russ called around and located an old Ford flatbed truck they could borrow. "Since it's got no sides, Reverennnd, you'll need lots of rope. I'll leave some on the front seat. I'll leave you some tarps too, in case it rains. Just come by the yard and take it when you're ready." It was Marty Williams of Williams Construction. He told Russ his grandfather, William

Williams, had helped build the church almost a hundred years ago, "You know how to double clutch, Reverennnd?" he asked.

"Sure," Russ said. He had double clutched an old school bus all over the Berkeley hills one summer, collecting kids for Daily Vacation Bible School at the big Presbyterian Church near the University.

Russ got in six calls by noon, went by Williams Construction for the truck, and he and Ellen were on the road a little after two. With Russ double clutching even more than he had to because he enjoyed it, the old truck roared through the Poconos. Threatening clouds were piling up in the west, and a blustery wind was blowing purplish brown leaves in great swarms across the road. Some of them appeared to hop along the highway like frogs. Russ cringed as he drove over them, but they crunched instead of squished and then swirled behind the truck in a dusty wake. Nothing like a good old adventure, Russ thought, but Ellen was more interested in seeing if the truck had a heater. It didn't. Heat from the manifold blew up through cracks in the floorboard. That was it.

They got to the seminary in time for dinner and joined the mob filing into the dining hall. Ellen looked at all the people she didn't know. Russ didn't know many either. His class was now at work in the fields of the Lord all over the world, actually. Hoppsy Hopple spotted Russ and waved him over. He was sitting with Gert Woodsen, one of three women at the seminary studying for the ministry. There were several other women in the School of Christian Education, making maybe a dozen all told. They made their way among almost five-hundred men.

Along with being tall and blond with biceps like a god, right then Hoppsy had a look about him that any second something important was going to happen but he wasn't quite sure what it was. A year behind Russ, he was in seminary, some thought, to get a handle on himself. He took a lot of psychology courses and had a hard time with what he called church junk. Almost two years ago, right after Russ' former roommate left seminary to become a trainee at a brokerage house in New York, Hoppsy knocked on Russ' door and announced, "I don't like the guy they put me with, I'm pitching my tent with you."

So Hoppsy and Russ had roomed together close to two years, a whole lot longer than Ellen and Russ had roomed together. It was Hoppsy's record player and Ella Fitzgerald records that kept Russ' ear for music alive during those years, and it was Hoppsy's pipes and tobacco ordered from Boston that got Russ smoking a pipe, actually walking around wearing a pipe, a practice he gave up soon after graduation.

"Hey Russ, you and Ellen come up to the old room after, will you? We're having a little gathering," Hoppsy said as dinner was breaking up. Ellen looked at her watch. She wanted to get the stuff on the truck and be on her way, but Russ sensed something was up and didn't want to miss it.

"We can come for a while," he said.

Their old room on the second floor of Hodge Hall was decorated with autumn leaves and a bouquet of flowers. On the coffee table was an ice bucket wrapped in aluminum foil, and in it were three bottles of German white wine and a bottle of champagne. About fifteen people were gathered there, which didn't leave a lot of space. The corks came out, plastic glasses emerged, and the wine was poured. It may have been the first wine ever poured in that room.

"Gert and I would like you to know that we will be married this Christmas vacation here at the seminary in Miller Chapel, and you're all invited," Hoppsy said, smiling his uncertain smile.

"Hear, hear, hip, hip," resounded from behind the raised glasses. In a green-toned gingham dress, her brown hair clipped just above the shoulder, Gert looked her pretty, self-assured self smiling next to Hoppsy. She calmly thanked everyone for being there.

It took an hour to drink up the wine. Then Hoppsy said, "C'mon, let's go down to the King's Inn for pizza. It's not even eight o'clock, the shank of the evening." Ellen winced, as if she knew darn well what would happen.

"We've got to load my stuff and get going." Russ said.

"We'll load it for you right now," Hoppsy shot back, "and then you can ride down to Kingston with us. We'll get back early, but we can't stop this party yet, Russer, you know that."

Hoppsy was on his way. He had risen up from whatever swamp of insecurity he often dwelt in and was taking charge.

Hoppsy's assertiveness reminded Russ of the time about a year earlier when the seminary was making plans to cut down a huge elm tree to save the others from Dutch elm disease. Hoppsy thought it was atrocious. He had petitioned Homey Homrighausen, Dean of Students, and President Mackay himself, insisting they could trim the diseased limbs and leave the tree standing if they really wanted to. He was all but alone in his protest. The tree came down.

The groundsmen spent a whole afternoon trimming the branches off the tree and carting them away. This left the trunk lying on the grass like an immense torso, dismembered, violated, debased. Hoppsy was livid. That night, toward eleven, when the study lamps began to flicker out above the quad, Hoppsy went around with two six packs of beer, some cokes for the teetotalers, of which there were many, and collected his crew.

"We're gonna stand that elm tree in the stairwell of Hodge Hall," he said. "You're going to help." No one refused him.

Hodge Hall, built in the nineteenth century and named for the premier Calvinist theology professor of the time, is a brownstone covered with ivy and bent in the middle where the main doors are. They open on a great circular staircase that goes up three floors with a huge empty cylinder around which the stairs climb. When you enter the building, you step immediately into the open cylinder of the stairwell. You learn to stick close to the walls, for occasionally a water balloon comes flying at those who meander casually across the open circle below. At the back, a door opens onto a service road.

Beer and cokes in hand, a dozen hearty seminarians went out to move the tree. It was maybe forty feet long, bigger around than a bass drum at the bottom, and weighed God knows how much. All together, this crew could budge it along the grass but an inch or two per grunt and shove. Two hours later, one end of the tree was off the grass and onto the road. It slid more easily over the pavement than on the soft lawn, and another half hour got it to the back door of Hodge Hall. Someone went out for more beer and cokes, but Hoppsy said no more drinking until the job was done. And so when the drinks arrived, nobody drank. Russ was amazed at how little Hoppsy was aware of his power.

"Hold those doors open," Hoppsy whispered, "and get the tree lined up, small end first. And nobody talk or even burp." Everybody did what Hoppsy said. The concrete floor was the best surface to push on yet. The tree was moving right through the door, and then BUNG! the whole thing stopped. It was stuck fast. A jutting stump of a branch had hooked on the sill.

"Back off, back off," Hoppsy hissed in a bombastic whisper. "We'll get a run for it." But there was no getting a run with a log like that. It got hung up time after time.

"I'll see if I can find a broom or something, and we can use the handle to get it to roll and then teeter it up," someone said.

"Screw roll. Screw teeter. Screw you neo orthodox jerks," Hoppsy hissed. "We're going to get this tree in there right now." With that he bent down behind the big end sticking out the door, spread his arms around it as far as they would go, and hissed, "You jerks get hold of it someplace, and when I say so, you jerks pull. You jerks got that?" He sucked in enough air to propel a space ship and exploded it in a rocketing "GO!" There are those who say the rest of the crew watched in awe, perhaps stunned by the blast of released energy, while Hoppsy lifted the end of the tree over the threshold and moved it a full foot all on his own. Others say it was a group effort. In any case, the tree was in the door.

The rest was easy. Many hands rode the smaller end up the curving banister until the truncated tree stood straight. Hoppsy produced ropes and lashed the tree to the stairwell from four directions so it wouldn't fall and crush someone. Like a mutilated statue, the tree stood in the stairwell and reached to the middle of the second floor, a huge and ponderous presence.

"There," Hoppsy said, "now you jerks can drink your beers and sodas." And that's what happened, all at Hoppsy's command. Somebody tacked up a crude sign that said "The Tree of Good and Evil, Native of Eden," but Hoppsy tore it down.

"All I want is this tree to stand here, no stupid Bible games," he growled.

Next day, the tree was both the joy and scandal of the campus. Students, professors, passersby, and neighborhood dogs stopped in to see it on their way around Princeton. The groundskeeper was furious, and he got President Mackay's ear. Black robed President Mackay, jowls quivering and reddening, spoke of "dire consequences for the perpetrators of this dastardly deed" in his announcements after his sermon in chapel that morning. All eyes turned toward Hoppsy, but his head was bowed solemnly in prayer.

After three days, President Mackay called Hoppsy into his office, not to accuse him of anything, of course, he stated, jowls flapping, but to point out that the grounds crew could not possibly get the tree out of Hodge Hall, so it would have to be done by professionals which would cost the seminary a lot of money. Hoppsy offered the President a deal. He would see what he could do about getting the tree out of the stairwell if that would settle the matter, no retribution of any kind upon anyone. President Mackay extended his hand, saying he would have to mollify the chief groundskeeper who was "demanding expulsion for any number of our finest students." Hoppsy shook hands and took his leave. Next morning, the tree was back where it started from, and again there were beer cans and soda bottles in the wastebaskets of Hodge Hall.

ON HIS ENGAGEMENT NIGHT, Hoppsy was in charge again. Russ drove the truck to the back of Hodge Hall, and out the same door through which they had moved the tree some months before, a similar crew carried Russ' belongings onto the truck. The old green couch, overstuffed pink chair, a table. two lamps, a typewriter and filing cabinet, boxes and boxes of books, cinder blocks and boards from which to fashion bookcases, piles of clothes, and his golf clubs, all this was on the truck in about fifteen minutes. They spread the tarp over the load and lashed it down with the ropes Marty Williams had provided. Then they headed out for pizza.

"It would have taken us two hours to do that ourselves. We've got time to spare," Russ said to Ellen as they rode in the back of Hoppsy's old maroon Plymouth. Ellen wasn't buying it. In fact, she was mildly put out that she had to sit on Russ' lap to make room for the eight people in the car. Hoppsy had insisted there was no need to take more than one car for such a short trip, and so that's what happened.

To loosen Ellen up, Russ began to scratch her back.

"Stop that, you pest," she said. Russ started to tickle her under her arms.

"Quit it, silly," Ellen said, talking high and whiny and trying to seem serious. Russ reached under her skirt.

"If you don't quit that, the next thing you know you'll be running my stockings," she said with full emphasis. The car exploded in laughter. Hoppsy had to pull off the road, he was laughing so hard, and the car shook in merriment for several minutes. Ellen gave up. She started giggling, and Russ kept tickling her, and people were quoting her famous words, "The next thing you know you'll be running my stockings."

"May that always be the next thing you know, Russer old boy," Hoppsy said. From then on Ellen seemed not to worry so much about the time this celebration might consume. Actually, they were done with their pizzas in an hour or so, and the party broke up before nine o'clock.

On the way back to Scroggtown, it began to rain. Russ stopped the truck and put his golf clubs inside, crowding Ellen a bit. She merely rolled her eyes. When he tried to start the truck again, it wouldn't go. The fuel gauge, always on full, had not warned them they were out of gas. While Russ set out a flare, Ellen got a ride to the service station up the road with a guy who had a statue of St. Christopher on his dashboard and pictures of naked women on his sun visors. He and Ellen were back in a few minutes with a gallon of gas, and he wouldn't even let Russ pay him for it. That got them to the gas station where they filled the tank, making the gas gauge correct for the moment.

"I probably shouldn't have gotten into that car," Ellen said, as they rolled along again.

"That's for sure," Russ said. "If it were me, I never would have brought you back."

Ellen liked that, and snuggled against Russ the rest of the way. Back in Scroggtown they parked on the street and went inside. Russ took his golf clubs in with him along with Professor Cailliet's history of philosophy and *A Little Treasury of Modern Verse* edited by Oscar Williams. He left everything else under the tarp hoping it would stay dry.

10

From the Coal Bin
to the Golf Course

NEXT MORNING WAS BROTHER HENRY'S BREAKFAST with the reverends at The Coal Bin. Seven AM, Lord have mercy. As they walked out the door together, Ellen told Russ she wanted him to pick her up at the bus station at four o'clock so she could get home early, and Russ said he would be glad to do that.

Ten minutes later, dressed in grey slacks and sport coat, blue button down shirt and maroon tie, Russ walked into that black and blue cave of a restaurant and paused so his eyes could adjust to the dimness of light fixtures resembling old time miners' lamps. Syrupy music came from speakers disguised as great lumps of coal in the high corners of the room. Many of Scroggtown's business-men were having breakfast, and they seemed to think it quite nat-ural for music to exude from lumps of coal. In the middle of the room were Carson Whitlock and Brother Henry, looking lonely at a table set for eight.

"Good to see you, Llewellen," Brother Henry said. "The others will join us directly, I'm sure." People came by and shook Brother Henry's hand and wished him a good day. Carson and Russ looked at each other, raised their glasses and drank their orange juice in a mock toast.

After a while, a young somewhat pudgy cleric walked in the door and made his way to the table. He wore a black suit and white collar that circled his neck all the way around. Brother Henry greeted him as Father Brundage and turned to acknowledge another of his Coal Bin admirers.

"I'm Russell Llewellyn," Russ said. "I just came to the Welsh Presbyterian Church."

"Oh, I see," Father Brundage said.

"And your name is Brundage? Did I get that right?" Russ went on.

"Father Brundage, St. Luke's Episcopal," he said.

"I'm not sure I know where that is," Russ said.

"St. Luke's is up on the hill in the Greenbrier section. Very nice there. You will have to come sometime." Father Brundage was not much older than Russ, but his manner seemed to indicate he considered himself much older or much wiser or much more something than the rest of them.

"How's married life treating you, Father?" Carson asked.

"Very well, thank you, we're making a splendid adjustment," Brundage said.

"Let's see, you've been married almost two weeks now, isn't that it?" Carson went on. "Llewellen here has been married almost a month. Maybe he can give you some pointers from his long experience." Carson blinked his eyes and stirred cream into his coffee.

Father Brundage turned to Russ and said, "I've found clerical pajamas very helpful."

Russ cleared his throat and looked at Carson who quick turned away, leaving Russ on his own. Russ couldn't tell if he was being primed for a joke or if this was on the up and up.

"May I ask about these clerical pajamas?" Russ said.

"Clerical pajamas are black with white trim around the neck." Brundage answered. "I got them for our honeymoon so we would always be reminded of my holy office. They have been invaluable in helping my wife achieve a proper sense of respect."

"I can imagine," Russ said. Brundage had spoken with what seemed like genuine seriousness, but Russ still wasn't sure how to take it. Thinking to enter these conversational waters at the same level, he said, "When I went to buy pajamas for our honeymoon, the fellow who sold them to me said I could get the cheapest ones because they just go under the pillow in case of fire."

"There, you see," Brundage quickly replied, "you Protestants just don't understand ecclesiastical matters." The waitress came by with the breakfasts. Russ had ordered waffles.

"You're from California, aren't you, Llewellen? I think I read that somewhere," Brundage went on. "It figures you would have waffles for breakfast. Fluffy, syrupy, and not particularly nourishing, like the theology out there."

"I took my theology at Princeton," Russ said, sorry as soon as he said it, feeling this had gone beyond friendly sparring.

"Oh yes, Princeton. Very Presbyterian, isn't it?" Brundage said.

"Very," Russ replied in a conclusive tone as Brother Henry was rising to his feet and beginning to speak in his inimitable bellow. The entire restaurant became quiet.

"Let us begin our day with prayer," Brother Henry announced in his booming voice. Everyone in the room stopped what they were doing, everyone at the counter, everyone in the black leather booths, everyone paying their bill at the cash register by the door, everyone. The waitresses stopped waiting, the busboys stopped bussing, and the cooks behind the ledge that separated the kitchen from the dining room stopped cooking. It was quieter than most empty churches.

Brother Henry tilted his head toward heaven, closed his eyes in a way that brought a great furrow to his forehead, and prayed: "O Lord, most merciful and gracious, once again you have brought your servants together to begin a new day." Russ peeked over at Carson who was sitting with his eyes wide open shaking his head. What with mentioning the glorious morning, the bountiful breakfast, and at least half the blessed trades and professions represented

129

by those who gathered at "this most virtuous establishment," it was a long, hard prayer. Near the end, Brother Henry even put in a plug for the clergy: "May these good citizens go forth to their places of labor and industry in the sure knowledge that the servants of the Lord here gathered in peace around this table will be toiling on their behalf in the holy vineyards of the Most High. Amen."

Applause rang out from all quarters of the room. Even the waitresses were clapping. Everyone was smiling and giving Brother Henry thumbs up. It was amazing.

"Say, Brother Henry, do they make good wine in the holy vineyards of the Most High?" Carson asked.

"It's a figure of speech, Whitlock. It gives no opening for imbibing, if that's what you are hoping to imply," Brother Henry shot back. Ah yes, Russ thought, together in peace.

A tall, dark-haired man with a full head of wavy dark hair in an impeccable brown suit came to the table. His temples were graying a bit; his eyes were clear and alive.

"Ah, Rabbi Steiner," Brother Henry said, "So good you could join us. We've just had the prayer, but I'm sure you can order a nice breakfast."

"I heard your prayer as I was coming in the door, Brother Henry," the rabbi said. "I must say you delivered yourself nobly this morning. Elijah himself could not have done better." He spoke well of everyone as he went around the table. When he came to Russ, he made a point to say he had read of his ordination in the paper. "I hear you Presbyterians put each other through a rigorous ordeal before the laying on of hands. I'm most impressed with your credentials, and I wish you well," he said.

"And you, Father, are looking extremely well. It's obvious God is smiling on you," the rabbi said to Brundage and gave him a pat on the back. Not a hitch all the way around.

On the other hand, the rabbi's stories left something to be desired. He had several about a rabbi, a minister, and a priest, all of which had been around for centuries, and one about a little girl in Sunday School who was crying while looking at a picture of Christians being attacked by lions in the Roman arena. "Why are you crying, Mary?" the Sunday School teacher asked. "Are you sad because of the brave martyrs?" "Oh no," said Mary, "I feel sorry for that little lion in the corner. He's not getting anything to eat." With that, Russ stuffed the last of his waffle into his mouth. Carson shook his head. Brother Henry looked the other direction. And Father Brundage gave a snort and appeared to be offended. Then the dishes were cleared away, more coffee was poured, and in came Reverend Wally.

Reverend C. Walter Wallace was pastor of the Free Bible Church that operated out of an old movie theater on the edge of the business district. Reverend Wally wore a red blazer and gray slacks, a white shirt, black tie, and beautiful black and gray two-toned shoes. The reddish tinge to his thick hair seemed to go well with the perpetual smile on his handsome face.

"God bless you now," he greeted each one in turn in a warm semi southern drawl. He was surely the most outgoing fellow for miles around, Russ thought. "I'm sorry I couldn't be here for breakfast with ya'all," Wally said, "but I had to meet with my own folks about the big rally we're havin' Saturday night. We've got a real good movie that shows a different way of how the world began than what the kids get in school these days, if you get my meanin'. Your young people should all see it so they don't drift away from the truth as they get on in life." Russ wanted to argue with this, but nobody else was paying any attention. Apparently Wally was always inviting them to his rallies.

Scroggtown was almost seventy per cent Catholic, so the assembled clergy at The Coal Bin got together out of a sense of being put upon as much as anything else. They made up the Scroggtown Ministerial Association which included most of the non Catholic clergy in the area.

"Perhaps, now that Reverend Wally is here, we can get down to business," Brother Henry said. "Can we have a treasurer's report, Wally?"

"Got it right here," Wally said. "Had my secretary type it up yesterday and run it off on our new copier. There's a copy for everyone and few extras for the record." Wally passed around gray papers that gave off ether fumes and on which the ink smudged if you barely touched it. The treasurer's report was all but illegible, but it showed a balance of several hundred dollars. The source of income was mainly from offerings at Lenten Noonday Services and Good Friday Services, in which all the churches participate. Expenditures were bulletins, printing, and advertising in the newspaper.

"We're getting a nice little balance," Wally said. "Next time we might think of some fancier bulletin covers. We can certainly afford it."

"Maybe we could contribute to the Salvation Army for the Thanksgiving baskets they take to the needy," Carson said, but Wally went right on as if he didn't hear him.

"I also have here an attendance report," Wally said. "It shows what's been happening at the Association's services the last few years." With that he produced more sheets of the smelly paper on which the reverends found every service or activity of the Association listed for five years running, the location of each event, what the weather was on that particular day, who preached, who read the scripture, who prayed, the number present, and the amount of the offering. Russ found himself admiring the report, though he could not imagine spending his time keeping track of all this.

"Who counted all these people?" Russ asked.

"I make it my business to know these things," Wally said. "How else can you tell what's goin' on. No reason we can't do as much to improve the Lord's business as they do to sell soap. I never have a meetin' of any kind but what I take a count and write down the particulars. That way you can adjust your program to what the people are responding to."

Russ looked over at Carson who was looking at the door and checking his watch.

All of a sudden, Carson got up and went to the door. He came back with a large African American man and introduced him as Reverend Ben Jackson, pastor of the Eighth Street African Methodist Episcopal Church. Everybody rose to shake his hand.

Six feet four and weighing at least two hundred fifty pounds, Reverend Ben wore a double breasted brown suit with a suggestion of a stripe in it, but he could never have buttoned the coat, and his neck stretched the collar of his white dress shirt. His tie was dark brown and tied in a way that seemed to choke him. His eyes had a huge filling sadness about them, fit for the size of the man. Streams of living water seemed to flow from his deep voice.

"How ya doin' there Wally, Brother Henry, all you. You just sit down now and go on with your meetin,'" Ben said, taking a seat near Carson.

Speaking deliberately Carson reviewed some of what everyone but Russ knew about Scroggtown. "As you know, Reverend Jackson's church is located in what is called Kentucky Town, a neighborhood near the railroad yard," Carson said. "I asked Ben to be here this morning in connection with my report on the Open Housing Covenant left over from our last meeting. I thought it would be good to have him help us get our statement in its final form," and he passed out carbon copies of a paragraph written on half sized paper. "I don't have one of those copiers like Reverend Wally here, so this will have to do," Carson said.

At the top was OPEN HOUSING COVENANT, and underneath it said, "Sponsored by the Scroggtown Ministers Association." The text read, "I hereby covenant with my Christian brothers and sisters and with others of good will to welcome into my neighborhood all persons without regard to race, religion, or national origin. I further pledge that, in selling or renting my house or apartment building, I will not discriminate against anyone on the basis of race, religion, or national origin." There was a place to sign and set down the date.

"Ben here is able to answer any questions we have about the need for the covenant and how it can help," Carson said.

"Well, Carson," Ben said in the friendliest tone Russ ever heard, "first let me thank the Association for invitin' me to speak with you today."

Reverend Wally, smiling his fixed smile, welcomed Ben profusely and asked if there was really a need for such a covenant in the fair community of Scroggtown.

"Well, as you know," Ben replied, "a lot of families in Kentucky Town have lived there for decades, often in the same houses their grandparents lived in. They just keep tackin' on rooms in back makin' it a long, skinny house. They call them shotgun houses because you could shoot a shotgun through the front door, and it would pass through all the doors and go out the back without hittin' a thing. Because of that kind of construction, those houses are impossible to heat unless you have a heater in every room."

"If I'm not mistaken, I've got houses like that in my parish," Russ said, "old company houses that got added on to over the years."

"I'm sure that's true," Reverend Jackson said. "It's not something only black folks know about. In fact, your people probably had it worse than many slaves did back in the day. On the plantations, there could be plenty to eat. They grew corn and okra, there were pigs and cows and chickens. There was fish in the rivers, crawdads in the creeks and all like that. For some, the main trouble with bein' a slave was just bein' a slave." All the ministers, including Russ, shifted uncomfortably in their chairs.

Reverend Ben went on, "Our people got up this way after slavery days and got jobs around the railroad yard, and that's where they found places to live. The women worked as maids up on the hill. It wasn't much different from the south except it snowed hard in the wintertime. But the thing is, a lot of these folks can afford to move to better houses now. Some have pretty good positions with the railroad, for instance, and many have good educations, our doctors and lawyers, our teachers. They would like to move up in the world, but they can't seem to buy or rent houses anywhere but down by the tracks. Nobody will rent to them. Nobody will sell to them. Some could pay cash outright, my deacon Charlie the coal dealer, for example. He's built up a good business. Same with Otto's Construction. He's built extra rooms onto most of the shotgun houses in Kentucky Town. These folks are gettin' tired of spendin' their extra money on Cadillacs and big rings, if you know what I'm sayin'. They would like to buy a nice house in a nice neighborhood for their families to live in. So, if you gentlemen can give us any help with this, it would be just wonderful."

"When do you propose to have this covenant ready for people to sign, Carson?" Reverend Wally wanted to know. "Is this something we can think about for a while?"

"I thought we had been thinking about it for a while," Carson said.

"Most of us are going into our fall campaigns right now," Father Brundage said. "We have our every member canvas next week, in fact. I'm not convinced these two activities complement each other very well."

"I was hoping it would be our Advent program," Carson said. "We could tie it to there being no room at the inn for Mary and Joseph."

"That sounds fortuitous," Brother Henry said. "Can I have a motion that we table this until Advent? We can take it up at our November meeting." Brother Henry got his vote, and the meeting began to break up.

"Do I get this right, that in this document Jews are referred to as 'others of good will?'" Rabbi Steiner asked. "We've been called worse, but I'm not sure my people will sign it if it doesn't sound more inviting to them."

135

"You're absolutely right," Carson said. "We'll change it to take care of that. Any objections?" No one objected, but then no one was paying much attention either. Chairs scraped back and napkins were tossed on the table.

Russ could not believe this discussion would end with everyone going off on their own after looking squarely into the heart of Scroggtown and finding racism there. "I hope we don't just let this drop. It's not right what Reverend Ben told us about. It's just not right," he blurted out.

"You will find, Llewellen, that many things in this world aren't right," Father Brundage informed him. Russ was about to quote one of the prophets when Brother Henry stood and offered a relatively subdued and uncharacteristically brief benediction, and the meeting was over.

Russ looked at Carson in sheer bewilderment. Carson said, "We'll talk about it Sunday. We're coming to your place, right? I've got to get to the hospitals." Indignantly, Russ slapped a dollar tip among the scattering of coins his colleagues had left.

"Thank you, Reverend," one of the waitresses said. "We all have to make a living, you know."

"I know," Russ said, but he was no more ready to practice his profession than dig sixteen tons of coal. He went home, changed clothes, and with a neighbor's help moved his stuff from the truck into the apartment. He drove the truck to Williams Construction and walked back home. Then he put his golf clubs in the Saab and headed for the Poconos, traveling right through Kentucky town on his way.

RUSS' BALL ROSE OFF THE TURF AND FLEW TOWARD the first green. Then it started bending, that sickening bend to the right of a miss-hit shot. Catching the October breeze, it floated higher and farther to the right until it landed on a mound near the second tee, took a right angle bounce, and headed for a clump of trees. Russ was playing golf for the first time in months and he wasn't on to it at all.

Artie's ball started off to the right and then hooked back low and mean, driving under the wind, hitting well short of the green, crawling up over the mound in front of it, and trickling to a stop no more than twelve feet from the hole.

"Seems like there's two ways to play this game, Artie," Russ called across the fairway. "The right way and my way. Nice shot."

"Thanks, Reverent, you'll get on to it after you've warmed up. Let's see if we can find your ball." Artie was smiling his wonderful smile, which, from what Russ could tell, would have been the same even if his ball was in the trees and Russ' was on the green. They found his ball in a fluffy lie amid leaves and twigs with a little opening to the flag, but his club caught the ball in the middle and sent it zinging on a low line past the pin and down an embankment, ending up on hard pan about fifteen yards over the green.. Now he needed to hit it up a steep bank that fell away to the flag.

"Yas got one of our famous mound shots around here," Artie said. "What you do is take an eight iron, play the ball way back off your right foot, smack down on it, and hit it into the bank and make it pop up over the edge."

Russ smacked it all right. Artie had to do a fast dance as the ball skidded under his feet and rolled down the hill in front of the green, still several yards away.

"Don't let me hold you up, Artie. You just go ahead and play through," Russ said, trying to be light hearted but not entirely succeeding.

"Here, Reverent, let me show yas how to play that shot." Artie took Russ' eight iron and dropped four balls from out of his back pocket. Playing a ball way back in his stance, he took a quick, short swing and nipped the ball so it flew into the bank, popped up in the air, and trickled down toward the hole.

"Try it, Reverent," and he handed the club to Russ. He hit the first one over the green fifty yards on the fly. He dumped the next one into the bank and it just stayed there in a clump of grass. The third one did pretty much the same as Artie's ball had done and almost went in the hole.

"There, now yas got it," Artie said. "We use that shot a lot around here."

So it went hole after hole, Artie thoroughly jovial whatever happened, glad to show Russ the ins and outs of golf on the public course south of Scroggtown. The par three seventh hole had trees around the tee and a pond in front of the green. Artie's low hook didn't do him any good on a hole like that. There was no place in front of the green to land the ball and let it run up. But he didn't worry about it. He just set his ball down, drew the club back, and fired away. Kersplash, right in the pond. He dropped another ball and plunk, off in the trees.

"Hell with it," he said with maybe the first hint that his disposition could be other than sunny. "Sorry about the bad word, Revernt. Go on, hit one."

Russ stepped up to the ball and caught it just right. It sailed between the trees, over the pond, and onto the green where it settled six feet from the hole. He missed the putt for birdie, which brought a momentary scowl to his face, but at least he was getting on to it after a long time away from the game.

White clouds were piling up in the west, and leaves were blowing around the course in the freshening afternoon breeze. Russ forgot all about the reverend clergy and their housing covenants. He forgot about elders with serious expressions on their faces and sick people waiting for him to take hold of their hands and say a little prayer. On the back nine, he started parring hole after hole, more and more relaxed all the time.

"Gee, yas play like a pro, Revernt," Artie said. "Maybe you're in the wrong business."

"Don't I wish," Russ said, and hit another shot right down the middle.

"We had a priest around here who played eighteen holes every day. His flock accused him of saying mass in his golf spikes. That'll be you, Revernt. They'll be after yas for chewing up the rugs at church with your cleats."

Playing quickly, they came to the eighteenth hole, a wide open par five up the hill to the clubhouse. A helping wind was blowing fairly hard.

"Play yas the last hole for a beer, Revernt," Artie said.

"You're on," Russ said, and teed up his ball. He gave it the best swing of the day, and the ball flew in a long arc better than half way to the hole.

"Wow, mention a little bet and the Revernt wakes up. I figure you been suckerin' me in all day." Artie said this while teeing his ball and giving it a mighty swing. Artie was the only one Russ ever saw who could talk and hit a golf ball at the same time. His shot was another low-flying hook that rolled almost as far up the hill as Russ' shot had gone. But Artie's second shot dove into the slope and didn't ever get rolling. He was left with well over a hundred yards to the green. Russ hit another shot just like the first, and his ball bounced onto the front part of the huge green. He could two putt and make birdie. As he walked up that last long hill, he felt pretty good about his chances of winning a beer from Artie. But then Artie, hardly breaking stride, hit a little punch eight iron to within four feet of the cup.

"How's about that one, Revernt," he shouted, a big grin on his face. "I'll probably sink that putt and beat yas." He probably would, too, Russ thought. He knew the course like it was his own, which, in effect, it was.

Russ' ball rested on the front part of two-tiered green, and the pin was way in the back on the second level. Russ looked at a putt that would go maybe seventy feet. When he bent over the ball, he couldn't see the hole.

"Hold the pin, Artie," he shouted into the breeze. "I need all the help I can get."

"It's going to break way left, Revernt, and you can hit it as hard as you want up that swale. It's terrible slow in there."

"Thanks, Artie, I'll probably sink it now," Russ said completely in jest. He had no idea what this putt would do, so he gave it a big rap and started it way right like Artie said. When he first hit it, he thought the ball would roll clear off the green. Then it bogged down in the swale, and he thought it would stop twenty feet short, but when it got to the smooth top tier of the green it began to roll in a big curve to the left and disappeared at Artie's feet.

Artie let out a whoop and ran around waving the flag. "You did it, Revernt! Good God almighty, what a shot! You're the greatest I ever saw. What'll yas have, Stegmaiers or Gibbons?" As he jabbered, he bent over his putt and stroked it on a dead hard line to the back of the cup for a birdie, letting Russ know he needed that long putt to beat him. But Artie was happier for Russ than Russ was for himself. He was simply an exuberant human being who took pleasure in everyone's good fortune.

In the clubhouse, Artie slapped everybody on the back and told them what a fine player Russ was. Guys in slacks and bright colored sweaters and others in dungarees and gray sweatshirts sat at the bar and the tiny tables scattered around the small room. The wood-paneled walls had old hickory shafted drivers and putters mounted on them here and there, along with the head of a four pronged buck over the bar.

"I'm treatin' yas all," Artie said, and got a dozen beers out of the cooler. "The Revernt and I had a great match, and then he goes and eagles the last hole. My birdie didn't count for nuttin'. Now what do yas guys think of that? Here's to your health, Revernt." It was toasts all around.

Russ was having a wonderful time. Everybody bought beer and wouldn't let him pay. "We don't take a newcomer's money," someone said. "Next time you'll roll the dice like anybody else."

"Fair enough," Russ said.

"Who wants hot dogs?" Artie called from back in the kitchen. "I'm fixin' 'em with chili sauce." Hands went up all around. "Good, nine redhots comin' up." The chilidogs came and more beer was passed around. Then the thunder hit, and Russ jumped and everybody laughed.

"What's the matter, Revernt? Ya think Christ is comin' back? It's only a thunder storm. You could see it buildin' all afternoon," Artie said.

Rain came in from the west in sheets, pounded the roof, dripped from the eaves, and splattered through the open louvered windows. Nobody cared. Hot dogs, beer, dice hitting the counter, laughter, and light hearted talk, it went on and on as if this was indeed what the day was for. Why worry? Why brood? Why preach good news or warn of bad? These men seemed to know how to live without any concern for the ultimate things Russ thought were so terribly necessary. They seemed to know their friendship was a gift and that being together was as important as anything on earth. With the memory of the eagle on the last hole and this newfound acceptance among the golfing nuts of northeastern Pennsylvania, Russ couldn't think of anything he needed to do.

11

$10,000 Gone Missing

FRESH FROM HIS GOLFING TRIUMPH, Russ drove home whistling as he went. He couldn't remember the last time he whistled a tune. He parked in front of their apartment where Ellen stood on the porch, soaked. She was rummaging through her big purse looking for her key.

"Where have you been?" she hissed as Russ got out of the Saab. "You were supposed to pick me up at four o'clock at the bus station, remember. I stood in the rain twenty minutes and finally took a cab."

"I'm sorry," Russ said, "I just forgot." As soon as he said it, he could tell it was not the best thing to say. But it was the honest truth. He hadn't remembered anything all afternoon, church, clergy, or his wife of barely a month.

"You forgot! You forgot! How could you forget? And what's that smell? It's like an old brewery. So you go off drinking and leave me in the rain, and the taxi costs a dollar eighty we can't afford, and my school clothes got ruined." Ellen was stomping water out of her shoes.

"I didn't go drinking. I went golfing."

"Where, down at Hughie Saloony's? That's wrong, Reverend, to go off drinking beer and leave your wife standing in the rain."

"Hey, I don't need you reminding me about that reverend business. I've got hundreds around here doing that. I was playing golf and having good time, I just plain forgot. I'm sorry. After the game we had a couple of beers."

"You having a good time, and I'm getting soaked. How could you play golf in weather like this?"

"It wasn't' raining earlier," Russ said. "I went out to the course after the meeting with Brother Henry and the gang. I just couldn't face church stuff after that."

"Does the Reverend realize that church stuff is his job around here, and picking up his wife when he's supposed to is one of the commandments?" She opened the door and stomped up the stairs. Russ dragged in behind her.

"I hope you know how to find some soup in that pile of cans your ladies left us, because I'm going to take a hot bath," Ellen said from the bathroom door.

"I had chili dogs at the golf course, but I'll fix you something if you want." Russ grabbed a can that looked like it might be soup, and sure enough, Campbell's Vegetable, a good sign in bad times. He put a pan on the stove, poured in the soup, added a can of water as Ellen ran water for her bath. The phone rang.

"Reverennnd, I hear a lot of water running." It was landlord Edgar Howells calling from downstairs.

"That's right, Edgar, my wife's taking a bath."

"A bath at six o'clock in the evening?" Edgar wanted to know.

"She got caught in the rain and got chilled."

"You sure she's not washing clothes up there? You know you go to the laundromat for that."

"She taking a bath, Edgar."

"You sure about that?"

"Do you want to come and look?" By this time the water had stopped running, and Ellen was in the tub.

"That's no way for a reverennnd to talk, Reverennnd," Edgar said and quick hung up the phone.

Ellen ate her soup and crackers and went to bed with her books to study. Russ went to his desk and tried to figure out Sunday's sermon, but being full of the day's good time, he got nothing done. He put on his coat and went outside, thinking a little stroll might clear his mind.

IT WAS DARK AND SULTRY. The rain had left the streets shiny wet and swirling whips of steam rose from them. Russ strolled past the little shops on Main Street. It seemed every other business was a beautician or a funeral home. "Lots of death and ugliness around here," he mumbled. His head began to hurt, so he went into the drugstore and bought some aspirin, then went across the street to the church, got a glass of water and took two of them.

He went outside and trudged down the hill. The cool air seemed to be the best thing for him. He turned the corner, and on a whim headed for Hughie Saloony's. He walked right in the barroom door. It had a sticky floor, plywood counter, neon beer signs all around, and a few of the cheaper brands of whiskey and gin lined up behind the old cash register. Six stools stood along the bar, and a few small tables and chairs filled up the rest of the room. Hughie sat in a corner by the coal stove dozing in his wheelchair. Mrs. Saloony sat on a stool at the far end of the bar stirring a cup of coffee and watching the television news. Other than that, the place was empty.

Mrs. Saloony was wearing black slacks and a white blouse and her bottle-enhanced auburn hair was rolled into a tight bun. By the look of her, Russ guessed she was way ahead of most of those who came in her door.

"Well, Reverend, what a pleasure. I hope you're not bringing us a summons," Mrs. Saloony said.

"I don't bring summonses, I bring good news," Russ said.

"That hasn't always been so, my friend. One of the old Welsh preachers of that church of yours got his elders to pass a resolution against us here, and he came over and read it out in his holy voice and then summoned Hughie and me to the church to be censored by the Session. I told him we'd be right over soon as he got his parishioners to pay their bar tabs." She was shaking her head and laughing about it.

"And what did he say to that?"

"He said, can you believe it, that if I would tell him the names of the parishioners that frequented my establishment, that's just how he talked, why he'd make sure they were churched at the next meeting of the elders."

"He was going to kick them out of the church for coming here?"

"He knew I wouldn't give him the names. As far as I'm concerned, nobody has to know who's in here. Hell, he knew the names himself. The whole neighborhood knows who comes and goes here. Everyone knows you're here right now. But that's all right. You're on a pastoral visit, aren't you? You've come to see old Hughie and have a little prayer." She led Russ over to the slouched and sleeping Hughie Hughes. Drool dripped out of the corner of his mouth onto his red and green wool plaid shirt. What was left of his straight black hair had been worn down like an overused brush. Russ patted Hughie's back and prayed for him. On hearing the "Amen," he opened his eyes to little slits and grinned.

"He sits there in his wheelchair and sucks down as many beers as he can get people to give him, Reverend," Mrs. Saloony said. "It's too bad the way he is. He was a good man in his time. Now the sugar's got his legs and the beer's got the rest of him." Hughie heard all of this, but continued to grin.

"How long ago did they come over here and read their summons to you?" Russ asked her.

"Not that long ago, Reverend, two, maybe three preachers back. The guy's name was Davis, I remember that. But they've had a ton of Reverend Davises at that church. This one was a pip though. His britches weren't big enough for him, to hear him tell it. Still and all, this last one was the cream of the crop. That Reverend Thomas, he would condemn this place at church then sneak in the

Ladies Entrance and ask me to put a 'bit of the sauce' in a coffee cup for him. 'A bit of the sauce,' he called it, in that Christian way of calling things other than what they are. Then he wouldn't pay. He thought we owed it to him because he was of the cloth, I suppose, and that after preaching down on us to his precious flock. It's a kick, Reverend, I tell you it's a kick." She actually did seem to think all this was a kick, an attitude worth cultivating, Russ could see.

"Did you ever hear anything about some money missing, some pretty serious money, around the time Reverend Thomas left?" Russ ventured. He could think of no one better than Mary Saloony to ask about the mystery of the $10,000 he had seen set down in the church records.

"Well, I suppose I can tell you what I heard, but I don't like to go blabbing about what is said by customers with a little something in their snoot. A couple of elders came in one night maybe a year ago, had a shot and a beer just like the old miners used to, and began whining under their breath about some money. I got ears like a hawk, Reverend, so I heard what they said. Those dummies, leaving money lying around with that two-faced minister of theirs in the room. All I can say is they got what they deserved."

"So you think Reverend Thomas took it." Russ said.

"I'm not saying that. All I'm saying is you've got some dumb elders there not to know what sort of man their minister is. What a kick they are. But that's enough of that. What can I do for you, after you've been so nice to drop by and say a prayer for us?"

"Well, to tell the truth, I had a couple beers at the golf course earlier, and my head's started to hurt. What do you recommend?"

"Some swear by the hair of the dog, Reverend, but I wouldn't do that to you. It'll make you into a rummy. I'll fix you a little fizz." She took a package of seltzer from under the bar and stirred it into a glass of ginger ale. When it stopped fizzing she gave it to Russ and told him to drink it down all at once, which he did. She's the kind of person who makes you feel she knows what she's doing,

146

Russ could see, and having run this place for all these years, she probably does.

When Russ finished the fizz, Mrs. Saloony swirled the glass in the sink, went over and locked the door, and put the "closed" sign in the window.

"If anybody comes, Hughie," she hollered into his face, "tell them we'll be open in half an hour. Now, Reverend, you come with me."

Russ wondered what he was in for, but Mrs. Saloony had such an authority about her he figured he'd better follow along. She went up the few steps behind the bar into the house where she and Hughie lived. Russ followed behind feeling better already. The fizz seemed to settle him down, or maybe it was that Mrs. Saloony seemed so sure she could help. They entered a pleasant modern room with a new stuffed sofa and chairs, a kind of Swedish looking low table, and potted plants growing healthily in the corners.

"Take off your coat, Reverend," Mrs. Saloony said, and she arranged pillows on the couch so he could lie down. "Now come over here and get flat on your stomach." Russ did as she said. She crossed his arms over his head and began to massage his neck. She moved gently at first but then harder and harder when she found a tight spot. Pretty soon his neck felt more relaxed than it had in weeks, and his headache, by golly, seemed to be going away. Then she moved down his spine, inch by inch, feeling each level and following the muscles out to his sides. Wherever there was tightness, she came in with expert pressure and the tension dissolved under her touch.

"You're very good at this," Russ said.

"Quiet, Reverend. Your job is to be quiet now. You spend all your time talking and thinking and trying to figure out what to say, but now you need to be still and let me work on you. I used to do this for a living. I worked on lots of gentlemen, some famous ones, in fact. And some nasty ones too. Some got a little upset when they found out all I was going to rub was their backs, if you know what I mean. But most of the time I enjoyed it." She went on working, poking, rubbing, squeezing the tension out of him. Then she started little tap-tap-taps up his back and down his arms, tap-tap-tap, until he was tingly and alert.

"Now let me help you sit up, Reverend," she said. "Don't you go moving too much on your own and getting all tense again." She sat him up facing her and laid his head back on the couch and massaged his throat and shoulders. No question, that's where he was tightest, from the vocal chords out, as if the pressure of saying things had him by the neck. Mrs. Saloony's hands found the little knots that his prayers and holy moments had not been able to find. Truth be known, his prayers and holy moments had probably caused them.

When she was done, Russ didn't want to move. He sat there in great ease. She looked at him with a satisfied smile, and then she got up and slapped him on both knees as if to bring him out of a trance.

"I'm going to send you on your way now, young man, but don't hesitate to come by if you need something done. I'm more than glad to keep you loose and comfy. It'll be my little contribution to the church. And," she went on, "if you get so you can't figure out what's going on around here with these Welsh, you might want to ask me what I can tell you. I know 'em pretty good."

"I bet you do," Russ said. "And thanks."

She led him back down the stairs into the saloon. Hughie was snoring in his chair. She flipped the "closed" sign to "open" as Russ went out the door.

THE FOLLOWING EVENING, THE TIME CAME for Russ to preside over his first Session meeting as Moderator. The meeting was at Hank Henry's house at eight o'clock. Hank had prepared an agenda that included an opening and closing prayer, which if not offered and duly noted in the minutes would merit an "exception" when the church's books were checked by the Presbytery Committee on

Sessional Records. Russ offered a brief prayer of thanksgiving for their church, asked for guidance in their deliberations, and they were off. Approval of minutes, all in order. Hank would not have it any other way. Then the financial report.

Billy Jones, Church Treasurer, said there had been a nice increase in offerings because of Russ' first service when the church was packed, but there were offsetting expenses due to the Ordination Service and reception. The offering at the ordination, Billy reported, was substantial, but, by custom, it went to the Presbytery. Mutterings of disapproval followed that comment. Russ learned the little blue leather *Book of Common Worship*, his ordination gift from the congregation, had cost them ten dollars. He considered it the bargain of the age. All told, finances were in fair shape, Billy stated, and there were a few thousand dollars in the bank owing to the church having been without a minister for a year and thereby only obligated to pay for Sunday sermons at ten dollars each.

It seemed to Russ' quick glance that the yearly offerings never quite met the actual expenses, and, if all goes as it had been going, in about three years the church would once again be broke. The record showed this was the case when his predecessor, Reverend T. Calvin Thomas, left.

Then Russ took a deep breath, coughed quietly and asked about the ten thousand dollars he had read about in the minutes of a year or so ago. A quick silence fell upon the proceedings. The elders looked around at each other as if this was entirely out of order. Finally, Buck Davies said, "Reverennnd, if you solve that mystery you can write your own ticket around here. We have our suspicions, but we have no way of checking them out."

"Where did the money come from in the first place?" Russ asked. Again, elders looked around at each other.

Hank Henry cleared his throat and came forth with, "Aunt Alice Morgan, a real estate lady in the church, sold a couple of old rental houses she owned, and for some reason decided to give most of what she got to the church. We were meeting in the church basement, and in came Aunt Alice and put ten thousand dollars cash money on the table just like that. All she said was, 'This is for the work of the Lord,' and turned around and walked out. It was a shock to us all. We spent a good while talking about it. It was lying on the table when we went to the kitchen for the little lunch my wife fixed for us. When we came back, the money was gone. Nobody can think what happened to it."

"I thought the minister would take care of it," Billy Jones said, "and since I'm the treasurer, he assumed I would take it, leastwise that's what he said."

"So, nobody picked it up from the table?" Russ asked.

"None of us did," Hank said.

"Did you look around to see if it fell off someplace?" Russ asked.

"We didn't think it was lost, Reverennnd." Billy Jones said. "I thought the minister had it; he says he thought I had it, and everyone else, I guess, thought one or the other of us had it, so nobody thought anything about it. Talk about a shock. You should have been at our next meeting when there was no record of a big deposit and no trace of the money. Ten thousand dollars would mean a lot to this church, Reverennnd, as you no doubt can see."

Russ ventured that it seemed to him this must have happened about the time his predecessor was leaving.

"That's one of our suspicions, Reverennnd," Buck said.

"You think Reverend Thomas has the money?" Russ asked.

"I'm just saying it's one of our suspicions. I know you revrennnds will stick up for each other; you're worse than the doctors about that, but you have to admit that it's quite a coincidence, the money is gone and the minister leaves town."

The rest of the meeting went quickly. Russ found out that "sparking," to the elders in charge five or six years ago, was holding hands while walking down the street, which apparently was permitted on any day but Sunday. Russ had noticed from the record that two of the present elders were on the Session during that time, and there was no mention of dissenting votes, so these two had voted for the rebuke. Davie Russell, one of the newer and younger elders, in a tone with a tinge of sadness in it, told how the rebuked young people had married, had two children, and never darkened the doors of the church again. Soon after that there was a motion to adjourn, and Hank Henry reminded Russ to close the meeting with prayer and give thanks for the "little lunch" they were about to enjoy, which he did.

The little lunch was cold cuts, sliced cheeses, potato salad, sweet pickles, sliced white bread, dark tea, and a large platter of Welsh cookies. Mary Henry, Hank's wife, had the reputation for the best Welsh cookies in Scroggtown, and Russ could see why. He could also see he would be needing bigger clothes if he kept eating like this at all hours.

Russ walked home in the crisp, autumn night. The Henrys lived a block and a half up the street from Russ and Ellen. Elder Davie Russell lived next door, and there were elders and deacons living just one block over and others a block down the hill. "Welsh Hill is also Elder and Deacon Hill," Russ mumbled as he walked along.

Russ noticed he was smiling to himself as it came to him that if, as was said, the money disappeared between the time the elders left their table to go to the kitchen for refreshments and the time they came back to the table, which couldn't have been more than fifteen minutes or so, then the person who took the money had to be in the church during that brief interval. And so, not only the former pastor, but all the elders, Hank Henry's wife, and whoever might have been helping her in the kitchen that night, are legitimate suspects in the case of the missing ten thousand dollars. The first thing to find out would be if these present elders were the ones on the Session that night, or if some of them had been elected since. He decided he would ask Hank Henry for another look at the Session's minutes.

"Maybe I should have been reading about Sherlock Holmes and Ellery Queen in seminary, instead of Irenaeus, and the Cappadocian Fathers," Russ chuckled to himself. "At least this job just got more interesting."

12

The Freedom of the Pulpit

IN EARLY NOVEMBER THE Scroggtown Ministers Association meeting at The Coal Bin decided the new minister in town should preach the sermon at the annual Union Thanksgiving Service at the Asbury Methodist Church. The idea was to have it there because the pastor, Dr. James W. Johnston, did not often attend Association meetings and maybe this would encourage him to be more active. The word about Dr. Johnston was that he wanted to be bishop, so he spent a lot of time at denominational gatherings in order to make himself known. Several times running, after the votes were counted for electing a new bishop, Dr. Johnston learned he had come in second. The further word was that many Methodists of the area did what they could to make sure Dr. Johnston always came in second.

Russ was initially pleased to be invited to preach the Thanksgiving Day sermon, but as the meeting wore on, he began to agree with the old theologians who designated pride as the deadly sin that triggers all others, for here he was barely getting one sermon done a week, and now he was signed up for two sermons only three days apart. Russ sensed that the old pros knew better than to crowd themselves this time of year.

Having been made aware that Asbury Methodist would be asked to host the Thanksgiving Service, Dr. Johnston showed up at the meeting after breakfast was over. A tall, thin man in his early sixties, he had the air of someone who not only expected to be bishop someday but imagined he already was. He was extremely fussy about the details of the service. He raised questions about who might or might not be offended if the Nicene Creed instead of the Apostle's Creed was said just before the prayer. Getting Dr. Johnston's approval for those who would read scripture and do the other parts of the service took up the better part of an hour. Thus, the assembled clergy did not have time to deal with the matter of the Open Housing Covenant that had been tabled at the previous meeting, even though Carson Whitlock had a whole stack of statements and signature cards ready to go. Russ suspected that the long discussion about the place of the creed and the assigning of parts may have been generated by those disinclined to deal with racial injustice in Scroggtown. When Carson muttered "typical" under his breath and got up to leave, Russ' suspicions grew stronger.

Russ walked out with Carson. "Why wasn't Reverend Ben here?" Russ asked.

"He probably knew this is what would happen." Carson was shaking his head and getting a cigarette out of his shirt pocket. Before he could light up, Russ took a couple hundred of Carson's Open Housing Covenant forms and went off to make hospital calls. He had the forms put into the bulletin for Sunday's service and, during the announcements, told the people to sign them and put them in the offering plate. He got one signature back—Auntie Sophie's. That evening, over cake and coffee in the Llewellen's apartment, Carson told Russ, "You have to work this kind of thing through your committees with several presentations," he said. "You have to soften up the opposition." Russ just assumed good Christian folks would naturally want to sign such a covenant. He was thoroughly stunned by the response he got, and it didn't help his faltering disposition.

BY THE TIME THANKSGIVING WAS ROLLING AROUND, Russ was still out of sorts over the Open Housing Covenant as well as being up

154

in the air about what to preach at the big service. Then he heard on the radio that a young Methodist civil servant had caused a flap among the cranberry growers of southern New Jersey. This man found too high a concentration of something toxic in several batches of cranberries he tested, and, rather than lowering the standards as had been done in the past, he condemned the whole crop. Not stopping there, he ordered a recall of the cans, jars, or boxes of New Jersey cranberries in all the grocery stores up and down the east coast. And he publicly stated his actions were based on Christian convictions he had acquired at his Methodist church. There were no cranberries for Thanksgiving after that, at least not at prices most people were willing to pay. Ah, Russ thought, here's something that has everyone's attention. He deiced to call his sermon "Thank God for the Cranberries" and phoned his title to Dr. Johnston in time to get it into the newspaper.

Russ wrote a sermon praising this Methodist civil servant for protecting babies, expectant mothers, and the entire population from dangerous poisons, even though the powers of this world wanted him to compromise his principles. Russ' text was from the Book of Genesis, the story of the destruction of Sodom, which, the story goes, would have been saved had God found one righteous person in the entire city. Russ likened the young civil servant to that one person God was looking for. Because that man took decisive action based on his Christian values, Russ wrote, countless people may have been spared long lasting harm.

Thanksgiving morning came, and Russ and Ellen were in each other's way trying to get ready for church. The service was at ten, and it was clear across town, so they didn't have nearly as much time as on Sunday when the service was at eleven, and all they had to do was walk down the street. Sharing the bathroom, dressing at the same time, it was all too distracting. Russ got rushed and nervous. He was combing his hair for the fifth time when Ellen yelled it was time to go. They sped across the mostly deserted town and got to the church with barely five minutes to spare. The organist had already started the prelude. In his haste, Russ had forgotten his robe. Dr. Johnston wouldn't hear of him preaching in his brown suit and forced a maroon choir robe on him.

Russ preached his way through his sermon determined to do justice to the young Methodist civil servant, God's man in New Jersey, who had warded off a sinister threat to health and wellbeing. Not having cranberries for Thanksgiving was a small price to pay over against such courageous and caring action, Russ proclaimed.

People left the church with hardly a comment for this new young preacher. Clearly, they came to Thanksgiving service to feel good about being grateful for their blessings, not to be reminded of current issues in the news. The ones who spoke to Russ, though polite, indicated they weren't happy to be doing without cranberry sauce. They hoped they could get some for Christmas.

"Nice try, Russ," Carson said while the reverends who participated in the service were at the door shaking hands with the people. Dr. Johnston didn't know quite what to say. Though polite as always, he seemed out of sorts that anything that could be construed as controversial would be mentioned from his pulpit, even though the courage Russ had extolled was Methodist courage. "You gave them something to think about besides their turkey," he offered. It was the kindest thing anyone said.

NOW THE FIRST SUNDAY IN ADVENT was coming on fast, and Russ was determined to do some good homework for a series of four sermons leading up to Christmas. He decided to give them an up-to-date rendition of the Virgin Birth, thinking it would help people feel less ill at ease with one of the more preposterous tenets of the faith. After all, it was a great help to Russ to learn in seminary that the Biblical authors are not at all unanimous about Jesus being born of a virgin. So, having been enlightened about the Biblical record at Princeton, Russ thought surely the good Welsh Presbyterians in the Lackawanna River Valley would appreciate being enlightened as well. With these assumptions buoying him, he stepped into the pulpit that first Sunday in Advent and preached his heart out. His main point was that it is the manner of Christ's life that is important for faith, not the manner of his birth, and he said it quite well, he thought.

Before the day was over the elders had met without him, which is against the constitution of the Presbyterian Church, and they decided to send a sizeable delegation to visit their new minister that very evening. Youth Fellowship had to be cancelled. Four of them came up the stairs in a block and sat together in the parlor of the little apartment. Russ offered them coffee and cookies, but they declined, saying they would only be a minute.

"Reverennnd, the elders decided we should come by to see you," Hank Henry said. Buck was also there, and Billy Jones, the Church Treasurer, who didn't say anything. Davie Russell sat quietly as well.

"Well, now what did I do wrong?" Russ said, figuring to plunge in, not knowing what it was about. He had been praying for the sick and holding their hands, he hadn't forgotten the offering in over month, and he hadn't been seen drunk in public, though maybe they found out about his golf match with Artie and the good time in the clubhouse afterward.

"It's your sermon today, Reverennnd," Buck said. "I hope we're not going to get any more like that."

"And why is that?" Russ asked.

"Well, Reverennnd, you know what it says in the Creed, 'born of the Virgin Mary', our people believe that. They don't want their minister telling them it might not be true."

"My point was that the Bible talks a lot more about Jesus' life than about his birth. I wanted to direct our attention to the whole story." Russ could feel himself becoming argumentative.

"Still and all," Buck said, "we're not used to hearing things like that. Nothing like that has ever been said from our pulpit before." The emphatic "our pulpit" was not lost on Russ.

"Are you saying I can't preach what I am led to preach?" Russ asked.

"Oh no, Reverennnd, we would never tell our minister what he can or can't preach. That wouldn't be right. You go ahead and preach anything you want, but try to consider the people, Reverennnd. We're just poor struggling folks here. We haven't been to school like you. We're simple people who believe the Apostles Creed just as it is in the hymnbook." Buck was half smiling the whole time. It seemed to Russ he loved to talk that simple humble talk, knowing full well he was putting the screws right into his new minister.

"I believe the Apostles Creed too, Buck," Russ said, thinking to himself, What a stupid thing to say, like being led to a lion's den, opening the door and jumping right in.

"Well, it sure didn't sound like it this morning, Revvverennnnd," Buck said. With Buck's extra lengthy "Revvverennnnd," Hank Henry could tell things were getting close to the edge. His position as Clerk of Session was to keep decency and order, and he knew, whether the other elders did or not, that this little exchange had been authorized at an improper meeting of the Session.

"Reverennnd," Hank said, "We are pleased with everything you're trying to do for us. We just want our church to grow and build. We need everybody we can get. If you want to discuss matters like you told us about today, go down to the seminary. That's the place for that sort of thing. Here in Scroggtown we need to have our faith encouraged, not put down all the time with these new ideas you ministers have."

"I didn't think I had been putting faith down all the time. I'm trying to help people think about some of the things they believe so they can believe in them more," Russ said.

"Well," said Hank, "many more sermons like that one today and you'll have everybody so confused they won't know what to think. People don't come to church to get confused, Revvverennnnd." Now Hank, the most conciliatory one of the group, was also coming down hard on the extra "v's" and "n's" in Reverend.

"So that's how it works," Russ said. "I can preach whatever I want, it's just that if I'm not careful, nobody will come to listen."

"That's how it works," Buck said. "It seems they might have mentioned that in preacher school."

"In preacher school they encouraged us to look into questions and discuss them," Russ said, thinking to himself, Why don't I keep my mouth shut? He knew what the books said about handling situations like this: Nod and listen and try to hear the message in, with, and under the words. He just couldn't do it. So the conversation stayed on its strident edge for the better part of an hour. Nobody really backed down, and even though Russ was by now determined not to waver, he was getting more and more scared. These elders could snap their fingers, and he and Ellen would be out in the cold. It occurred to him that a minister who gets thrown out of his first church after a few months isn't going to find another one any time soon. The power they had over him was definite and sure, he could see. He had no place to make a stand, but still he made one.

"Gentlemen," Russ said finally, "I will continue to preach on matters I feel are important."

"But you said you don't think the Virgin Birth is all that important," Buck pointed out. "Why not leave it alone then?"

Russ could see Buck's point. He could also see that Buck had a marvelous way of twisting things so that you don't notice all the implications until a while afterwards. In any case, Russ was getting too frightened to pick up on the fine points, and he just wanted this whole thing to end somehow.

"I appreciate your telling me the feelings of the congregation, and I'll take that into account. I hope you will think about what 'freedom of the pulpit' means as well," and he gave a quick jerk of a smile in Buck's direction. "It's a basic principle of Protestant Christianity, you know."

"Oh, we will think about it all right, Reverennnd. You bet we will," Buck said. He got up to go and the others followed.

Hank was obviously troubled that a nice resolution of the matter had not occurred. He stood on one foot and then the other and finally said, "Give our best to the Missus."

When they left, Russ noticed he was shaking. He sat down for a minute but it didn't help.

"Ellen, I've got to talk to Carson," he yelled into the other room. He was dialing the Whitlocks to see if it was all right to come over, which it was.

"I'm coming, too," she said. "That was pretty good what you did."

"Pretty good! I probably got myself fired and us thrown out in the street."

"You stood up to them. They'll respect you for that," she said.

"You're crazy. Get your coat."

CARSON WAS IN HIS BASEMENT REFINISHING another old chair. Judy and Ellen went into the kitchen and Russ went downstairs.

"What's up, Llewellen?" Carson said. "You look a little shook."

"Yeah, well, I just had a visitation."

"From an angel?"

"From four elders."

"Oops, four of them, huh? When one comes, he's got trouble. When more than one come, you've got trouble. What'd you do, try to pick the hymns?"

"No, it's not the chorister," Russ said, "I wish it was."

"Don't say that, Russer. There's no trouble like Chorister trouble in a Welsh church. God, Christ, Chorister, that's the Holy Trinity around here. The minister comes in far down the list." Carson kept on scraping paint off the chair. Underneath was a smooth, light wood, delicately grained.

"What kind of wood is that under all that paint?" Russ asked, glad to have his mind on something like a chair for a moment.

"This is a New England pine chair. Has to be a hundred and fifty years old. It'll finish out really nice."

"Where do you find stuff like that?"

"It's all around, especially out in the country, but you have to be careful or you'll get gumwood or something worse. We'll go on up now and talk about your visitation. While I wash my hands, you go back in the coal bin there and open up the orange crate you'll see by the far wall. Pull out one of those soldiers and bring it upstairs," Carson said.

"What?" Russ said.

"Just go. You'll see what to do." Carson was moving about slowly, like a man of great wisdom, Russ thought, which was just the kind of man he wanted to see right then. In the corner of the coal bin farthest from the chute were two orange crates. Russ opened one and inside was a case of Gibbons beer in quart bottles. Figuring these were the "soldiers" Carson had spoken of, he picked one out and headed for the stairs.

"Better bring two of those soldiers with you, Llewellen. The ladies might be thirsty too." Carson called. So Russ went upstairs with a quart of beer in each hand. He turned out the lights with his shoulder. Judy was popping corn, and everybody gathered at the kitchen table.

Carson had a "soldier" in the refrigerator already, so he put the two fresh ones in as replacements. He poured his beer down the side of his glass so carefully he didn't raise a bubble. Russ dumped his in and watched it foam. Carson scowled at that.

"It's the way I like it," Russ said.

"Well, to each his own," Carson said and reached over and pulled the shade down. "The neighbors are always looking to see what we're up to. They'd like nothing better than to spread it around that the four of us were in here having a big drunk, especially after I preached on that Genesis business again. I keep trying to get them to stop bothering the schools about evolution, but it doesn't do any good. They expect me to argue with the Board of Education over the science books, get Darwin repealed. Weird. These Christians today, driving around in cars with heaters and defrosters, for God's sake, and they want to keep their religion in the Middle Ages. It's hard to figure."

Carson reached into his shirt pocket and reached again. No cigarettes. He went to the cupboard, opened a new carton of Kools and took out a fresh pack. He tapped all eight corners of the pack lightly on the table, got a cigarette out, lit it, and put the pack carefully in his shirt pocket. He patted the pocket twice, and was set to converse.

"You know, Llewellen, there are two things we should never preach about, Adam and Eve and the Virgin Birth," Carson said after his first good sip of beer.

"Well, I preached on the Virgin Birth," Russ said. "After all, it's Advent."

"Yeah, Advent," Carson said, "that's what I thought, too. What could be more Advent than the creation story, the biggest advent of them all, even if it did take ten or twenty billion years to pull it off? Well, aren't we a couple of dummies? I should have known better, but I always think maybe this time they'll understand. They never do."

"You mean it just goes on and on like this? You preach for, what has it been, twenty years for you, and they still think the same way as when you started?" Russ asked.

"You got it, Russer, my friend. With rare exceptions, that's it. It's the exceptions that keep you going. If I always preached the way most of them want me to I'd drive the few thinkers away. I figure the crusty old hunkers will always be in church anyhow, so once in a while I try to give something to those who can't swallow that stuff in a literal way. Today, I preached to the precious few, I guess."

"I don't have this preaching business worked out that clearly, I'm afraid," Russ said. "And there's never enough time to do the job right. Today I felt I had the material pat. It came mostly out of a theology course notebook."

"Yeah, well, we do better not to refer to that stuff too much," Carson said. "But my God, we can't live in the Middle Ages forever. So what'd they do, threaten you with an inquisition?"

"Well, yeah, in a way that's what they did. They said for me to discuss my ideas with the people at the seminary and tell the people in the pews what they want to hear."

"And what did you say?" Carson asked.

"Like a dummy I told them I'm going to preach the way I felt led to preach. What possessed me, I don't know." Judy started laughing. Carson was grinning a big grin.

"Freedom of the pulpit, huh?" Carson said. "Why that's absolutely brilliant, Russer. I wish I'd thought of it a long time ago. I can preach anything I damn well please because that's why I'm here. That's fantastic."

"That bad, huh?" Russ said, and took a good swig of Gibbons. "Well, at least the Presbytery put me here, and only the Presbytery can make me go, but my hunch is that these elders could make me want to leave long before the Presbytery got around to holding a hearing."

"Russ, I'm serious," Carson said, still grinning. He took a long pull of his beer. "You did the one thing they won't be able to explain. You stood your ground. Welsh respect that. You'll see."

"That's what I told him," Ellen said. "He just wouldn't let them get the upper hand. I thought it was great what he did."

"It sure doesn't feel like I did anything great. Not only that, I don't even care about standing my ground on this point. I just wanted to say there's more to Jesus than his birth."

"Oh spit, Llewellen, it doesn't matter what the issue is. You let them know that they can't have a little meeting, send four of their biggies to see you, and make you do whatever they want." Carson was positively beaming. He raised his glass in a toast and sipped again.

"What if they go to Presbytery and complain?" Russ asked.

"What are they going to complain about?" Carson said. "Are they going to say, 'He told us what he learned at Princeton and we don't like it?' Princeton's supposed to be the powerhouse seminary for Presbyterians, isn't it? Llewellen, you got 'em. Don't let them think they got you." Carson was emphatic. He went to the refrigerator and got more beer.

"What's all this 'got them', 'got you' business?" Russ said. "I don't want to play gotcha."

"You may not want to play it, but it's part of the game. Seems to me you play it pretty well," Carson said. "You may have a knack for this business." Carson put out his cigarette and they sat around the table and finished the popcorn and the beer.

THE FOLLOWING SUNDAY, RUSS WAS READY. He stuck close to the text from Matthew out of Isaiah that says the Messiah will be one who speaks good news to the poor, sets the captives free and proclaims the acceptable year of the Lord. He looked right down into the Holiness of Holinesses at the elders when he got to the part about God anointing one to utter the Word beyond all human control.

"Christ is coming not only with a load of Christmas presents," he said, "but with promises and possibilities. We can have new thoughts, new understandings, and new lives." The people seemed to take it pretty well, but there were noticeably fewer in church than the week before.

"Fine sermon, Reverend," Buck said as he went out the door. "You know, I respect you for the way you stood up to us the other night. Never had a minister do that before." Russ was all but bowled over. So Ellen was right. And Carson was right too. It's a power game. Russ allowed himself to think that maybe he had won a round, but then, even though the end of November was long past, his check hadn't come in the mail. When it was ten days late, Russ phoned Treasurer Billy Jones to ask about it. It was under Russ' door the very next morning.

"Typical," Carson said when he heard about it. "That's what they do."

13

The Most Venerable Elder of Them All

FOR TWO WEEKS AFTER THE VIRGIN BIRTH INCIDENT, all Russ did was serve communion to shut-ins. Everyone on Welsh Hill wanted communion for their poor old Auntie Jennie who never came to church much but who was always a believer and anyway now she can't climb the steps anymore so would you go by and see her before Christmas. It means so much. That poor old Auntie Jennie can still walk up the hill and climb the steps to the social hall of St. Elizabeth's for Friday night bingo seemed to be no contradiction.

As Advent pressed on, Russ and all the reverends made the rounds. They bumped into each other in hospitals and nursing homes. Sometimes two or three of them were seeing people in the same room. Russ suggested to Carson that they combine their services, let him take one ward and Russ another and get done in half the time.

"They want their holy food from a familiar hand," Carson said.

So every morning Russ filled the little bottle with grape juice, cut bread into small cubes, packed it all in his Communion Kit, took hold of his *Book of Common Worship*, and made his calls, checking names off a list as he went.

165

"You must be sure to get in to see Jacob Jones, Reverennnd," Buck said on the phone after Russ had gotten back from a day of communions. "He's the venerable elder of the church, over ninety years old now. He served on the Session fifty years, until the sugar got him and made him blind."

"Is tomorrow all right, or should I go over there tonight?" Russ asked.

"Oh no," Buck said, "tomorrow will be fine. But allow a good hour. You'll need it. And be sure to speak up. Old Jacob can hardly hear a thing." Buck also said Jacob's son Isaac worked for the IRS in Scranton, his wife was a high school teacher, and their daughter was in college in Bloomfield some distance to the west, so only Jacob would be home. "Just let yourself in. You'll probably find Jacob in a chair by the window." Russ noticed that Buck was being especially helpful and he was grateful for that.

That night, Russ plowed through the Sessional Records again, looking for entries about the missing money. There was only the one mention of it he had seen before. But clearly the elders on Session at the time of the gift's disappearance were the same ones as now, and, according to the list of attendees at each meeting, none of them had been absent in the last couple of years. "At least that simplifies it some," Russ mumbled to himself.

Next day, Russ set out to see Jacob Jones, venerable elder.

Jacob lived on Locust Street directly across from the church in an old two-story house done over with aluminum siding. It had a steep pointed roof and seemed squeezed between a double house with reddish sesame seed siding and the drug store on the corner. Russ cranked the old fashioned doorbell and let himself in. Hardly anyone on Welsh Hill locked their doors. It was mostly family coming and going. If a stranger showed up in the neighborhood, dozens of pairs of eyes peered out from behind curtains; then the phones started ringing, and the pedigree of the newcomer was found out or else he was confronted and asked to state his business.

Some recent remodeling had been done to Jacob's house, Russ could see. Partitions had been removed opening up the downstairs rooms, and there was a large parlor facing the street. Birch paneling covered the walls, making the room look like one you might see in a ranch style bungalow in the suburbs.

Dressed in gray slacks, white shirt, dark green tie with a red Welsh dragon embroidered on it, and a red cardigan sweater, Jacob was sitting by the parlor window that looked upon the west wall of the church. Rays of sun streamed upon his face. Russ said a loud hello and touched his shoulder to let Jacob know he was there.

"Ah, is that you, Revvverrrennnd. They told me you would be coming," Jacob boomed in his resonant voice. When he spoke it was like listening to a baritone sing a solo, lilting and melodious, Welsh through and through.

"I'm pleased to meet our new minister," Jacob intoned. "I cannot rise up very fast, Reverennnd. The legs you know, takes me a time to get them going, so I sit here by the window. I cannot see the light of the sun but I can feel its warmth. Please come and sit across from me here. This is where I meet my visitors."

Jacob turned and greeted Russ by extending his gnarled right hand. He was a giant among the Welsh, almost six feet tall with a great shock of white hair that, because of its coarseness, had resisted being neatly combed. His angular, strong-featured face seemed stately, even noble, and his broad shoulders and lean torso gave him an athletic look. Clearly, he had been a powerful man.

Two thick canes leaned against Jacob's chair and his left hand rubbed the polished wood of one of them. Russ sat in the corner of a little couch that had been arranged to put visitors close to Jacob and directly in front of him. Jacob tilted his head to the right and pointed to his hairy left ear.

"I do better from this one, Reverennnd. If you speak right into it, I should be able to hear your good words." So they got arranged and made the usual kind of beginning: Where Russ came from, how he liked it in Pennsylvania, how he was finding the church.

But when Jacob said the word "church" the room seemed to shake. It was a huge rumbling word in his mouth. "Ah, the churrrrch, the chuuurrrccch," he said. "How I love the churrrch." He told Russ he loved the church since he was a boy in Wales. "My mother would read to me from the holy book, and now I spend my time thinking about those old stories. When they told me I would be blind, I memorized the Psalms so I would have something to read in the darkness."

"That's a wonderful thing to have done, Jacob," Russ said, finding himself totally impressed with this old man. He almost mentioned that he knew no more than two or three Psalms by heart, but quickly thought better of it.

"Ah yes, I wouldn't want Isaac to have to pamper me. He's got too much to do for that." Jacob was smiling broadly. "Now that's something, isn't it Reverennnd, I'm Jacob with a son named Isaac, while in the Bible it's the other way around."

"Maybe you're getting closer to the source," Russ said, not really knowing what he was trying to get at, but Jacob was right on it.

"Ahh, yes," he intoned, "if Isaac had a son, we could call him Abraham which would get us back to the beginning." He laughed out loud, and so did Russ. This man truly was venerable, it seemed. The time flew by with Jacob telling about how he went to work as a boy in the breakers and then became a full-fledged miner and then the foreman of a crew. "I tried to do right by my men, Reverennnd, but I had the big bosses to contend with as well," Jacob said, his tone more subdued. "It was hard to show support for my men and please the bosses too. I hope I did not displease my Lord." Russ could not help but think this sounded something like the position he was in, caught between his sense of his calling and the elders' sense of what a minister should be, though without the coal dust, noise, and constant danger Jacob had endured.

Then Jacob leaned back and spoke in utter determination. "For many years, Reverennnd, I have wondered about something. I have wondered about the book of Genesis. It says there that God created the heavens and the earth in six days. Six days! Imagine! And then God rested on the seventh day. Do you believe that, Reverennnd?"

Here we go, Russ thought. If he said what he really believed Jacob would throw him out of the house and the elders would throw him out of the church. He was sure of it. And so there was a long pause. Russ began his answer much as he had begun answering Dr. Clark at his ordination trials. He said how it was well established that the first creation story in Genesis was written quite late in holy history, that it was an enlightened writing from the tradition of the Hebrew priesthood, and that its purpose was to put the history of Israel in a cosmic setting. It was the priests' rendition of the science of those times, Russ explained, and he wished out loud that religious leaders today, himself included, were as versed in current science as the ancient priests were in theirs. Russ went on to describe the various orders of creation laid out at the beginning of Genesis—light, heavens, earth, water, land, fish, birds, animals, and finally humans. He noted the artistic parallel between this and the theory of evolution.

"There is nothing finer for us to contemplate," Russ said at last.

"Ah yes, but we read how God created the heavens and the earth in six days and then rested on the seventh day. Six days, Reverennnd. Do you believe it?" Jacob asked again.

Russ treated Jacob to a second song and dance much like the first one. He spoke of a great hymn to the creation, of the formlessness of all beginnings, of the tender image of the Spirit of God brooding over the face of the deep like a mother hen brooding over her chicks. Russ lifted up the fact that Genesis shows the world to be created by divine speech and went on to highlight what he called the marvelous insight that language creates imaginary worlds for our spirits to dwell in.

"Yes, yes, Reverennnd," Jacob boomed, "I suppose that's something, but it says God created the world in six days and rested on the seventh day. Now tell me, do you believe it or do you not believe it? "

"Do you mean do I believe that we must take the passage literally, that one day a few thousand years ago God sat down and began creating everything and six days later God was done and took a day off?" Russ asked, hoping against hope that Jacob's answer would let him off the hook.

"Yes, Reverennnd, that's exactly what I mean. Do you believe it? Yes or no?"

Russ gulped and said, "No, Jacob, I do not believe that is how it happened. I believe…," Russ was going to cover his tracks with some more talk about the poetic quality of the passage and how poetry opens up the soul and prepares us to experience mystery and grace, but Jacob broke right in with a great surge of sound.

"Ahhhhhh, Reverrrennnnd," Jacob nearly shouted, "I never believed it either. You're the first minister who ever agreed with me."

Russ sighed audibly. What a relief. Here is the most venerable elder of them all thinking like a contemporary theologian. He had come to his conclusions on his own, because no minister up to that moment had told Jacob what they teach in seminary. They told him what they thought he wanted to hear.

"We'll keep this just between us, Reverennnd, I think that would be best," Jacob said, chuckling a bit. And so right there Russ knew how this way of thinking about the Creation Story sits with the bulk of the congregation.

Russ got out his little communion kit and opened the *Book of Common Worship*. He poured grape juice into two tiny cups and placed two little pieces of bread on the small chrome plate the kit provided for that purpose. "Commune with the people you bring communion to," the Pastoral Ministry Professor had said. "Help them feel they are part of a congregation." As Russ began to read the opening verses, Jacob pointed to his left ear, and Russ moved closer. Jacob pointed again and put his hand behind his ear to catch every word. He leaned toward Russ. He didn't want to miss a syllable. Finally Russ put the book down, cupped his hands around Jacob's ear and shouted the words of the communion service from no more than an inch away.

"The Lord Jesus took bread," Russ shouted into Jacob's left ear.

"Ahhh yes, the Lord Jesus took bread," Jacob said right after Russ did and nodded his head vigorously up and down.

"And when he had blessed it, he broke it," Russ went on.

"Ahhh yes, he blessed it and broke it," Jacob said. Phrase by phrase they chanted their way through the ritual.

"And Jesus said, 'Take, eat. This is my body broken for you.'"

"Yes, we take and eat, Reverennnd."

"'This do in remembrance of me.'"

"In remembrance of our Lord. Our precious Lord."

Jacob's voice was trembling. His whole body, still strong and masculine, full of years in the mines and full of years in the church, seemed to heave toward heaven. For almost seventy years longer than Russ had lived, Jacob had been nourished by this bread. From Wales to Pennsylvania, from deep in the mines to his pew in the Holiness of Holinesses, this had been his help and stay. And it was still so on this very day as the two of them sat by the window, the sun turning gold in the afternoon sky.

Jacob took the little piece of bread gently in his thick hand, lifted it to his mouth, tossed it to the back of his throat and swallowed it without chewing. Then he folded his hands in prayer. For several minutes he prayed silently. When he looked up, Russ placed the cup in his fingers, and shouted into his ear the holy words, "Jesus said, 'This cup is the new covenant in my blood. Drink from it in remembrance of me.'" Jacob repeated the phrases much more quietly this time, whispering them to himself. Russ had never seen such open, forthright devotion.

After the benediction, Jacob prayed for Russ and Ellen and for the church, a prayer full of grace and encouragement. For the first time in a long time, Russ felt ministered to. He had communed in a way he had never thought possible, and his eyes were misty when he left Jacob sitting in his chair by the window, a look of total peace on his sun-bathed face.

14

"It's quite a haht you're wearing..."

THE SUN WAS FADING FAST WHEN RUSS STEPPED into the brisk Advent air after visiting Jacob Jones, and the wind whipping around the corners of the parish was biting cold, hitting Russ square on the forehead. It felt like the top of his head was being pried off. When he got to the apartment he went right to the boxes of things from seminary and found the cap Hoppsy Hopple had lent him. It was one of those "pancake" hats, they call them, flat with a small visor in front. This one was wool tweed, and it fit Russ just right. He put it on and walked up the street to do one more communion for the day, but Amy Prichard's poor shut-in Auntie Maud was out somewhere.

Walking back home, Russ came across Hank Henry, Clerk of Session, who had just gotten off work and was about to go into his house.

"Good evening, Hank," Russ said. "It's gotten cold, hasn't it."

"Ah, Reverennnd," Hank said, "it's quite a haht you're wearing there." The word "hat" came out with a soft "a" and an uplifted tone.

"Thanks, Hank," he said, "my roommate in seminary lent it to me, and I never gave it back. I'm glad to have it on a day like this."

"It's certainly quite a haht," is all Hank would say.

That night a good snow came in, and, next morning, Russ and Ellen looked out on a changed world. All the slightly askew ledges and angles of Scroggtown were trimmed with an inch or two of white. The old houses seemed lovely and cozy with snow on the banisters leading up to the porches, snow on the windowsills, and snow just about covering the roofs.

Wrapped in the warmest clothes she had, including a six-foot long black and orange scarf Russ had gotten for her at the Princeton University Store, Ellen stepped into the cold and caught the bus for school. Russ found the Harris Tweed topcoat he had at Princeton, zipped in the wool lining, put on Hoppsy's wool cap, and walked down to the church. All along the way, men were scraping snow off their car windows as the engines idled and tailpipes sent white smoke into the frigid air.

"Ah, Reverennnd, that's quite a haht you're wearing now," Russ heard from any number of them. No "Good morning." or "How do you like the snow?" just "That's quite a haht you're wearing." They said it just like Hank Henry had, as if these were the words of a song they all knew. Some of these men Russ had never seen before, but they all took special interest in his hat. "Ah, Reverennnd, it's quite a haht you're wearing, that one."

Russ didn't know what to make of these comments, but he appreciated how musical they sounded coming from these Welshmen's mouths.

THE FOURTH SUNDAY OF ADVENT ARRIVED a bitter cold day. Russ donned his tweed topcoat with the zip-in lining and Hoppsy's little wool cap. With Ellen bundled up beside him, they set out for the church, walking in other people's shoeprints in left-over snow on the tipped and slippery slates of the sidewalk. There was hardly anyone out that morning. The few parishioners they came across didn't greet them in any usual way but remarked about the cap: "Quite a haht you're wearing today, Reverennnd." It was the only greeting offered. For many of these parishioners, the typical

Sunday salutation was "Blessed Sabbath to you, Reverennnd." Their attention to his hat was clearly a change from the norm.

When he and Ellen got to the church, Russ hung his hat and coat on one of the hooks on the back wall where all the coats and hats were being hung, some on top of others in precarious heaps of wool. He got into his preaching robe which was almost as warm as his topcoat. Ellen kept her coat with her, saying she was still chilled from the walk to church. Actually, the church was almost full. People were getting their souls ready for Christmas it seemed.

On this Sunday, green boughs appeared around the pulpit, and they sang standard carols instead of those minor key Advent hymns that preachers and musicians love and most parishioners hate, except for the Welsh, who sing in minor keys all year long. But even the Welsh like the happy carols this time of year, and they sang them with gusto and warm feeling, which made the service seem fine no matter what else happened.

Everyone was friendly and cheerful shaking Russ' hand at the door, and Buck and his wife Ginny invited Russ and Ellen for dinner afterwards. However, when Russ went to get his hat and coat, the hat wasn't there. He looked all around for it, asked the people still there if they had seen it, and even went up to the balcony to see if the two teenagers sitting there holding hands knew anything about it. No one seemed to know what he was talking about. They had not known him to wear a hat, they said. Some of these were among those who had recently remarked, "Ah Reverennnd, that's quite a haht you're wearing."

Russ looked down in the basement rooms as well, but found no hat. When he got back upstairs, all the coat hooks were empty, and there was no little wool cap in any of the pews. Hatless, he went off to dinner with the Davies, and a fine dinner of chicken and dumplings it was. Tommy and Jimmy, the Davies' teenage boys were perfect gentlemen at the table, as if they had been inoculated against any adolescent behavior so long as a minister was on the premises. Russ thanked the Davies wholeheartedly for their

175

kindness and was told, "Now Reverennnd, don't be writing us any thank you note, you have enough to do without that." They probably meant it Russ thought, but on the way home Ellen said, "I'll write them a note. It was a wonderful dinner. And we wouldn't want the Reverennnd to have too much to do."

At the Whitlocks that night, over beer and popcorn, Russ asked Carson if he had heard anything about the missing $10,000 that had somehow vanished around the time the former minister was leaving for another parish. Carson had not heard about it, but he knew Reverend T. Calvin Thomas through the Ministers Association, and he could entertain the possibility that Reverend Thomas knew more than anybody about what happened that night in the basement of the Welsh Presbyterian Church. "Those Welsh preachers know everything that's going on," Carson said, "and they don't necessarily tell the people everything they know, especially about money. He came over from Wales, you know, and that put him in the driver's seat right there. I doubt if they asked many questions about him before he got here, and I doubt if he told them everything about why he left the dear old homeland." Russ decided it might be a good idea to look up Reverend Thomas in the Presbyterian Ministers Roster and see if he could talk to him. After all, the elders themselves had their suspicions, and Mary Saloony didn't think much of him either. Of course, there were hardly any ministers Mary Saloony thought much of, though Russ hoped he might be one of the exceptions.

NEXT EVENING, ON HIS WAY TO BRING COMMUNION to one of the shut-ins, Russ heard the choir practicing as he walked by the church. Christmas tree lights glowed from the front windows of all the houses round about. There were patches of snow on the ground, on the roofs, and in the crotches of the leafless tress. It seemed like an old fashioned Christmas card to him, with the added beauty of a Welsh choir singing songs of the season in the background. He stood hatless in the cold air and listened for a time.

"Ah, Reverennnd," he heard Billy Jones say from the steps of the drugstore, "you shouldn't be about without a haht on a night like this. You'll catch your death of something now." Russ told Billy he was absolutely right, and as soon as he found his little cap it would be firmly on his head.

By this time, Russ had several versions of the communion service memorized, short version for those most debilitated, long version for those who could tolerate it, and in between version for others. Tonight would be the short version for old Tommy Thomas, who suffered from the black lung. After his visit with Tommy, it was even colder out, and Russ was glad he didn't have a long walk home from the Thomas' house. His bare head felt like it was being squeezed by the cold.

Later that evening, Ellen got a call from Mary Henry, wife of the Clerk of Session. "Oh Mrs. Llewellen," she said, "I'm told the Reverennnd is going about without a proper haht. I'm so afraid his head will get terribly cold and it will affect his sinuses. We can't have that now, can we, Mrs. Llewellen. So, I've been thinking, it would be so nice if you would go to Reese Haberdashers up on Main Street and get the Reverennnd a proper haht for Christmas. They have wonderful gentlemen's hahts there, and I am sure you will find one just right for the Reverennnd. I hope you don't mind my making this little suggestion, but I am so concerned, Mrs. Llewellen. In this cold weather, the Reverennnd needs a proper haht."

"Have I got a surprise for you, Reverend," Ellen said as she hung up the phone.

"What's that?" Russ said. "And don't call me Reverend."

"Even if that's your name now?"

"It's not my name. What's the surprise?"

"You'll have to wait for that. Christmas is coming you know."

"Boy do I know that." Russ was working on his sermon for the Christmas Eve service, trying to get a bit ahead of the game for a change. "It's the holiest service of the year, Reverennnd," people had told him,

THE DAY OF CHRISTMAS EVE DAWNED with snow flurries, and it snowed off and on through the morning, changing the hard brown ice on the sidewalk slates to a flecked, powdery and slippery white. At a steep discount, Ellen and Russ got a little Scotch pine at a tree lot near the church and spent most of the day trimming it. It was the first Christmas without a crowd of family around, and it felt strange to realize that they could have whatever kind of celebration they pleased, so long as they got to church by 11:00 PM for the Candlelight Communion Service.

They decided to start their own tradition of red lights and red ornaments tied with red ribbons onto a tree sprayed white here and there to give the impression of a tidy, indoor snowstorm. Russ went to the drugstore and got a can of white stuff to spray on the tree, while Ellen bought the other things at a five and dime down the street. She came back with some silver ornaments too, for a little spice and shine, she said. They had no old ornaments that had to go somewhere, no special angel or star for the top, nothing but what they came up with on their own. Russ made a terrible mess spraying the tree and had to get another can of the white stuff and start over. Then he knocked most of the fake snow off stringing the lights and had to get a third can to touch things up. By then real snow was falling and starting to pile up on the sidewalks and roofs and fences and everything.

As Russ and Ellen worked on the tree, they had the radio tuned to Christmas songs, and Ellen sang along with them just like she sang in the car coming east. She knew all the verses to "The Twelve Days of Christmas" and could do the complete "Little Drummer Boy," not to mention easy ones like "White Christmas." Russ knew the carols, and this time Ellen seemed pleased he joined in.

It was getting dark outside when they got the tree done. They turned on the red lights and sat down on the rug to admire their work. It was absolutely beautiful in their eyes, a somewhat less than artful tree glowing red but with just enough silver to give it sparkle and reflect a bit of light into the far corners of the room. In each other's arms, they rolled around on the floor right there in front of their marvelous tree, a kind of religious observance it seemed to them, even if it was more in the way of a pagan rite beneath a canopy of green branches. Ellen's skin became a deep pink in the glow of the lights. Completely happy with each other, they pulled pillows down from the couch, covered themselves with their scattered clothes, flipped the corner of the rug over themselves, and slept.

They woke to the ringing of the phone. It was Edgar from downstairs asking if they wanted to come by for a Christmas drink. Russ said, "Sure, give us a few minutes, we need to get ready for the service tonight."

"Even Welsh landlords become human on Christmas Eve," Russ said as they went downstairs.

Edgar and Margaret Howells had never been to church since Russ had come to Scroggtown, but they were dressed up and ready to go. With Ellen and Russ in their church clothes, the four of them looked very civilized and proper.

"We never miss Christmas Eve, Reverennnd, holiest service of the year," Edgar said. "Margaret likes the candles and all. What can I fix you?"

"If you have Scotch I'll have it with water," Russ said.

"Well now, a reverennnd who drinks Scotch whiskey can't be so bad, can he, Margaret? And what for the missus?" Edgar was being the most solicitous of hosts. It was hard to believe this was the man who had accused Ellen of washing clothes in the bathtub.

"Something with a little gin in it, please," Ellen said, not really knowing what gin was, having grown up in a dry Christian home.

"Why, Mrs. Llewellen, that's what I like to drink. Reverennnd drinks Scotch like my Edgar, and I take a little gin like you. I think that's very nice," Margaret said. She seemed to be smiling more than this or almost any occasion could possibly call for, but her hair was immaculately done by one of the neighborhood beauticians, her nails were polished, and she wore a black dress and a string of beads that could pass for pearls. Ellen, also in black, still glowed from the recent roll on the floor.

"Here's to Christmas," Edgar said as he brought in the drinks. He looked quite a figure, sharp-featured, thin and fit in his gray suit and maroon tie, a nice wave in his dark, slightly thinning hair. The drinks were strong enough to keep the horse from kicking. "What were you two doing up there this afternoon?" Edgar said.

"We decorated our tree," Russ said. "Our first one."

"Sounded like you were beating the rug or something," he said, beginning to growl like the Edgar Russ and Ellen were familiar with.

"Oh Edgar, leave them alone, they're still young you know, not like us." Margaret said. She got all red and Ellen got redder, and Russ took a quick gulp of his Scotch in order to keep from snorting out a laugh.

"You'll have to come and see our tree," Russ said. "We did a right good job for beginners."

"You two aren't beginners," Edgar said.

"Edgar, they're still young. Everything's new to them. I wouldn't mind being young again myself," Margaret said and smiled her huge smile.

Edgar began to talk about his days in the merchant marine. As he spoke he became increasingly spirited, until he was spinning out yarns about ships and ports and, yes, women and captains and crews, each one a perfectly told tale.

"I remember a Christmas off Cape Horn," he said, smiling as he seldom did. "I thought we would lose her sure. I don't pray very often, Reverennnd, but I tell you I prayed that night. The Captain had gone below with his Christmas bottle and left me in charge on the bridge, and then the storm hit." Edgar went on to describe a battering and tossing to and fro that rivaled the fantastic storm in

Joseph Conrad's novel *Typhoon* that Russ had read in college. "But then," Edgar said, "Christmas day broke calm and clear, and when I wrote in the log about the storm, the captain wouldn't believe me. He'd slept right through it with his Christmas bottle by his side, but it was a hell of a storm."

Edgar looked thirty years younger as he told his story. Russ could see him for a moment as the hard-driving first-mate he must have been. There he was at the helm again, seeing his ship through the piling waves. Now he had this little house in a caved in coal town and tenants living above him who were young and passionate and could never really appreciate that he is First Mate Edgar Howells, second in command of ships at sea.

"Edgar," Russ said, "you tell a great story. It's all true to me whether the captain believed it or not."

Edgar was pleased. They finished their drinks and left for church, walking through the steadily falling snow.

15

The Holiest Service of the Year

Russ was not prepared for what he saw when he got to the church. The organ, the pulpit, the choir loft behind the pulpit, the communion table, the gate to the Holiness of Holinesses where the elders sat, the pulpit chairs, the platform on which the pulpit rested, were wrapped in aluminum foil. Everything sparkled with reflected light. The whole church twinkled.

The only light was from candles, and candles were everywhere. They stood in tall candlesticks that must have been borrowed from every household in the parish. Four tall candles stood on the pulpit surrounding the big Bible. To give organist Richie Evans the light he needed, at least a dozen candles glowed on top of the organ console so that it looked like Richie was playing his prelude in the midst of a bonfire. Russ wondered if there could be any oxygen left in the room.

A huge plywood cross covered with aluminum foil leaned back against the pulpit from the floor below. Holes had been cut in the plywood and potted poinsettias had been placed in the holes to form a red and green Christmas Cross. Russ had never heard of a Christmas Cross, but Christmas and Good Friday, Bethlehem and Golgotha, birth and death, all this and more bloomed together in that cross.

Russ put on his black robe and, because it was Christmas Eve, his academic hood as well, red velvet around the neck and over the shoulders, blue satin in back. Red for theology, blue for Princeton Seminary, and black just for the sake of black, Russ supposed. He was ready to start the service when Buck handed him a typed list of names. "If you don't mind, Reverennnd, will you read the dedications?" he said. Well, Russ did mind. The list was three pages long, but Christmas Eve was clearly not the time to discuss it. He went forward, stood next to the Christmas Cross, and began to read what Buck had handed him:

> Poinsettias have been placed in the sanctuary this evening by the following:
> Mrs. Henry Morgan in memory of Henry Morgan.
> Mr. and Mrs. John James, Jr. in memory of Mr. and Mrs. John James, Sr.
> William David in memory of David Williams and Mrs. William David.

THE LIST WENT ON AND ON, THE NAMES OF THE WELSH who had lived in the neighborhood and had died wherever they died, in Scroggtown, in California, back in Wales. It didn't matter; they were represented by a red poinsettia on Christmas Eve. People dead for fifty years and more were represented by a poinsettia. The most recent to die were given places in the Christmas Cross. Others had their poinsettias on the floor beside the cross, around the communion table, in front of the organ, and along the walls. Poinsettias in memory of elders were lined up against the partition that marks off the Holiness of Holinesses. So long as somebody put a poinsettia in the church for you, you were still a member of this community, you were called to mind and grieved for again, no matter how long ago you had been laid to rest. Russ wondered if anyone would put a poinsettia there for him when the time came. It would depend on many things, he supposed.

When he finished reading the list of dedications, Russ went to the back of the church where the choir was waiting, picked up a bulletin, got in line, and marched down the center aisle to the strains of "O Come All Ye Faithful." He was loaded down with clothes—shirt, tie, wool trousers and vest, preaching robe and academic hood. He felt like the man from the mountains caught indoors.

There had been no time for dinner, and Russ was a little light headed from Edgar's generously poured Scotch. It wasn't until he got into the pulpit that he realized he didn't have his sermon notes. They had left from Edgar and Margaret's place, so the notes were no doubt upstairs on his desk at home. Not to worry, he thought, with all the extra readings and anthems there wouldn't be much time to preach anyway. Russ stood there in a warm Christmas glow singing the hymn. The church was full to the brim. Everyone was smiling, and Russ got to feeling nothing could go wrong. After all, it was Christmas.

Then it hit him—a blast of heat like a furnace. The church was a reflector oven, and Russ was at the center of it. All that glitter glittered his way. The candles kept generating heat, the foil kept sending it toward Russ, and those packed bodies out there left no place else for it to go. He began to sweat like a man in a steam bath. Sweat poured from his hair, around his ears, down his cheeks, and dripped off his chin onto the holy pages of the pulpit Bible. The liquids of a lifetime oozed out of him, and with them his confidence oozed as well. His eyes hardly focused in the glittering light. Young Richie Evans at the organ caught the situation and played another chorus of the hymn while Russ shuffled through the Bible trying to find the second chapter of Luke, the main Christmas story. Every time he turned one of those huge pages, the flames of the candles on the pulpit hissed into the wax and threw off bigger flames. Russ thought he might set the whole place on fire just looking for the Gospel Reading.

Sweat ran into his eyes faster than he could brush it away. Though he could see the titles of the various gospels and the big Roman numeral chapter headings, he couldn't read the smaller print of the text. He called for the Prayer of Invocation and Lord's Prayer, and while the people prayed he got out his handkerchief and wiped his face.

Then the choir sang its first anthem, and Russ was able to sit down a little bit away from the flames. He bent over behind the pulpit where no one could see and felt for a cool place to breathe. A few deep breaths seemed to help. After the anthem, he rose up into the inferno to read the story of Christ's birth. The idea was to read a portion of it and then pause for an anthem or a hymn. Then read the next part and so on until the whole story has been told in scripture and song. Russ could see the words now, but he could barely tell what they were. Figuring he could do it from memory, he started in.

"And it came to pass in those days that a decree went out from Caesar Augustus that all the world should be taxed." It was going well, Russ thought. He got Cyrenius, governor of Syria, in the wrong place, but nobody noticed. It was so dark on the other side of the wall of candles, Russ couldn't see anyone out there anyway. He got Mary and Joseph and the babe all in the manger together by leaving out that little pause he had been drilled on in speech class: "They came and found Mary and Joseph...and the babe lying in a manger." Leave out that pause and you get a real manger full.

Richie Evans at the organ, bless him, plowed right into "Away in a Manger," and somebody pushed a bunch of little kids up to the front of the church to sing it for the people. The little ones seemed timid about getting close to that much light and heat, and Russ couldn't blame them. While they sang, he wracked his brain for the words of the story of the Wise Men from the Gospel of Matthew, but all that came to mind was the opening of T. S. Eliot's "Journey of the Magi," which he remembered from a wonderful day in college when the professor ended the term with a stirring reading of the poem and, to a standing ovation, sent the class off to Christmas vacation or what was called Winter Break at U. C. Berkeley. At the end of the song, Russ launched into Eliot's lines as if they were canonical scripture: "A cold coming we had of it, / Just the worst time of the year / for a journey...."

Well, that got their attention. There was an audible murmur from the darkness beyond the candles, and, from what Russ could tell, they weren't all that pleased out there. Furthermore, he began to stumble after the line about "silken girls bringing sherbet" and quickly jumped to the end with its life-in-death phrases and other such themes that both college and seminary had urged Russ to hold in high regard. "After the first death there is no other," he fairly shouted into the blackness, and quickly sat down. Only then did he realize the line is from another Eliot poem altogether.

The choir launched into a long, involved version of "While Shepherds Watched Their Flocks by Night," and Russ recalled his seminary colleagues' version of that carol: "While shepherds washed their socks by night / All seated on the ground, / The barmaid of the inn came by / and poured another round, / And poured another round."

Glancing at the bulletin, Russ was relieved to see there was no sermon listed. But he had the reading for the first chapter of John to go, and he still couldn't see the words clearly enough to read them. He stood up, took a deep breath, and, again from memory, began like this:

> One Christmas was so much like another,
> in those years around the sea-town corner now
> and out of all sound except the distant speaking
> of the voices I sometimes hear a moment before sleep,
> that I can never remember whether it snowed
> for six days and six nights when I was twelve
> or whether it snowed for twelve days and
> twelve nights when I was six.

A number of appreciative oos and ahs could be heard. Many of them knew Dylan Thomas' "A Child's Christmas in Wales" in this valley of transplanted Welsh. From college days, Russ knew several long passages of it, and they came back to him one after the other. He gave them Mrs. Prothero beating the dinner gong to call the fire brigade, Auntie Hannah in the backyard "singing like a big bosomed thrush" because she had gotten onto the parsnip wine, and the caroling party where a "thin, small, eggshell voice" came back at the carolers through the keyhole. Then came the final lines:

> I could see the lights in the windows
> of all the other houses on our hill and hear
> the music rising from them up the long, steadily
> falling night. I turned the gas down, I got
> into bed. I said some words to the close and
> holy darkness, and then I slept.

The lines filled Russ' voice and poured out into the shadows of that twinkling room. The people could hear the cadence and ring of their own true sound. These were their words, and Dylan Thomas was their poet, and these were their people in the poem. And their Jesus was all wrapped up in Welshness, Russ could see. When Dylan Thomas' words faded away, Richie Evans at the organ moved quietly into "Watchman Tell Us of the Night" to the tune Aberystwyth, as Welsh a tune as there is. They sang like wind from the sea against cold mountains. They sang like a cry from the mines. They sang like they knew peace and truth were breaking forth in a grand new light right there amid the glowing candles that surrounded them. Even Russ felt it might be so.

The custom was for communion to be served at twelve midnight on the dot, but Russ could not see the clock on the balcony wall in the flickering light. He gave the Prayer of Consecration and Richie Evans hit twelve chimes with all the authority of the royal timekeeper. So far as he and Russ were concerned, it was midnight exactly.

Elders materialized out of the darkness and passed the bread to the people and then the little cups of grape juice. When they brought the trays back there was hardly any bread or little cups of juice left on them, a sure sign of a full house. Then Elder Buck Davies approached the Communion Table and, from the tall candle burning there, lit a little candle he carried in his hand. It had a paper doily around it to keep the wax from dripping on his Christmas suit or onto the renovated church carpet. Everybody had a similar candle, and Buck lit the elders' candles from his, and they went out into the congregation bearing their little lights. One by one, candles were lit all around the room. Russ could see the glowing faces of his parishioners and their friends and neighbors, each one a golden presence in the darkness. The choir began to sing "Silent Night" and the people joined in. They sang it in English first, then some few sang it in Welsh, and one man with a delicately pleasing voice sang it in German. Then everyone sang it in English again. They drew out the phrase "All is calm, all is bright" so that it seemed like a wail, a protest against all that is not calm and bright. They sang it again and again until all the candles were lit.

Then Hank Henry, Clerk of Session, rose from his pew in the Holiness of Holinesses and walked slowly forward in time to the music. He motioned for Russ to join him in front of the communion table. Hank handed Russ a candle, lit it from his own candle, and presented Russ with an envelope on which was printed in big letters, "FOR OUR PASTOR." Hank and Russ stood there holding their candles and singing in front of the people. The song got quieter and quieter and finally it faded out.

"Now pronounce the Benediction," Hank whispered.

Russ raised his arm and said, "May the light of these candles, the love of the Christ Child, and the holiness of this night remain with us through all our days. Amen."

As if by one breath, the little candles were blown out and everyone sat together in an instant of darkness. Then the lights of the church snapped on, and Richie Evans boomed forth with

"Joy to the World" on the organ with all the stops wide open. The people stood and moved through the song like an army on the march. They smacked into the chorus going full bore as if they really meant to make heaven and nature sing. Russ just stood there and listened, smiling and nodding to the people. It was another glorious moment among the Welsh.

"Nice service," Buck said on his way out the door, "except for that part about the Wise Men. Hard to tell what you were grabbing for there." Russ was willing to admit Buck was right about Eliot's poem.

WHEN THEY GOT HOME, RUSS AND ELLEN OPENED the envelope Hank Henry had presented to Russ in the flickering candlelight and found a Christmas card with a picture of a country church on it. Snow sparkled, and the lights coming through the church windows glowed. Inside the card was the interior of the church with a Nativity scene in the chancel. There was a long verse about how "OUR PASTOR" is all but perfect and that's why we love him so. There was also a check for twenty-five dollars, a Christmas blessing if there ever was one.

Next thing they knew, people were singing Christmas carols on the front porch. "My Lord," Ellen said, "it's going on one in the morning." They went down and opened the door. All the teenagers of the church and surrounding neighborhood shouted "Merry Christmas, Reverennnd."

Annie Griffiths, a bright cheeked girl of maybe fourteen, pressed forward and announced, "C'mon, Reverennnd Llewellen, you're supposed to go caroling with us while Mrs. Llewellen fixes the hot chocolate and cookies. It's the custom."

Ellen sagged. "I don't have any cookies," she said, "and how am I supposed to fix chocolate for that gang in our little pots."

"We'll figure out something," Russ said, "but let's change the custom and you come singing too." They got their coats on, their boots and scarves and gloves, and went out with the kids. Ellen had a stocking cap, but Russ was bareheaded. The snow had stopped falling. It was turning into a dark, star-filled night. Wisps of clouds reflected back the Christmas lights of the town, or maybe it was smoke rising from the culm dumps. Either way, it was lovely.

"Be sure to give Chester Lewis 'Hark the Herald,' somebody said, "he loves 'Hark the Herald.'" So they sang to Chester Lewis from the sidewalk in front of his little tipped house at the bottom of Locust Street just up from the mine. The curtain opened and an old man peered out, his constantly working mouth bunched up into what tried to be a smile. Then he began to cry.

"He does that all the time since the stroke got him," Annie said, "but he likes to hear us sing to him." When they finished the song, Chester Lewis' daughter came to the door with a sack of Welsh cookies.

"Thanks for coming, Reverennnd. Papa looks forward to this all year. Insists on staying up until the youngsters come to sing. He won't be worth a darn tomorrow, but it's what he wants. Why Mrs. Llewellen is with you there! It's the first time the minister's wife has come caroling on Christmas Eve. What a pleasant surprise for us!" She ducked inside and got another handful of cookies to put in the sack. "Merry Christmas to the both of you," she said, and the kids sang, "We Wish You a Merry Christmas and a Happy New Year."

They stopped where there were old people who couldn't get out or where people were sick or where there were handicapped children. The kids knew exactly where to go. Up and down the dark bumpy streets they went, singing as they walked, spreading a deep kind of cheer. People came to the window and waved to the youngsters even when they didn't stop at their house to sing. Everyone was waiting for the carolers to pass by. Every place they stopped they got more cookies or a Christmas cake or a breakfast roll, all homemade. Ellen didn't need to worry about not having cookies for the kids; they had several sacks full already. She had gotten into the spirit of it anyway and was singing at the top of her lungs everywhere they went.

"What a nice voice you have, Mrs. Llewellen," one of the young fellows said. "You must be part Welsh." Ellen smiled and thanked him. She didn't look much older than he was. That young man and one or two others, especially Buck Davies' sons, had clear tenor voices. You could hear them singing their parts above the others, but there wasn't one of them who didn't know how to stretch out and really sing.

Maudie Williams in her wheelchair smiled and waved from the window. Clarence Davis, who used to play cards like a demon, the kids said, came stumbling out the door on his crutch. He'd lost his left leg to diabetes. Blind Sally Morgan was led to the porch by her son, and she tilted her head and smiled a wonderful smile into the dark night. Blind and deaf Jacob Jones came out and waved his venerable blessing. And even old Goosie Thomas, Sr., big Goosie they called him, who had the black lung so bad he couldn't lie down, came jerking out on the porch behind his walker and tried to sing along on "Silent Night." The kids began to hum and let Goosie sing the words. He used to sing solos in church, someone said. It was eerie and moving and beautiful. A band of youngsters, an old dying man singing his heart away, snow on the ground, the air cold as ice, shadows cast by streetlights and Christmas lights, and young voices humming a song about a mother and her special child. That was Christmas on Welsh Hill in Scroggtown.

When they got back to the apartment, Ellen began heating milk and cocoa mix in all the little pots in the kitchen. Some of the girls spread cookies on plates and the rest of the kids crowded into the tiny living room and sat on the arms of the sofa and chairs and on the floor in front of the glowing red Christmas tree. In this neighborhood, Russ could see, it was a sign you had passed a life threshold when you could go out caroling with the minister on Christmas Eve. One of the kids got some Christmas music on the radio, and they gossiped and teased each other and seemed to have the time of their lives.

"How about Big Goosie singing 'Silent Night' at the top of his lungs?" one of them said. "His mouth looked like an owl's nest," said another.

"You know why they call him Goosie, Reverennnd?" And they all laughed.

Russ told the kids he knew, and they laughed louder. It seemed terrifically funny to them that their minister would know Big Goosie got his name from honking like a goose and grabbing the ladies' ankles as they went up the steps to church.

Another kid imitated Big Goosie's breathing—huge heaves of the chest and shoulders, then a long pause, then another huge heave and gasp, then a squeaky, croaky, expiring rendition of the first lines of "Silent Night" complete with the coughs and spits that come with the black lung. The kids thought it was hilarious, and Russ had to admit it was funny even if in terrible taste.

"Revernd's going to have a big funeral pretty soon," one of the young boys said. That's how he said it, "Revernd," the short version. He got up and shuffled around imitating old Chester Lewis coming to the door to hear the singing better. Everybody laughed at that too, and saw nothing uncharitable about it. Russ didn't try to straighten them out on that score either, though he was tempted to.

There weren't enough cups for everybody, so they had to take turns using them. A grabby kid spilled chocolate on the rug, and two or three jumped on him and made him clean it up. Kids were wandering around all four rooms of the apartment, getting hold of Russ' golf clubs now stored in his study till spring. Playing with his putter, they slammed golf balls against the walls and into the nooks and crannies of the room, where they stayed. They nosed around his desk and shelves, but didn't seem to disturb anything there. Girls went in and out of the bathroom in pairs for reasons that Russ found a mystery ever since high school. The boys pushed and pulled on each other, dropped cookies on the floor, and stepped on them. Ellen cringed. There is something pretty awful about a stepped-on Welsh cookie. It spreads like putty and grinds into the rug and the currents break open and form splotches of thick brown paste.

About five in the morning, the phone rang. Probably Edgar from downstairs, Russ thought, fit to be tied for all the ruckus, but it was Martha Griffiths wondering where her Annie was. Russ took that for a sign and announced it was time to break up the party. Lo and behold, the kids settled right down, got into their coats and hats and headed out the door, full of appreciation for a wonderful Christmas Eve. Several stayed and helped clean up, which took another hour or so. As the last ones left, the first light of Christmas morning was breaking over the hills to the east.

"Hey, Ellen," Russ said, "you tired?"

"Hey, Reverend," she said, "you kidding?"

"Let's watch the sun come up before we go to bed."

Ellen brought coats and blankets and they wrapped themselves in them and stood on the porch in the ten-degree morning. The world was absolutely quiet. A misty light crept over the town and fell on the snow on rooftops, wires, old fences, and on the broken metal frame of the breaker standing by the entrance to the abandoned mine. The natural shapes of hills and trees seemed connected to the angled geometries of what humans had fashioned. In that light, it all blended together, tree shape and house shape, limb line and power line, everything a variation on the same color and texture. The steep roofs no longer seemed severe. The long snow tinged wires drooping gently from pole to pole looked as if they had evolved there. Even the TV antennas high above the houses seemed to be there to tell the world there really might be a harmonious arrangement that our very souls inhabit.

"Ellen, look," Russ said, "look at this town right now. It's different. It's beautiful. Nobody sees it like this but us." But Ellen was asleep, leaning against his shoulder. He lifted her as best he could and tried to carry her upstairs, but couldn't manage it. Too many clothes and blankets. They stumbled up the stairs together and got into bed.

On Christmas day they got up late and opened their presents to each other. Ellen was happy with her new warm coat with what looked like a mink collar but wasn't. Russ unwrapped the large round box containing Ellen's present to him and found a gentleman's brown felt hat much like Brother Henry wore, except his had a wider brim and was black. It seemed like the strangest thing in the world to Russ, and he doubted he would ever wear it except maybe to a costume party.

THE SECOND DAY AFTER CHRISTMAS, Ellen and Russ took the train from Scranton and rode through the Poconos to Hoboken, New Jersey, where they caught the ferry to Manhattan. Christmas cards from family had brought in a total of a hundred thirty-five dollars, and they put that with the twenty-five dollar bonus from the church and decided to blow it on a couple of days in the big city. Ellen wore the new, fur collared coat Russ had gotten her for Christmas at the Globe store in Scranton, but the new felt hat from Reese Haberdashers remained in its box back home.

They stayed two nights at the Hotel Taft, went to the Guggenheim, ate at Momma Leoni's, and saw "Camelot" with Robert Goulet making his Broadway debut. They also bought Ellen a red and blue wool skirt and jacket at B. Altman's and listened to an unknown, young, and terribly emaciated woman jazz singer at a joint in Greenwich Village. In all this, Russ found himself to be the only bareheaded male in New York City, and his head was freezing.

Their adventure ended at one in the morning with them eating hamburgers costing six dollars each in the bar of the Hotel Taft, which was about the last of their money. It was all rush and push and get out of the way, and they suffered from indigestion and exhaustion and enjoyed themselves immensely. Then they took the train down to the seminary for Hoppsy and Gert's wedding in Miller Chapel.

It was windy and sleety when they got to Princeton Junction and caught the shuttle that took them to the edge of the university. They walked to the seminary just as darkness was falling. No one was around. The empty campus quadrangle, the leafless, snow-packed trees, and the white colonial chapel seemed severe and overly Calvinistic. The old Princeton feel of being among books and comrades was not there at all. Maybe it was the weather or maybe it was that Russ was being weaned from school by the realities of Scroggtown, he didn't know. The chapel was open, so they went in and sat down.

By a bit after six o'clock, twenty or so people had gathered in the cold chapel and sat here and there in the pews. Professor Beeners of the speech department came out from a side door in a plain black robe and stood in the center of the chancel as Hoppsy and Gert marched down the aisle toward him. The sound of their heels hitting the floor was all that was heard. The emptiness of the place, the coldness of the room and the stark ring of heels on tiles gave the sense of a huge stone cathedral that Protestants were somehow desecrating with their simple ceremony. The guests were invited to form a circle in the chancel, everyone holding hands for the final prayer. Then the bride and groom and their guests went to the Princeton Inn for a fine dinner, a little wine, some proper toasts, and the most intelligent of best wishes ever expressed, all very Princetonian.

Russ was glad when it was time to leave. He and Ellen took the little tram out to Princeton Junction where they caught the train back north. Scroggtown, not Princeton, was home now. It came to Russ like a discovery.

"I can't remember anything at the seminary being so restrained," Russ said as they rode along. "It didn't seem like Hoppsy at all."

"I don't know why they didn't have music," Ellen said. "That chapel is cold and has a spooky ring to it."

"It never did before," Russ said. He wondered if he had been captured by the warmth and singing of his congregation and, maybe, by his role as one through whom blessings flow. For all their foibles, he was willing to admit, his parishioners were lively and interesting, and they were putting up with him, for which he was grateful.

NEXT DAY, IN SCROGGTOWN, THE WEATHER WAS even colder than in New York. There was nothing for Russ to do but wear his new gentleman's hat. It stood on his head like a dark brown model boat, he felt, its crown seeming too tall for its narrow brim. Russ felt ridiculous wearing this hat, but it was that or freeze the top of his head off. As he walked about the parish, he could see that the ladies looked at him approvingly, and he fell naturally into tipping his new hat to them. "Good morning, Mrs. Morgan, Good morning Mrs. Davis, Mrs., Lewis, Mrs. Williams, Mrs. Jones, Mrs. Jones, Mrs. Jones," speak a greeting, tip the hat, and receive a respectful nod and smile. Russ was getting his exercise just by tipping his hat.

When the men came home from work and saw Russ walking about in his new hat, they expressed approval. "Ah, Reverennnd, now you are wearing a proper haht," Hank Henry called out as Russ came down the sidewalk from a late afternoon pastoral visit. So did Buck Davies and any number of others. "A fine haht you're wearing there now, Reverennnd. A fine and proper haht," they said.

The very next Sunday, his little wool cap was hanging on the hook at the back of the church where he had left it on the fourth Sunday of Advent.

16

Money Matters

JUST BEFORE THE SERVICE ON THE FIRST SUNDAY of January, Russ got a note from Billy Jones, Church Treasurer, asking him to announce from the pulpit that the Annual Report would soon be published. Simple enough, Russ thought, so that's what he did. Then he began to wonder what this Annual Report reported. After the service, he asked Clerk of Session Hank Henry, and good old Hank hemmed and hawed and told Russ it's not anything he needed to be concerned with, it happens every year about this time.

"It seems to me," Russ said to Hank, "if I'm making an announcement to the congregation, I should know what it's about."

"Well, you got a point there, Reverennnd," Hank said. And he explained that this was a financial report that told how much was given to the church during the year, to which was attached a list of every member's name showing the amount they had contributed.

"Hank, that's wrong," Russ howled, "you can't let everyone know what people give. It's confidential information, between them and God."

"The ministers always say that," Hank said, "but hell, Reverennnd, excuse my French, if we tried to do it confidential, we wouldn't raise enough to pay you." That this decent and orderly Clerk of Session would use the word "hell" in his minister's presence showed Russ he was dead serious. And Russ was serious about getting paid, which made for a complicated situation.

"So what happens, Hank? I make this announcement, and then they all get a report in the mail with all the giving spelled out for everyone to see. And that's what keeps the money coming in?"

"It's something like that. Next week, I expect, you'll be asked to announce the Annual Report has been delayed a week, so if people want to make a donation it will count for last year and they won't have a "none" after their name. Sometimes I think we've got more "nones" than they got at St. Anne's Monastery over in Scranton." Hank chuckled at his pun.

"I'm not going to say that, Hank," Russ said. "No power on earth could make me tell the people to get their money in to avoid being a 'none.'"

"No, no, Reverend, you don't have to tell them that. Just say, 'The Annual Report has been delayed a week.' They'll know what it means. It's the only way, Reverennnd. It usually takes two or three delays to make the budget, but this year, since we were without a minister most of the time, I think one delay might do it."

"Yeah, I expect it would," Russ said. "If you didn't have a minister you wouldn't have to publish the report at all, isn't that it?"

"Now c'mon, Russ, don't get like that," Hank said. It was the first time he had called Russ anything but Reverennnd, the first time any of them had. "We've had lots of ministers here, and like I say, all of them, except the ones from Wales, they hated the Annual Report, but it's the only way we could get the money to pay them. We need a minister. Without a minister there's no church. And we're tickled to death to have you and Mrs. Llewellen here. It's wonderful to have a young Welsh couple leading us. That Reverend Thomas before you, he was Welsh in name only. People didn't take to him. You, we can tell you're Welsh whether you know it or not. It's how you talk to us, and how you appreciate the hymns. You're doin' us a lot of good you know."

"Frankly, Hank, most of the time it seems like I'm just bumbling through. I wonder if I'm cut out for this at all," Russ said.

"It takes time to learn," Hank said. "You're doin' just fine, but don't make a big fuss over the Annual Report. It's just the way it's done. You've heard of the Scotchman bein' tight? Well, you haven't even got close to bein' tight 'til you meet a Welshman. But you ought to know that, your name bein' Llewellen, like it is." Clearly, making a stand against the Annual Report was more trouble than it's worth, the new minister began to feel. Little by little they get you, Russ could see. They make you one of them, and then how are you supposed to uphold the power and purity of your calling like they taught you in preacher school?

"Hank," Russ said, "is there anything else I should know about this? So long as it's going to be done this way, no use my fouling it up because I don't know what's happening?"

"Well," he said, looking out of the corner of his eye and grinning a little knowing grin, a trait of most of the elders, "there may be one thing more worth knowing about. Don't give more than Buck."

"What?" Russ said.

"Don't give more than Buck. He gives the most. He's done it for years. Buck considers it his place to give the most that anybody gives to the church. I would hate to see him if he got embarrassed about that."

Russ could see that if he hadn't taken Hank aside and shaken all this loose, he wouldn't have known any of it. He decided to see if he could find out more about the unseen workings of the congregation.

"Hank," he said, "tell me what the deal was about my little wool cap going missing and then turning up again on the hook in the back of the church where I left it. It seems to me that wasn't just a matter of lost and found."

"Oh that," Hank said, a big smile on his face. "It's like this, Reverennnd. You have to realize that your little cap is the kind of hat coal miners wear into the mines. They roll it up and put it in their pocket while they're wearin' those miners' helmets, then put their caps back on when they go to the saloon for their dustcutter. That's not the kind of hat for a minister to wear. A minister should wear a proper hat and tip it to the ladies as he passes them by. That's why your hat turned up missing for a while, Reverennnd." Hank nodded as if hiding the minister's hat was perfectly normal church policy and practice.

"So why didn't someone just tell me?" Russ asked.

"It's not our way," Hank said.

Russ thanked Hank for his time. It was probably the most valuable conversation he'd had up to then. What a hopeless mixture of faith and pettiness it all is, he thought. And he could see his mother was probably right about professional clergy. If it weren't for feeding and housing the minister, the church could get by very nicely. The whole budget was but $10,000, of which Russ cost them about half when you add in pension and medical insurance. And there were over three hundred people on the rolls, more than a hundred households. A hundred pledges of a hundred dollars a year would do it. There must be a lot of "nones" in this congregation, Russ figured.

"Guess what," Russ said to Ellen when he got home, "they consider us Welsh"

"Wonderful," she said, and went back to studying.

IN THE THIRD WEEK OF JANUARY, with a break in the weather, Russ got up early and headed the Saab out along the Susquehanna River through Wilkes Barre, Berwick and on to the college town of Bloomsburg where, in a suburb just to the north, his predecessor, Reverend T. Calvin Thomas, was now Senior Pastor of the Westminster Presbyterian Church. Russ had looked him up in the roll of Presbyterian ministers and then called and told him he would be passing through Bloomsburg and wondered if they could get together for coffee. Reverend Thomas said he was very busy, but would be glad to give Russ an hour at eleven the next morning. And so at that very hour, in an impressive brownstone building with a huge stained glass window of Jesus at prayer, Russ found the receptionist and was announced to the busy pastor in his office behind double oak doors.

"Come in, Reverend Llewellen," Reverend Thomas said, extending his hand, "how are things among the Welsh of Scroggtown?" His speech had a lilt to it, but it also hinted at a patronizing tone.

"Well," Russ said, "it's hard to tell. We had a lot of people in church during Advent and Christmas, but now it's half empty every Sunday, and there's some pettiness going on."

"Typical, typical," Thomas said. "Those Welsh, they sing like angels and fight like snakes. But then you must be Welsh yourself, with a name like Llewellen."

"I'm just learning about being Welsh," Russ said. "I never considered myself anything in particular before coming to Scroggtown. But then with a name like Thomas, there must be some Welsh in you too."

"No, we're English," Thomas said. "My people left Wales behind before Saint David's time, and nobody in the family remembers when that was. Owing to my name, I suppose, I served a church in Wales and managed to learn a bit of that impossible language." He chuckled as he picked up his phone and ordered coffee brought in. The receptionist appeared almost immediately with a tray that held two cups of steaming coffee, sugar and cream, and two small ginger snap cookies.

"Thank you," Russ said, as he took a cup and a cookie. "This is the first coffee I've had without a Welsh cookie in a long time."

"Oh, those Welsh cookies," Thomas said, "how do you find them? They seemed to drop into my stomach like ingots of lead."

"Some are better than others, all right," Russ said, "but Mary Henry's are very good, and the ladies use her recipe for the ones they sell at the church, as you know."

"Ah yes, Welsh Cookie Wednesday and Clam Chowder Wednesday on alternate weeks. The church goes forth on Welsh cookies and clam chowder. I never could break them of the habit of selling their wares for the glory of God. I'm glad to be away from there." Thomas was on the edge of being derisive, as if he considered it better to be English than Welsh and so for that reason it was necessary to express an aversion to Welsh cookies.

Russ asked some questions about what Reverend Thomas knew about Buck, about Hughie Saloony and the refusal to take money from him, about the ministers in the Ministers Association, and about the workings of the Presbytery of Lackawanna. Reverend Thomas did not have much to say about any of it, except that he advised Russ to make short his stay in Scroggtown. "If you stay very long in a place like that, you can get stuck there," he said.

Finally, Russ asked, "What's this business about a missing $10,000? It seems strange to me, from what little I've been told."

"I thought that might come up," Thomas said. "Did they send you out here to ask me about it? They probably think I took it and then left. Well, you need to know I was trying to leave that church for a couple of years before the money turned up missing. I never saw it, in fact. If there was $10,000 on the table that night, it wasn't in plain sight. I think the whole story may have been made up to put their Welsh hex on me, if there is such a thing." Reverend Thomas, then turned his face squarely to Russ and said slowly and emphatically, "You go back and tell them to stop accusing me of this. I'll not stand for it. If word of their implication gets out, they will have a suit on their hands. I can promise you that." He let his hands fall onto his knees with a slap, and nothing was said for a time.

"If there was money on that table, and it disappeared," Russ ventured at last, "who there might have taken it?"

"To me, that's a hypothetical question. But if I were in your place, I might ask myself, Who among the elders bought a car recently, or put up aluminum siding, or any number of things, remodeled the kitchen, got a new roof, went on a trip?" Reverend Thomas was exasperated. His tone was becoming shrill, and he was looking at his watch. Russ could see he had ruined the good pastor's morning. "And you, Llewellen," Thomas went on, extending his hand to end the conversation, "you do well to get your dossier in order and start soon to pave the way for a quick exit from Scroggtown. It's the kind of place that can bring you down."

"Thanks for your time, and thanks for the coffee," Russ said, and quickly left.

Walking to his car, Russ wondered why Reverend Thomas would say he hadn't seen the money. To protect himself perhaps, but according to the elders' account, he would have seen Aunt Alice lay it on the table. And, Russ was aware, one elder has a new stove, another has new siding, and one talks about a two week fishing trip to Canada last summer

With Russ mulling such thoughts, the Saab putted along the two lane concrete road, and every tar separator sent a bump through the shock absorbers. He stopped for lunch at a silvery diner alongside the road and had some good chili and a piece of apple pie with ice cream and coffee. With the late afternoon traffic through Wilkes Barre and Scranton, it took him the rest of the day to get home.

ON WELSH HILL, THE SEASON OF THE EPIPHANY was the time for people who were sick a long time to get it over with and die. It was as if they were hanging on until after Christmas but weren't all that interested in Lent with its forty days of solemnity, even if Easter waits there at the end of it all. It's just too much trouble, apparently. Or maybe spring is too burdensome if you're on your way to the grave, better just relax, leave off breathing, and be lowered into the snow covered, half-frozen ground. In any case, Russ was called to attend operations, heart failures, assorted cancers, the last stages of emphysema which come with black lung disease and then to officiate at the funerals. First hospital, then nursing home, then funeral home, then back to the house for a "little lunch," then do it again.

Many of these folks never came to church, but they were connected to someone who did. That seemed to mean Russ was expected to give them the best of Presbyterian prayers and the finest send-off he could muster, which he found himself more than willing to do. He took on these responsibilities with a growing sense of usefulness. He also noticed that often the family of the unchurched deceased would be in church after the funeral. They were just the opposite of solid church members who were likely to stay away from church for a time after a death in the family, giving themselves a chance to gather courage for facing a host of sympathizers.

And so Russ learned the Funeral Service almost as well as he knew the Communion Service from yelling it into Jacob Jones' left ear. That in itself was something, he allowed. And he got ten dollars for just about every funeral he conducted, which gave him and Ellen a little extra to go to the checkered table cloth Italian place in Old Forge once in a while and have some good pasta and maybe a half bottle of Chianti.

"These raviolis are in loving memory of Maude Lewis," he would tell her, "and this Chianti comes to us by way of the grieving relatives of Mr. Robert Roberts."

"Cheers," Ellen would say, and they laughed little devilish laughter.

17

Jacob Jones Is Laid to Rest

A ND SO IT WAS DURING THE COLD AND SNOWY season when death stalked Welsh Hill that Jacob Jones, the venerable elder, slipped away from this world. He didn't fall. He wasn't sick. He gave no sign. He simply got up one bright morning near the end of February, dressed himself in gray slacks, white shirt, and red cardigan sweater, ate his ample breakfast of eggs, sausage, toast, and dark tea, sat down in his chair by the window, held his head, gave out a groan, and quietly died.

"What a way to go," people said. "Leave it to old Jacob. He knew how to live and he knew how to die." Russ suspected that his parishioners' admiration for Jacob's way of dying came, in part at least, from their fear of spending their last years in a nursing home strapped to a bed, as any number of their loved ones were doing.

The day of Jacob's funeral dawned blustery cold. The snow wasn't so much falling as blowing sideways, stinging the faces of those entering the church for the service. Reverend Rhys Jeremiah Davies had been asked to preach the sermon. He was an old friend of Jacob's, well into his eighties himself, having retired in Scroggtown from parishes in Scranton and other parts of the hard coal country. Why anyone would retire in Scroggtown, Russ didn't know. A Welshman wanting to be near the Welsh, he guessed.

Born in Wales, Davies had been a Calvinistic Methodist, a major church body there. He immigrated with his family to Scranton where his father dug coal all his life. But RJ, as they called him, was spared that fate. He finished high school with excellent marks and got a scholarship to Lehigh University and then to Princeton Seminary. At his ordination, he became a member of the Welsh Presbytery in Northeastern Pennsylvania. At the time, the Presbyterian Church allowed ethnic groups to have their own jurisdictions that transcended Presbytery boundaries, and so the Welsh Presbytery included congregations in a large section of eastern Pennsylvania. Up until about 1950, most all these churches held services in the Welsh language. No more than five years before he arrived on the scene, Russ learned, the Welsh Presbyterian Church of Scroggtown had an evening service in Welsh each Sunday, and Reverend R. J. Davies often led them. In the old days, Russ was told by several parishioners, people went to church at ten in the morning and after services they sat for two hours of Sunday School. Then they went home and ate a huge dinner, slept and belched through the afternoon, and returned to church at about five for the Welsh service of preaching and songs.

"All we did the whole day was go to church," the women told him. "We cooked on Saturday night for Sunday. No cooking on the Sabbath, no, no. It gave us the whole day for church and family, which was nice. And the ministers prepared two sermons and a long Bible lesson every week."

Russ didn't see how they did it, but Reverend R. J. Davies was one who did. He and Jacob, in fact, had resisted the encroachment of the English language into the Welsh congregations. They started a Welsh language school in the church basement so the youngsters would be taught what they called the "idiom of the angels." "They'll need to be able to speak to the heavenly host when they get to paradise," Jacob once said to Russ with a smirk, "so we teach them Welsh. That doesn't mean they shouldn't know English. No, we have to bend with the times, Reverennnd, but we give up the old ways to our peril."

By Russ' time, the churches of the Welsh Presbytery had been absorbed into the regular Presbyteries, and only rarely, when someone born in the old country was available, was a service held in Welsh. Yes, the old sounds and syllables were dying away. Jacob's funeral brought them back to life again, at least for an afternoon.

People dressed in black, heads bent against the blowing snow, streamed into the church on the corner of Locust and Main. They found pews, squeezed in, sat down, and promptly at two, without announcement, Organist Richie Evans began to play beloved Welsh hymns. They sang Aberystwyth, "Jesus, lover of my soul, / Let me to thy bosom fly," in all its ponderousness. They sang "Lead, kindly Light, amid th'encircling gloom," to the tune Sandon, the hymn that was sung after an explosion in the mines. Reverend Davies sang in Welsh, as did a number of others. It seemed to Russ that though the language appears to be all consonants, it sounds like all vowels in tones particularly suited to reaching into the heart of sorrow in song.

The tunes were slow and weighty, but also steady and sure. Many dipped into minor keys. When the Chorister directed the congregation to draw out a note at the end of a line, it was like an animal howl— hurt, defiant, strong. The music cast a shadowy, Celtic spell, and the people drew upon their heritage of privation and survival to give homage to Jacob, the benevolent mine foreman and venerable elder of the church. Russ could hear it in every note they sang. The words of the hymns were often deep mournful chords rather than segments of lines in a poem.

At the front of the church, there was a huge, bronze colored open casket. Jacob reclined in it, slightly propped up on a white satin pillow, his large black Bible lying open in his gnarled hands. Flowers in rising banks towered above the casket so that much of the choir loft could not be seen. Russ had nothing to do with these arrangements, and had not been told about them. It was, apparently, what was done for a venerable elder.

Soon the sanctuary overflowed with people, many of them of the older generation. The doors into the sanctuary were left open so extra chairs could spill out into the narthex. Younger people got up and stood in the corners of the room, around the organ, and on both sides of the platform where Russ and Reverend Davies sat in the velvet covered chairs behind the pulpit. Ninety-three year old Jacob had not outlived his community or his sterling reputation.

When the final falling notes of Sandon drifted into silence, Russ went to the pulpit and read several of the Psalms, every one of which Jacob had known by heart and, in ringing tones, had recited to Russ time and again during their visits. Russ put all he knew of Jacob into the magnificent Psalm 90, which says the days of our years are threescore years and ten, but even if they are four-score years, their strength is soon cut off. Russ wished to say this was only partly true in Jacob's case. His blindness was certainly a sorrow, but light still shone in him right to the end. When he came to "So teach us to number our days, / That we may apply our hearts unto wisdom," Russ brought into his voice all the purpose-fulness he could muster, for surely that is what Jacob had done. He had applied his heart and had become wise. And then, with Jacob before them as the example, Russ concluded quietly, "And let the beauty of the Lord our God be upon us: / And establish the work of our hands upon us; / Yea, the work of our hands, establish thou it." And he spent a few ticks of the clock looking upon Jacob's work scarred hands holding his precious Bible opened to the very Psalm Russ had just read. The people followed Russ' gaze and focused on Jacob's hands and the holy book they held.

Charlene Jones Latinsky, her huge voice trembling throughout, sang an impassioned Penparc, the simplest and most profound of Welsh funeral hymns.

> Jesus I live to Thee,
> The Loveliest and Best,

> My Life in Thee, Thy life in me,
> In Thy blest love I rest.

The tune is so simple, most of it seeming to be the same note with a minor chord here and there, the third line rising into a cry of longing and then falling into the quieter fourth line. It seemed to take her five minutes to sing those four lines. Russ had never heard anything so moving.

She sang even slower when she came to the second stanza:

> Living or dying, Lord,
> I know not which is best
> To live in Thee is bliss to me,
> To die is endless rest.

Russ shuddered a little. It felt to him like these words rose up from the earth itself, rose up from the lives of those who went down into the mines.

CHARLENE WAS A DISTANT RELATIVE OF JACOB, but, Russ could see, there is little distance in these kinds of Welsh connections, especially at funerals. It seemed like down deep everyone had the same last name, and that name was Wales. Charlene sang her soul away for the venerable Jacob, and her trembling heart pulled upon every heart in the room.

Then Reverend Davies rose to preach. He was a little man, thin and thin faced, gray hair still thick and slightly wavy. In his black, well pressed suit he seemed a slight presence among the large crowd and teeming flowers. He stood silently, looking upon the people, fixing this one and that one with his eyes, acknowledging old friends with a slight nod, not saying a word. His manner spoke of the gravity with which he took this moment. The longer he stood there, the more power he seemed to absorb. It was as if he was increasing in size, taking up more and more space in everyone's attention. Pretty soon, little R. J. Davies was the central figure in the room. The heaviness of the heated air and the closeness of the crowded quarters became details rather than forces upon the scene, and the flowers and the casket and even Jacob Jones lying there with his Bible in his hands were no longer the main attractions. By the very way he stood and looked into the eyes of the people in the congregation, Reverend Davies communicated significance. Something profound was about to happen, he seemed to indicate. What was coming was worth everything.

"Ahn old mahn, full of years, is gathered into the lahnd of his people," he began. His voice was high pitched, flowing, on the edge of song. "This is a text from the Book of Genesis describing the burial of Abraham." "Ahbrrahahm," is how he said it, with all the "a" sounds soft and drawn out, a light trill on the "r" and a lift on the last syllable. "Ahn old mahn, full of years, is gathered into the lahnd of his people," he said a second time.

Looking upon Jacob Jones, Reverend Davies said, "This mahn was an Ahbrrahahm among us. He heard the voice of God. He received the promise. And he came to a new lahnd to seek a better way. And he was a Jacob too, the father of many clahns." Davies stretched the history of Jacob the elder of the church back to those earliest Biblical days when forebears of the Hebrew people left their home in Ur of the Chaldee Mountain to seek a land flowing with milk and honey, and he pressed it forward to the days when the Welsh came to northeastern Pennsylvania hoping for better lives. He went back and forth from scriptural times to present day Scroggtown until any distance between them was gone. Then he paused and looked upon Jacob's family sitting in the Holiness of Holinesses, which the elders had given to them for the afternoon. "You and I are members of Jacob's clahn," Davies said. "We mourn him, yet we also honor him as a patriarch of our people. An old mahn, full of years, is gathered into the lahnd of his people."

The phrases rolled off the preacher's tongue like a brook flowing through a meadow, Russ thought. There was never a hitch or delay, only rising and falling tones and reliable cadences. It was as if a musical score was in the preacher's mind. Davies was a magnificent preacher, but little by little, the fact that he was a magnificent preacher didn't matter, which made it all the more magnificent. What mattered was what he said and how it sounded as it reached for the people's souls. It was all that mattered to him, and thus it became all that mattered to those who heard him.

"Ours is a heritage of countless persons," Davies proclaimed. "The God of Abrrahahm, Isaac, and Jahcob is our God as well." He paused again and looked here and there at the people. He looked toward the family and caught the eye of Jacob's son, Isaac Jones, and said it again, quietly. "The God of Abraham, Isaac, and Jacob. The God of our Lord Jesus Christ." Davies moved from Jacob of old to Jacob Jones of Scroggtown in a flash, as if it was a most natural way to describe human reality. The identifications were by now so close it was possible to feel that all these Biblical figures, including Jesus himself, were right there in the room. In a matter of minutes, Davies had spun out a world in which all of history is in the present moment, and the present moment is charged with possibilities engendered by all of history. Jesus and Jacob of old are part of the same story, he was saying, and so is Jacob, the venerable elder of the church and foreman in the mines, and so are those gathered to mourn him. "This story does not end in our dying. It never ends. We are born to it anew breath by breath." Davies not only said this in words, his very posture made it seem to be so.

"The dead do not leave us," Reverend Davies went on, "they bind us to themselves, to those who have died and those yet to be born. They speak the fullness of their lives in the silence of their death. We find we are as much influenced by the dead as by the living. We find the dead speaking to us every day, even as old Jacob speaks to us today of all his living taught him and all it teaches us. We find that life has a completeness that could not exist without our dying. 'An old mahn, full of years, is gathered into the lahnd of his people.'"

Then Davies turned again to the chief mourners at the front of the church and said softly, almost in a whisper, but with enough support beneath it for everyone to hear, "Our grief is also a satisfaction. Our sorrow tells us that we have cared deeply, even as my sorrow for my friend Jacob speaks to me of my love for him. Our humanity consists of more than breathing for a time, it is also participation in the breath of God by which we live and move and have our being."

With a full heart, Reverend Davies brought the ancient words of faith and the lyrical sound of his Welsh soul together before the gathering, and the people were absorbing it all. The little man took leaps of meaning as if one thought led naturally to the other in ways that go well beyond neat reason. He moved from ancient text to current life, from Wales to Pennsylvania, and from person to person around the room, weaving an immaculate wholeness of spirit and flesh. "This divine oneness is blessedly ours to inhabit, if we but pause long enough to behold it," he said. "And in the beholding we live new lives day by day. This can never be taken away from us. We are part of life eternal, just as Jacob Jones is now. Ahn old mahn, full of years is gathered into the lahnd of his people. And so are we gathered with him this day to be among all those who live and die. Let us give thanks and sing praises for this eternal oneness with those who die that is ours by the grace of God. We sing our praises here and now as Jacob sings with the angels forever and ever. Blessed be. Ahmen and ahmen." The people nodded. They smiled slight smiles. And a kind of peace settled upon them, it seemed to Russ.

Russ could see, at least for the moment, why he would want to be a minister. Tenuous as it is, this sort of thing happens. An intimation of a blessed comprehensive reality comes forth in a preacher's utterance. Try to put a value on it and you're lost. Try to explain it to somebody and they have a right to think you're crazy. Try to prove it's literally true, and you fail. But, as Reverend R. J. Davies preached for his friend Jacob Jones, a blessed world emerged, and Russ knew he wanted to be part of the process that helps bring this about. If only such things as this wouldn't happen, he thought, if only faith was always froth and phoniness and flim flam, if only it was nothing but empty ritual and mind-numbing meetings down at The Coal Bin, then I could get out clean. I could leave this silly profession and get a real job. But then somebody dabs an eye when I break the communion bread, or somebody sings Penparc and it feels like the sky is going to open up and weep, or somebody preaches into the heart of grief and everyone feels resurrected somehow, feels it even if there isn't any way to explain it, even if they don't what is called "believe" it. It is more than mere believing, Russ could see, but what is it?

Russ could tell he was on dangerous ground. If he let Davies get through to him, it would be hard to break loose from the jello mold of being called "Revvverrrennnd." But there was no help for it; Davies was getting through. There was something about the sound of those words, the tone of that voice, the purposeful cadence of inspired phrases that Russ couldn't shake free from. Maybe dangerous ground is holy ground, he thought.

With the sermon ended, they began to sing Cwm Rhondda, the hymn Russ had been overwhelmed by in his first service in Scroggtown. This time the singing was slower and more controlled, a measured march through "this barren land" to the "healing streams," to the "verge of Jordan," and finally to safety on "Canaan's side." Then Chorister Jenkins asked for more volume and even a slower pace. "Songs of praises, songs of praises, I will ever give to Thee," they sang over and over, slower and stronger each time. It seemed to Russ they would sing this one phrase on into the night. Among these folks, ever and always, whatever else there is, there is always this overriding call to sing songs of praise. Russ was glad it was up to Reverend Davies to pronounce the benediction. Once again, he would have found it hard to speak.

Almost everyone at the church got into the funeral procession to the graveyard high up on Welsh Hill. A long line of cars with their lights on wended their way through town. Russ and Reverend Davies rode in the hearse at the head of the line. As the retinue passed by shops and stores, everything stopped. People stood quietly. Men took off their hats until all the mourners' cars were gone. This was the way of death in Scroggtown. Everyone, of whatever heritage or tradition, paid respect to the one in the hearse and the mourners following behind in their cars. For Jacob, it was a good long pause in the activities of the day.

The graveside service among mounds of icy snow took but a few minutes. The grave, like many of the older gravesites there, lay beneath the outstretched arms of a huge white wooden cross that towered over everything around. Welsh Hill rose to its peak behind it in a bramble of woods and low brush. The ground was frozen, so Jacob's grave could not be dug that day. His casket rested above ground with flowers strewn around it, some beginning to freeze where they lay. Reverend Davies read the verses of assurance and committal, and Russ was given the nod to say the final blessing. He raised his arm and projected the words as fully as he could into the cold air: "O Lord, support us all the day long, until the shadows lengthen, and the evening comes, and the busy world is hushed, and the fever of life is over, and our work is done; then, in thy mercy, grant us a safe lodging, a holy rest, and peace at the last, through Jesus Christ our Lord. Amen." Even with that brevity, people were shivering and eager to get into their cars.

THE "LITTLE LUNCH" BACK AT ISAAC JONES' HOUSE across the street from the church was the full spread of ham, hot potato salad, cold potato salad, beets and beans, pickles and olives, and several platters of Welsh cookies. No beer or booze of any kind, just coffee and Welsh tea that is blacker and stronger than coffee.

People talked in little groups and told stories of the old days, remembering what their parents or grandparents had said about the boat trip from Wales and about starting out in Pennsylvania. "These were all company towns in those days, Reverennnd, and the stores were company stores," somebody said. "They worked all

214

week and found they owed the store more than their pay. Still they did it, and here we are."

And they talked about the church and the former preachers who preached in Welsh and had voices that seemed like the angels singing the tenor part. They talked about the Gymanfa Ganus, grand gatherings for singing Welsh hymns, and the Eistedfodds, the singing competitions where the winning singers, while standing in front of the crowd, would have small leather purses full of money hung on little ropes around their necks. Russ just took it all in, collecting elements of his own heritage in this indirect way. My name isn't Llewellen for nothing, he thought, and now I'm learning what that means.

Buck was holding forth with a group of men around Jacob's favorite chair by the window. "Reverennnd," he said, "listen to this one," and he told one of the stories about an old Welshman with the death rattle that seemed to be high humor on Welsh Hill. "'Maud, Maud,' the old man shouts from his bed to his wife downstairs," Buck said in a hoarse and halting voice, "'is that ham your cookin' now? Is it hahm you're cookin', Maudy dear?' And Maud hollers back, 'Shut up, old mahn. It's for your funeral.'" Though they surely had heard it many times before, the men around Buck laughed. Russ wondered if there was an undercurrent of darkness in these people. "Jacob became foreman in the mines right after Davy Williams threw himself in the slag pond," an old friend of Jacob's was saying. "O that Davy, what a black spirit of a man. A terror to work for, too. It's not good to say, Reverennnd, but it was a pleasure to see him go. Then Jacob took over for him and treated everyone right."

"It was the drink got Davy," Buck said. "He and my old man used to tie one on every night after work. They were the best customers Saloony ever had. Ma would throw a bucket of water on him as he came up the back porch. 'Get the water ready, Buckie, your father's comin' home,' she would say. It washed the coal dust off him and sobered him up in one big splash. Though sometimes it would make him mad, and he would chase us with whatever he could pick up, chairs, sticks, brooms, it didn't matter. Bad as his condition was, he could run pretty good. But we wore him down before he got us."

So that's how Buck came to be Buck, Russ thought. "We're just simple folks here, Reverennnd, never had all the advantages," he would say. He felt cheated out of what could have been. He was a bright guy and had to go to work early to keep his father in drink, and then the old tippler would stumble home and chase him around with a broom or something worse. Buck had a big ball of resentment stuck in his craw, and who could blame him? And here comes the minister of his church with all his degrees and his gentleman's hat which must be a constant reminder to Buck of what he might have become had things been different. Buck was angry with his father, Russ realized. The minister, whatever age he happened to be, was the closest thing to a father Buck had, and his resentment landed right there. Buck was sitting in Jacob's chair revealing the deep truth about himself without really knowing that's what he was doing. Yes, Buck was sometimes a self-righteous ass, but he was also sharp and articulate and had a story to tell, Russ could see.

"What did the ministers say about drinking in those days? Did they preach temperance? Did they support Prohibition," Russ asked.

"To a man," Buck said, "even though a lot of them met for coffee of an afternoon and drank their whiskey out of proper cups and saucers. In a Welsh coal town there's two kinds of drinking, open heathen drinking and the secret Christian kind. I think the secret Christian kind is worse." It's amazing what you can learn, if you just ask questions and then shut up, Russ noticed once again.

As Russ made the rounds, he met the Welsh from other congregations, people named Davis, Thomas, Jones, Williams, Roberts, Morgan, Reese, and all the rest of those Welsh names that Russ had thought of as basic American names until he got to Scroggtown. They had come from miles around to honor Jacob by singing great hymns, hearing a magnificent sermon, and now talking, laughing, and eating as much ham and potato salad as could be carried from the kitchen. Russ sat down on the couch to drink tea, eat a Welsh cookie and listen to what was being said. Standing behind him, Billy Jones, the Church Treasurer and Hank Henry, Clerk of Session, were talking about the missing ten thousand dollars.

"If we had that money," Hank was saying, "we could think about buying our new minister a house to live in, maybe that place next to Aunt Sophie's near the church. Aunt Alice rents it out, but I heard she wants to sell it. Of course it would take some fixin' up, but we could do that ourselves." Billy Jones agreed that with ten thousand dollars the church could probably buy that house and have some money left to pay the chorister a little more of what he deserved. Aware of Carson and Judy Whitlock's experience, Russ wasn't sure he wanted them to buy a manse for him and Ellen to live in, but it would be good not to have old Edgar Howells listening for every squeak of the bedsprings and calling about every drop of water they used. Russ leaned back into Hank and Billy's conversation while seeming to pay attention to what Buck was saying across from him. For one thing, it meant these leaders of the church were interested in keeping Russ around for a while.

"It's a total mystery what happened," Billy Jones said. "The money was there on the table, and then it wasn't there. We've swept and cleaned that basement a dozen times, and there's no sign of it. Unless one of us took it, somebody else had to be in that room. The only other one I saw was your wife, Hank, and she was in the kitchen fixing our little lunch. That's it, though I still don't trust that minister who says he'll sue us if we start asking him questions. Can you imagine, a reverennnd suing his former church?"

"If he's got the money, he's got us over a barrel," Hank said. "If we go after him, he sues us, and we can't afford to defend the suit. But I don't think he took it, Billy. He maybe wasn't the best minister we ever had, but there was never any sign that he was dishonest."

"It's one thing to be honest about fifty bucks in the plate collection; it's another to be honest about ten thousand dollars laying there on a table when everyone else is in the kitchen," Billy said.

"That could be said about a lot of us, I suppose," Hank said.

Billy visibly bristled. "I don't like your implication, Hank," he hissed.

"Now Billy, take it easy here. I'm includin' myself in my remark. Ten thousand dollars is a lot of money to any of us, is all I meant. But I don't think any of the elders know anything about it."

Billy relaxed some. "Who then? If not the minister and not the elders, who? Did your wife see anybody else in the church that night?" Billy's question made a lot of sense, it seemed to Russ.

"Naw," Hank said, "she would have told me if she did."

Still, Russ thought, it might be a good idea to pay a visit to Mary Henry, the champion Welsh cookie baker. The worst that could happen is he would be served a couple of her fine Welsh cookies or even a homemade cinnamon roll. In fact he was eating one those rolls at that very moment and sipping the last of his black Welsh tea.

18

Y Gymanfa Ganu

As Russ was walking up the hill from the little lunch after Jacob's funeral, he met a portly man of about fifty with gloriously bushy eyebrows and slicked down black hair. He was dressed in a dark brown suit and green wool vest, his black topcoat flapping about him unbuttoned. He extended a stubby Welshman's hand and introduced himself.

"Lewis Lloyd Llewellyn here, minister of the First Continuing Calvinistic Methodist Church. They call me Ellell for short. I've been looking for you, my young friend. They told me you would be down here about your duties."

Russ had never met him before. His congregation was a gathering of descendants from those Welsh Presbyterians who had not joined in when the Welsh Presbytery was absorbed into the various Presbyteries it had previously spanned. Calvinistic Methodism had long been a strong Protestant tradition in Wales, and they wanted it continued. Ellell, in keeping with the people he served, was an independent sort and did not attend the ministers' meetings at The Coal Bin, which Russ considered to be in his favor.

Ellell wanted to talk about Saint David's Day, which was coming up on March 1st. "I desire you to know, my dear namesake, though I understand you spell it differently, we'll have the celebration at our church, as is the custom. You must extend our sincerest invitation to all your fine people." Full of quaint locutions, Ellel's way of talking stayed close to old country formalities, it seemed. His voice was a bit gruff, yet with natural Welsh lilt and cadence. Russ had heard the rumor that Reverend Llewellyn smoked, but no one had ever caught him at it. Russ had also heard that every Sunday after church he took the bus to Scranton and caught the train for New York. He was not seen again until Tuesday evening. Since he was a bachelor, the stories about what Ellell did in New York were rife with lurid imaginings, none of them confirmed.

Russ got out his little date book from Westminster Bookstores and put First Continuing Calvinistic Methodist down in the space for March 1, 1960.

"There'll be a rabbit supper and a Gymanfa Ganu," Ellell said, "and maybe a surprise or two." The Welsh words came out as Gahmahnvah Gahnee, and again Russ marveled at the lyrical sound of the language. Ellell went on, "As you must know by now, the Gymanfa Ganu is a festival of Welsh hymn singing, the most important one of the year being the one on Saint David's Day. Perhaps you would be so kind as to grace us with a prayer, not too long, of course, before the start of the singing."

"I would consider it an honor and privilege to do so. Thank you so very much for the kind invitation," Russ said with as many circumlocutions as he thought he could get away with. Then Russ asked Ellell who Saint David was.

"Ah yes," Ellell said, clearing his husky throat as if for a little speech. "Saint David harkens back to the sixth century. Legend says he was a Welsh knight at the round table of King Arthur, who was also Welsh you know, or so we say. Dewi Sant, or Saint David, slew dragons with his lance, and he was the devout protector of all things good, especially fair women. He reportedly ate nothing but leeks and drank nothing stronger than pure spring water, and from this came the virtue to ward off all would-be conquerors of Wales. He is said to have driven out the dastardly English with little more than a stick and a prayer.

"Now, to be honest, I must tell you that our historians find much evidence that Saint David was a bishop who, like Saint Patrick in Ireland, founded schools and hospitals. And, sad to say, the historians also find Wales was conquered many times before, during, and after Saint David came and went, but to a Welsh heart this is entirely beside the point. Whatever is true about any of it, the Welsh gather on March the first each year to honor the good Saint David by eating copious amounts of fricasseed rabbit with side dishes of rutabagas and parsnips. Potato leek soup is also served and, of course, we drink tea instead of spring water and down a few Welsh cookies into the bargain. Your Mrs. Henry always brings the best ones, so I hope you can prevail upon her to get right to her baking once again. In honor of Saint David's supposed eating habits, we wear the blessed leek on our lapels that day and decorate the tables with bouquets of daffodils, signifying the splendors of springtime in dear old Wales. Then we raise our voices to sing our splendid Welsh hymns. It's a glorious occasion, my dear Llewellen. I'm surprised you have not participated in such celebrations, given that your name is Welsh as Welsh. There's no mistake in that."

"I was raised in California," Russ said. "Out there we have Cinco de Mayo, not Saint David's Day."

"I suppose that explains it then. Well, you are in for a Welsh treat, my new friend. Until March the first, then." With a parting phrase in Welsh that Russ took as more or less "God be with you till we meet again," Ellell nodded and strode off.

NEXT DAY, RUSS DROPPED BY to see Mary Henry. His visit was ostensibly to tell her that Reverend Llewellyn of Continuing Calvinistic Methodist had specifically asked for her Welsh cookies for the Saint David's Day celebration. Mary had already bought the ingredients and had them ready. She had baked cinnamon rolls for breakfast that morning and placed a big one on a plate along with a fresh pot of tea for Russ where he sat at the kitchen table. The dark tea and wonderful roll energized Russ for delving the mystery of the ten thousand dollars, but Mary was telling Russ how she had been a Henry before she was married. "That happens with us Welsh," she explained. "There are only so many last names, so some of us girls don't have to change our names when we walk down the aisle. It's that way with Betsy Davis and Naomi Williams, and I don't know how many others. It's kind of nice. I'm glad I'm still a Henry."

She told Russ her two grown children, a son and a daughter, were doing well and lived nearby, one in Old Forge and the other in Scranton. They see each other often, Mary said, and she loved taking care of her one grandchild. She hoped there would be many more, though her twenty-three year old son was still single. She had a sense of peace about her, as if her life had turned out just the way she hoped it would.

"Mary," Russ said, "I would like to ask you something, if you wouldn't mind. The elders have told me about the missing ten thousand dollars, and though I probably shouldn't even think of it, I find I get more curious all the time. I've poked around here and there and even went to see Reverend Thomas about it. From everything I can find out, it seems there must have been some-one else in the church that night besides the elders and you. They were all in the kitchen eating your fine Welsh cookies. With such a treat as that, I can understand how they wouldn't pay attention to what was going on in the other room. So, I'm wondering, Mary, did you notice anyone come and go during the little lunch you were serving that night? Did you hear anything, a door or footsteps or anything?"

"Reverennnd, you're a great flatterer aren't you now, praising my cookies like that. You will go far, I can see. But yes, there was another person there. Aunt Alice was there."

"Well, yes. I'm told she brought in the money and laid it on the table and left."

"She didn't leave right away, actually. What I remember is I came in the front door of the church that night because I left my scarf on the rack after Sunday services. When I went in to get it, I saw Aunt Alice in one of the back pews. She looked like she was much at prayer, head bowed and leaning forward where she sat. She didn't even know I was there. I didn't want to disturb her, so I just went downstairs and began fixing the lunch for the elders. During the first part of the meeting, Aunt Alice came downstairs, and I guess gave the elders the money. Then she went back upstairs again, I suppose to pray some more."

"You mean she didn't leave the church after she put the money on the table? She didn't go out the basement door? She went upstairs and sat in the dark and prayed?"

"I don't know what she did up there, but I know she went upstairs after she gave the elders the money."

"Well, that's the first I've heard of that. It's all very puzzling, isn't it Mary."

"You can say that again, Reverennnd."

"So Aunt Alice might have been in a position to know if anyone was lurking around the church that night."

"Well she wasn't up there very long. When the elders were having their little lunch she went out the basement door in a big hurry. She's a funny one, you know. But we're all kind of funny here, if you think about it."

"I'd say interesting, at least." They both chuckled about that. "Do you think Aunt Alice knows the money has turned up missing?"

"She would storm the Holiness of Holinesses with a torch if she did. She's not the easiest to get along with. The elders have tried to keep the whole thing quiet, hoping to get the money back before anyone knows it's gone, but it's been over a year now, and nothing's turned up. It's an embarrassment to them. I'm surprised they told you." Mary seemed on the verge of smiling like so many on Welsh Hill often do.

"So," Russ said, "Aunt Alice may be the only one with an inkling about what might have happened that night, but we can't ask her about it because we're afraid of what she'll do when she finds out the money's missing. That's a fine situation now, isn't it?"

223

"A rock and a hard place, Reverennnd. If I were you, I'd leave it right there."

"You're no doubt right, Mary. Thanks for the cinnamon roll. It was scrumptious."

"Gwan, now Reverennnd. You're going to flatter your way into heaven, aren't you? You be careful now and watch yourself. The church will get by without that ten thousand dollars. We got by without it up to now. The elders would be mighty upset if this gets out, and we don't want to be lookin' for another minister any time soon. We've still got a lot to teach you."

"That you do, Mary. That you do. And I'm a slow learner." With that they said goodbye.

LIKE MOST OF THE DAYS SINCE CHRISTMAS, March the first dawned cloudy and cold, and, by midafternoon, a heavy snow was blowing through the streets of Scroggtown. Nevertheless, that evening the huge basement of the Continuing Calvinistic Methodist Church was packed with Welshmen in dark wool suits. Bright yellow daffodils graced each table in honor of the coming springtime in dear old Wales.

For reasons Russ never learned, the annual Saint David's Day Dinner was served to men only. Cigarette smoke hung heavy in the room and Ellell seemed to hover where the smoke was thickest, inhaling for all he was worth, but not lighting up on his own. The rosy cheeked women of the church brought in tureens of rabbit stew, platters of fried rabbit, and some chicken for those who would not touch rabbit even if it was Saint David's Day. They also carried in bowls of cooked cabbage, carrots and green beans along with rutabagas and parsnips. For dessert some lemon cakes appeared as well as several platters of Welsh cookies, Mary Henry's among them.

Somebody had stoked the furnace with extra coal to make sure the revelers didn't suffer from the cold. Thus, the basement became a steam bath. Mist from boiling vegetables in the kitchen mixed with cigarette smoke and the sweat of wool-clad Welshmen, and it all coalesced into a light-colored haze swirling above the diners.

After dinner, Ellell got up and called the ladies out of the kitchen for a round of applause. Then the committee on arrangements had to be introduced and duly appreciated with more applause. It seemed like Ellell was taking a long time to get the honors done. He looked at the watch on his thick hairy wrist every few seconds, and he grabbed little glances at the door. Finally he whispered to one of the men at the head table, and the fellow quickly got up and left the room. While he was gone, Ellell announced that the surprise of the evening was a speech by Bill Scranton, the Republican candidate for Congress in that district. The snow must have delayed him, Ellell said, and so he wondered if there was anyone who would like to say a few words or tell a story or sing a song while they waited.

Nobody volunteered, and they all sat there in the steam for a minute or two. Finally, Buck stood up at his place across the table from Russ and told the assembled gathering that he knew of a new minister in town who did funny skits for the young people and maybe that minister would favor the Welshmen of Scroggtown with his humor. The man who had left the room came in and whispered to Ellell who turned and told the assembly that Bill Scranton was on his way and should arrive within half an hour. Russ shook his fist at Buck and got up on the little platform behind the head table and proceeded to do his pantomime of a mad doctor operating disastrously on a patient. Then he did one that mimicked a dumb sergeant trying to get his troops to line up alphabetically even though he didn't quite know the alphabet himself. For a grand finale, he did the pantomime of his wife getting dressed in the morning, including hooking her brassiere by reaching around her back with her mouth full of hairpins, one of which she swallows. The first skit got some snickers. The second some guffaws. And the third brought down the house.

With the marvelous sound of laughter and applause still roaring in the room, Bill Scranton walked in with one of his aides, and Russ was introduced to a thoughtful-looking man who seemed to need a shave. He was impeccably dressed in a dark blue, subtly striped suit. His blue tie had tiny white dots, and a small daffodil was pinned to his lapel. He shook Russ' hand and flashed a quick, natural smile. It was Scranton's family for which the town was named, the biggest town in northeastern Pennsylvania even if it was on the skids, as was everything in Northeastern Pennsylvania at the time. There hadn't been a Republican from that district in Congress for over thirty years. So Bill Scranton was a white knight to these put-upon, held-down, out-of-power Protestants, even though he was management and they were mostly labor, laid-off labor in some cases. The Welsh Protestant Republicans blamed the Irish and Italian Catholic Democrats for everything wrong in Scroggtown, and everywhere else, far as that goes.

Scranton spoke quietly and to the point. He told of the plight of old people in the hospitals and nursing homes, spoke of the neglected schools and roads and the sad condition of the parks and libraries. He didn't attack the incumbent directly, but everyone knew he was not worth attacking. Hardly ever on the job, he was pretty much a puppet for what was called the Democrat machine. The story was you could find him almost any afternoon in the dining room of the best Italian restaurant in Pittston lingering over a long lunch and a bottle of red wine.

"Where is our congressman?" Scranton asked, "I've been trying to see him for days and they keep telling me he's out. Well, he's out all right. Let's get together and vote him out." He said it without great emphasis, yet a blast of thunderous applause erupted that made the applause Russ had received seem like silence.

"I'm in the wrong business," Russ mumbled to himself. "I work all day on a sermon and preach my heart out, and nobody says 'boo' unless I mention something that offends a cherished understanding. Then I get a visit from the elders. Scranton lists some obvious lacks, and they get red in the face from enthusiasm." Even though he liked what Scranton said, it seemed to Russ he could use a good speechwriter. He thought about applying for the job.

After the speech, Ellell invited everyone upstairs for the Gymanfa Ganu. The large and very plain sanctuary was already filling with people. The wives of the men coming upstairs from the dinner had arrived early and saved seats for their husbands on the hard brown pews. The walls, carpets, and ceiling were deep brown as well. Except for the big picture behind the pulpit showing Jesus knocking at a door, the room could have passed for the inside of a warehouse.

Since Russ was to offer a prayer, he was escorted to a seat on the platform close behind the harp. A tall thin young women dressed in a flowing golden gown was strumming quiet notes with her long fingers. It seemed to Russ her hand went by in front of his face like a huge spider on a giant web.

Promptly at eight, Ellell strode to the pulpit. He shook his little Welsh finger at those still filing in and said, "It pays to be on time, you know." For him, the snowstorm was no excuse, and the fact they were bringing in folding chairs to accommodate the overflow was no excuse either. He introduced the imported chorister, one Morgan Henry Prichard Reese from Wales by way of Pottstown, Pennsylvania, who smiled, raised his arms and brought them sharply down. The piano and organ boomed forth, and the singing began.

"There really is nothing like it," Russ mumbled to himself. He could hear the lilting voices calling from heart to heart in that cavern of a room, calling from the heart of Wales where grand preaching and magnificent singing had ruled the day. When it was time for him to pray, he rose and bowed his head as if in another world. He prayed for the wonder of music and the splendor of song, for the courageous spirit of old Saint David, for all those who had ever sung hymns on Saint David's Day, for Bill Scranton and all who work for a fairer world, and for uplifted spirits among those gathered to raise their voices in praise. The harp made little ripples in the background during his prayer, like a brook over smooth stones, so that Russ could hardly keep his mind on his words. He noticed his voice taking on a higher pitch and moving toward the cadences he heard among these people and their preachers, his sentences rising in tone at the end. He drew out a long Ahhhmennn and sat down.

The chorister had an idea how each hymn should sound, and he took time to speak of its tone and feeling. He got the women singing high descants, and he had the basses rumble down below with deep and powerful chants. One hymn after another came forth from over five hundred Welsh throats. Then a soprano soloist sang an absolutely thrilling rendition of the Welsh lullaby Ar Hyd Y Nos, which in English is "Sleep, my child, and peace attend thee, / All through the night." She sang it both in Welsh and English, and it was entirely beautiful. The chorister mentioned that his mother had sung it to him when he was a lad, and most of the congregation nodded, affirming their mothers had done the same. Then more congregational singing. Then the harpist played an exquisite solo, and Russ closed his eyes to avoid seeing her spidery fingers crawling a foot from his face. Then it was singing far into the night.

Here we are in an old battered church in old battered Scroggtown, Russ thought, and the music is worthy of a famous hall in a great city. After a while, he just sat there behind the harp and listened. He didn't care how long it lasted.

When Russ got home it was almost eleven. On the television news were pictures of Bill Scranton speaking to the Rotary Club in Clark's Summit that noon. The Scroggtown speech wasn't covered, but it was much the same as the one to the Rotarians. Then there were pictures of John Kennedy speaking to a large rally in Chicago, his right hand chopping the air as his words flew swiftly off his tongue. Kennedy wanted for the country what Scranton wanted for Northeastern Pennsylvania, it seemed. They both wanted jobs for workers and help for the elderly and a better shake for every-one. They spoke similar words, but Scranton was much quieter and less at home before a crowd. Still, from what Russ could tell, it would be hard to distinguish between their platforms. In an inter-view after his speech, Scranton assured the people of northeastern Pennsylvania, who were mostly Democrats, that he would work closely with Kennedy if he became president. "Our area needs help to get back on its feet," he said, which was certainly true.

19

Mildred Morgan's White Dress

THE WIDOW MILDRED MORGAN WAS FAMOUS for her grief. Russ learned about her bit by bit in his visits around the parish. She had mourned seven years for her dear husband Mousie. They called him Mousie after his father, the first Mousie Morgan, who had been a small, hairy man. He was often sent into the tiniest crannies in the mine to see if there was more coal there. Mousie Senior was known to have been a disagreeable sort, but he would help out in spite of himself. When the congregation was able to afford a bell, he volunteered to crawl into the church tower and make sure the rope was in its groove on the pulley because he was the only man small enough to get into that tight space.

Mildred's Mousie was large and good natured. Still, he was called Little Mousie, and his diminutive father was Big Mousie. Little Mousie was also called Mousie Junior. Mousie Junior had worked at the mine, but above ground, managing the transfer of coal to train cars and such. When Little Mousie married Mildred, the bell Big Mousie had helped place in the church tower was rung a hundred times as the bride and groom whisked themselves out of the church. They wanted to do the same after Mousie Junior's funeral, but the pulley high in the tower broke at about the fiftieth ring, so when Russ came to town, the bell hadn't rung for seven years.

Mildred and Mousie had lived all their married lives on Eynan Street, two blocks over and one block down from the church. They had no children of their own and so became the favorite aunt and uncle of a large crop of Morgans and Davises and Joneses, the family names of their brothers and sisters, as well as the unofficial aunt and uncle to all the kids on Welsh Hill. They had put on strawberry socials for everyone in the neighborhood every summer. Mousie brought the strawberries, Mildred brought the makings for homemade ice cream and an old fashioned, hand cranked ice cream freezer. They got the kids in a line to take turns with the crank and let the church charge people for the ice cream and strawberries to help with the budget. The kids got their ice cream free for turning the crank.

After much urging from the deacons of the church, Russ went to see the widow Mildred Morgan. "Reverennnd," they said, "all the years since her Mousie died, Mildred's sat in her living room with the shades drawn. None of the ministers have been able to help her. Maybe you can get her going again." If none of the other ministers have been able to get her going, why do you expect I can? Russ would have liked to ask.

He stopped by on a blustery afternoon in early March. Mildred's was a white wood frame house, a perfect square, with a small front porch. The paint looked thick and new, so somebody was taking care of the place. But the doorbell didn't ring, so Russ knocked several times. After some minutes, the shade on the small window in the door was lifted and two dark eyes peered out.

"Who are you?" said a crisp voice from behind the closed door.

"I'm the minister, Mrs. Morgan, I've come to pay you a visit."

"I'm not receiving visitors today," she said.

"Mrs. Morgan," Russ said, "I walked down the hill especially to see you, and I sure would like to have a little visit. Not only that, it's cold out here."

The window shade went down and the there was a rattle as one lock after another was unbolted. A tall, thin woman in her early sixties stood in the open door. She was dressed entirely in black, not a speck of any other color to be seen, and her dress reached the tops of her coal black shoes. Her gray hair was rolled into a tight bun.

"We can't have the Reverennnd catching his death of cold on the porch, can we now?" she said. "Nobody would talk to me if I let that happen. You can come in." In the dark parlor an old fashioned lamp dangled from a wooden arm sending a dull glow through a brown shade. It showed the outlines of exquisite pieces of furniture obviously handed down in the family for generations.

"You have lovely things here, Mildred. It must give you pleasure to sit among such fine old pieces of furniture," Russ ventured.

"You have a good eye, Reverennnd. This old table, for instance, came over from Wales with my dear husband's family, and it wasn't what you would call new then. Yes, it is nice to have these things around me. Comforting, you know."

"We don't see furniture like this in California," Russ said.

"No, I don't suppose you would. Everything's new and shiny out there from what we can tell from the television." So, she doesn't sit entirely in darkness, Russ noted. She watches television, and it seems she could be drawn into some chit-chat. But then her face turned serious and she said, "I sit here a lot all by myself." After a quiet moment she went on, "But Reverennnd, you should have some tea to take the chill off. I'll call Dorie. She's my dear niece. She comes by almost every afternoon with the things I need." She spoke in a subdued Welsh lilt, but still it was a lilt.

Dorie Davis came in from the kitchen and was introduced by her aunt. She was a small, dark haired young woman with flashing eyes. Her dress was pale blue and very plain, but she seemed like one who, on other days, might wear stylish and colorful clothes. She went back into the kitchen to make tea.

"Dorie will be married to Davie Jones, the one they call Locker, for Davie Jones' Locker," Mildred said, her face brightening noticeably. "Dorie's mother is my sister who married Charlie Davis, who they sometimes call Sammy because he is so dark complected. Dorie is light complected though, like her mother. Isn't she a picture, Reverennnd?"

"She is that, Mildred. When is the wedding?" Russ asked, his head spinning from all the names and nicknames.

"It'll be sometime soon. They need to talk to you and set a date, but they're waiting to make sure when young Locker gets out of the Army. His two years are about up."

"Well, that will be a day to look forward to. Davie home, Dorie married. The church will be packed for that one." Thinking, What the heck, she knows I know she's been in mourning for seven years, so why not play the cards early, Russ asked, "Will you be coming to the wedding, Mildred?"

"I'm considering it, Reverennnd, for Dorie's sake, you know. I don't know what I'd done without her through this hard time."

"I'm glad to hear it," Russ said. There was a pause. Russ decided to wait it out. Tea was on the way so the silence couldn't last forever.

"Oh, Reverennnd, I know folks think it's silly of me to go on like this for all these years." Mildred said finally. "I just can't help myself. I lived for that Mousie's footfall on the porch when he came home at night, and for that whistle of his as he went down the steps in the morning on his way to the mine. I still hear that whistle every day. A happy tune, 'You Are My Sunshine,' it was. Well, he was my sunshine, and then he just dropped dead one day at work. I still don't know what I'm going to do."

"Your Mousie is a lucky man. We all should have someone to remember us so well," Russ ventured.

"Oh, don't wish that on anyone, Reverennnd. It's too hard and too lonely. Other widows have gone on trips, have gotten married, even, but I can't force myself to get to church. Mousie and I hardly ever missed church, but now I can't go. It would make me too sad."

Dorie came back with tea and Welsh cookies. The teapot was an old one from Wales, a red and green quilted cozy over it to keep the tea hot. The cups and saucers were old too and elegant and gave forth a cheerful clatter in the shadowy room.

"I hear you plan to be married before long, Dorie." Russ said.

"Yes Reverennnd, as soon as we know when my Davie gets home. I'm having a hard time to wait."

"I'll bet he's having a hard time too," Russ said. Dorie sat in the dim glow of the light and was for a fact pretty as a picture.

DAVIE GOT HOME LITTLE MORE THAN A WEEK AFTER RUSS visited Mildred, and he and Dorie wanted to get married right away. The date was set for noon on the third Saturday in March. It would be a simple wedding, they said, no need for a rehearsal.

The day of the wedding dawned with a late winter storm coming in. Six inches of snow had fallen and new snow was still falling. At seven in the morning, the phone rang. "Reverennnd, I don't know who to call. My Aunt Tillie Reese is a member of your church, and she said you would come help us. Our baby needs to be baptized, Reverennnd. He's in the hospital. Something's wrong with his spine. They're going to operate at ten, but we want him baptized first. Can you come and do it?"

"I'll be right down," Russ said. By the time he was ready, another inch of snow had fallen. In the alley behind the house snow had drifted a foot deep. Russ had to shovel to get the garage door open, and he had to travel a couple hundred yards of alley-way before he could reach the street. He revved up the little Saab, backed out of the garage, and headed down the alley. With front wheel drive, he had good traction, but he got caught in snow-filled chuck holes and spun his tires. It was back off, rush forward, splash and slide. It took nearly half an hour to get to Main Street, which hadn't been plowed. He inched along the middle of the road trying not to touch the brakes. It took another half an hour to get to the hospital.

"Sorry to take so long, the storm fouled the streets," Russ said to a young, heavy chested towheaded young man, who looked horribly worried.

"We're just glad to see you, Reverennnd. I'm Johnny Williams. Sue's with the baby. I've never been through anything like this. I'd rather be shot at than go through it."

The baby, born just the day before, was in an oxygen tent next to his mother's bed. She reached through a slit in the tent, patting him gently with her rubber gloved hand. "You better hurry," she said. "I think he's getting worse." She looked drawn and pale, her dark hair was matted against her head

The nurse brought gloves and a basin of water for Russ. He said a quick prayer and baptized the little scrunched up creature in the name of the Father, Son, and Holy Spirit, said a blessing, and turned to see big Johnny Williams crying helplessly in his wife's arms.

"Thank you, Reverennnd. If you think of it, pray for us, huh," she said. Russ touched both of them on the shoulder. "I'm sorry to have to leave, but I have to be at a wedding," he said.

By now some of the streets were plowed and some weren't. Russ got home a little after ten. He put water on for tea, thinking to work on next day's sermon. Then he saw the note stuck to his study door. "Get over to Big Smokey Griffith's on Academy Street. His mother is dying. I've gone to the grocery store. Love, Ellen." Every Griffith in the world must be named Smokey, Russ thought. Big Smokey, a good sized man, had a coal truck. His son, Little Smokey, who was the spitting image of his father and exactly the same size, drove it. They lived side by side in a double house. Sarah, Big Smokey's mother, lived with him and his wife, and by the time Russ got there, Sarah Griffiths was gasping and rattling.

"She just started doing this," Big Smokey said. "The doctor told us she might last for days." Russ bent over the bed and said a prayer. He sang a quiet stanza of Penparc, "Jesus, I live to thee," and Sarah's eye opened a little and her gasping paused for a second and resumed. Then, as he sat on the edge of the bed holding her hand, Sara Griffiths took a deep breath and died. No more rattling and struggling, just quiet. Smokey's wife started crying, but Smokey covered his mother's face with the sheet, and said, "That was a godsend, Reverennnd, your prayer put her at peace."

"Smokey," Russ said, "I'm glad I got here in time, but I really have to get back for Dorie's and Davie's wedding. I'm sorry not to be able to stay."

When Russ got to the church all the lights were on and Richie Evans was getting the organ warmed up. Snow still fell and piled up in the streets. Cars and delivery trucks were stuck everywhere. People walked toward the church bent over into the wind and snow. Eddie the janitor swept the steps but snow swirled in behind the broom and stuck there. Richie began to play his prelude at ten till twelve, but there was no bride, no groom, nobody from the family around and only a few people scattered in the pews. Russ put on his robe and got the satin ribbon bookmark in the right place in his *Book of Common Worship*. At ten after twelve the groom showed up with his best man who said their car was stuck and they had tramped several blocks through the snow. Davie "Locker" Jones, a fairly tall, fairly hefty young man with a short cropped U. S. Army haircut and a worried look on his face, was all decked out in a black tuxedo, but his trousers were stuffed into galoshes and he had a thick brown scarf around his neck.

"Cars are stuck all over town, Reverennnd. The others will be along soon as they can," Davie said. Russ went upstairs into the sanctuary and announced to the few who had gathered that there would be a delay because of the storm. Richie at the organ rolled his eyes and kept on playing. He was going through his prelude music for the third time. When he got back downstairs, Russ asked Davie for the wedding license so at least they could begin to fill that out. Davie looked startled.

"Gees, Reverennnd, I haven't seen it since last night. We were showing it to all the folks after dinner. We had a little family party, you know. Dorie has it, I bet. I'll go see."

"You stay here, Davie," Russ said. "Send your best man. That's what he's for."

The best man took Davie's scarf and threw it around his own neck and trudged off into the snow. People were filling up the balcony by now, but the downstairs was almost empty. On Welsh Hill, it was understood that anyone in the neighborhood could come to weddings and sit in the balcony, but the family and invited guests got first call on downstairs. Russ looked out the door and saw people standing on the steps and down the sidewalk.

"Did you invite all these folks, Davie?" Russ asked. "I'm not sure the church will hold them."

"Naw, we invited maybe a hundred. Everybody wants to see what Aunt Mildred's going to wear." he said.

"Ah, she's coming then," Russ said.

"Yeah, she's coming. Hell, she wouldn't miss it in a hundred years. The bets are she'll wear her black dress though. Sorry for swearin', Reverennnd. I picked up some bad habits in the army."

The balcony filled up and the uninvited were spilling into the downstairs. Wearing her beige honeymoon dress, Ellen slipped in and sat in the back.

The best man came into the church puffing and said Dorie was stuck about two blocks away, and she thought the wedding license had fallen in the bushes last night as they left the party and by now it was probably under a foot of snow. Russ figured he'd better call somebody at the county office to find out what to do. All he could get to answer was an emergency number. The guy on the line said, "This number is for emergencies only." He sounded cross,

"Well, the snow buried the wedding license," Russ said, "and I've got a church full of people here and a bride and groom ready to get married, and I need to know what to do." He gave Russ the County Clerk's home phone number.

When he came to the phone, Robert E. Roberts, Clerk, sounded like he was already in his cups. He was not pleased that Russ had bothered him.

"How'd you get this number, Reverennnd?" he wanted to know.

"They gave it to me at Emergency," Russ told him.

"Those bastards," he said. "I'll get them for this." Russ told him the situation and asked what he should do.

"Marry the little fools, Reverennnd," the Clerk said. "I can't remember if I issued a license to 'em or not. Davis and Jones, huh. Welsh. Can you imagine how many Davis and Jones weddings we have in Scroggtown? Us Welsh, we never worried about getting a license to screw anyways." He laughed and hung up. Russ went upstairs to announce another delay. Organist Richie Evans was making his way through the hymnbook now and had gotten to "Just as I Am without One Plea," which is often sung during the altar call at evangelistic rallies.

At one-thirty the bride and her party arrived. Russ ushered them into the narthex. Aunt Mildred walked in wearing an ankle length black coat. Dorie was next to her in her white bridal gown that looked much like an evening dress. Russ noticed her dress was unzipped half way down the back.

"Can you help me with this, Reverennnd?" she said. "I can't get it zipped. I must have eaten too many cookies waiting for Davie to come home."

Russ yanked on the zipper but it didn't budge. Dorie sucked in and Russ yanked again. Zing, the zipper slid up into the flesh between Dorie's shoulder blades and drew blood. A red streak began to run down the smooth white satin. Dorie didn't seem to feel a thing, and Russ didn't mention what happened. The bleeding soon stopped. "Praise God for that," Russ murmured.

"Let's get the family into their places," Russ said. All the pews were full but the first row. Richie at the organ had gotten through all the hymns he could stand and was starting in on "Danny Boy" as the widow Mildred Morgan took off her black coat, hung it on one of the hooks at the back of the church, and walked down the center aisle.

Every head turned toward her. There was an audible gasp. She wore a black hat, black gloves, black shoes, carried a black purse, and her dress was sheer black rayon, but scattered here and there in it were the tiniest white polka dots anyone had ever seen.

"Mildred's wearing white," people whispered, "Mildred's wearing white." The buzz over Mildred's dress continued while the groom, best man, and Russ entered from the side door and stood in front of the communion table. The murmur continued as the Maid of Honor walked down the aisle and took her place. Then the Wedding March brought Dorie in on her father's arm. Everyone stood to honor the bride, but all eyes were on Aunt Mildred's amazing dress.

The wedding was fine once it got started. Davie just beamed the whole time, and Dorie trembled and shook but was able to say her vows well enough. Almost all the women except Aunt Mildred cried. She sat quietly with her hands folded in her lap as if it was the most normal thing in the world to attend your niece's wedding, which, of course, it is.

As they got near the end of the ceremony, Russ noticed a large reel to reel tape recorder turning slowly under the front pew on the groom's side of the aisle. A gentleman there was holding a microphone all but hidden in his folded hands. Russ hadn't noticed it till right then. He pronounced the couple husband and wife according to the ordinances of God and the laws of the state, and right at that moment the tape ran out, and the machine made a high pitched noise and began to flutter and slap. A terrible screech—eeeeeah- screetascreetascreetascreeta— pierced the holy joy, drowning out the benediction.

"Now kiss the bride, Davie," Russ said over the noise of the machine. "Play, Richie, fast and loud." And so, to screeches and a double time recessional, the wedding party left the church. Everybody laughed and clapped and even Aunt Mildred smiled.

"Lovely, wedding Reverennnd," people said as they went out the door. "And didn't Mildred look nice in her new dress."

Russ just smiled. All weddings are lovely, he could see, no matter what happens.

20

You Had to Be There

THE WEDDING RECEPTION WAS AT THE DRUIDS HALL, a large low lying cinder block building two streets south and one street west of the church. Before putting in an appearance, Russ went home to get at his sermon, but it was a bad try. Birth, death, official cynicism, and a wedding, it all came rushing into him mixed together and overflowing. He wondered how he could ever sort it all out. What do you preach about in a situation like this? He couldn't think of a thing.

"Let's go to the reception," Russ said to Ellen. "We may as well walk." They bundled up and headed out into the snow. No more fell, but flakes blew off the trees and wires and whipped around the neighborhood. The whole town was muffled by the snow and hardly any cars moved on the streets. People trudged along carrying sacks of groceries from the store. When they passed, Russ tipped his hat and nodded. They seemed to appreciate it.

"I thought I would scream when that tape recorder went off. How could you let him do that?" Ellen said as they walked along.

"Let him! I didn't know it was there until I heard it. Not everybody can have a perfect California wedding like we had."

"Ours wasn't perfect. My underwear fell off in the church because you knelt too close to me and tore it loose."

"First bride who started undressing going up the aisle toward the door." Russ said. "Now that's eager."

"I think I was more eager than you were," Ellen said. Instead of disagreeing, Russ took Ellen's hand, and they walked the cold streets in silence the rest of the way.

In the fading afternoon, the Druids Hall glowed with little lights along the entrance way. People were crowded inside and all of them wanted to congratulate Russ on the lovely wedding. All of them also remarked about Mildred Morgan wearing a white dress even though it was mostly black. She didn't come to the party though. That would have been too much.

A band made up of piano, bass, drum, and saxophone, was up on the stage doing music like Chubby Checker. Charlene Latinsky, maiden name Jones, star soprano of the church choir, grabbed Russ by the hand and led him to the floor where she started to twist.

"What's this?" Russ said. "When I went to dances we either held each other or jitterbugged. At least we touched."

"No touching, Reverennnd. Just twist. We touch later when we get home." Russ noticed every head in the place turned his direction.

"Charlene, all these people are staring at us. Am I supposed to be doing this?" Russ asked.

"Forget them. They're all fuddies. Even Jesus had a good time at weddings," she said, and they twisted even more furiously. When the music stopped, they went over to Ellen. Charlene's husband Hal was there. He handed Russ a cup.

"Here, Revrend, I brought you some special tea," he said. The cup was half full of bourbon. Ellen was already sipping from her cup, looking amazed.

"Any chance of getting some ice and ginger ale in this tea?" Russ asked.

"Revrend, I think you better drink it like that for now. Some of these Welsh don't cotton to their minister having a drink with them. Now if it was us Polish, why we could fix it however you want. Our priests are regular just like us. In fact, most of them can drink us under the table. And that's saying something." Ellen and Russ sipped their "tea," and Hal took them around and introduced them to his family. Dorie's mother's brother, they found out, was married to Hal's sister, so there was a Polish contingent at this affair.

They all said, "Nice wedding, Revrend." And offered Russ something to drink from flasks in their pockets, which he declined. "'Revrend' must be the Polish version of my title," Russ mumbled under his breath.

The Polish were on one side of the hall, drinking, helping themselves at the buffet table, getting up and dancing, laughing, and partying royally, while the Welsh were sipping tea that was really tea and chatting quietly on the other side. Clearly, by getting out on the floor with Charlene, Russ had broken through a little line that he hadn't even seen. He took a long sip from his cup and asked Hal if he could find him some more tea. For Hal, that was no trouble at all. He had a flask in his back pocket.

Ellen's cheeks were beginning to glow, and Russ began to feel less and less concern about whether he was being approved of or not, a dangerous state of affairs for a minister in a Welsh church, or any church, for that matter.

They had a dance where you pin money to the bride's dress and then take a spin around the floor with her. Russ slipped a five dollar bill under her sleeve just like he could afford it.

"Thanks for everything, Reverennnd," Dorie said.

"How's your back?" Russ asked.

"What do you mean, how's my back?"

"Oh, well, I shouldn't have mentioned it, I guess, but when I zipped you up I caught your skin in your zipper, and I wondered if it hurt."

"I haven't felt a thing." She danced off and the next man put a bill down Dorie's back, right where the red spot was on the dress.

The party gyrated on into the night. Charlene and Russ twisted once more, then the band played a slow one, and the floor got crowded. Russ and Ellen danced together for the first time ever. Their cross county airmail courtship had not included dances or parties. It was a marvelous feeling, everyone together on the floor, even some of the Welsh. Then the band moved into a faster number, and people stayed on the floor and hopped around like trained fleas. Nobody touched. The whole floor moved in a boom da boom steady beat with everyone dancing with everyone else, young and old, Welsh and Polish. Russ was on his third cup of tea and found himself feeling at home with this whole crowd and particularly attracted to lithe and lovely Ellen.

When they sat down to eat, Russ and Ellen went to the Polish section and were plied with sausages and breads and cabbage rolls from the long table that many of the guests had helped fill with their family specialties. The Welsh had brought ham and potato salad and Welsh cookies, but Hal said that was funeral food. "Eat Polish tonight, Revrend, it's a wedding."

During a break in the band music, somebody brought out a concertina and played a lively Polish dance. Three young women with arms around each other's shoulders skipped and hopped across the floor and all the Polish clapped to the beat. Over in a corner, some of the men began to sing Polish songs. The Welsh sat quietly eating their ham and potato salad and sipping their tea.

About ten o'clock Ellen and Russ got up to go. He was concerned about his unwritten sermon. Hal came over and insisted on driving them home. Charlene came too.

"Now when we get to your house, Revrend," Hal said, "I want you to go in the front door, turn on some lights, wait a few minutes, then turn off the lights as if you've gone to bed, then meet us out back in the alley. You and the Missus need to get out and see what Pennsylvania's really like."

"Do what he says you two," Charlene said, "or I'll spread it all over the church that we had to take you home drunk."

Russ and Ellen did as they were told and met Hal and Charlene in the alley where they waited in their car with the lights out. There were three more cars behind them. Hal headed out of town to the west and north toward Tunkhannock. The roads were plowed by now, and Hal's snow tires rumbled as they went. Ellen and Russ cuddled in the back seat like a couple of kids. After half an hour, Hal pulled into a scraped off parking lot next to a huge red barn with Chinese lanterns swinging across the doorway. Inside, along one wall was a bar, and Hal headed straight in that direction. He came back with a shot and a beer for himself and a highball for Russ. He knocked off his shot, drained his beer, and got everyone to a table.

There was a ten piece dance band playing tunes like "Stardust" and "Sentimental Journey." Ellen and Russ danced with each other and with half the people there. Before the night was over, a belly dancer slithered among the tables, and everyone tucked bills into the top of her billowing trousers well below her bare navel. It was just a raucous good time, and it went on and on. Russ and Ellen didn't get home until well after two in the morning, stumbling up the back steps trying to be quiet.

"Shh, you'll wake Edgar," Ellen said.

"Nuts to Edgar," Russ said, "let's run the water and take a bath." They got in the house, scattering their clothes in the hallway as they made their way to the bedroom. Having better things to do, they didn't sleep much that night.

AT EIGHT FORTY NEXT MORNING, RUSS WOKE UP realizing he had to go to church and preach a sermon which he had not prepared. He didn't feel all that well, and he had no idea what he was going to say to the people that day. He didn't have the nerve to pray to God to bail him out. Instead, he drank some orange juice and took a hot bath. Toast and coffee and three aspirins were next. That helped some, but as he got dressed his stomach began to churn. He drank some milk. By then it was going on eleven o'clock.

"What a dummy," he mumbled to himself. "What a damn fool. Drinking in public, dancing the twist, staying out late on a Saturday night. No wonder people miss church. How could they stand to listen to a sermon feeling like this? And you've got to preach one, you dumb twit."

"What did you say?" Ellen said from bed.

"Nothing, I'm just talking to myself."

"Well, have a good service. I'm sleeping in." She rolled over and that was it. Russ never envied anyone more.

Russ had maybe half an hour to get ready for the service. People were probably already gathering. The choir for sure was warming up at that very moment. He poured himself some more coffee and opened his Bible. He couldn't remember the scripture for the service, had no idea what the hymns were going to be, and was completely blank about the sermon title he'd phoned in. The Bible opened about in the middle, and Russ flipped over to the 139th Psalm.

> Whither shall I go from thy Spirit?
> Or whither shall I flee from thy presence?
> If I ascend to heaven, thou art there!
> If I make my bed in hell, thou art there!

"Whoever wrote that was probably feeling the way I do right now," Russ mumbled to himself.

He put a book mark at the place and headed out. The shock of cold air braced him. He breathed deeply and trudged on. The sun was bright and the shadows of houses were clear lines in the snow. It was a day of outdoor clarities, and he hoped he could find some inner ones between then and the second hymn.

"Oh, well," he mumbled, "there won't be anyone there. They'll all be as washed out as I am from the party."

THE CHURCH WAS PACKED. People Russ had never seen were there. Even Mildred Morgan was back in her pew across from the Holiness of Holinesses wearing the dress she wore to the wedding.

No one was missing from the choir. There were but a few seats left in the balcony, and they were filling fast. "Look at the crowd," Charlene said from her place ahead of Russ as he lined up behind the choir. "They probably want to see if the Reverend can preach as well as he can dance."

"I hope they didn't let anybody in with tar and feathers," Russ said.

As they marched the congregation sang "All Hail the Power of Jesus Name," to the Welsh tune Diadem. The sopranos sang their descant high above the others, and, in the refrain, the basses dove into deep affirming reverberations down below, the sound swelling, rising and falling, the Welsh in full song.

Russ had them turn to the 139th Psalm in the back of the hymnal. He let his voice linger a bit on each of the words, giving full value to the vowels: "O Lord, thou hast searched me and known me." The people responded with the next line: "Thou knowest when I sit down and when I rise up!" Russ's voice was calling to their voices. Their voices were lifting up his. Each exchange became more intense, it seemed. When they got to the end, Russ repeated the phrase three times: "And see, and see, and see if there be any wicked way in me." And they responded in a deep, pleading tone: "And lead me in the way everlasting."

The next hymn was "Jesus Lover of My Soul" to the tune Aberystwyth, last sung at Jacob Jones' funeral. The final lines reach for the fullness of Welsh pain and longing:

> Hide me now my Savior hide,
> Till the storms of life are past;
> Safe into the haven guide,
> O Receive my soul at last!

With the long, drawn out Amen sung at the end of the hymn, Russ moved forward to preach. He had no notes to spread out on the big Bible on the pulpit. He simply placed his hands there and noticed that his left thumb was beginning to twitch.

247

"A long time ago," he said, full of discovery's own force, "someone wrote a poem that tells us God is always close by. It tells us there is no place we can be where God has not already been. We read the poem together just a few minutes ago." And then he leapt away from the text and toward the people. "Where did you learn how to read the Psalms like that?" he asked. "It sounded so strong and real. Does it come along with the way you sing? Sometimes the sounds I hear in this church are so magnificent I can hardly stand it." Every head jerked Russ' direction. Every face looked up, waiting on what would come next. Russ took another leap

"We are all aware that we had a marvelous wedding here yesterday. Dorie Davis and Davie Jones stood right here in this church and made promises that bind their lives together. Nothing we do is more important than that. It seems like a miracle, doesn't it? Two people come together with every intention of sharing a long and happy life, and they pledge themselves to it, not knowing what life might bring them. We know the pitfalls and dangers of such high intentions, but still we affirm them here in the sanctuary of faith. Why do we do it? Why do we take that chance on a future we cannot know? Why do we take any of the chances that living through life entails? As things turn out, we may make our bed in heaven or we may make it in hell. We all know this is so. But, either way, the Psalm says, God is there.

"Before the wedding I was called to baptize a baby who had a troubled birth. I put my hand into the oxygen tent and placed the water on that tiny head and said the words we all know, the very words that were said at our baptisms. All that pain and all that hope and all that prayer, it's almost too much to think about, too much to bear. But the Psalm tells us God was with us there in the hospital yesterday."

It seemed to Russ he was rambling and filling, but everywhere the heads were nodding up and down, and quiet smiles could be seem across several faces.

"And then, just before the wedding, I watched Sarah Griffiths die. We had prayer, I sang Penparc to her, she opened her eyes, seemed to be at peace, then she died. A birth, a death, and then a wedding, all within a few hours on the same snowy day, and all of it so normal in a way, and all of it so profound. And the Psalm tells us God was there in it all.

"Somehow, it seems to me, you people know all about this. You know more than you think you know. I go around with my Bible and my book of prayers, but you have the words before I get there. You know them in your hearts. You sing them in your songs. I hope you realize this. I hope you know how great a faith it is you have here. Sometimes I feel I'm just along for the ride."

This brought a little chuckle. By now Russ' left thumb was hopping up and down on the Bible and making a little thumping sound. He took hold of it with his right hand.

"And then we had a party," he went on. "A troubled birth, a peaceful death, a marvelous wedding, snowstorm and all, and then a party. We're supposed to have parties, you know. The Bible says to praise God with timbrel and dance." This brought laughter, the preacher doing the twist with the choir's lead soprano much in their minds, Russ was sure. "In the Bible, God is always throwing parties. God throws parties for victories and defeats, for plantings and harvests, for prodigals when they return, for apostles when they leave on long journeys. But the main parties in the Bible are wedding feasts. We read that Jesus turned water into wine at a wedding feast." This brought more laughter. "In the last book of the Bible, the final resolution of all things in heaven and earth is likened to a wedding feast. With everything else that happened yesterday, we ended with a wedding feast, and the Psalmist says God was there too. God is in our laughter and in our tears. God is in our victories and defeats. God is in the grieving heart and joyful heart." Russ glanced toward Mildred Morgan in her black and white dress. She seemed just fine.

"When you sing, you show that you hold this to be true," Russ went on. "The sound of your singing rises up from the pain of those who came to this valley decades ago to work in the mines. Your songs come from the bowels of the earth, from all the danger and sweat that brought forth the coal that formed the steel that built the cities of this land. I think you sing the way you do because you know when your men go into the mines, no matter how dirty and dangerous it is, God goes with them, just as the Psalm says.

"Our houses, our schools, this very church, are all tilted this way and that because of the mines. There's fire underneath us and sulfur gas around us. There's the black lung and tuberculosis, and all of this is in the sound of your singing. Your glorious, ponderous songs are more than all your troubles. As you sing them, they tell you God is here. Even when the ground cracks and heaves and crumbles beneath you, God is here.

"Your songs were sung when the men went into the mines and when they came out again. They were sung when explosions trapped men below and they were brought home wrapped in shrouds. In all of that misery and glory, God was there, and your songs are evidence it is so. These songs will be sung when we are lowered into our graves telling the world God is with us even then, especially then. This is what I hear when I hear you sing. Never let it go. Never doubt the power you have here. Your songs will triumph. Your songs will win for you. Whatever life can bring, these songs will rise up in our throats, and we will sing and dance and feast, just as we did yesterday after the wedding. It is all so wonderful, and we are here together to feel the wonder of it, and the joy."

Russ had gotten the words flowing and was unaware of how long he had spoken. The clock on the balcony wall showed it was almost noon. He had gone on for forty minutes, and he had more to say. He wanted so much for them to know his sense of their strength, their devotion, the fullness of their spirit. He stood and looked upon them, and let a long pause linger as he gathered in what to say next.

"Amen," somebody said. "Amen and Amen," people said around the room. And then somebody started to clap, most likely, somebody who hadn't been to church much and didn't know it wasn't done, a tentative, inhibited clapping that was joined by others here and there until it began to swell and grow and move through the congregation. The latecomers in the balcony seemed especially enthusiastic. Then Hank Henry, Clerk of Session, a stickler for propriety, stood up. Russ thought Hank would quiet this unPresbyterian display, but he stood clapping. Others joined him until the whole congregation was on its feet clapping in response to what they had heard. Russ stood at the pulpit holding his twitching left thumb, totally exhausted. Tears formed in his eyes. Finally he said, "I don't know what the final hymn is supposed to be, but let's sing Cwm Rhondda."

Once again, the hymn rose up and lifted itself above the singing congregation. The quiet places were quieter than ever, the booming places even more triumphant. They were not showing off their voices this time. They were singing for their souls. That wailing Welsh cry of pain was there, but also the thundering bass notes that affirm the faith that accompanies the cry.

They moved to the second stanza and sang "Open now the crystal fountain / Whence the healing stream doth flow," and Russ said to himself, "The healing stream is the sound of these voices. That's just how it is. Just how it is…." In the midst of Russ' meditations, the congregation came to the final chorus which felt to him like a forceful wind blowing in from beyond the hills:

> Songs of praises, songs of praises,
> I will ever give to thee,
> I will ever give to thee.

Russ couldn't sing. He was through for the day. He let the sound buffet him and thrash him and flay him with its force. He let tears fall off his chin onto the pulpit Bible open at the 139th

Psalm. When it was quiet, he pronounced the briefest benediction ever, "God bless us all. Amen."

WHEN RUSS GOT HOME, ELLEN WAS FIXING BACON and eggs for a proper breakfast. "How was it?" she wanted to know.

"You had to be there," he said. "It's too much to figure out."

"Why do you have to figure it out?" Ellen said, hovering about with more toast and coffee.

"I guess I always thought you had to figure things out," Russ said. "Let's go to bed."

"I just got up," Ellen said.

"Let's go to bed anyway," Russ said. And that's what they did.

21

"Not My Will, But Thine Be Done"

RUSS WAS NOT ALL THAT KEEN ON LENT and its forced somber-ness, but the Wednesday Lenten Noonday Services sponsored by the Ministers Association and arranged for at a meeting at the Coal Bin that Russ didn't attend were well underway at Brother Henry's church. They lasted but thirty minutes, a fast shot at the downtown working people. Russ was glad he had not been asked to participate. He attended one service and was surprised so many people gave up half their noon hour to be at First Presbyterian Church. All Brother Henry's fans from The Coal Bin were there to see him plop down on his knees to pray and pop up to preach a stirring word, his arms flailing and the walls shaking from the roar of his voice. He didn't disappoint them.

On Palm Sunday, Russ stood before a full church. The sun was shining, and people were glad to be out. Tall palm branches stood on either side of the pulpit and palm fronds were given to all the worshippers. The kids in the balcony waved the little green whips or were fully absorbed with making them into crosses, as there were taught in Sunday School.

The service had not gone well, it seemed to Russ. It was like starting over with a new crowd. Where were all these faithful when the snow was falling and the church was more than half empty? he wondered. The point of Russ' sermon was that Palm Sunday is about the mob that wants to get in on the celebration but hasn't been around for the teaching on which it is based. It fit the occasion, but Russ could see he had harangued people who had made the effort to be there about not being there. Half into the sermon he could tell it wasn't a good idea.

After church Russ got a call from Brother Henry telling him the schedule for the Union Good Friday Services. His voice came in loud honks as if he was in a rush.

"What are Union Good Friday Services, Henry?" Russ wanted to know. He figured to have enough trouble getting ready for Easter.

"You should have been at the meeting where this was discussed. We have three services for the people, Llewellen. One downtown, one on the heights, and one over your way. It's your turn, so you will have the last word at Welsh Church."

"Don't I wish," Russ chuckled.

"What's that, Llewellen?" Brother Henry shouted.

"Henry, what is this last word business? What's going on?"

"I think you better come by and get a copy of the service, dear man. We do Jesus' Seven Last Words from the Cross at three different locations. You're scheduled for the first word at the Methodist Church downtown, the fifth word over at Father Brundage's up on the hill, and, of course, the seventh word at your own church. It's customary for the host pastor to conclude."

"That's three more sermons, Henry," Russ groaned.

"Not sermons exactly. We've got to get all seven words in between 12:15 and 2:45, so people who work can get in and out. You can have your choir sing as well. So, these are brief meditations on the cross. But preaching is a wonderful opportunity, Llewellen, no matter how brief, I'm sure you would agree. We always look forward to the choir at Welsh Presbyterian."

Brother Henry was all excited. "Lord, how he likes church services," Russ mumbled. "How can anybody stand so much of it?"

Bad as that news was, Russ didn't know the worst was yet to come. When he went to get the Good Friday bulletins, Brother

Henry told him that on Maundy Thursday, the Thursday before Easter, it is customary for the two Presbyterian churches in town to come together for worship and communion. The guest minister gives the sermon and the host does the rest. This year, Russ learned, he would be the guest preacher in Brother Henry's pulpit. Then, Russ found out, there's a sunrise service at six in the morning on Easter. If the weather's nice, people gather at the big white cross in the cemetery for singing, Bible readings and prayers. When he learned there was no preaching at that service, Russ had to stifle a "Thank God," which Brother Henry would not want to hear. Totaling it all up, between Palm Sunday and Easter, Russ figured he had six services to get ready for, and five fresh sermons. Lord help us all.

"Pour the beer," Russ said to Carson on the phone that evening. "We're coming over early and leaving early. I've got to get a running start on Holy Week."

"I hear ya, Russer," Carson said. He chuckled like he often did when he saw Russ coming up against more of the ministry's requirements.

NEXT DAY, RUSS CALLED CHORISTER JENKINS and asked him about the special music for Good Friday.

"Aye, we've been workin' on it for a month now, Reverennnd," he said in the Welshest of lilting voices. "We have a quartet for when you go to the other churches, and, of course, the whole choir will sing here at the Last Word on that holy day. We wouldn't let you down Revvverennnnd." He seemed to sing as he said it.

"Thank you mightily," Russ said. He sighed his relief into the phone, and the Chorister chuckled.

"You just nod to us, Reverennnd, when you want us to sing. And, oh, on Easter, we have a second anthem, one before the sermon and one after. Now I'm not tellin' you your business, understand, but on Easter there's lots of them who aren't used to sitting in church, if you get my drift. It's worth it to consider a little extra music and a little shorter sermon perhaps."

Russ said he couldn't agree more.

As soon as he hung up, Russ started flipping through whatever material he had on Jesus in the garden, Jesus at the supper, Jesus on the cross, and Jesus risen from the grave. Most of it was heavily theological stuff gleaned from the gray-headed, bespectacled professors at seminary. By Tuesday night, Russ could see that if he was to get something out of the cross and resurrection, he would have to get it himself. He reached for his Bible and read the texts in a desperate need for preachable meanings. It hit him how the gospels show Jesus hanging there and uttering quotations from the Psalms and prophets, the holy writings of his people. Jesus did what Russ had seen scores of people do; he clutched his Bible to himself when the end was near, and he let the Bible's words be his words in those moments. Russ thought of old Jacob repeating the Psalms to himself in his blindness, his cloudy eyes tilted toward heaven.

And Russ was impressed by the contradictions in some of the sayings attributed to Jesus in his last hours. He didn't get the picture of Jesus as a calm soul resigned to his fate. There is anguish, resistance, the sweating of blood. In the garden, Jesus pleads with God to let him off the hook, for heaven sakes. He is reported to have said, "Not my will, but thine be done." But before that, he says, "Let this cup pass from me." To Russ it seemed the Jesus presented here doesn't want to face what is coming any more than anyone would. Maybe we try to get to the second part of that prayer too soon, Russ thought, jotting things down as he went. Maybe we pray for a lot of things because we think we're supposed to pray for them rather than letting on how we really feel.

"Damn it, God," Russ said under his breath, "if Jesus could tell you he didn't want to die, maybe I can tell you I don't want to go on like this not knowing what I'm doing. And there's a lot I do want that may or may not have anything to do with your blessed will, which I find inscrutable anyway. I want to learn more about this preacher thing I'm part of. And I want to be with Ellen more. And I want time for poems. And I want time to play golf if the weather ever warms up around here."

In the inadequacy of his knowledge and the rushing eddies of his young life, Russ was reading the Bible for purposes of his own. He could see he wasn't ready for "Thy will be done," but he had an inkling about "Let this cup pass from me." And he could talk about living between these two phrases. He pored over the verses and jotted down thoughts as they came. He let the texts speak, and he spoke back to them, and in an hour's time he had several sheets of paper full of notes. They weren't well organized, and they weren't all that scholarly, but he sensed a kind of inner connection between the Bible verses, the state of his soul, and the thoughts he jotted down.

He got out some envelopes and distributed his notes around to where they might best fit—Holy Thursday, Good Friday, Easter. He had little if anything for the Easter envelope, a small slip of paper with "it seems something like a dream" written on it. He could see he was stronger on crucifixion than resurrection, and he decided to let it be. He decided not to try to explain the meaning of things he wasn't close to explaining to himself. When it came to the last word on Friday "Into thy hands I commend my spirit," he would have to say, "I don't know about that. I haven't experienced it except as something waiting for us when we are able to lay aside much of what we struggle for." He welcomed the clarity, such as it was.

Maundy Thursday turned out all right. Russ preached a quiet sermon into the old stone sanctuary at First Presbyterian Church. The pulpit, a shiny marble monument to someone long gone, was gloriously carved with eagles on the sides and a Celtic cross in the middle. The hard surface caused his voice to bounce up at him, and Russ got the feeling he was preaching to himself, which, it occurred to him, isn't such a bad thing.

He gave them what he had gotten from rubbing up against the story of Jesus in the garden and from meditating upon the prayer Jesus is reported to have uttered there: "Let this cup pass from me; yet not my will but thine be done."

"We live in the space between the two phrases of this prayer," Russ said. "We live between our daily lives and what our deepest nature calls us to be. It's not always comfortable, but in that discomfort we have a sign that we are more than our self-interested needs and desires. In that discomfort we become aware of a divine dimension in our souls." So, the only good news Russ offered his hearers was that by identifying with Jesus' struggle in the Garden of Gethsemane they can become clearer about their true nature and, by extension, their connection to God. A lot of folks seemed confused or put off as they came out the door. But Russ got some strong, even tearful gestures of appreciation from a few who looked as if they dropped in on the service after dinner out because there's not much else to do on a Holy Week evening in Scroggtown except go to church. For once, Russ felt it really didn't matter what people thought about what he said. He had been as honest as he could about it without loading them up with all of his uncertainties.

So it was on to Good Friday. Along with the glowing phrases and the universe-transcending ideas of his esteemed colleagues, Russ set out his quiet little thoughts. At the Methodist Church, where he started with the First Word, which is "Father, forgive them, for they know not what they do." Russ said it seemed like Jesus' final words were in character with what he had been saying all along, that the rule of God embraces a lot we would like to leave out of it, including our pains and griefs. "We live, as Jesus did, on the cusp between what is called heaven and earth, darkness and light, life and death. Jesus knows about this, and we can look to him as one who has been where we are and felt as we do."

Russ had said nothing at all about forgiveness, but he shrugged that off and sat down. In fact his remarks were so brief that Carson, who followed him, had over forty minutes before Father Brundage would show up to do Word Three. Russ stuck around to see what Carson would do with the time he was not prepared to fill. Good old Carson, in sport coat and tie, his high forehead gleaming, was calm, calm, calm. He plugged into the hymn with which Russ' section ended and went on for fifteen minutes about who was there when they crucified our Lord. He got everyone there—angry people, sad people, the mighty and the frail, the confused, the hurt, the religious and irreligious. He looked upon the gathering, and wove the people of Scroggtown into the scene around the cross. Scroggtown at Golgotha all of a piece. It was the best preaching that day so far as Russ was concerned, and it came because filler was needed.

At Father Brundage's church, Russ gave them his less than inspiring musings about Jesus taking a chance on God at the end. He said Jesus didn't know that Easter was coming as he hung there facing the stark possibility that everything he had tried to do was crumbling around him. "Sometimes it feels like Easter will never come," Russ said, "like Good Friday just goes on and on. Jesus knew such feelings, the gospels tell us, and Good Friday afternoon is the time to let such feelings have their place." He pretty much left it right there and was on his way to deliver the Last Word.

At the Welsh Church, the choir was magnificent in its version of the ponderous funeral hymn Penparc. They stretched it out and came down on the minor chords like a chorus of blues singers. The uncertainty at the heart of Russ' sermon seemed to be imbedded in the heart of the song. "Living or dying, Lord, I know not which is best." Russ just left it hanging there, and it was not a good place to leave it, he could tell, but he had done all he could do for that day.

Buck didn't think so. He couldn't wait to get at his minister. He was fairly well glaring when he made Russ face him in the close quarters of the empty narthex.

"What is your purpose, Reverennnd, to weight us down?" he asked.

"What do you mean, Buck? Seems to me Good Friday is a pretty heavy time," Russ said. Strangely enough, Russ found himself calm and composed, a Good Friday calm, perhaps. Considering what happened to Jesus that day, Russ thought, why should I worry about what Buck can do to me?

"Christ died to save us, Reverennnd, to give us hope. Why didn't you say something about that instead of shove our faces into our graves?" The madder Buck gets, the more articulate he becomes, Russ noticed.

"In the war, Buck, did you ever face death?" Russ asked, thinking to dive in under the religious language if he could.

"Day after day we faced death, Reverennnd. You sort of got used to it. You got to feel like Jesus must have felt, 'Not my will but thine be done.' But then I never felt more alive than when I was being shot at."

"You know, I think that is something like I was trying to say. But you're right, I didn't do much with feeling more alive when facing death. Well, I've never been through that, Buck. I don't know what it's like. If we're going to have that message in this church, you'll have to be the one who brings it."

"Oh no, not me, Reverennnd. You're the minister," Buck said, and turned away scratching his thick neck. Maybe it dawned on him that we all can't have the same experiences, Russ thought, and that I can't hit his soul square every time and pound it into shape for him.

Russ hummed a chorus of "O Sacred Head Now Wounded" as he walked home.

RUSS HADN'T BEGUN TO GET AN EASTER SERMON READY, and he was all sermoned out. Right off he realized that what got him through Holy Week wasn't going to work for Easter. He could see that the proclamation of Easter faith cannot be controlled by one's doubts and questions or by anyone's particular experiences, including Buck's or the learned professors at the seminary or even blessed

Jacob Jones sitting by the window reciting the Psalms. Who has experienced Easter so they can tell about it, as if it happens on typical mornings and people with cameras can take pictures of it? Well, according to the record, the apostles did, and there's a fairly detailed description of the empty tomb in John, Russ was aware, though his professors said John was probably written at least a hundred years later. In fact, it seemed to Russ, the way the story gets told in the gospels, it's hard to tell whether Easter is something that happened to Jesus or to his followers. A lot of them had run off and hid when Jesus was arrested, and it is reported that at least one of them denied ever knowing him. Nobody, not even the women who stuck by Jesus, expected what happened to happen on the third day after the Crucifixion. But what happened? Is it what the hymns and anthems say: Christ arose? Or is it that the apostles started preaching and the church got started and the ancient world included a community that wouldn't give up on what this dead rabbi said and did, and eventually this changed everything? These were Russ' thoughts as he stared at the blank page before him in his typewriter.

Though he wasn't getting anywhere with his sermon, Russ felt he was learning things he needed to know. And he sensed himself slipping away from the need to please all of his hearers all the time. He had gotten past Holy Week without getting through to everyone who heard him, and it wasn't so bad. Displeasing Buck wasn't so bad. "Imagine that," Russ said to himself.

ON EASTER, RUSS AND ELLEN got up early and drove to the Sunrise Service in the graveyard. There was no sun, only mist, fog, culm smoke, and rotten vapors. Ellen got chilled and started shaking, so Russ took her home right after the service and told her to take a hot bath while he put in an appearance at the Annual Easter Ham and Egg Breakfast, all you can eat for two dollars, proceeds to the church. About nine, when he got back to Ellen, she was in bed with a slight fever and a cough, but listening to the Hallelujah Chorus over the radio from Saint John the Divine in New York.

"I'm staying in bed," she said. "Something's got me. I feel rotten." Still, when Russ went out the door, Ellen was singing along with the radio choir. "Hallelujah, Hallelujah, Hal...le...lu...yah!" She sounded awful, but the effort was there. Something of Easter in that, Russ felt.

Though he got there early, the church was already filling up. People Russ had never seen crowded around him and pushed him aside as if he was going to get in ahead of them and take the last available seat. The widow Mildred Morgan's Easter dress had broad white stripes making it as white as it was dark, and the darkness was dark blue rather than black. Furthermore, she wore a new blue hat with a few tiny white flowers on it. This woman speaks to the world about her inner life through her wardrobe, Russ observed, and took it for a good sign.

Then there was that huge plywood cross again, this time the Memorial Easter Cross full of potted white lilies like it had been full of red poinsettias on Christmas Eve. And there were lilies around the pulpit, lilies on the organ, and lilies in the choir loft. Same deal, buy 'em cheap and sell 'em dear, give people honorable mention, and give the profits to the church. Again, Buck handed Russ the list of dedications which was even longer than the Christmas list, for which Russ was grateful in a perverse way. It meant his sermon could be a short one, which is all he had.

The whole thing seemed like a circus to Russ: People all dressed up, wearing flowers in their lapels, pushing and shoving to get into church, kids crawling around between the pews, some of them fussing, and several folks, with no place to sit, standing in the corners in the back and along the walls. The sun hadn't bothered to come out yet, and Russ could hardly blame it.

Russ decided to get into the spirit of the occasion and hurry it along, but that wasn't easy to do. The choir was in a dither over their robes. They had been sent to the cleaners as they are each year just before Easter, and the collars had gotten separated from the gowns and the sizes were steamed off the labels and nobody knew whose robe was whose. Russ told them that, whatever else happened, they were going to start on time. He got his robe on, threw on his red and blue Princeton hood to give the crowd a thrill, and bellowed to the choir, "Let us pray."

"No. No. No. We're not ready," came the reply. "We got four minutes yet anyhow. Hold your horses, Reverennnd. You don't want to try it without us do you?" They had him there. He wanted both anthems, all the hymns the people could sing, a quick look at the resurrection story, and then home to Ellen. He had already learned all he could learn this Holy Season, and he had already preached most of it. Here it was Easter, and he wanted it over with. "What kind of minister is that?" He mumbled. Five minutes later, he was behind the choir marching up the aisle, and everyone was singing "Christ the Lord is risen today, Ah...ah...ah...le...lu...iah."

With the "Amen" of the hymn still lingering in the air, Russ got right into the Prayer of Invocation. Then quick into the responsive reading. He didn't inflect. He didn't change tone or pace. He didn't gesture. Taking a cue from Dr. C. Calvin Clarke of Wilkes Barre, he pressed his left shoulder forward and preached over his red velvet hood and his coal black sleeve. He employed the Gatling gun approach, shooting his crisp phrases just above the people's heads, not really looking at anyone. The main thing in his mind was to get done on time. And that's what he did.

Everybody thought it was grand. "Your voice had such a holy sound today, Reverennnd," someone said. "It brought chills to my spine." Even Buck was beaming. It was just what the preacher professor said not to do, and people were taken with it. Spit the words out. Make it seem like they're hitting something even if they aren't, and whatever you do, keep it moving, and you can say anything or nothing at all and they love it, Russ was thinking. "My best work seems to confuse them, and the corniest stuff I do seems to find a home in their hearts," he mumbled to himself. "I give up. Enough's enough."

Several families asked Russ and Ellen to Easter dinner, but he said Ellen was sick, and he had to get right home, grateful to her for providing such a valid excuse. He wanted no more of them for the rest of the day, but all afternoon people concerned for Ellen came by with pots of soup, casseroles, left-over slabs of Easter lamb, and, of course, Welsh cookies, which make the wounded whole. There was enough for meals for the week, which was just as well, because Ellen could do nothing but lie around wheezing, and Russ could barely boil water.

Ellen wore a boxy flannel night gown, wrapped a green wool cloth around her neck, poked tissue paper up her nose, and pleaded with Russ to spread Vick's Vaporub on her back. Russ wanted her to take aspirin and decongestants, but she wouldn't hear of it. She doesn't like pills, she whined, so Russ dipped two fingers into the Vicks bottle and pulled out a wad of pungent goo.

"It reminds me of what my mother did when I was sick," Ellen whimpered with her face in the pillow while Russ rubbed Vicks on her back.

"My mother did the same thing," Russ said, a gob of Vicks oozing between his fingers. "I tried it on myself once when I was in school, but it didn't do any good."

"It doesn't work if you do it to yourself," Ellen said. "It has to be someone else, someone who loves you."

"It probably has to be your mother," Russ said.

"You're my mother now, Russer," she said, and closed her eyes and wheezed off to sleep. Russ bent down and kissed her on the ear behind her matted hair. A shaft of sunlight slanted into the room and fell upon her. "Lo and behold, the sun is shining now that Easter is all but over," Russ mumbled. "Still, it's nice to see."

22

It's Spring

"THE SUNDAY AFTER EASTER YOU PREACH to the pews. No wonder it's called Low Sunday." Russ mumbled as he stood behind the pulpit. The choir took the day off. The soloist wasn't well prepared. The service seemed to be a ragged web of readings, hymns, thoughts, and prayers without catching anything substantial. The offering was disappointing. And yet, somehow, Russ liked it better than Easter.

Among the few, Buck was there, and Hank Henry, and Jacob Jones' family, who had become regulars because Russ had visited Jacob several times to shout the communion service into his ear. The widow Mildred Morgan was there in her Easter dress and her Easter hat as if to say she was not slipping back into her morass even if it was Low Sunday. Auntie Sophie sat all by herself, smiling. Every day was the same to her, every day was the Lord's Day. She seemed to feel that if there was an Easter once, then each day is Easter. Mary Hughes, also known as Mrs. Saloony, who was becoming more or less a regular, was there in gray slacks, white blouse, and a red sweater, the only woman who did not wear a dress to church. Nor did she wear a hat, letting her brighter than natural auburn hair catch the sunlight slanting in through the tall windows.

And there was Ellen, her first time out of the house since she got sick. She wore her Easter clothes because she hadn't had a chance to wear them the week before, a turquoise dress of Italian silk, tightly wrapped, tucked here and there at the waist and shoulders. She had bought the material and made it herself on the old sewing machine she'd had since she was a little girl. They had brought it with them in the trunk of the Saab. Her wide-brimmed hat, also homemade, was trimmed with the same material as the dress. It seemed to Russ there was hardly any distance between her pew and the pulpit where he stood looking upon the sparse congregation. It seemed like she was the main one there that day. He couldn't keep his eyes off her.

She was pale from her illness, seemed feathery light and leaned forward so the pew ahead braced her as she stood for the hymn. It must be something of a strain for her, Russ thought, living here now where it's so different from anything she's used to and expected to become a clergy wife in the course of a six day drive from Los Angeles to Scroggtown.

Russ spoke briefly and quietly of the ongoing, every day goodnesses that stretch past great celebrations like Easter. He tried not to look at Ellen, but he couldn't help it. Her head was bowed, but she seemed to be smiling the faintest of smiles. Russ knew Buck wouldn't like the sermon, but he was cordial as they shook hands at the door.

After church Russ and Ellen drove into Scranton for dinner at the big hotel in the middle of town. The dining room had water goblets and fresh red tulips in small green vases, on white tablecloths; chairs of deep cushioned green velvet, and huge old paintings of Pennsylvania woods in ornate gold frames hung on dark green walls. It was the most elegant place they had ever been together, including the trip to Manhattan. They hardly spoke, but they touched hands often, brushing each other's fingers.

They ordered lamb chops, which came with white paper bonnets on them, mint jelly, and a side dish of good German-tasting dressing. Ellen said she loved mint jelly. There were carrots, peas, onions, and potatoes sliced thin and sautéed, everything nicely seasoned. Russ and Ellen were alone except for a large family several tables away occupied in some sort of celebration. The two of them ate and sipped burgundy and let their silences lap against them like lake water on a calm day.

Finally, Russ said, "It's very pleasant to be here with you," not to start a conversation, but merely because it was true. He was struck by how deeply he felt those polite sounding words.

Ellen smiled and said, "I was thinking the same thing." And then, after a time, she asked, "What would you have done, Russ, if I hadn't come east with you? If I had decided to finish school in California?" She tossed her head back slightly so Russ could see her whole face, her gleaming eyes, her broad forehead beneath a swirl of blond hair. Russ took the question in and said nothing for a minute or so.

"I don't know what I would have done. Gone to graduate school, I suppose."

"Do you ever wish you were in graduate school?"

He gave it time, and finally said, "Yes, I suppose I do sometimes," and glanced out the window where sunlight was turning gold in the fading afternoon.

"I sometimes wish I was back in California in my old school," she said with a tenderness that made them both shudder. They touched hands and tears swelled in their eyes. So there it was. There, in great honesty, they looked together at what they had given up in order to be where they were. They dabbed at small soft tears. Waiters stayed away. The rest of the room seemed to retreat into far dark distances. Everything seemed to revolve around that white tablecloth and their empty plates and their wine in little purple pools in the bottoms of their glasses. Exactly together, they felt the enormity of what they had done, leaving all they had known and ending up in what turned out to be a strange and complicated world.

"Ellen," Russ said, "I'm glad we did it. I'm glad we ended up here together. We're doing something important. We're doing something we couldn't do any other way, and we're learning things we could only learn here. That's what I feel. I'm glad we're doing this. I'm glad you came with me."

"I'm glad, too, Russ," she said. They both breathed deeply and sighed. "It was a wonderful dinner. Thank you," Ellen said. She got up and walked to the ladies' room. She seemed to glow in the darkening space around her. Outside the light was a deep reddish gold, and there was hardly any traffic going by.

THE FOLLOWING SUNDAYS WERE JUST REGULAR church days with the basic faithful there. By the end of April, the roads through the surrounding hills were entirely passable, and people went to see relatives in New Jersey or western Pennsylvania. When relatives came to visit, neither they nor their Sroggtown kin came to church. People would actually say, "We couldn't come to church today, Reverennnd, we had company." Besides this, families with cabins at nearby lakes began to spend weekends getting them ready for summer, and whole flocks of Presbyterians were busy in their gardens during church time. As Russ walked to church on these Sundays, gardeners ducked indoors until he passed by, leaving their trowels stuck upright in the soft, dark earth. When Russ got to the next block, they reemerged in their wide brimmed hats, sweatshirts, old trousers, and puffy cloth gloves.

There was less and less to do. Russ was caught up on pastoral visits. The phone hardly rang. Those who were sick had either gotten well or died. The steady turning of the season brought a surge of human health along with a smattering of yellow forsythia, tufts of green, and swelling buds on the trees.

And then at nine forty-five on a bright morning early in May, huge creamy magnolia flowers began to unfold on trees in several front yards, pink and white dogwood blossoms showed among the evergreens on the hillsides, mock cherry, flowering pear, and everything pink or white or lavender bloomed forth. It was as if someone had flipped a switch. Within an hour, the slate hued world of Scroggtown was transformed into a blend of blossoms and colors that seemed a premonition of glory. By noon, people felt the heat of the sun for the first time in seven months. Sweaters came off, convertible tops came down, windows flew open, and formerly solemn citizens breathed deeply in the fragrant air and found themselves smiling. "It's spring!" people said to each other. "It's spring!" as if there had been some doubt about its arrival.

Instead of taking Ellen to catch the bus for her trip to school, Russ turned north out of town and drove the narrow roads through greening meadows and chartreuse woods. Ellen didn't even begin to object. They had lunch at a roadside diner near Montrose, wound their way home through the hills north of Tunkhannock, and got back to Scroggtown in time for Russ' Session Meeting to which, Lord be praised, fewer than a quorum showed up. He said a brief prayer for the church and everyone went home.

ON WEDNESDAY AFTERNOONS RUSS MET with the Communicants Class, six twelve year olds who, if they stayed with it, would become full-fledged voting Presbyterians on Pentecost Sunday, a celebration sometimes called the Birthday of the Church because, in the book of Acts, the Holy Spirit comes upon the Apostles like tongues of fire, and they go forth preaching, teaching, and healing like Jesus did.

Russ had a slick little booklet he gave the kids. *Your Church* it was called, put out by the Board of Christian Education. It summed up things in a hurry. Right off, the kids had to draw the sign of the fish and write the Greek word for fish, IXTHUS, inside it, and in this way learn that the fish sign stood for "Jesus Christ God's Son, Savior" and was used as an early code so the Romans wouldn't know where the Christians were meeting.

Then the little book depicted the Shield of the Blessed Trinity. God is Father, God is Son, and God is Spirit, it says, but Father

269

is not Son, Son is not Spirit, and Spirit is not Father, which the kids seemed to understand but Russ found puzzling. "Someday I'm going to have one of you tell me exactly how that can be," he chuckled to them. They didn't see anything difficult about it at all.

Then there was a history of the faith from Abraham on, which Russ improved upon in lessons that flew through several centuries a minute beginning at 2000 B.C. Abe, Ike, and Jake, he called the patriarchs of the tradition, and he got Joe in Egypt in a great hurry, and told them how good old Joe resisted the advances of Potiphar's wife, thinking this tidbit might get the kids to read the story for themselves. Then he took off running through the Exodus from Egypt, the great leader Moe receiving the Ten Commandments at Mount Sinai, and the twelve tribes wandering across the wilderness to the Promised Land. Then they learned how Josh "fit the battle of Jericho, and the walls came tumblin' down." Russ brought in a recording of the song by a black gospel choir, but he couldn't get it to play on the old phonograph he borrowed, so he tried to sing it for them, and they considered it hilarious.

They went down the list of the kings of Israel and Judah, pausing only for one or two of the more interesting ones. The kids really liked the queen who drove a spike through her royal husband's head, and they giggled about King David looking upon Bathsheba while she was taking her bath. They were surprised and pleased to find the Bible had such interesting parts. The Babylonian exile and the Hebrew prophets were kind of a drag, except maybe Hosea whose wife was supposed to have been a prostitute and whose sons had impossible names like "God's-going-to-get-you-if-you-don't-watch-out" and "The-little-guy-sometimes-may-just-have-a-chance."

"Was that really their names?" one of the kids wanted to know.

"Oh, I translated freely," Russ said, grateful there was no follow up question.

They spent a whole session on Jesus, and Russ was surprised at how much they had gotten from their years of Sunday School. They knew not only Christmas and Easter but also the healing of the

270

blind man, the walking on the water, Zacchaeus, the little guy up in the tree whom Jesus called down and joined for dinner, a story they liked a lot because they identified with the little guy. None of it bothered them. Five thousand people fed with five loaves and two fish, ok, that's cool. When Russ asked if it seemed possible one of them said, "Maybe the fish was whales."

Maybe so, Russ agreed, but went on to suggest maybe it's an old story. Maybe it's like "Goldilocks and the Three Bears." Maybe it's there to tell us something even if it didn't happen. But no, they said, it's in the Bible, so it has to be true. It seemed to Russ neither the time nor place to get into demythologizing the New Testament, as the seminary had taught him to do. It seemed he had come up against bedrock religion in the coming generation, like a strong seam of coal that had been forming under great pressure for a long time. He wondered if they would feel the same five or ten years later.

The kids didn't much care for the Apostle Paul except for the shipwreck story in which he shook the fangs of a poisonous snake out of his hand and went on to light a bonfire. It stimulated a discussion about copperheads and rattlers they'd seen or heard of in the woods around Scroggtown, none of it having anything to do with the Apostle Paul.

Then they came upon the creeds, and Russ told them about the Nicene Creed and showed them an artsy filmstrip of the historic Council of Nicaea in 325 A. D. With the lights out and the blinds drawn, Russ almost lost the class. He couldn't keep them off the floor, where they piled on top of each other with abandon while a picture of the forceful and fiercely orthodox Athanasius stared at them from the screen. Russ told them they better shape up because if they want to join the church they've got to memorize the Apostles Creed. Three of them said they already knew it, so there.

Their study book skipped clear up to 1054 AD and got the Eastern Orthodox Churches split off from Rome and then jumped to the Reformation. The attitude of the Presbyterian Board of Education seemed to be that it was no use cluttering up young minds with all that Catholic history of the Middle Ages. His seminary didn't do much with that history either. It would be easy to conclude, Russ could see, that there was a millennium or more that isn't all that important to Protestants. In teaching these kids, he noticed glaring gaps in his own knowledge.

Going through it fast like this, Russ was hit by how much the history of Christianity is strife and bloodshed. He could see the heroes of Protestantism were intense schismatics, brilliant to be sure, but full of ego, belligerence, and national pride. Condensing the Reformation and its aftermath into an afternoon, Russ could feel the huge force of conflict at the heart of his theological way. With Luther and Calvin, Zwingli and Knox, all of them there in a heap of his own rushing words, Russ saw how these men were driven, pushed and pushy, fierce at times, and terribly productive. They organized movements, translated scripture, formulated doctrines, wrote comprehensive theologies, composed hymns, and changed the course of the western world. There's no hint they ever played golf, though Russ liked to think reformer John Knox might have, along with other venerable Scots. It came to him that the upshot of it all was a driven culture, people of avid faith competing on the basis of faith, often at each other's throats and at times spilling each other's blood, with a zillion grand attainments thrown into the mix.

Russ sputtered a lot during this part of the course and finally got to the missionaries who, in the eighteenth and nineteenth centuries, went off to India, China, Africa, and the Pacific Islands to make it a Christian world. But, he wondered, who's going to tell these kids that in the process, the missionaries learned there are many religions in this world, most of them older than the Bible, and many of them gentler than Christianity?

What am I selling these kids anyway? he asked himself. How are they going to learn there is no complete answer in any tradition however sweeping and grand? Who is going to tell them? Certainly not the Board of Christian Education. "How shall they hear without a preacher? How beautiful upon the mountains are the feet of the one who brings good tidings," came to Russ' mind. Ah yes, that night which now seemed so long ago when he looked down at his dusty shoes, shook his head, and wondered what he was getting into.

"Reverennnd Llewellen," Nancy Lindsey, a thin, dark-haired girl, nervously alert, said quietly, "you haven't said anything for five minutes. Does that mean we can go home?"

"Oh, sure, Nancy, I'm sorry. Yes. Class is over. Be sure to work on the Apostles Creed."

They left him standing by the blackboard where he had drawn the timeline of four thousand years of Jewish and Christian history. It was all there in his energetic stabs of chalk: Abe, Ike Jake, Joe, Moe, Sol, and Dave, the prophets and JESUS in big letters in the middle of it all. The undulating line touched Egypt and Babylon and Jerusalem and Rome and Constantinople and Geneva and Jamestown and Boston, highlighting what the Board of Christian Education designated the mighty acts of God. It seemed to Russ it also designated something else. He extended the line one segment further, pressing hard and breaking the chalk. He printed in thick capital letters, SCROGGTOWN, and underlined it and circled it and put check marks all around it. Then he sat down and looked at his lesson.

The chalkboard showed the whole blessed tradition ending right there in Scroggtown. Culm. Industrial waste wafting its odors into the afternoon sky, hollowed out mines and hollowed out men and women. Exiles. Pilgrims needing bread. That's why the grandfathers and grandmothers of these kids came here, bringing their songs. They were starving in Christian Europe, for God sakes. And they just about starved here. The entire list of holy places and holy names led to a squalor overseen by networks of callous industries,

273

most of them owned by Christians and Jews doing all they could to heap up fortunes on the backs of impoverished workers.

What is it I represent? Russ wondered. He mulled over how the little book didn't even mention slavery, skipped right over the Civil War and the fearful churches finding ways to let good Christians keep their slaves under the noble right of property. "Dear God, history is embarrassing," Russ muttered. "And here I am pushing the embarrassment into the next generation." Russ went out, slammed the church door shut, and drove out to the golf course to practice his putting for an hour or so before the sun went down.

23

Aunt Alice Morgan

SPRING MOVED TOWARD SUMMER, the chartreuse leaves became shiny green, and Russ arranged to pay a call on Aunt Alice Morgan to see if he could learn more about the missing $10,000.

Aunt Alice lived high on Welsh Hill near Saint Elizabeth's Catholic Church in what was called a "mixed section" of nicer homes, which meant Catholics and Protestants in the same neighborhood. She came to the door dressed in a brown slack suit that made her seem businesslike, which, of course, she was. She appeared younger than her fifty-five or so years. Her hair was dyed dark brown and rolled into a tight bun, as if she wanted to make herself look severe, but her face was full and friendly looking. She had tea ready to pour and Welsh cookies on a platter when Russ got there in midafternoon. Even though it was a bright warm day, he wore his rust colored Harris Tweed sport coat, white shirt, and tightly knotted brown wool tie.

"Well, how are you liking Scroggtown by now?" Aunt Alice wanted to know. People were always asking him that, and his answer was always, "Scroggtown's just fine."

Sensing this was a stock answer, she pushed on. "We're kind of a weird bunch, don't you think? I mean, have you ever been around people like us? I'll swear, if it weren't for those folks in that church singing like angels, there wouldn't be much to commend us I'm afraid. Me, I can't sing a lick. Can't keep a tune in my head. One of them told me to keep my mouth shut, I was ruining the hymn. So that's what I do."

"Far as I'm concerned, church singing doesn't have to be pretty. It just has to be felt," Russ said.

"You wouldn't say that if you heard me sing, Reverennnd. I'm plain awful. People doubt I'm Welsh. But I'm close with money, and that's Welsh, as you have no doubt discovered."

"I don't sing well either," Russ said, "but I like it. It's the main thing I like about church, truth be known. And I can be interested in money too." Taking the opening at hand and throwing caution to the winds, he went on. "In fact, I read in the Session's minutes about that ten thousand dollars you gave the church some time ago. The elders have tried to keep it a secret, but I expect you've heard it's turned up missing."

"Yes, I know about it," she said. "Those elders are idiots." Russ let go an inward sigh of relief. It would not have been good for him to be the one to spill those beans to Aunt Alice.

"I went to see Reverend Thomas about it," Russ said, "and he considers the elders to be culprits in the matter. I hate to think that about them."

Aunt Alice looked down, pushed the platter of cookies toward Russ, and stirred her tea. They sat in silence for some time. She turned and faced the window that looked upon Saint Elizabeth's Church, a sturdy brownstone with a high steeple and a sprawling one story school nearby. The church grounds were a great expanse of green grass with huge oak trees leafing out, framing the medieval looking buildings.

"I look at that holy ground every day," she said. "I say my prayers here every day. It gives me a good feeling, though it never got me a husband. The Lord got me some money, though. He gave me ways to accumulate property, and I worked hard, and I did it. I wanted to give something to the church in thanksgiving."

"You were more than generous," Russ said.

Aunt Alice took a quick sip of her tea and went on. "Also, when I was young and away in New Jersey for a year, I did some things I'm not proud of. I put all this feeling into that $10,000 bill and gave it to the elders, and those idiots left it lying on the table like it was scrap paper."

"It was a $10,000 bill?" Russ said. "I didn't know such things are available."

"If you're a good customer of the bank, they do things for you. I went to some trouble about it. And those elders treated it like it was nothing."

"Yes, it does seem they were pretty careless. As I understand it, they all just went into the kitchen when their little lunch was ready. The call of Mary Henry's Welsh cookies was too much for them, I guess. Those were expensive cookies."

"You got that right, Reverennnd." She gave a quick smile Russ' way and turned to look out the window again.

"Alice, someone said you were up in the church praying before you gave them the money."

"That's right, Reverennnd, I was."

"And then you went upstairs again to pray? Is that right?"

"That's right, too, you've been around asking questions haven't you Reverennnd."

"I guess I have, Alice, off and on." Russ decided this was the time to reach for the moon. "Someone also said you came back downstairs and left by the basement door while the elders were having their little lunch in the kitchen. Did you notice any..."

"Oh they did, did they?" Alice cut in.

"Is that so, Alice? Did you come back to the basement that night and leave by the side door?"

"So you're putting me at the scene of the crime, Reverennnd. What are you, a Welsh Sherlock Holmes? You think I gave the money and took it back? Why? To get credit for giving something I didn't give?" She fairly spit the words out between tight lips.

"No, no, I don't think that at all, Alice, I appreciate your generosity. I appreciate your wanting to help our church. God knows it needs it. But if you were there in the church later that night, I wonder if you saw anything that no one else saw. Somebody no one else noticed." Russ spoke as slowly and calmly as he could.

"Reverennnd," she said quietly, "you have come here to this funny place from out in California where it must be much different. You and Mrs. Llewellen should have a home of your own. Living above old Edgar Howells must be a kick. I would be proud for them to take that money and buy you a house with it, a nice house up here on the hill, not the kind of houses they have down by the old mine. So, I'm going to tell you something, but before I do, you have to promise me that you will not ask me any more questions about this. You have to promise that you won't tell anyone about our visit today and what was said here, ever." She turned and looked directly into Russ' eyes.

"I promise, Alice," Russ said.

"All right then, here's what you do: Open the New Testament. That's all I'm going to tell you." She turned again toward the window.

"I open the New Testament every day just about," Russ said.

"That's all I'm going to say, Reverennnd. We speak no more about it. And don't you tell a soul about our little chat or I'll get that money back and haunt you for all eternity." She was dead serious.

After some minutes, Russ asked, "Would you like me to say a prayer?"

"I do my own praying, thanks. I have my own ways."

"That you do, Alice. That you do." They both smiled at that. She began picking up the tea things. Russ thanked her for her time and took his leave.

He walked down the hill to the church and sat in a back pew to ponder what Aunt Alice had told him. If she was not leading him on a round-about chase to nowhere, Russ realized she had just revealed that she did, in fact, know where the money was, and she wanted the church to have it. And yet, for her own perplexing reasons, she was going to make a peculiar kind of game out of it, and the clue was somehow in the New Testament. Russ sat and pondered this, looking at the back of the pew ahead of him where there was a rack with the hymnbook, prayer book, and pew Bible in it. Would she have gone downstairs that night, seen the money lying there unattended like a piece of scrap paper, as she put it, then would she have taken it off the table and put it in one of the pew Bibles, somewhere in the New Testament? If so, what if somebody found it there and went away from church so much the richer that day? But little chance of that. Russ had never seen anyone, not even the elders in the Holiness of Holinesses, open a pew Bible during services or any other time, for that matter. He had never seen any of his parishioners with an open Bible in hand except for Jacob Jones lying in his casket. So how did they know so much scripture? Russ wondered. Must have gotten it from the hymns and from the sermons the old Welsh preachers fairly well sang to them.

Feeling a little silly, Russ opened the pew Bible in front of him and flipped through the New Testament. Nothing. He opened one pew Bible after the other, flipping those sacred New Testament pages. It was kind of exciting, actually, each Bible brought another chance to hit the jackpot. It took a while, but he went through every Bible in the pew racks, and no $10,000 bill came fluttering out. He went through the Bibles again with the same result. He sat down to think about it some more. He ran up the stairs, but there were no Bibles in the balcony at all, only a few hymnbooks scattered around on the seats.

It was getting dark. He started to leave the church, but then bounded up the center aisle and leapt onto the platform where the huge old Bible rested on the pulpit. He turned all the big pages from Matthew through Revelation. He held the Bible by its spine and shook it, making the pages flap back and forth. Nothing. Russ went home thinking maybe it's not in a Bible. Maybe there's a clue in the New Testament that needs to be ferreted out. He also felt sure Aunt Alice knew exactly what he had been doing after he left her house and was laughing her head off.

At home, he got out *Young's Analytical Concordance*, that huge book that lists every word in the King James Bible, gives the word in the original Hebrew or Greek from which it was translated, and then cites the books, chapters, and verses where each word can be found. He looked up every word having to do with money, words like "riches," "wealth," "coin," "denarius," "silver," "gold," "mammon," and "money" itself. There is much about money in the New Testament, he discovered. Jesus talked about it a lot. In one story, a fellow takes the money with which his master entrusts him and buries it in the ground so it will be safe. Russ thought of looking around the church for fresh dug dirt, but then he thought, heavens, with the snow, ice, wind, and rain that had fallen over the months, no trace would be left. Still, next day he decided to take a look and found some promising places and pushed some of the dirt around with his shoe, all to no avail. He went home and tracked his way through the concordance some more. Ellen had to interrupt him for dinner.

"My goodness you're engrossed in your studies today. Did you get a second wind on the preaching business?" she asked.

"Something like that," Russ said. "It's amazing how many sermon ideas come when you open the New Testament," he joshed. But it was true. Along with crossing off verses as clues to the Aunt Alice mystery, Russ was making notes for a series of sermons on Jesus' words about what money can mean to people.

In the days that followed, Russ checked the ground around the churchyard more thoroughly. Grass was growing now and covering the earth with delicate green blades. It all seemed uniform in color and texture, no obvious upheavals, no places where the grass seemed thicker or thinner than other places and so more than likely undisturbed for a long time. He remembered there were Bibles in the basement for the Sunday School. He flipped through them and found nothing. It was hard to think about anything else.

He even gave up some fine golf days to look through Bibles, walk the churchyard, or sit in a back pew and ponder. He felt it must be like any good puzzle, that in, with, and under everything, there was one clear answer, and it was probably staring him right in the face, but he couldn't see it.

Sunday by Sunday, the people remarked that his sermons were being helpful. He was retelling Jesus' stories involving money in Scroggtown terms. Local ethical quandaries were addressed if not settled, like the one brought to him by the florist Robert James when Russ, a couple of weeks late, ordered flowers sent to his mother for Mother's Day. The florist wanted Russ to tell him if it was right to advertise "Free Delivery" when it really isn't free and has to be paid for in the price of flowers bought by all customers, including those who come into the shop and get no free delivery at all. And yet, florist James pointed out, if he didn't advertise free delivery, he would suffer from competition with florists who did. Russ wondered if this fellow was maybe a bit too exacting in his moral make up, but he was also intrigued by the question. Disguising the florist's question as arising from a pizza parlor, Russ set it over against the Golden Rule and the verse in Second Corinthians that speaks of "the hidden gains of dishonesty." Russ found he didn't have to say what the owner of the pizza parlor should have done; he just allowed the Bible passages to rub against the situation and let people come to their own conclusions or no conclusion at all. They seemed to like to think about such things and discuss them during their dinners when they got home from church. Even Buck was happy. "Your sermons have become much more Biblical, Reverennnd. Good for you," he said and slapped Russ on the back.

24

O God, Save Our Church

EVERY DAY NOW, THE SUN WAS a bit warmer than the day before. White clouds piled high above the valley, and the sky was bright blue. On one of these afternoons, Russ was gazing down the hill in the warmth outside the basement door of the church, having just dismissed the last meeting of the Communicants Class. It included the final exam on his timeline of God's dealing with the world so far as the Board of Christian Education was concerned. All the kids passed, which is the main goal of such education. In individual interviews, each youngster assured Russ of a desire to be confirmed as full-fledged Presbyterians next Sunday, Pentecost, the feast of the Holy Spirit, the birthday of the Church.

Happy that this whole process was over, Russ allowed himself to slide into a late spring reverie. Fresh green leaves adorned the trees in the valley, red and yellow tulips bloomed brightly in people's yards, and a light breeze tickled the new grass at the bottom of the hill. Russ took a deep breath and exhaled slowly. Though not a habitual thing for him, he muttered a little prayer, "Thank you, Lord, for this beautiful afternoon."

While gazing at nothing in particular, Russ heard the CH-CH-CH of a steam locomotive as it puffed heavily into view from around the bend east of town. Blasts of white steam shot out the sides of the locomotive as a slow train made its way down the tracks along the river at the bottom of Welsh Hill. It was a coal burner and a coal puller like most of the trains in hard coal country. The rolling bins of anthracite came into sight one by one. "They're still mining coal somewhere," he said to himself. Russ took to counting the cars. He got up to thirty-seven before he lost count.

As the engine approached the old coal yard where an out-of-use company road crossed the tracks, it gave a long blast of its whistle that echoed against the hills up and down the valley. Russ looked down upon the train and contemplated the shapes and colors of the scene: slate river, green grass, white steam, dark smoke, blue sky, and carload after carload of black, black coal. It took some minutes for the train to pass, and when it was gone, it seemed like steam lingered behind. Wisps of white blew up behind the wooden fence around the coal yard and the defunct chemical plant a hundred yards or so downstream from the mine. The wisps became puffs and the puffs became billows. That seemed strange, but looking down on it, it appeared a distant, quiet thing.

Then Russ saw the flames. Dry matted grass was on fire under the new shoots, and the old fence was beginning to burn. Russ ran for the phone, but as soon as he picked it up, he heard the siren. He put on his tweed sport coat and headed down the hill. "Good afternoon, Reverennnd," people said. "What do you suppose the trouble is?"

"There's a fire in the coal yard. I was watching the train go by, and then the fence started to burn."

"Probably a spark from the locomotive, Reverennnd. You be careful down there." A small crowd was running down the hill toward the excitement.

By the time Russ got to the bottom of the hill the fire had eaten through a good length of fence and was chewing up old boards and trash on the other side of it. When touched by any breeze at all, last year's clumps of dry grass hidden under this year's green shoots smoldered and flamed up. The spreading fire found more

283

trash piles and woodpiles and set them ablaze. Flames were moving toward the old breaker and were heading for the chemical plant as well. Russ could hear the fire trucks whining along Main Street. From the sound of them, it seemed they cut through tiny Boyles Avenue toward Locust, the shortest way. Then it seemed they may have gotten stopped by cars parked across from each other among the former company houses and had to back out and go around the long way. "Locust and Boyles," Russ chuckled to himself, "they must have named the streets around here for the plagues of Egypt."

Finally fire trucks roared up to the gate of the coal yard with sirens screaming and lights flashing, but huge metal beams blocked the way, and a rusty lock dangled from a chain that kept the beams in place. The firemen ran to their trucks and got sledge hammers, axes and crowbars, yelling and cursing and giving each other hell. It took three or four minutes to break open the lock, smash the gate apart, and lift the beams away. Two red fire trucks roared across the bumpy field toward the chemical plant, but a wheel on the lead truck broke, and the truck tipped sideways and stopped. The other truck backed up and inched around it.

By then one wall of the chemical plant was on fire. By the time they got the hoses laid out and the water turned on, loud pops could be heard from inside the plant. Canisters of something or other were exploding in there. Whatever was in the little bottles stored in that old plant was heating up and letting go. The walls of the chemical plant were burning on two sides and flaming missiles flew through the collapsing roof. Pop. Boom. Boom. Pop. The projectiles flew up through the burning roof and sailed out over the field, starting new fires everywhere they landed. Flames spread all directions and each time something popped and flew through the roof, people cheered like it was the Fourth of July.

"Everybody back," the fire chief yelled. "Clear out of here. We don't know what's inside that old plant. It all could go." People moved back up the street some, but nobody really cleared out. Phosphorus or something like it was tracing through the blue sky behind every missile. The hotter the fire got, the further the missiles flew. "OOOO, look at that one, just like a Roman candle," somebody said.

Then came a deep rumble shaking the ground, then BABABAROOOOM, and the entire roof of the chemical plant blew off in a white-hot blast. Everyone turned tail and ran up the hill, burning stuff falling behind them. When they turned around, they saw fiery material flying into the neighborhood of old company houses at the bottom of the hill. Grass was burning in several vacant lots and in a few back yards. Two roofs were smoldering. Russ ran down the hill and pounded on rickety doors. Some of the houses had bedridden old miners in them. Firemen ran in, wrapped them in blankets and carried them out to the street where younger neighbors took hold and got them up the hill. "Get the kitty, get the kitty," one of the old miners said. But there was no time to get the kitty. Firemen were hauling huge hoses from their trucks. They pulled them uphill and attached them to hydrants on Main Street. There was good water pressure, but there were too many fires for the hoses at hand. Sirens roared in the distance as trucks from other towns raced toward Welsh Hill.

By now, flames crackled along several fences, got to garages, and began to burn the houses which were no more than a foot or two apart. Most of them down by the river were made of wood that had been beaten on by all sorts of weather for more than sixty years. They went poof in a burst of flame, and in a matter of minutes they were mostly gone. The firemen attempted to make a stand halfway up the hill. "I want all these houses vacated," the fire chief shouted over a loudspeaker. "Everybody out. We can't save them." He pointed toward a dozen houses. Russ went over and told him the people could use the church to sleep in.

"I'm not sure we can save your church, Reverrrnd. If you ever did any praying, now's the time." Russ noticed that the chief's badge said his name was Murphy and that the Irish have their own way of addressing the clergy, trilling the r.

Down the hill, it was a fury just to get the people out. Up the hill, people carried their furniture into the street. Some of them set couches, chairs, tables, and TVs out on Main Street, and arranged it all like in a room. It was eerie. Nobody seemed to move very fast, just a methodical in and out like on moving day. They got their cars out of garages and drove them up the hill, weaving around piles of furniture. Dolls were important, and pillows and blankets. Russ noticed just about everyone had a Bible someplace among their belongings, whether or not they ever came to church.

Russ ran to the church and got the big Bible down from the pulpit, grabbed the candle stick off the communion table and went outside. What else? There's no way to move the organ, he could see that. He set these holy things on the sidewalk.

A house with aluminum siding stopped the fire half way up on the far side of Locust Street, but there were only wooden houses on the side the church was on. One by one, these houses smoldered and crackled and burst into flame. They couldn't get enough water between the houses to cool things down. Every few minutes another shocked family moved slowly up the hill, faces shattered in disbelief. Wordlessly, Russ put his arms around them and wept along with them. "Oh God, Reverennnd, I'm glad you're here," they said. Why, Russ didn't know. He obviously wasn't keeping their houses from burning.

The house next to the church started to smolder. Within two minutes flames popped alive inside it and smoke poured out the windows. Flames came through the roof and licked at the stucco back wall of the church. Even though the church grounds made for some open space, the billowing heat was too much for the amber glass window behind the choir loft. With a sickening crash, it shattered and fell in.

"Oh God, save our church. Save our church!" a lady Russ had never seen before cried out. The firemen threw heavy streams of water on the back wall and into the gaping hole where the amber window had been. Smoke sucked into the church, but none was coming out.

"Thank God for that slate roof you got there, Reverrrnd," the fire chief said. "If we can keep your back wall cool, we have a chance." They got two hoses working on the threatened wall, and they poured water on the church's roof as well. The churchyard gave them room to maneuver. They hooked up more hoses and splashed the church mightily from all sides.

They stopped the fire at the back wall of the church. It was singed but did not burn. It had taken four hoses going full bore, and they kept at it long after the danger was past, it seemed to Russ. Where the church faced Main Street, water poured down the front steps like a waterfall. Finally, the firemen left the church alone and went back to hose the hot spots along Locust street. They soaked everything that smoldered, smoked, or glowed, and black water flowed in torrents toward the river.

From all over the valley, pickups appeared to help people get their furniture off the street. Families were taken to relatives in other parts of town. There was fresh weeping each time the burned out ones faced someone who hadn't been there. Their wails were heard over the noise and bustle on all sides.

Buck the Elder came up behind Russ and said, "Now you can see what it was like in the war, Reverennnd. We went through this every day over there."

"You got time to go look at the church with me, Buck?" Russ asked him.

"That's what I came over for," he said. "I figured you shouldn't have to look at that by yourself."

"Thanks," Russ said. And they went in the front door and slogged through a half inch of running water. Inside, everything was blackened, soggy, and smelled of smoke. Water dripped from the light fixtures onto the pews. Shards of amber glass were every-where, that lovely amber glass that let in just the right amount of light behind the choir loft. The carpet hissed like a sponge everywhere they stepped. The lightened renovated walls were streaked from smoke and water. The pulpit had been tipped forward by blasts from the firehoses. It rested on the communion table. All the chairs on the platform and choir loft were tipped over. Buck held his side as if he had been pierced with a sword.

"Looks sort of like it used to look before the renovations," Buck said, "all dark and everything." They started to laugh, but then didn't. They went around kicking at stuff.

"Buck," Russ said finally, "let's try to worship here next Sunday. I think it's important."

"I think you're right, Reverennnd. Let's do it somehow," Buck said quietly

Russ turned and saw Carson in the doorway. Solid Carson. "You're going to need help cleaning this up. Let me know when you want a crew here," he said.

"Thanks, Carson," Russ said. "We're going to start tomorrow. We're going to have services here Sunday if we can."

"Not if we can, Reverennnd," Buck said. "We're going to do it. They can put it in the paper if they want."

"You all right, Llewellen?" Carson said.

"Yeah, I'm all right. A lot of people down the hill aren't all right though. Thank God everyone got out." Buck was up on the platform looking around.

"I got the pulpit Bible out, Buck, if that's what you're looking for," Russ said. "We better get the hymnbooks someplace where they have a chance to dry. And we better check the organ."

"Now you're talking like a Welshman, Reverennnd. If we got a Bible, some hymnbooks, and an organ, we got a church." Buck started going through the pews picking up hymnbooks. Some were soaked and would have to be thrown away, but others had been protected from the water by the backs of the pews. The pew Bibles were mostly ruined. Russ was glad he had gone through them twice in his attempt to follow Aunt Alice's clue.

"I'll call my brother to come down and take these hymnbooks to his place. He's got a nice dry basement, should be perfect for them," Buck said, and he disappeared down the stairs.

"PRAISE THE LORD. GOD SAW FIT TO SPARE HIS CHURCH." Brother Henry's booming voice echoed through the darkening room. "It's a sign, Llewellen, for the future of your ministry here."

It's a sign all right, Russ wanted to say, but "Thanks for coming by," is what he said.

"We'll pull together with you, Llewellen. You'll see. We'll not let disaster overtake one of our sister churches. I think we should have a meeting of the Ministers Association tomorrow, don't you think so, Carson. How about it, Llewellen? Tomorrow at seven at the Coal Bin. I'll get on the phone. You just be there, my treat." As the sound faded away, so did Brother Henry.

"Well, that's a first," Carson said.

"What's that?" Russ asked.

"Brother Henry treating someone to breakfast."

"I'VE ASKED REVEREND WALLY to lead us in prayer," Brother Henry bellowed next morning as the ministers gathered around the table at The Coal Bin. There was noticeable disappointment all around. Scroggtown's finest weren't going to hear Brother Henry perform that day. Wally stood up and, in his smooth, friendly drawl, said, "Oh precious Lord and Savior, we lift up today the pain and suffering of your people on Welsh Hill. Their houses lie in ruins, Lord, and even their precious church has been smitten by the flames." Russ was pleased to hear Wally refer to his church as precious. Russ had the impression Wally didn't think any church except his was worth much.

"And now we have gathered, dear Lord, to join our hearts and our hands in the alleviation of suffering and the rebuilding of our fine city. May there come forth upon thy people, Lord, a great outpouring of thy Spirit. May the latent generosities of the multitudes be loosed. May there be a veritable plentitude of willing arms and strong backs for the toil that awaits us. And may we have funds, dear Lord, an offering pressed down and filled up, thousands and thousands of dollars for the rebuilding of homes and the preservation of families, so that out of the ashes an even fairer Scroggtown may arise to please you. In the name of our Lord and Savior Jesus Christ. Ayyyumen."

"Amen," echoed all over the room. No applause, like when Brother Henry prayed, but what happened next was even more overwhelming. People started to come by with money in their hands—tens, twenties, even fifty dollar bills. Wally emptied a little wicker basket of its muffins and put the money in it. "Thank you kindly, folks," he said. "Lord bless you now, ya hear." People all over the restaurant lined up to put money in Reverend Wally's basket. "Here, Llewellen, give me that other basket. Pass it around folks. No use having to stand in line to give your money to the Lord." At every table in The Coal Bin breakfast rolls were dumped out of baskets, and the baskets were passed around like offering plates. People who had no intention of contributing had to go digging as a basket got close to them. And every basket seemed to get started with big bills. No small change in sight. Some put in napkins or slips of paper with a pledge for a hundred or more dollars and signed their names. It was amazing.

"Let's count it up," Wally said after everybody had a chance to contribute. Wally stood up and moved around the table counting and stacking as he went. "Twenty, thirty, eighty, a hundred. Ten, fifteen, thirty-five, fifty-five, sixty, eighty, a hundred." He made little stacks of bills, each one adding up to a hundred dollars. Russ counted ten, fifteen, twenty, twenty-two stacks of bills and a separate stack of pledges.

"Here ya go Llewellen, twenty-one hundred and sixty-five of Uncle Sam's dollars plus twelve hundred more in pledges. It's not a lot, but it should get you started." Russ was dumbfounded. How could he do that? A prayer about the "veritable plentitudes" full of the "venerable platitudes" and he collects almost thirty-four hundred dollars on the spot. Here was an aspect of his calling Russ didn't know much about, he could see.

"Gee, Wally, thanks," Russ said. "I sure wouldn't have expected anything like this. I thought you'd have done well if you got a hundred dollars."

"Well, Llewellen," Wally said, "when it comes to raisin' money for the Lord's work, it helps to do a little preparation. So I called a few of my healthier deacons, if you know what I mean, and told them to be down here this mornin', sort of out in the audience like. Most of the ones who got things started with those big bills were folks I called. The others just sort of naturally followed along as the Spirit led. I thought we might do even better, tell you the truth." He paused and scratched his head and looked deeply at his fingernails. "One thing about us Bible-pounders, Llewellen, we know what to do when it comes time for the offering."

With that, Wally excused himself and scooted out the door. Brother Henry also had to go. Russ figured Brother Henry knew Wally's prayer would bring in some money, and he opted for an offering for the Lord over applause for himself. Ah yes, in adversity we come through.

Father Brundage shook his head and muttered, "That was the most disgusting business I've ever seen. Why he staged the whole thing."

"I wonder, Father, if what we have just seen is a form of the sacrament," Russ said.

"A sacrament of dollar bills?" Brundage harrumphed.

"It may be Wally knows something we forget. When he gets people to give their money, he's helping them feel connected to God. Isn't that what a sacrament does?" That Russ was holding almost $2200 of Wally's sacramental dollars plus over a thousand dollars in scribbled promises added credibility to his argument.

"I'll have to ponder that one, Llewellen, but it doesn't seem right somehow. And it was all so unspontaneous really," Father Brundage said.

"Is the Eucharist spontaneous?" Russ asked.

"You've got a point there," Brundage nodded. "Kind of ironic when you think about it, wouldn't you say. He plans the offering and leaves the rest of the service to chance, and he rolls in the green. We plan everything else and leave the offering to chance, and we can't even get our roof fixed." They had a good laugh about it, the first time Father Brundage and Russ saw anything the same way.

"So, Llewellen," Brundage went on, "I'm sure our people will want to do something to help. I don't do Wally's sacrament very well, but is there something you can think of? An altar cloth maybe? Or candlesticks?"

"You know, the pulpit got knocked down on the communion table and banged it up pretty bad. If you have some kind of cloth we could put over the nicks and scars, that would really be nice. We want to try to have services there Sunday, communion and all."

"I'm sure we can find something suitable. It will be our pleasure to help out in that way," Brundage said, and they shook hands on it. Lo and behold, Russ noted, a terrible fire and we all start acting like Christians.

Reverend Ben Jackson scraped his chair back, got up, went over to Russ, and put his big arm around his shoulder. "Sounds like the church is going to be all right, Russ, my friend."

"I think you're right, Ben," Russ said. "But a lot of people are hurting. I expect only a few of them have much insurance. I don't even know what to think about that."

"Maybe that's not your problem, Russell. You can't solve everybody's problems for them, you know."

"What do you mean, Ben? It seems to me we've got to worry about what happens to these people. What good's a church if it just worries about itself?" Russ said.

"Oh, I'm not arguin' that. But you know, worryin' never solved things. I'm just wonderin' if there might be more that could come of all this. Hard times seem to bring folks together. Seems like some of the barriers around this table are beginning to fall, if you know what I mean."

"Yeah, kind of a good feeling, isn't it," Russ said. "Why Brother Henry even paid for my breakfast."

"He did?" Ben smiled. "Why then for sure a new age is dawnin'. Anyway, I'm thinkin' that some of us folks down in Kentucky Town could drive up to Welsh Hill in some of our trucks and help haul away debris, if that would be a help."

"That would be great, Ben. First thing that has to happen is get rid of all that mess we have up and down the street," Russ said.

"Well, you probably should be aware that my folks haven't always been welcome on Welsh Hill, Russell my friend."

"That's one thing I'm not going to worry about right now, so long as you're not," Russ said. "And if it fits into your schedule, why don't you join us for the service on Sunday. If we can make the church habitable, we're going to start praising the Lord about eleven o'clock."

"Well now, I thank you for that kind invitation, but let's see how our haulin' and helpin' go. I wouldn't want to cause you more trouble than you already have these days, but it would be something for all of us to praise God together for once, that's for sure." Ben flashed his great open smile.

Carson and Rabbi Steiner were standing there listening to this conversation.

"You know, Llewellen," Carson said, "you may be onto something. This could be the one chance we have to get everyone together in the same church. What if the whole town comes out to show its support? It wouldn't be as if we were trying to integrate folks that don't want to be integrated. Just a groundswell of compassion for the victims of the fire."

"You know, Russ," the Rabbi broke in, "there could be people upset with something like this. You probably ought to give it some thought. But if you want me there, I'll come and bring some of my people along. It fits our schedule fine. There's not much going on around the synagogue on Sunday morning."

"Let's do it," Russ said. "You all come. What the heck, the neighborhood's in ruins. The church barely scraped by. The people aren't paying attention to this old stuff right now. Nobody has to know we had this conversation. Right?"

"Right," they said all around, and joined hands in a little pact.

25

Church at Its Best

T HE SAME DAY THE MINISTERS MET AT THE COAL BIN, Williams Construction sent machinery for pushing the charred remains of houses on lower Welsh Hill into huge piles. Black folks from Kentucky Town were all over the pile, throwing the rubble on trucks and carting it off. Singed and soggy, couches, easy chairs, and mattresses were scooped up along with the rubble, bringing on more weeping and gnashing of teeth. With the many trucks and willing hands, it took but two days to turn the places where twenty houses had stood into empty basements, concrete foundations, and chimneys standing here and there like the crumbling towers of an ancient ruin.

Rabbi Steiner sent a cleaning service to work inside the church. The walls were scrubbed and began to lighten as the plaster dried out. The great gaping hole where the amber window behind the choir had been was boarded up, and the boards were painted a pale purple which made it all seem a little less oppressive. Carpets were ripped out and thrown away. Pews were scrubbed and set back in place on the bare wooden floor, which was slowly drying out. No matter how many times they swept or vacuumed, more shards of amber glass appeared in cracks in the floor and in the corners of pews. Carson and Judy organized a food brigade so volunteers could keep working without having to drive home for meals. People worked through the lunch hour, through dinner-time and into the night.

Father Brundage came by with some ladies of his parish to measure the communion table. "We decided to make you a new altar cover, Llewellen. All of our extra ones have been folded so long they have terrible creases. It just wouldn't do."

So it was looking like there would be a service at Welsh Presbyterian on Sunday. Time to start thinking about what it would be, Russ could see. He wanted to talk about the scene he saw as he walked around the neighborhood. The town was together without bothering to notice. The Welsh, the English, the Irish, the Polish, the Jews, the Afro Americans, they were swarming, salvaging, cleaning, repairing, helping. No one seemed upset about who was doing what.

The main thing, Russ knew, would be the songs: Diadem, "All Hail the Power," maybe Sandon, "Lead, Kindly Light," and of course, Cwm Rhondda, "Guide Me, O Thou Great Jehovah" with its mighty chorus "Songs of praises, I will ever give to Thee."

Dawn broke clear and cool that first Sunday in June. Russ had forgotten it was Pentecost until he saw the liturgical calendar on his desk as he gathered up his notes to head for the church. "Pentecost," the calendar said, "liturgical color: red, signifying fire," and there was a small picture showing tongues of flame blazing over the apostles. Under the picture it said, "And they spoke in the languages of all the earth's people and everyone understood them."

Russ left the house at nine, two hours early. Buck was bringing in the hymnbooks that had been taken to his brother's warm basement, and Russ gave him a hand. They were dry, but the pages were waffled and the bindings looked like they would burst. They wouldn't fit in the pew racks anymore, so they placed them on the pews.

Buck opened all the windows to keep air circulating. The walls were still streaked with dampness. On the communion table, a white linen cloth covered the dents and scratches. Where it hung down in front there was an embroidered Celtic cross done in a tasteful light beige.

The organ couldn't be fixed, but a music store lent the church a Baldwin grand piano that stood to the right in front of the Holiness of Holinesses, black and gleaming. Richie Evans was there adjusting the bench and strumming chords. The clock on the balcony wall said four-fifty, the time last Wednesday when water poured into the church, stopping the clock. Russ thought it made sense to leave it just the way it was.

About ten, Rabbi Steiner pulled up in a sort of airport limousine full of people from the Jewish Temple. They got out and sent the limo back for more of their congregation.

"We knew parking would be scarce," the Rabbi said, "so we hired a car. We'll just sneak in at the back, Russell. Don't pay any attention to us." Russ knew a couple of them from the golf course, but they seemed content to remain inconspicuous. He nodded to them and let them be.

The choir robes were ruined, and the stacks of music for the anthems were a mess. "Share now," Russ said as they gathered to rehearse. "You can look on two or three to the same sheet. We're Welsh, you know, we shouldn't need the music written down." The choir gathered around the piano to see what it could do. Russ' robe was damp and wrinkled, that black, felt paneled ordination gown. His academic hood was beyond hope. It looked like a drowned red and blue furry animal. He took it out and threw it in the garbage bin across Locust Street and quivered a little. He'd worked hard to earn that thing.

Billy Jones the Treasurer was polishing the offering plates, which, being brass, were not affected by the water, only a bit spotted. The Deacons cut slices of white bread into little squares and filled the tiny cups with grape juice. "You might want to have extra on hand today," Russ told them. "I have a hunch we may get a pretty good crowd." They put an additional platter of cut-up bread

297

and a pitcher of grape juice in the cabinet under the communion table and looked at Russ as if he was crazy.

There were no bulletins to say what was going to happen, no robes to wear, not enough hymnbooks or choir music, and all this in a water streaked church with a boarded up window painted purple.

Just after ten, an hour early, people started coming. Some of them had never been there before. All the kids from the Communicants Class and their parents came in, even though a couple of those families had been burned out of their homes. Two Catholic priests from St. Elizabeth's walked in quietly and stood in the back, their hands folded in front of them. Some people sat down and cried. Richie Evans played the chords of Aberystwyth on the big piano, deep and rumbling, the tune's imploring tone a tug on the heart.

The church filled and people still came. The balcony became a crush of folks mostly standing. Russ hoped the old struts wouldn't give way, adding disaster to disaster. Other people pressed in and stood around the piano. Black folks peppered the crowd with a new complexion. Carson and Judy and the Congregationalists crowded along the side aisles and out the front door onto the steps. People stood in the aisles so the choir had to slip in from the side door rather than march down the aisle singing the first hymn. When Russ saw the ministers, he motioned for them to join him on the platform. When Brother Henry got there, Russ asked him to have the opening prayer right after the first hymn, and he agreed enthusiastically.

People spilled out past the steps to the sidewalk and around the churchyard and in back of the church behind the wall that had almost burned. Buck and some elders left the Holiness of Holinesses and pried the purple ply wood off the back window and let the light and air stream in. The people outside behind the church cheered. Elders opened all the side windows as wide as they could go so those in the yard and on the street might hear something of what would go on inside. Russ saw Ben Jackson out in the crowd and motioned him up on the platform. Ben whispered that his choir was ready whenever Russ wanted to call on them.

"Let's begin by singing 'All Hail the Power', Welsh version," Russ shouted to the crowd. People were tentative, uncomfortable, a little reluctant to sing in the midst of so many strangers, perhaps, or because they never heard of the hymn or didn't know the Welsh version. The Welsh didn't need hymnbooks, so they passed them around to the visitors, and more and more people began to open their mouths to sing. The first stanza came forth in a halting wail. Richie picked it up a little faster, and the voices started to blend, "All hail the power of Jesus' name, / Let angels prostrate fall." They sang the first stanza again and again until even the folks outside joined in, hitting the notes an instant or two behind the people singing inside. It gave an odd stuttering effect. But it was happening. People from every facet of the town were singing a hymn together. Sopranos picked up the descant over the chorus, and the basses came down on "crown Him, crown Him, Crowowowown Him" and by the end of the hymn it seemed people were feeling better about where they were and what they were doing.

Russ nodded to Brother Henry, and he dropped to his knees just for a moment and rose up to pray a huge, bellowing prayer. He stretched his hands to heaven, stood on his tiptoes and craned his neck as if to give God a better look at him. He prayed for the neighborhood "charred and smoldering with earth's fierce sorrows;" he prayed for "flames which turn dross to gold" and for the "limited wisdom of humankind that leaves old substances rotting in forgotten places waiting, waiting, waiting for the appointed time to remind us we are not gods." The man was magnificent. A few of the Afro Americans shouted "Amen" when Harry turned a particularly potent phrase. When he bellowed his great final words, "And now to the One who brings hope out of ashes and sends the spirit of triumph over hell's own fire, all glory and power, dominion and praise...," the people outside started shouting, "Way to go Brother

Henry. Amen! Amen!" Brother Henry, for maybe the first time in his life, sat down before he was quite finished and allowed the people's amens to culminate his prayer.

Time for another song, Russ felt, and he pointed to L. David Jenkins, Chorister. Jenkins fairly jumped up before the choir and led it in a haunting rendition of Ton-y-botel, a tune in which the notes roll up and down the scale in steady, ponderous waves. The words by the poet James Russell Lowell tell of momentous happenings which bring humans to times of decision: "Once to every man and nation / Comes the moment to decide." The last stanza delves into mystery, raising the deep dark question, Why do hard things happen? but does not answer it. Instead it ends with God in the shadows keeping watch "o'er his own." A people who can sing that way about things like that will surely endure, Russ thought to himself.

Then Russ called up the Communicants Class, six crisply clad kids in a sooty church, girls in white dresses, boys in well pressed black trousers, white shirts and red ties. He asked them the questions of the faith from the *Book of Common Worship*. They were pretty much the same questions Russ had to answer when he was ordained, he noticed. They answered "I do" to them all. He prayed for the kids and promised them they would get their Bibles soon, because the ones they had ordered for them were ruined by the water from the firemen's hoses that saved the church. Right then Russ determined he would look through those very Bibles in search of hidden treasure.

The youngsters seemed so straight and proud as Russ shook their hands and welcomed them as full-fledged Presbyterians, little men and women who would never waver or flinch, no not them. The congregation sang the hymn "Blest be the tie that binds our hearts in Christian love" just for the kids, and they went proudly back to their parents.

What next? Russ didn't know. The pulpit Bible was lying open about in the middle at Psalm 107. Since there were too few pew

Bibles to read the Psalm responsively, Russ gave the people their response, "They cried to the Lord in their trouble, and He delivered them in their distress," and asked them to say it every time he paused. They pulled it off with a great rumbling of words flowing out the windows and flowing back in when the people outside caught on to what was going on.

After that, Russ motioned to Ben, and that great presence moved to the pulpit and calmly, without a word, waited for everybody to look his way. All he said was, "We just decided to come on over to be with you all because we know it helps to have someone pray with you and sing with you when things go hard." The Welsh people nodded, and the Jews and the English and the Polish and everyone else nodded too.

Ben motioned to his choir to come up front, and they wove themselves through the people standing in the aisles, climbed up into the choir loft and squeezed in by the Welsh choir. A tall, thin older black woman with short gray hair and wearing a long black dress with a white carnation pinned to it, glided forward and sat down at the piano as if approaching a shrine. She paused, raised her hands, and hit a bluesy chord that became the first note of "Amazing Grace." It seemed like that choir took ten minutes to sing the first stanza. Every syllable ripped and festered and spread a mixture of pain and balm. Wretchedness and graciousness crashed into each other, struggled and blended note by note. Seven people were the whole choir, but they sounded like twenty. Each singer took a coursing solo flight into the dark feeling of the song, and then they came to the third stanza, "Through many dangers, toils and snares, / I have already come; / 'Tis grace that brought me safe thus far, / And grace shall lead me home," and the hymn came alive in those seven voices, their groaning, glorious sounds filling up that damaged holy room.

Then it was "Just a closer walk with Thee, / Grant it Jesus if you please. / Daily walkin' close to thee. / Let it be, dear Lord, let it be." People began to clap, mostly the blacks and the whites who don't go to church much. The old regulars kept their hands folded in their laps.

The service had started late and was already almost an hour long. Some of the other churches in town were letting out, and some of those people were joining the crowd outside. Russ caught a glimpse of Pastor Wally on the sidewalk and motioned for him to come in and stand with the other clergy on the platform. Wally came in dragging The Reverend Doctor James W. Johnston of the Methodist Church, who had apparently been outside as well and looked as if he was being led to the lower reaches of Purgatory. Wally had his white shoes on and a powder blue linen suit. Johnston, of course, was impeccable in dark gray suit with a folded white handkerchief in his breast pocket, a little gold cross in his button-hole, and not one of his graying hairs out of place. Ellel didn't come. Russ imagined he was probably settling into his seat on the train to New York, lighting a cigar.

"Let's sing the one they used to sing when there was trouble in the mines," Russ said. Richie took over the piano and struck up the slow aching tune Sandon, "Lead, kindly Light, amid the encircling gloom." Now it was the Welsh turn. Hank Henry went forward, took out his cigarette lighter, and lit the one candle in its brass candlestick on the communion table. It flickered in the air moving around inside the church but stayed lit.

The song stretched itself over the congregation. The Welsh didn't improvise like Reverend Ben's choir did. They sang what was written on the page. They held the notes steady and long until all the qualities of the various voices began to fuse together in a continuous movement of musical phrases. The sound arose from the wrongs their people suffered over decades in that valley, their chill and hunger, the potato leek soup getting thinner and thinner as winter wore on. Russ wondered if the African Americans and the Welsh knew they have pains in common.

"Now here's one we all know," Ben said when the Welsh hymn ended. Piano players changed and the room filled with the first chords of "Swing Low, Sweet Chariot." The rhythm was so strong that even white people began to clap on the second beat without thinking about it, puh SLAP puh SLAP puh SLAP, puh SLAP building up a steady, unfailing pulse under the song. In huge rumbling sounds that seemed to come from chambers deep inside him, half preaching, half singing, Reverend Ben called out the verses and the people answered back with the refrain.

> I looked around Scroggtown and what did I see?
> Comin' for to carry me home.
> Smoke and fire a comin' after me.
> Comin' for to carry me home.

Ben went on to tell the story as he sang.

> The fire burned up the great and the small.
> Comin' for to carry me home.
> Cause the Lord don't have no favorites at all.
> Comin' for to carry me home.

Ben's voice became louder and his pace slower, the clapping congregation right with him.

> Then God looked down from heaven above.
> Comin' for to carry me home.
> And doused that fire with the waters of love.
> Comin' for to carry me home.

Now faster and still louder, Ben called out, and the people answered back, hearing what they knew already, but still wanting to hear it.

> So the people gathered round in the mornin' to pray.
> Comin' for to carry me home.
> Now ain't we got one real fine day,
> Comin' for to carry me home.

The piano rolled into the chorus and slowed it down to a walk, a saunter, a pulling on the soul, and the congregation took the simple well known song into themselves as one people together.

> Swing low, sweet chariot,
> Comin' for to carry me home.
> Swing low, sweet chariot,
> Comin' for to carry me home.

Applause rang out from everywhere. Ben clapped, and all the ministers clapped back at the applauding people. They were cheering each other and themselves as if they knew they deserved it.

"Now, Llewellen," Wally whispered, "the offering. This is the time. You do it." Russ got the plates and handed them to four elders who stood in front of the communion table. "Better get the bread baskets from the kitchen," he whispered to Buck who took off through the crowd. Then Russ looked out over the packed congregation and let his arm sweep slowly in front of him.

"Thank God you are all here," he yelled to the rafters. "We know what the needs are. We know so many have suffered. Let us give so the healing stream may flow through Scroggtown. Let us praise God with our offering. Amen." Wally almost kicked him. He muttered to Russ and shook his head about missing an opportunity the Lord doesn't often provide.

The offering took a while, and so Russ publicly acknowledged all the clergy and thanked their congregations for the help they had given to cleaning up the church and neighborhood. He made a special point of the new altar cloth, and Father Brundage beamed. Russ acknowledged the two priests from Saint Elizabeth's and invited them to the platform, but they nodded their thanks and stayed where they were.

Then Russ called for the hymn Penparc, and when they heard the minor key notes, many people cried openly, the falling chords mixing with all their losses. Only the Welsh sang the words, but Ben's choir hummed it behind them, and on the second stanza,

Richie Evans played the simple old tune ever more softly on the piano and finally stopped playing altogether. A ponderous combination of Welsh, African American, and many other voices carried the song forward, blending human pain with deep affirmation of something more in the midst of all the ruin around them.

There was no way to serve communion in an orderly fashion. All the ministers helped out as runners, taking the plates down to the elders, refilling them, stretching out to receive them back. Getting everyone served who wanted to be served was the main thing. It wasn't quiet, it wasn't pious, but it was sacred and real. There wasn't nearly enough bread. A couple of elders' wives came down front and cut the bread laid by in reserve into smaller and smaller pieces. For the grape juice, Russ could see they were going to be at least two hundred cups short. People passed the little cups to each other and they dipped their bread in and got it pink, and thus they ate and drank in memory of Jesus and for the renewing of the town. Russ noticed that the Rabbi and the two Catholic priests took communion, which he knew was a stretch for them. "New occasions teach new duties," as the hymn the Welsh call Blaenhafren puts it.

Then Cwm Rhondda. Chorister Jenkins raised his arms, and the people stood, took in breath, and lit into "Guide me, O thou great Jehovah, / Pilgrim through this barren land." A rhythmic swaying began. The notes of the song and the bodies in the room wove into a moving whole. A huge abundance of feeling poured out with uninhibited singing of this great Welsh hymn. Russ sang at the top of his lungs. Carson did too, and though they were standing side by side, they couldn't hear each other for the swell of sound. Rabbi Steiner didn't know the song, but he swayed along with it as he realized it was based on the story of the Exodus from Egypt. Reverend Johnston was singing more or less joyfully. Wally sang all out. Brother Henry too. Father Brundage with his red stole around his neck in honor of Pentecost, sang for a while and then stopped, looked around at the swaying people and smiled. Certainly some moments redeem all others, Russ thought. This was one of them.

For the benediction, Russ had the people join hands. All up and down the aisles, in and out the pews, on the stairways, in the crowded balcony, outside on the steps, sidewalk and lawn, everyone held hands, likely the first time some of those white hands had touched black hands and vice versa, or some of those gentile hands had knowingly touched Jewish hands. Russ said to the ministers, "Let's do 'The Lord bless you and keep you' together." They shouted it out more or less in unison, and the people said a staggered series of "Amens" that went through the church and out the doors and windows and rose up from the streets outside.

"If church could be like this all the time, there would be no question it was worthwhile," Russ said to Carson.

"Russer, it's worthwhile if it happens once," Carson said, and gave Russ a rib bending hug. Ellen, when Russ found her, had tears in her eyes and a big smile on her face. Lots of people did. It was that kind of morning. Actually, it was past one in the afternoon.

26

$10,000 Found

FOR TWO WEEKS AFTER THE BIG SERVICE, the church was crawling with sheet rockers, electricians, plasterers, carpenters, glaziers, painters, and the like. A new amber window was set in place behind the choir loft and new lavender wall paper with little gold florets was hung around the window, and new paint, new carpets, new light fixtures replaced the old. New choir robes were ordered. Choir music was ordered. At an expense approaching the original cost, Russ got his ordination gown cleaned and reshaped. He decided not to send away for another academic hood.

Somebody got the organ working, though it took replacement parts from a shop in Scranton. How sure they are of themselves, these who work with their hands, Russ noticed. Most of them gave discounts because it was for the church. What did it matter? The offering Reverend Wally had looked upon with disdain totaled about thirty-three hundred dollars and I.O.U.s for maybe a thousand more. It was the biggest offering ever taken in that church, by far.

And money was still coming in. The insurance claim was being processed. The Presbytery made an appeal to its sixty some churches, and a couple of thousand dollars in checks of various amounts arrived in the mail. One day a Father Dominic, a young Catholic priest with dark wavy hair showed up at Russ' door with an envelope. "The people at Saint Elizabeth's want you to have this," he said. It was a check for $1400 made out to Russ. He endorsed it over to the church and gave it to Billy Jones, who was happy as punch with the unheard of balance in the church's bank account. The Session passed and sent a resolution of thanks to St. Elizabeth's, to the churches of the presbytery, and one to the "Good and Generous People of Scroggtown" which was printed in the newspaper.

The church basement was the last place the workers got to. Down there, water had found its way into cupboards and cabinets. It was still pooled in the pots and pans in the kitchen and in the spoons in the silverware drawer. The dishtowels, the soaps and cleansers, and the linoleum floor were ruined, as were the Sunday School materials. The only thing to do was toss it all into one of the big bins the disposal company left on the street. The men of the church gave all their spare time to the basement, and the women spent hour upon hour cleaning up the kitchen. Before they were tossed into the dumpster, Russ looked carefully through the warped and soggy Bibles for the Communicants Class, making sure no $10,000 bill was lodged inside.

Then, early one evening as Buck was carrying a pile of ruined Sunday School books out of the basement, one of them dropped off the load and fell to the floor. Russ noticed a soggy copy of Floyd Filson's *Opening the New Testament* lying at his feet. Just like that Aunt Alice's clue came rushing to mind. "Open the New Testament," she said. "That's all I'm going to tell you."

Opening the New Testament was a hard bound book of the costly *Faith and Life Curriculum* written for high school kids by a well-regarded Bible scholar. In accessible language, it summarized the latest findings about those little pamphlets and letters Christians call their scriptures. Truth be known, Russ and his seminary classmates used the book to study for exams in the New Testament course, and they all passed. The book was that good.

He picked up the book and flipped through its pages. Nothing. He rushed to the cabinet where those light green books had been stored. The shelves were empty. Trying to appear casual about it, Russ went over to where Buck was gathering up soggy posters of Jesus surrounded by children and asked if he knew what had happened to the books that were in the cabinet.

"I threw those out a couple of days ago, Reverennnd. They were pretty bad. Would have gotten moldy if we left them in here."

"Are they out in the bin across the street?" Russ asked, trying not to seem anxious.

"That's where I threw them. Why?"

"Those were pretty nice books. I just wondered if we might save some of them."

"Nobody ever used them, Reverennnd. You'd have to have advanced degrees to make use of those books."

"Still, I think I'd like to save some of them if I can. Have they emptied the bin yet?"

"Not for a couple of days. If you want those books, they're probably in there."

Russ went out the door with an old mop and the Filson book he'd picked up off the floor. He reached over the edge of the garbage bin and stirred around with the mop handle. Then it occurred to him this wasn't a good idea. He might stir that $10,000 into a place where he would never find it. The only thing to do was climb in there. It was, of course, a wet, stinking mess of charred asphalt shingles, broken boards, shards of glass, soggy clothing, and all manner of cleansers now combining their chemicals into God knows what kind of volatile or poisonous compound. Still, after making sure no one was looking, Russ climbed into the bin and ducked down so as not to be seen.

He carefully picked through the stuff, trying not to make noise, and trying not to get cut by something sharp. Underneath some wet underwear, a hardbound book appeared, but it was a *Readers' Digest Condensed Book*, thick and squat and soggy. Under it were some charred shingles, and, under them, he picked through copies of *The King Nobody Wanted*, the *Faith and Life* book for younger kids, and laid them aside. Digging further, he came across a copy of *Opening the New Testament* and tried to look through it, but pages were stuck together, and it was getting dark. Pushing more debris aside, he found five more copies of the Filson book pretty much stacked on top of each other, a good sign, he thought. He decided to get all those books out of there and look through them at home. He wondered if this was all there were and if there was any way to find out. They likely would have ordered half a dozen, Russ thought, but then there was the one he'd picked up from the basement floor, which made seven. Seems like a funny number. He counted the copies of *The King Nobody Wanted* he had uncovered, and by golly, there were seven. That could mean he had all the Filsons. He felt around as best he could and came across nothing else that seemed like a hardbound book.

One by one, Russ dropped the six books over the side of the dumpster as carefully as he could, then got himself quietly onto the street. Druggist Jimmy James was locking up his store and saw him.

"Find what you were looking for, Reverennnd?" he wanted to know.

"I hope so," Russ said. "I would like to save at least one of these books."

"Seems to me you wrecked some good clothes going after it. Must be a wonderful book, is all I can say."

"I didn't think it would be so much trouble," Russ said, and slouched off down the street carrying the soggy books.

"You can't come in here like that," Ellen said when he got home. "What have you been doing?" Russ took off his shoes and socks and left them on the front porch. He carried the books upstairs, spread some old newspapers on the floor of his study, and set the books down there. Then he went to the back porch, took off his clothes, and got into a hot bath.

In his pajamas and robe, Russ went into his study and shut the door. He quickly flipped through the books, but no $10,000 bill fell out. He held each one by the binding and shook it. Still nothing. He washed his hands and went to dinner. It was wonderful homemade soup from somebody in the parish, potato and leek to keep a Welshman whole. And Mary Henry had sent over a plate of Welsh cookies. Russ ate his soup, took a couple of cookies and a cup of strong tea, sat down in his study, and contemplated the pile of soggy light green books on the floor in front of him.

He went over what he knew: Clearly, Aunt Alice had admitted to knowing where the money was by giving the clue about opening the New Testament and by saying she would take the money back if Russ mentioned their conversation to anyone. She also admitted being down in the church basement that night while everyone else was in the kitchen. The Filson books were on a shelf in the cabinet almost within arm's length of the table where the money had rested. The door to the cabinet was probably open; it almost always was. In her disgust for the elders, Aunt Alice could have picked up the money and put it in one of those books in less than five seconds. Unless they happened to be looking that way, nobody in the kitchen would have seen her. The more he went over it, the more convinced Russ became that Aunt Alice's clue led to one of the books lying on the floor in front of him. Ah, but I don't know for sure how many of those books were on the shelf that night, he thought. The only way to know is to go through the garbage bin inch by inch. It was more than likely they would pick up the garbage in the morning and haul it off to the landfill. In a few hours the mystery could be buried forever.

He went through the books in his study again, shaking them more vigorously this time, but still no money appeared. There must be more of these books to find, he thought, and this thought was too much for him. He went to the back porch and took off his pajamas and put on his damp, reeking clothes. Then he went around the house to the front porch, put on his socks and shoes, and walked out into the clear night. He took the flashlight out of the glove compartment of the Saab, pleased to find it was still putting out light, though it wasn't all that bright.

By the time he got to the garbage bin it was almost midnight. The streetlight shined down into it, which Russ took for a good sign. He went up over the side of the dumpster and began to lift things out. He let them down to the street as gently as he could. The shingles made little whooshing sounds, but the boards could get away from him and clunk to the pavement. When that happened, Russ scooched down and waited for anyone who might have heard the noise to leave off being curious about it. He also ducked when he saw the headlights of a car. He found a book but couldn't tell what it was other than it was not Floyd Filson's *Opening the New Testament*. He threw it over the side and it landed with a pop on the street. He determined to be more careful.

After an hour of this, the bin was still almost a quarter full. It was becoming harder to see as he got further down into it, and the debris that was left was bigger stuff, so that Russ was standing on what he was trying to lift. Clearly, this wasn't going to do it. He climbed out of the bin and tried to push it over, but he couldn't even get it to rock. He walked down the hill looking for something to use as a lever and found a thick metal rod that had probably been part of a garage door. He also gathered up blocks of wood of various sizes. The rod fit under the bottom of the bin where there was a little dip in the pavement. He tipped that side of the bin an inch off the street and slid a thin board under it. Now the rod would go a bit further under the bin, and he slid a thicker board under it.

This process went on until, at almost one in the morning, he gave the bin a mighty push and GA-BOING-BONG-BUMBLE RATTLE BANG jangled through the neighborhood. Russ ran for the churchyard and hid behind the sign that announced the Sunday services. Doors of the few houses left across the street opened and closed, porch lights came on, and beams from flashlights scanned the walls of the church. Russ scrunched down and waited. The church loomed above him, a huge bulky shape in the night, darker than the surrounding darkness. Russ wondered why he cared about it, but, at that moment, at least, he knew he did.

After half an hour, Russ ventured onto the street to see what he had uncovered. It was mostly wet asphalt shingles, soggy sheetrock, and sections of linoleum flooring. Every book he saw gave him a little flutter, but they were all Reader's Digest Condensed Books. He poked around for another half hour, turned over everything on the street, beamed his flashlight inside the bin, now completely empty, and dejectedly walked home. He again left his clothes on the back porch and went to bed.

"OOO," Ellen noted, "you stink," and she rolled over as far from Russ as she could.

By eight in the morning, bathed and dressed in clean clothes, Russ was on his way to the church thinking it would be good to pick through the contents of the bin in the light of day, but when he got there, a crew of folks was already swarming around. They had righted the garbage bin and had most of the debris back inside it.

"Can you imagine, Reverennnd," one of them said, "somebody came down here last night and turned this bin over and scattered stuff all over the street. Cars couldn't get by for all the junk here. People are nuts, Reverennnd, don't you think?"

"You make a good point there," Russ said. "Imagine."

Russ went into the church basement where people were sweeping and resweeping, cleaning and recleaning, washing things and drying them off, then washing and drying them again. My people are wonderful cleaners, they don't need any help from me, Russ thought, and went back home.

He sat down in his study, picked up the Filson book on top of the stack, and began turning each page. Pages were stuck together with something that seemed like prehistoric permanent glue. He got a knife to slide between the pages, often tearing holes as part of one page stuck to another. He peeled the stuck pages apart and made sure no $10,000 bill was hiding between them. By noon, he had only three books done. Ellen brought him a sandwich and a wet towel to wipe off his hands.

"I don't know what you're doing, Russer, but you've got to eat something while you're doing it. What did you put in those old books that's so important anyway?" she asked.

"I didn't put anything in them, and they're brand new books nobody ever read. I'm trying to solve the mystery of the ages," he said, wishing he had said nothing at all.

"And the solution to the mystery of the ages is in those books?" Ellen asked, rolling her eyes.

"I think so," Russ said.

"Why do you need all of them? Aren't they all the same?" Her eyes rolled even further.

"I think one is different," Russ said and turned to his task. Ellen left the room, shaking her head.

THE NEXT BOOK WAS ESPECIALLY WET. Pages were stuck together in gobs. Russ got a razor blade and cut pages away from the binding. Then he tried to pull the pages apart from back to front. This caused tearing, and he ended up picking at the edges of stuck pages with tweezers. In this way Russ picked his way through Filson's discussion of the Synoptic Problem, which deals with the long-noticed fact that the first three gospels have a lot in common. He tweezered his way through Filson's introduction to the Gospel of John, the Acts of the Apostles, the Letters of Paul, and the Pastoral Epistles. He threw the jaggedly shredded pages into a paper sack next to his chair. He was not only opening the New Testament, he was tearing it apart. He flipped to the back and was about to cut the chapter on the Book of Revelation free when he noticed a little corner of something protruding between the back cover and the blank last page that was stuck to it, a tiny irregular triangle of whitish green. He took the razor blade and began to slice between the cover and that page. If what he hoped was there was really there, he realized he could easily rip it apart and make it unrecognizable.

He went slowly, slicing and pulling gently, hoping to get a confirming glimpse. It was two in the afternoon before he could see that sure enough money stuck there. By two thirty, he could see it was a $10,000 bill.

Russ quick put the book, such as it was, in a clean paper sack, washed up, changed clothes, and took off for the Bank of Scroggtown in its imposing brownstone building on the square in the middle of town. He got there a few minutes before closing time and asked to see the president of the bank. He was told he would have to wait, which he gladly did. Finally, out of the president's office came Father Brundage who, friendlier than ever, shook Russ' hand and introduced him to his parishioner, Avery Effington.

"This is Reverend Russell Llewellen, Avery," Father Brundage said. "He's the pastor of the Welsh Presbyterian Church which is doing so much for the people affected by the fire. You may remember we provided them with an altar cover which they consecrated on Pentecost Sunday." Russ did not realize he had consecrated anything on Pentecost Sunday, and he bit his lip against letting them know that Presbyterians don't have altars, only communion tables.

Tall, graying, and nicely attired in his dark blue business suit, white shirt, and subdued maroon tie, Avery Effington asked Russ how he could help him, and Russ said he needed to talk to him in private. Father Brundage excused himself and Effington ushered Russ into his spacious office with its large, shiny, mahogany desk and black leather chairs. After a bit of explanation in which he did not mention Aunt Alice, Russ showed Effington the Filson book and the portion of the $10,000 bill he had uncovered. Effington looked both interested and amused.

"This money belongs to the church," Russ said, "and I'm wondering how to get it in usable form again."

"How do you know it belongs to the church?" Effington asked.

"I can't tell you without breaking a confidence. In fact, I must ask you to keep this whole matter to yourself," Russ said, to which, after of moment of quiet thought, Effington agreed, so long as nothing criminal was involved. Russ told him it was all legal and related a sketchy version of the story about the bill being given to the church at a meeting of the elders, of it being left on the table when they went for their little lunch, and of it being missing when they got back. He told of his trip to see Reverend T. Calvin Thomas, whom Effington knew as a former depositor. He told of tracking down the money by talking to various unnamed parishioners and said he came to believe the money had ended up in one of the books on the shelf in the church basement. And he told about climbing into the garbage bin to retrieve the book and even about going back at night and tipping the bin over. At various places in the story, Effington chuckled, which Russ took as a sign he was being believed.

When Russ finished, Effington said, "Well, I always knew the Welsh were a bit different, but I was not aware they were quite this different. No offense to you, of course, Reverend."

"What I would like to do," Russ said, "is have this bill replaced so I can present a fresh one to the elders and then, if I can be permitted, enjoy what happens."

"Well, that might take a little doing, Reverend. We don't often have a bill of that denomination on the premises. I've heard they're going to do away with these large bills to thwart counterfeiting, you know. You will have to go to the Federal Reserve Bank in Scranton, and you will have to keep at least half of the bill intact."

"That's why I didn't try to pry the page off any further."

"Let me call our Chief Teller in for a moment. She knows everything that goes on here." Effington got on the phone and the Chief Teller came in almost immediately, a middle aged woman in a gray skirt and sweater who seemed pleasant, confident, and all business.

"Do you have any recollection of cashing a check for ten thousand dollars and getting a bill of that denomination to give to the party? It would have been something over a year ago," Effington said.

"I do recall something like that, Mr. Effington. We don't often have cash transactions in that amount, as you know. I'm sure we made a record of it in the ledger," she said. Effington asked her to check the ledger if she had time. Within ten minutes, she came back with the date of just such a transaction, the check number, and even the serial number of the bill.

"We had to get the bill from Scranton," she said. "It took a couple of days, as I recall." Effington thanked her and told her she had been very helpful. If the Chief Teller had the name of the person who cashed the check, she did not mention it, for which Russ was grateful. But it was not lost on him that the name was likely on record and Effington would soon know it too, if he had any curiosity at all. Russ hoped Aunt Alice would be merciful if any of this got back to her.

"It would help to see the serial number of the damaged bill, Reverend," Effington said. "If we had the serial number, and it matched our records, I see no reason why we couldn't write you a receipt for what you have here. Even better, we could send you over to Scranton with all the papers you need to get the bill replaced."

"Can you watch me tear this page away from the back of the book, so I have a witness to what we find?" Russ asked. Effington glanced at his watch.

"Let's see what we can do with it," he said. Apparently a money mystery intrigued him.

Russ took the book out of the sack, flattened the sack on the desk top, and put the book on the sack. Effington moved the lamp over so it gave strong light to the operation. Russ gently pulled at the stuck page while Effington held down the cover of the book. The papers separated with a tiny hiss. Russ pulled the page up to the edge of the ten thousand dollar bill and then came at it from another direction. Bit by bit he lifted the matted page. Part of the serial number appeared. He could see clearly the last number, a six, and he called it out to Effington.

"It matches, Reverend," Effington said. "I think we're on to something." He was having a great time of it now.

Russ lifted some more paper. The next to last number appeared, a nine. He called it out to Effington who excitedly confirmed it. Two more numbers were confirmed this way, and then the bill ripped. A piece of it was stuck to the page being lifted, and the rest was stuck to the book's back cover. Russ went at it from the far end, and progressed slowly as before. In time, it was possible to see every serial number except the one that had been ripped through. All the numbers matched, but the ripped one could not be fully confirmed, it was either a five or six. The number it needed to match was five.

Effington looked at it from every angle. He got a little magnifying glass out of his desk drawer and peered at the number like a watchmaker over a tiny watch. "I would say it's a five," he said, "and that would clinch it, but I can't be absolutely certain. The odds are overwhelmingly with you though. I'll tell you what we'll do; you take your book home, I'll draw up an affidavit, you come back tomorrow, we'll both sign it, have our Notary guarantee the signatures, and send you off to Scranton. You should be fine." Effington seemed actually excited to be participating in all of this. He shook hands warmly and told Russ to be back at ten in the morning.

Russ told Ellen she had to take the next day off from school, and Ellen said OK without a word against it. She seemed to sense big things were going on, and Russ was in on it.

THE SAAB BUMPED ALONG THE ROAD to Scranton on a bright cheerful morning. Ellen sang along with the radio just as she did when they had come east from California. But Russ was on edge hoping it all would turn out the way Avery Effington said it would.

The big bank in Scranton had marble pillars and tile floors and tellers behind little cage-like stations with bars separating them from the customers. It seemed a secure fortress but not as friendly as the Bank of Scroggtown. When Russ finally got past the teller, he found that Avery Effington had called ahead and explained what Russ would be bringing in.

The President of the Bank, a portly older man dressed almost exactly as Avery Effington dressed, led Russ and Ellen into a especially spacious office and offered coffee or a late morning brandy, both of which they declined. Again, there was some question about Russ proving that the torn bill was legally his to exchange, so Russ signed a document that pledged him to come up with ten thousand dollars to be put in escrow if anyone challenged the ownership of the bill. He had no idea where he would get $10,000 if such a case ever developed. But the head of the bank agreed that the serial numbers matched except for the smallest chance otherwise, and he had a younger officer bring in a crisp ten thousand dollar bill. Russ handed over the damaged bill, some of it still stuck to the back cover of *Opening the New Testament*, and asked for an envelope. He placed the new bill in it, and slid it into his inside coat pocket just as if he always carried ten thousand dollars there. Handshakes all around, and Russ and Ellen were on their way.

Outside the bank, Russ was sure the money bulged his coat so that everyone could see a lot of money was in there. A little bump, and a pickpocket could have the haul of a lifetime. He stayed away from people as they walked to the parking lot where the Saab sat waiting.

"I don't think we should stop for lunch," Russ told Ellen. "I want to get this money home."

"I'm with you, Rev.," she said. "This is way over my head."

"Well, one of the implications of this is that the church might build us a house. Now that so many houses have to be torn down, there will likely be some lots for sale down the hill by the railroad tracks."

"Do you want to live down by the tracks, Russ?" Ellen asked.

"I'm not sure I want to live in Scroggtown. I'm not sure I can be Reverend Llewellen forever."

"Russ," Ellen said, "You're good at it. You've done some wonderful things. You've taken that church through hell fire, for heaven's sake, and these people, they love us. They cook for us and pray for us and now you tell me they want to build a house for us. What more is there?"

"There's being at peace with one's self, I suppose." Russ said softly.

"What's that supposed to mean?"

"I don't know. But I do know I feel weird about this ten thousand dollars. I feel weird about their using it for a house for us when so many people in the parish are burned out of their houses. I'd feel even weirder if the church buys up distressed property cheap and puts a house on it for us. There's something not right about that."

"Russer, you worry about things too much."

"That's probably true, but here's the deal. I'm not going to let them spend their money on a house for us while people around us need places to live. If the money in the church treasury doesn't get used for the people who need it, we're leaving."

"Russ, I've still got another year of college. I don't want to start over someplace else, even if I could. I've made friends at school. I know the professors. I want to graduate with my class here."

"I have to say you make a good point there," Russ said. "Let's just see what happens."

When they got home, Russ called the elders to a special meeting at the church, eight o'clock, one item on the agenda, no little lunch. Then he went to see Aunt Alice and told her what had happened. She was especially tickled about all the trouble Russ had gone through to get copies of *Opening the New Testament* out of the garbage bin.

"You're a persistent young Reverend when it comes to money, aren't you. It proves you're Welsh as Welsh. Lord bless ya, young fella," she said and patted him on the back as he left.

27

A Streetlight Shining through a Stained Glass Window

Russ got to the church early and laid the ten thousand dollar bill on the table from which one just like it, except for the serial number, had disappeared something over a year before. As the elders came in, their mouths dropped open. They asked all kinds of questions, but Russ said all discussion would have to wait until everyone was present and the meeting was called to order.

After the opening prayer, Russ announced that the purpose of this special meeting was to discuss the financial situation of the church in light of the money that had come in because of the fire and in light of the found ten thousand dollar bill. He told the elders that he was not free to say how it had been found, but that this was indeed the money Aunt Alice wanted the church to have. Every time an elder asked about where the money had been or who had it, Russ ruled him out of order. Clerk of Session Hank Henry nodded his head and noted in the minutes that the Moderator, Reverend Russell Llewellen, allowed no discussion of any matter other than the one for which the meeting was duly called, just as the Book of Order requires.

"Gentlemen," Russ said, "the church now has a sizable treasury. I expect we have contributions that exceed our repair needs. We'll need a full report from the Treasurer at our regular meeting.

321

Tonight, I want us to think about what we should do with our resources in light of the needs of the people in this neighborhood. I'm asking for a discussion on a proposal that we use the money to help people get their houses rebuilt."

Silence. This was not what they expected. Finally, Treasurer Billy Jones said, "Though a lot of bills aren't in yet, I would estimate we'll have around twenty thousand dollars over what we need to repair the church, and now with this ten thousand here tonight, we've got more than this church ever had before. I don't know how you did it, Reverennnd, but I'm grateful to you. I'm sure some thought the worst of me." That opened a round of congratulations and gratitude for Russ' persistent sleuthing.

"Did it have anything to do with those books that were in the cabinet here, Reverennnd? You seemed mighty interested in those books all of a sudden," Buck observed.

"Can't tell you anything about it. Sorry," Russ said. "The question before us is what to do with our money, and I'm proposing we make our surplus into a fund to help rebuild the neighborhood around the church."

"Reverennnd, some of us thought we could use the money to buy you and Mrs. Llewellen a house to live in. The church should have a manse, don't you think," one of the elders ventured.

"Ellen and I appreciate that very much," Russ said. "If it hadn't been for the fire that would be a wonderful idea. But we wouldn't feel right living in a nice house when so many others don't know if they have a roof over their heads."

"Reverennnd," Buck said, "Your sentiments are admirable, but maybe you could consider that it's more complicated than that."

"What do you mean, Buck?" Russ asked.

"I mean, for instance, is it right to bail out those who didn't insure their houses, didn't pay the premiums others paid, and now they've lost everything, and we come along and make them whole again, while those who paid insurance premiums don't get anything from us? Seems to me there's something wrong with that."

Hank Henry chimed in with the fact the railroad company may be liable for a lot of the damage, and it could take years to straighten it out. This kind of talk went on for some time, and Russ could tell he was in over his head. These men knew about the complications only too well. Russ could see it was one thing to have a big service praising God in spite of dungeon, fire, and sword, and quite another thing to actually set up a process for helping those who needed help.

Russ said, "All right. You raise good points. I can see it will take more consideration than I thought. But here's the situation: Ellen and I will not live in a house the church buys while there are families with young children or older folks that need houses. On the basis of everything we stand for here, the church has to do what it can about these folks."

"You Reverennnds tend to be an idealistic lot," Buck said, "and that's commendable in its way. But there has to be some reality in the picture, wouldn't you say. What makes you think giving that money away is the best thing to do? Either way, we've still got to pay for your housing."

"I accept that you are raising good questions," Russ said, "and I don't expect us to get this settled tonight. I do expect it to be on the agenda for our next meeting. And, I'm telling you, Ellen and I won't agree to move into a manse until we know those who lost everything are being helped to get back in their homes."

The meeting ended shortly after that. Russ sensed things were different. He and the elders were disagreeing, but not in a threatening way. The elders could tell Russ felt strongly about what he was saying, and he let them know he didn't expect unanimity with his view of things. For the moment, they were on a new and more promising understanding with each other.

WELL BEFORE MORNING LIGHT, everyone in the parish knew the ten thousand dollars had been found, and that their minister had been the one to find it. Welsh cookies and potato leek soup arrived at the Llewellens' door by the hour. The ladies who made the clam chowder on Wednesdays, for the time being in Mary Henry's kitchen because the church kitchen was still being fixed up, left two quarts on the porch with a little note that said, simply, "no charge."

Russ got busy on his sermon, but it didn't matter what he said or didn't say that week. People came to look upon this young miracle worker who found lost money the way Jesus found lost sheep. They sang a lot of hymns, and the chorister called out others, several not even Welsh. "Now Thank We All Our God" was the last one, a down home marching hymn with uplifting music and phrases, thanking God "with hearts and hands and voices." Yes, voices. The congregation turned to it with all the gusto they gave to Cwm Rhondda. It sounded wonderful.

People crowded the church the following Sundays as well. They wanted to see the progress being made on the repairs, and they wanted to see what the minister, now baptized by fire, would do next. It's all they talked about in their noisy gathering before the first hymn.

A couple of the smaller men climbed into the bell tower to make sure the new electric chime apparatus was protected from the weather. They got that one by Russ. Those chimes were not a replacement. Nothing like that had ever been there before, but somehow about a thousand dollars worth of electric chimes came forth right out of the insurance money. No meeting, no approval, they just did it, completely out of order. Still, for half an hour every noon and before and after church on Sunday, the neighborhood rang with Welsh hymns chimed over a loudspeaker. "It's a magnificent, hope-building sound floating over the troubled world below," Brother Henry bellowed upon hearing it one day, and Russ could only agree.

Two old Welshmen crawled under the floor of the church and stuck rods into the earth to see if all the water the firemen had poured on the place had found any cracks that might cause trouble. They suspected there was a mined out cavern under there that might be closer to the surface than it should be, but their test was inconclusive.

One Sunday, Russ preached about the rebuilding of the Temple in Jerusalem after it had been destroyed, noting it was not only the Temple that got rebuilt but also a way of life among the people. They renewed their commitments to a just and caring community, he said, "which is what needs to happen here in Scroggtown." People smiled and nodded, seeming to agree.

Another Sunday, Russ preached about the "new heaven and new earth" envisioned in The Revelation, the last book in the Bible. The following week, trying to move attention toward a sense of rebuilding faith as well as the choir loft and amber window, Russ preached a sermon about Jesus saying, "I speak of a temple not made with hands." Rebuilding and renewing the church's service to the community was his consistent theme, but though they seemed to agree with him, none of it seemed to matter much to the people smiling his way from their pews. What mattered to them was their church was being put back the way it was, and their minister was up in his pulpit urging them on, and the choir was singing more forcefully than ever. "Now we have a church again," Buck said, shaking Russ' hand at the door after the service. Russ wanted to get into a discussion of the difference between form and substance, a good seminary topic, but that wasn't what the Welsh Presbyterians wanted at all. They were happy their dear church had survived, and they were packing it out every Sunday as summer came on.

The second Monday in July the bustling activity in and around the church stopped. There was no more pounding or grinding or testing things out. The church stood quiet and empty in the bright morning. No one could tell that anything unusual had happened there except in the back where the heat from the fire had baked the stucco a darker color, like toast left in the toaster too long. The church was just there again, the big difference being that every noon those magnificent Welsh hymns pealed forth from its stubby bell tower.

The men of the parish commuted to their jobs from their cabins at Lake Henry or Lake Sheridan or wherever their families had summer places in the nearby hills. Even the ones who didn't have jobs seemed to have cabins to go to. They were mainly old white frame houses with mossy roofs surrounded by white birches and an occasional evergreen where years ago clans had pooled their meager resources and bought a bit of property an hour or so out of town.. Generations of do-it-yourself improvements and tack-ons had produced houses large enough for twenty or so family members to spend several weeks together at lakesides in the woods. His people had left for another world, and Russ was left to hang around Scroggtown and think about going on a vacation he and Ellen couldn't really afford. He went out to the golf course some, but was terribly rusty and played badly.

The next two Sundays were worse than the dead of winter. People were just gone. Those who were still around argued over the best use of the funds now in the church treasury. Russ was always getting phone calls about it, to which he said "These are matters to be discussed with the full Session in a duly called meeting. The next meeting is in September." So far, they hadn't spent a penny of their new found wealth on anything but the chimes.

So, less than two months after Pentecost, it appeared the best darn church service in the world hadn't caused much lasting change. What really goes on when we're singing those hymns and praying those prayers? Russ wondered. Are we trying to get hold of our more compassionate selves and not doing a very good job of it, or are we just projecting our hopes into the sky where they blow away in the breeze? It was more of a puzzle to him than ever, except now he had a growing body of experience about it which included Mildred Morgan's white dress, a little cap stolen from the church to teach the new minister a lesson about his role among the people, countless communions for the sick and shut ins, Christmas

Eve with the church an aluminum foil reflector oven, the caroling party, the Communicants Class with its unanswered questions, Easter's folderol, a Pentecostal fire if there ever was one, a ten thousand dollar mystery solved, Ellen, lovely Ellen, making the best of it all and now wanting to stay the course. It was all such a puzzle to Russ, but it was no longer an entirely theoretical puzzle. Now it had substance to it. That much was for sure.

As July wound down, Russ and Ellen made plans for a little trip into New England, maybe see Cape Cod, Gloucester, Plymouth Rock. They had the whole month of August for a vacation but figured about one week of touring was all they had money for. Then, Russ thought, they might go down to the seminary and see about his getting an advanced degree. Unbeknownst to Ellen, he had been looking at various programs of study. Theology and literature was becoming an accepted academic field, and Russ had several applications ready to mail to schools around the country. About ten o'clock on a warm and sultry night, he walked to the mailbox by the drug store and mailed those applications, fully aware that, depending on the responses he got, he and Ellen had an issue to discuss.

A light was on inside the church, and he went to turn it off and save himself a phone call later. "Reverennnd, it's eleven o'clock and a light's on in the church. You got stock in the power company, Reverennnd?" He went in, turned the light out, and sat down in the dark, in the front row where the elders sat, the Holiness of Holinesses.

"What is it about these people?" he wondered more or less out loud. "I hear them singing and it reaches into me as if I was born to it, as if I'm Welsh through and through. Much of what they do exasperates me, and much of it lifts me up. Why can't it be one or the other?" Russ felt he was close to the core of it. He could soar with the spirit of Wales in song, but when he came down it was to his own particular mixture of faith and unease.

"I preach and pray and visit, meet with the elders, marry and bury, meet with Presbytery, with Brother Henry and the bunch at the Coal Bin, preach, visit, pray some more, and do it all again, and nothing changes. It's an ever-rolling stream. It goes on and on."

Through the stained glass window, light shined into the church from the streetlamp across the street. The room took on a lavender glow. Light. Let there be light. The light shines in the darkness and the darkness does not overcome it. God is light. Lead, kindly light. Phrases came. Phrases from songs, from Bible verses, the prayer book, the creeds. I believe in God, the one true light. The light of the world is Jesus.

Russ became very still. He looked up at the pulpit with its big Bible lying open to last Sunday's gospel reading. There, where he must stand again next Sunday, he wanted to see a little light, a flicker, a sign of some kind, even a dim swell in the darkness. But there was none. He was just sitting there in the dark empty church with a streetlight shining through the stained glass window. At least it was restful. At least he didn't have to worry about saying something right then. All he had to do was sit there. And so he sat and waited and nothing happened.

It was no longer possible for a light to cast God's own light into his soul, apparently. He had learned too much at seminary for that, and he had learned even more in Scroggtown. And this long-suffering church had assumed a place in his loyalties by processes he didn't understand. What am I doing here and what will it amount to, he wondered. He remembered someone saying, "You ministers, you come and go, but the church goes on forever." It could have been Buck who said it, his kind of thing. The gospel according to Buck the Elder, as true as any gospel Russ could think of.

A shape in the darkness darker than the other darkness seemed to gather from the corners of the room and settle behind the pulpit, a gently curved and kindly shape it seemed to Russ. And what came to him was the simple realization that he was pastor of that church because he decided to be.

"I came here for reasons of my own, whether I understand them or not," he said to himself. "I plotted my way. I filled out the forms and took the tests. I made the phone calls and checked the map. I decided to be a minister for reasons that are not clear to me, perhaps not even valid, but they are my reasons and not somebody else's. Somehow I wanted it. I wanted to be in front of people in that pulpit. I wanted the mixture of aloofness and closeness that being up there brings. Whatever there is about being the one to help people look for meanings, I wanted it. The fact that I now know it includes a lot I don't want doesn't detract from the fact that I wanted it. Years ago I saw a light. Now I peer into a darkness. Maybe they're the same, in a way, whatever that means." He sat there a long time with such notions meandering through his soul.

When he got home, he reached for the lectionary and looked up the text for Sunday's sermon. He read it carefully three times. Then he wrote down chapter and verse on a large manila envelope so he would be ready in case a relevant idea hit him during the week.

About the Author

Robert Jones was pastor of Presbyterian and Congregationalist churches in Pennsylvania, Kansas, and California. He also taught at Pacific School of Religion in Berkeley, served as a hospice chaplain and as chaplain of an Episcopal retirement community. All along he wrote down his observations on the people and places he has served which led to several books and articles. He lives with his wife Arline in Western Sonoma County about an hour's drive north of San Francisco. His column "Keeping the Faith" has appeared in *Sonoma West Times & News* for decades and has won several state-wide awards.

Made in the USA
Middletown, DE
26 October 2021